Twisted Shadow

A cynical novel of politics

Volume 3 of the continuing adventures of
Glen Wilson…

Other books by Ken Coffman

Fiction

Steel Waters, by Ken Coffman
Alligator Alley, by Ken Coffman and Mark Bothum
Glen Wilson's Bad Medicine
Hartz String Theory

Nonfiction

Real World FPGA Design with Verilog

The Armchair Adventurer
www.ArmchairAdventurer.net

Books can be ordered from:

www.bytechservices.com
1500A East College Way #554
Mount Vernon, WA 98273

Twisted Shadow

A cynical novel of politics

Volume 3 of the continuing adventures of
Glen Wilson...

Ken Coffman

with

Mark Bothum

ISBN 0-975-43142-0

Published by:

The Armchair Adventurer
1500A East College Way #554
Mount Vernon, WA 98273

Dedication

Ken: For Gary Croft who is a continuous source of inspiration, inventive tonalities, good humor, wry commentary, bizarre flights of fancy and potentiated convergence. If anything else could asked of a friend, I don't know what that might be.

For literary inspiration, I thank Nelson DeMille who writes a hell of a good yarn (particularly The Gold Coast, check it out).

Mark: To my family for loving support...

We wish to thank our editorial board for encouragement, guidance, proofreading and commentary.

Judy Coffman
Stacey Kennedy
Ken Lomax
Dock Brown
Gary Croft
Dale Edwards
Kathy Kennedy
Colleen Bowen

Author notes on Twisted Shadow

When I worked on Alligator Alley and Steel Waters, for some reason, I really tried to make them pure brainless entertainment. I didn't want any science, politics, philosophy or social commentary to creep into the mix. How successful I was I will leave for the reader to judge. Looking back, I can't exactly explain why I thought this way. There was no way a guy like me, with such wide-ranging interests, could ever stay away from 'serious' topics. I suppose I was thinking that areas where I have strong opinions would just cause problems in marketing the books. However, I just couldn't keep it up. This book is a political one, but I hope an amusing, entertaining and fast-paced one.

I want to thank the editorial board for encouragement and support, but above all, for some scathing and withering criticism. The work gains no improvement from proverbial 'damnation by faint praise'. I appreciate someone who dislikes the books and can coherently explain why. I also appreciate hearing from the folks who, like me, are enthusiastic fans of the continuing adventures of Glen Wilson and his eccentric team. Mark and I have grand plans for their future, so stay tuned.

KLC – August 2005

You can email me at kcoffman@sos.net if you have questions or comments. As always, online reviews, good or bad, are greatly appreciated.

Typographical, punctuation and grammatical errors are very pernicious and annoying. We proofread and edit and catch a lot of them, but some still sneak through anyway. Here's your chance to make some money. Be the first to report an error, and as long as the dollars in my pocket hold up, I will send you a buck. I reserve the right to withdraw this offer at any time and will be the final judge of whether an error is worthy of payment.

2000 ALASKA PRESIDENTIAL ELECTION RESULTS

58.6% George W. Bush - REP
27.7% Albert A. Gore, Jr – DEM
10% Ralph Nader – GREEN
1.8% Pat Buchanan - REFORM
0.9% Harry Browne – LIBERT
0.4% Write-in (Scatter votes)
0.3% John Hagelin – NATURAL LAW
0.2% Howard Phillips – CONSTITUTION

Registered Voters (November 2000) 473,648
Total Popular Vote (November 2000) 285,560

Statistics from Federal Election Commission website (www.fec.gov) and
the Alaska Governor's website (www.gov.state.ak.us).

Now, if we can't ignore the law or exempt ourselves from it, we play games with the process. Do you know how we got our pay raise? Now, the senators voted no. Terrific. And by the way, thank God we got the pay raise. I'm happy. I need the money, and I earn the money. But do you know what we did in the House? We waited, under the guidance of the stage director over there, the Speaker, until 30 days had elapsed, until it was vested, it could not be unvested and then we got a vote on it. We waited until it was locked in, and then we voted. And we could all tell our constituents "I didn't vote for that pay raise." That's the way we — we do things. So — so there's much to be learned from watching us.

- Congressman Henry Hyde, R – Illinois

As recorded in the transcript of the testimony of Lieutenant Colonel Oliver L. North before the Select Committee on Secret Military Assistance to Iran and the Nicaraguan Opposition.

I recoil, overcome with the glory of my rosy hue and the knowledge that I, a mere cock, have made the sun rise.

- Edmond Rostand

INTRODUCTION

Glen

Glen Wilson and Bonnie Periera sat at a table in the International Controls Corporation lunchroom. Bonnie spoke with her mouth full of almond croissant. She made a wide gesture with the remnant and scattered almond slices across the table. The sun streamed through the windows; it had been raining and outside the window a spider web was outlined with droplets of water that glowed like sapphires.

"So I told her," Bonnie said, "if she'd let me ship 10K units by the end of the quarter, I would have the distributor pick up the product on the loading dock, we'd issue a credit, and the product could sit on the truck for a few weeks so it would not show up right away on the distributor inventory, then we'd take the material back on a return material authorization in next the quarter."

Glen grinned as he pared the skin off an apple with a jack knife. His left hand was missing two fingers, but he could handle the knife with no problem.

"I have trained you well, young flower," he said. "Do anything to make this quarter's budget, score the bonus, then you can figure out how to make everything work out next quarter. You don't learn strategies like that in MBA school. For lessons like that you have to go to Glen Wilson's Academy of Dirty Tricks, Under-Handed Methods and Abject Absurdity. You cut the buyer in for a point?"

"Half a point."

"Outstanding!" Glen exclaimed as he gave her a high five salute.

Bonnie turned serious for a moment. She looked out the window and the sunlight glistened on a hint of moisture in the corners of her eyes.

"It won't be the same around here without you prowling the halls," she said.

"I know," Glen said as he wiped a crumb of pastry from the corner of her mouth with the two fingers on his mutilated hand.

"You never said where you are going. Which company picked you up?"

"I told you, I'm going freelance, running for Congress."

"You've been saying that for years. Are you serious?"

"Oh yeah, baby, serious as a ʿcockroach. It's time to quit screwing around with six-figure side-deals and step up to the big league. Tax dollars," Glen said dreamily, "the most beautiful form of 'other-people's-money' there is, glorious and majestic piles of tax dollars. All I need are one hundred thousand Alaskan voters on my side. Less than that if I can Perot[1] the race somehow." Glen glanced at his watch. "Gotta run, babe, I just need to pick up my last commission check, then that's it," he said as he patted her on the cheek. "See ya on the tube."

Glen walked through the hallways and leaned over Peggy who sat behind the receptionist's desk. She was a busty young girl of about 18 who wore heavy eye makeup and a V-necked sweater. She handed over an envelope which Glen immediately tore open. The total on the check was all it should be. Glen whipped out his cell phone and 'direct-connected' to his lawyer.

"All's well," he said into the headset, "stand down." He flipped the phone closed and placed it back in its holster.

"The boss wants to say goodbye before you go," Peggy said.

"Okay," Glen said.

He walked down mahogany row to President Parker's executive office and breezed by his executive assistant who pretended not to see him. She was still mad about the time he left her at the Indian casino and she had to bum a ride home with one of the exotic dancers. In his office, Parker looked up from his PC and motioned for Glen to shut the door behind him. They looked at each other in silence for almost a minute.

"So, this is it?" Parker asked. "Seventy-eight months and here we are."

"I guess so," Glen replied, examining a picture of Parker's wife. She had a pouty expression that made Glen wonder why he hadn't taken a run at her. Probably something to do with Parker's extensive collection of antique samurai swords.

"Did you leave us any time bombs?" Parker asked. "Something that will explode in our face after you walk out the door? Computer viruses? Worms? Trojan horses? Something that will bring the IRS to our door? BATF? Revenuers? Auditors? More FBI agents? Some wretched treachery from your sinister mind? A plague of locusts? Anything?"

"As long as this check clears the bank," Glen said idly fanning his face with it, "you'll have no injury from me."

---

[1] Ross Perot collected 19% of the votes in the general election of 1992, mainly from conservative voters, which cost George H W Bush the presidential election.

"Okay then," Parker said, slumping down in his leather executive chair. "Can I ask you a few questions, just out of curiosity?"

"Sure, fire away."

"You leave behind an incredible legacy, like the largest expense report I've ever seen. Twenty-seven thousand dollars in miscellaneous expenses? How the hell do you run up twenty-seven grand over a weekend? Where did you find a thousand-dollar-a-night hotel in Sioux City, Iowa? Four thousand dollars in postage in one day? What about the bandwidth?" Parker waved a piece of paper. "You used four million times the bandwidth of all my other employees combined. That's a lot of Jessica Alba pictures, Glen. I figured it out. In seventy-eight months you cost the company 17 million dollars and change. It's mind-boggling. It's insane. It's..."

"Whatever, boss," Glen said in a bored tone. "What was the profit on the Digital Dynamics contract? If I recall correctly, and I believe I do, one hundred and seventy million, six hundred and forty thousand, eight hundred and fifty dollars, give or take a Susan B. Anthony or two. The engineering changes for the Phaeton project were worth what, about three-point-nine mil, all pure profit? What was this company netting before I came on board? Nothing but red ink? What did we do last year? Enough to buy you a new Gulfstream and float you a big loan to build that ski-in castle in Kellogg."

Glen got up and started putting Parker's golf balls on his practice green.

"Don't touch my Callaway putter, asshole. Sit back down, I have something for you."

Parker passed over another envelope. Glen slit it with a thumbnail and admired the check.

"If you're really running for Congress, then that check is deductible, right?" Parker asked.

"Absolutely," Glen grinned. "I'll deposit it into my PAC account right away. Thanks."

Glen walked to the door and then paused. "Your administrative assistant should have a FAX by now," he said.

Parker, with a tense look on his face, got up and followed him out the door. He was handed a few FAX pages. Parker looked at them and then sat down heavily.

"Oh my God, we got the Allied Technologies contract. If this is real, thanks Glen," he said to Glen's retreating back.

Glen waggled his fingers at Parker without turning around.

"Get my stock broker on the private line," Parker whispered to his assistant.

She got Parker's broker on line one and her own broker on line two. In the lobby, Glen stuffed the second check into his pants pocket and leaned over the receptionist's desk.

"You're a pretty little thing," Glen said looking down her cleavage and admiring her tattoos. "Is there any chance you'll run off and marry me?"

"No," she said firmly.

"Okay," Glen said. He walked out the front door into the sunlight, got in his battered old Mercedes and drove away without a single glance backward.

Elke and Murphy

On Manasota Key the sun drifted toward the water; the tinted clouds were gaudy like Las Vegas neon.

"Why didn't Glen pick me to be the arm candy?" Elke asked. "My boobs are better than yours." She lay on her back and watched the ceiling fan twirl in hypnotic circles. It was slightly out of balance so it swayed and clicked as it whirled.

"I know exactly why," Murphy said while dipping the little brush into a nail polish bottle. Murphy was painting Elke's toenails with a pale pink enamel.

"So tell me."

"Because he knew I'd be jealous and dangerously out of control if I saw you two together all the time."

"Oh."

"Did Glen pick Alaska just to torture us? What do you do if you're attacked by a polar bear? I don't even know where Alaska is exactly, is it by Hudson Bay?"

"No, it's on the other side, all the way across Canada. It almost connects to Russia. Glen's statistics team in Bombay says he has the best chance of getting one hundred thousand votes there. Once you're elected you just have to go back every two years to campaign again, it's no big deal."

"Isn't there like six feet of snow all year around up there? You gotta dogsled everywhere and the moose are as thick as sandflies? This really doesn't sound like a barrel of laughs to me."

"It will be fun for a change. You already said you'd go, so shut up about it."

"Did Glen say anything about the rest of the team?"

"No, we'll meet everyone at the kick-off meeting on Friday." Murphy looked around the room. "We sure have a lot of packing left to do."

"Let's order in some pizza," Elke said. As she reached for the phone the sheet fell away and exposed the breasts that were definitely more firm and attractive compared to Murphy's.

"Stop trying to distract me," Murphy said, "and hold still, I'm not done yet. Besides, we still have pizza around here from last night. We can microwave it."

"Yes, but it's gross," Elke stuck her bottom lip out and pouted.

"Alright, ya big baby," Murphy said, blowing on Elke's toes to dry the enamel. "We'll get you some damn pizza. Now hold still before you get polish on the sheets."

Benjamin Franklin Jackson

Bennie Jackson sat on the edge of a metal chair. The dirty tennis shoes on his feet did not quite reach the floor. Bennie was small for his 12 years, skinny, and his skin was as black as an eggplant. He grew up in the slummy part of Orlando with his mom who held two jobs; she spent her mornings cleaning hotel rooms and her evenings tending bar. Needless to say, she was rarely home to take care of Bennie and his brothers. His dad wasn't around at all and it was more than obvious that his mom did not want to talk about him. Bennie's fingernails were nibbled to the quick and he wore a Tampa Bay Devil Rays T-shirt that was three sizes too large. The most striking thing about Bennie was his brilliance; Bennie's IQ tested out at 165 on the Internet test he found. His guidance counselor, Miss Tabor, was also black; her hair was frazzled and graying and she wore an old ladies' business suit and a scarf around her neck. She was frustrated with Bennie for several reasons, the main unspoken one was that she needed Bennie to stay in school to skew the required state achievement tests.

"You can't just quit, you're only in the 6th grade," Miss Tabor said.

Bennie handed over an envelope.

"I took the tests and got my GED," he said calmly.

"You need more than a GED to get into Harvard, you need to finish school here and land yourself a scholarship. Don't throw away your future like this."

"I have a job," Bennie said.

7

"You're too young to get a job. Horse manure, boy, you can't get no job."

Bennie reverently handed over a dog-eared business card and Miss Tabor examined it.

"Glen Wilson? He's all the way up in Washington State. What kind of job?" she asked suspiciously. "Is he some pervert you met on the Internet?"

"I'm going to run his Information Technology while he runs for Congress in Alaska."

"How do you know anything about Information Tachometers? You're just a kid for cripe's sake."

Bennie thought about it and decided to answer her question.

"Instead of watching television, I took some home courses over the Internet. Glen paid the bills. I passed the MCSE test, then enrolled at the Phoenix online university and got a Bachelor's of Science in Computer Engineering. Just for the heck of it, I sent my senior thesis, some sample code, and some resumes I threw together to IBM, Intel and Microsoft. The only thing I lied about was my age. The best offer I got was from Microsoft where they offered $125K to start and a stock grant of 5,000 shares. The Intel offer was almost as good."

Miss Tabor looked skeptical. "Okay, what's an MCSE?" she asked.

"Microsoft Certified Systems Engineer," he replied calmly. He slid off the chair, reached over, and tugged Glen's business card out of Miss Tabor's grasp.

"You can't work for Microsoft, you're only twelve."

"I took a test for Microsoft that was timed and proctored. They wanted Itanium assembly language code for rendering six-dimensional polygons. It was scored on execution time and compactness. Instead of factoring through the geometry, I searched the hard drive for subroutines that I needed. There is so much code in XPx that no one knows everything that is in there. In an hour, I was rendering over four-thousand polygons in 11 milliseconds with 800 lines of assembly code. Of course, what I did was cheating, but they look for people who can work outside the rules. If you can do work like that, they are completely equal opportunity, it doesn't matter if you're black, white, chartreuse, male, female, gender-confused, a hermaphrodite, transgendered, a mass murderer, have three heads or wear your sister's underwear on your head. Being twelve is not an impediment at Microsoft if you can write C[#] code."

"Okay, Mister Smarty Pants, just how do you intend to get to Alaska?"

Bennie pulled an envelope out of his back pocket and waved it at her.

"First class with a stopover in Denver," he said, waving the tickets. He walked to the door.

"Wait Bennie, let me ask you something before you go. Did you have anything to do with Paul Brennon's hair falling out and his skin turning blue?"

Bennie turned and gazed at Miss Tabor for a moment.

"Yes," he said serenely. Then he pulled open the door and disappeared into the hallway.

Doctor Zalooq

The main stage at the Luxor in Las Vegas was painted with strobing lasers and backlit with pastel floods that illuminated smoke into floating gobs of fluorescent cotton candy. Doctor Zalooq was resplendent in his fur cape and top hat. This was a private show and the audience was preselected for age (21-45), income (all had available credit limits more than $10,000) and all the pregnant and menstruating women were given free passes to the Chippendales show instead.

"This is our last show here at the Luxor as next week the Blue Man Group takes over again." The crowd made disapproving noises, but the Doctor waved his arms to settle them down. "Don't fret, they will take good care of you. We have a special show for you tonight. Doctor Zalooq does the impossible as a matter of routine, but I want to leave you with something noteworthy to remember me by."

He pointed his cane at a curtain where the lovely Angela was standing in her high heels and feathery headpiece. The curtains parted and rotating holograms of the Egyptian pyramids hovered. Fractal images were projected on their sides. There was nothing magical about the hologram, but it held the mass attention.

"We travel the world in search of the unusual, the transcendent and lost secrets of the sorcerers. This parting gift comes to us from a series of Mayan hieroglyphs, so dangerous the mural was destroyed in 1934, but I found a set of tracings that were hidden in a government office in the Yucatan. I warn you that this magick probably resulted in the demise of the Mayan empire."

"Make her clothes disappear," a kid shouted from the audience. Doctor Zalooq just smiled patiently. *I'll get to that later,* he thought. He raised his arms and the music swelled in response. This music was laced

9

with subliminal chants and incantations as the fog machines sprayed hypnotics into the air. Zalooq and the crew wore nasal filters against the hypnotics and dark glasses to reduce the effect of the strobe lighting. Most of the crowd drifted deeply into a cataleptic state, but there were several unaffected who were knocked completely out with mist guns carried by the crowd control crew. Once the crowd was either hypnotized or unconscious, the girls started at the back and helped the audience get undressed. All the cash went into a canvas bag and the clothes were piled in huge mounds on the stage. The crew gathered at stage right and looked at the dazed nude people staring at the holograms. Angela handed Doctor Zalooq a laptop computer, all that remained was to press the enter key to run the final sequence. The Doctor looked at his crew, the girls were slipping into their jeans and their elaborate costumes were added to the huge piles of clothing. When everyone was ready, Doctor Zalooq said "It's party time," and pressed the enter key. The orgy started slowly. The crew filed out through the back door and got on the rented bus, while Angela and the Doctor were ushered into their limousine by the driver. The small caravan pulled out smoothly.

In the rooms they had rented at the Hyatt, Angela counted the receipts while the crew counted and banded the cash. Angela totaled up the take on an adding machine. She tore off the tape and handed it to the Doctor.

"This can't be right," the Doctor said.

"Not bad, eh?" Angela replied.

"They really came through on the suggestion to bring lots of cash, very nice indeed."

The Doctor popped the top on a beer and stood on a chair. He waited for everyone to notice and quiet down.

"Before I give you the total, I will say that we did very well tonight. I want to thank each and every one of you, the last few years have been a total joy. We've been lucky and we've done some outstanding work, but tonight we cash out and hang it up for a while. We've stayed a few steps ahead of the FDA, the BATF, and the IRS, but we can't stay as visible as we are and still beat them forever, so we have to go underground for a while. Doctor Zalooq hangs up his cape." The Doctor raised his beer. "I salute you all!"

The girls and the crew raised their drinks and clicked their glasses with their neighbors.

"What's next for you, Doc?" Red asked.

"It's North to the Future my friends. Angela and I are going to try Alaska for a while," Zalooq replied. "Now to the bottom line. Angela?" Zalooq gestured for Angela to hand him the adding machine tape. He looked at it. "Red got a good price for the trucks and we sold the show gear to Copperfield. So you're each walking out of here with seventy-seven thousand dollars and change. That ought to keep pinto beans on the table for a while. The rooms are paid for tonight and the room service tab is on me, so pick up your envelopes from Angela and have fun!"

The Doctor stepped down from the chair and his crew patted him on the back and hugged him. There were a lot of sloshed drinks, but even the girls did not seem to mind the mess. The crew lead, Red, set up a Karaoke machine and, after a little coaxing, the Doctor made an ass out of himself swiveling his hips and singing Heartbreak Hotel. At 2:30 AM, the Doctor found Angela nodding off in a corner. He took her drink and finished it himself. He caught the eye of a few of the crew gyrating on the dance floor and waved goodbye. He was sad that Doctor Zalooq needed to disappear, but it had to be done. Helping Angela to her feet, he guided her though the hotel lobby. Outside, he gestured to the waiting limousine.

Reclining in the back seat he helped himself to a diet soda from the refrigerator and pressed the can to his aching head. The bright lights of Las Vegas slid by; as they passed the Luxor he saw the advertising for his final show still on display. Some of the revelers, milling on the sidewalk, were partially dressed and disoriented as they hailed their taxis. He saluted with his soda, and then pressed the buttons to raise the privacy screens. The last outside light that streamed came in from the moon as it was being guillotined. He lay his head on Angela's shoulder and fell asleep.

Holly

The Florida State Institute of Mental Health stands three stories tall and occupies four acres provided by federal grant along the Ochochobee River. The board of trustees included several prominent local businessmen whose concerns were divided between the financial health of the Institute and the mental health of its patients. The Institute's director, Dr. Winston Fisk, was chronically frustrated by the board's decisions and had half-decided to tender the therapeutic resignation letter that he kept in a desk drawer. Fisk faced the Institute chairman, the esteemed Mr. Barton Thomas, across a plain, laminated desk covered with a jumble of papers, some discolored with spilled cola.

"She's whacko and that's an official diagnosis?" Chairman Thomas asked. He was a 54-year-old self-made millionaire, recently retired from running a chain of scrap yards. He held the firm opinion that hard work and immersion in a wholesome environment would straighten out most of today's youth, particularly if the rules included prayer and an outright ban against body piercing and rap music.

"No," sighed Dr. Fisk, "I'm just saying it's too soon to release her. She has earned my sympathy. Her father was a Green Beret, then a cop and then a criminally insane serial killer. The things he did to her... it's really, really sad. It's perfectly understandable how she turned out. However, she is a severe danger to the public." He paused to consult his notes. "Some of her test results are extremely disturbing, such as the traumatic psychological stimulation of the cortex — "

"In English please, Doctor," Barton interjected with a scowl. Fisk, disconcerted, pushed his heavy glasses further up the bridge of his nose.

"Okay, very well then. When we expose her to images of graphic violence she exhibits no discernible physiological indications..."

"That's not English, Doctor," Barton interrupted again. Fisk blinked, then shrugged.

"Okay, yes. We showed her photographs of a mangled human baby." He flipped an eight-by-ten glossy towards the older man, who visibly flinched at the grotesque image. "Her blood pressure didn't change, her pulse rate didn't twitch, her temperature remained constant, there was no capillary response, her pupils didn't dilate, and her epidermal conduction —" he paused and raised a hand before Barton could interrupt, "— I mean to say she didn't even raise a sweat."

"Was she awake?" Barton asked, flipping the photo over so he wouldn't have to look at it. "Look, I'm no shrink, but you don't get to where I am today without learning a thing or two." He stabbed a finger in the doctor's direction. "What you have there is *negative* data, and you can't prove a thing with negative data. Plus, it says here," he tapped a finger on the clipboard in his lap, "that you have her on enough Trazadone to drop a racehorse in its tracks." He glanced at the Rolex on his wrist. "Hell, you could probably chop off her arm with an axe and get the same result."

Dr. Fisk stared at Barton's clipboard and pointed. "Where'd you get that report? That's confidential."

Barton chuckled. "No, it's not." He got to his feet and retrieved his ivory-handled wooden cane from beside his chair. "The bottom line, Doc, is the bottom line. That little welfare cracker is tying up a room I can fill with a trust fund bedwetter." He limped for the door. "If she's cured, then she doesn't belong here. If she's incurable, she doesn't belong here either." At the door he turned and aimed the clipboard. "You show me evidence of violent psychosis before her hearing next week or she's drawing a Get-Out-of-Jail-Free card." He impolitely left the door open when he left the room.

A week later Dr. Fisk stood outside the hearing room with a very junior Assistant District Attorney.

"Can he really do that?" the ADA asked.

Fisk shrugged. "She gives the right answers and finds a third party custodial sponsor — game over. Barton sits on three boards and chairs the trustees." They watched Holly approach wearing a blue pastel hospital gown. She had a matching blue ribbon in her hair. She was escorted by a large male orderly. Her blonde hair was cut short, she wore no makeup and her face was expressionless. From 50 feet away, she looked very young and fragile.

The ADA lowered his voice to a whisper. "Doesn't exactly fit the profile, does she?"

The doctor started to sigh, but cut it short, as he knew sighing was becoming a habit, nearly a mannerism. "There *is* no profile for this one." He shook the ream of paper in his hand. "She's one of a kind."

The ADA presented the facts concisely, making no effort to hide his desire for Holly's internment to continue indefinitely as he concluded the state's presentation. "You can see we have a frightening pattern of behavior displayed here; a complete disregard for human life in an individual who cares for nothing but her own ambitions and who will employ the most extreme violence in the pursuit of those ambitions." He glanced over at Holly, who sat in a straight-backed wooden chair behind a small table with a plastic pitcher and cup. She slowly shook her head while staring at the floor. A tear rolled down her cheek and she slowly brushed it away. The young ADA looked at each of the seven people seated at a heavy wooden table. Behind them, sunlight streamed through the window and outlined their figures, making it difficult to see their expressions. He nodded in their general direction and returned to his seat beside the doctor. The chairman cleared his throat and raised a hand towards Dr. Fisk.

"Doctor? You have something to add?" The doctor stood and approached a central podium with a thick manila folder in his hands. He adjusted his glasses and spoke directly to Holly.

"Holly came to us via the court system with the extensive criminal record outlined by Mr. Lewis," he said, gesturing toward the

ADA, who sat with his hands steepled under his chin. "We feel we've made significant progress in determining the root causes of some of our unacceptable behavior," he turned to Holly, "haven't we, Holly?" She raised her eyes to Fisk and gave him a watery smile. Their eyes locked for several seconds, with the doctor breaking away first. "But," he said, pausing to open his folder, "a great deal of our progress in modifying that behavior would seem to be," he stopped as if searching for the proper word, "artificial," he concluded. A silence fell over the room, finally broken by Barton Thomas, who sat at the center of the bench.

"You're saying she's faking?" Barton asked.

Holly gave a small, disbelieving gasp and stared at the doctor with wide eyes. 'No,' she mouthed soundlessly, shaking her head. Tears brimmed in her eyes and her face crumpled, then she shook herself and bravely faced the panel. The doctor closed the folder and removed his glasses, finally parting with one of his stereotypically heavy sighs.

"Holly is very intelligent; her standardized test score is 139. She is an excellent actress and finds the desired responses to most of our tests to be painfully obvious." He allowed himself a thin smile. "But the physiological responses are not so easily faked." He indicated the folders in front of each of the panelists. "Holly has *no* empathic responses," he said. "She could field strip you down to the bone marrow with a pen knife without blinking an eye. She exhibits a total lack of even rudimentary compassion. She does not recognize our reality. We exist in her perception only as objects to be manipulated, as obstacles to be overcome, and as tools to be employed." He pointed to the pitcher of water. "In Holly's world view, you or I have no more human value than that pitcher, perhaps less if she were thirsty."

He slapped the folder onto the table in front of Holly, who now sat motionless and staring at the floor. "You've all had opportunity to study our test results and any decision you make today will be with the full knowledge of the sad reality those results reflect." He left the folder lying in front of Holly and returned to his seat beside the ADA. Holly raised her head and idly traced a finger across the folder. She bit her lower lip and looked at Barton Thomas.

"It's okay," she said softly. "I don't have anybody as a third party custodian, anyway." One of the other panelists coughed softly. Barton crossed his arms and leaned forward with his elbows resting on the bench.

Dr. Fisk groaned under his breath and leaned toward the ADA. "Oh, she's good," he whispered.

Barton Thomas could glare mildly at people. He glared mildly at Holly. "Young lady, this is a very serious matter, probably the most serious matter of your life to this point." He nodded toward Fisk. "You understand what the doctor and Mr. Lewis have told us?"

Holly nodded. "I think so." She also looked quickly back at the doctor and the ADA. "I understand what Mr. Lewis has said, and," she hesitated and dropped her eyes to her hands, which were clasped tightly in front of her, "and I have to agree that I did some terrible, horrible, ugly things." She raised her eyes, they were red with and filled with barely-controlled tears. "But now I *know* those were awful, awful things, and that's the point, isn't it?" She turned to the doctor. "Isn't it? I didn't know then, and now I do? Isn't that something?" She turned back to face the panel. "I can't undo the things I've done, I wish I could, I wish I could just start over as a child, be born to different parents, with a father that didn't, didn't..." she shuddered and gathered herself with a visible effort. "But I can't. I can only start here and now." She swallowed and held her head higher. "If I get the chance, if you give me that chance." She blinked rapidly, looking at each of the panelists in turn, then lowered her head. Paper rustled as several people fidgeted with their folders.

"This hearing is adjourned," said Barton Thomas. "We will render our decision this afternoon. Good day." He stood and smiled at Holly. She tried a brave but faltering smile in return.

"Mr. T-Thomas?" she stammered. "Could you possibly be my third party custodian?"

Barton Thomas opened his mouth, closed it, and then blinked a few times. "Well, Holly," he said, with the ghost of a smile, "that would solve one of your problems, I suppose." Fisk and the assistant ADA exchanged a look of utter disbelief.

Dr. Fisk waited for Barton Thomas in the hallway. His voice trembled. "I hope you're not doing this so you can wear that child's ass as a hat," he said.

Barton's eyes narrowed in anger. "That is way over the line, Winston," he snapped.

The doctor spun on his heel and stalked away. Barton Thomas watched until he turned the corner, thinking, '*but that little girl's ass would be a mighty fine hat, wouldn't it?*'

The next few hours seemed an eternity to Holly, but she finally found herself standing on the street outside the complex with her belongings stuffed into a plastic garbage bag. The thought of simply bolting crossed her mind, but the security thugs were watching from the designated smoking area. A young Hispanic driving a black van stopped, but before he could get the passenger window completely down to talk with her, Barton pulled up in his Lexus and laid on the horn. Unhurried, the kid waggled a large doobie at her and wiggled his eyebrows in invitation. Holly casually waved him away and he eased his van back into the traffic flow. Holly smiled, clearly this was a kid smart enough to stay clear of traffic cops. Dangerous. Barton pulled up and reached over to open the door for her. After she tossed her bag in the back, they were on their way.

The air conditioner fan teased at the hem of her thin dress and Barton had trouble keeping his eyes on the road. He'd run a comb through his hair and wore a snazzy pair of sunglasses that looked expensive.

"Please put on your seatbelt," Barton suggested.

Holly reached over and took off his sunglasses and decided that central Florida looked better to her through them. Barton gave her an exasperated look and opened a compartment and took out a spare pair. Holly opened the glove box and looked through the contents. She found a pack of gum, unwrapped out two sticks and shoved them into her mouth. She threw the wrappers on the floor.

"Stay out of my stuff," Barton warned, but his heart was not in it.

Holly continued her inventory. Under a stack of oil change receipts, Holly found some blister packs of drug company samples. She looked through them until she found a familiar name, Midazolam. She pressed out two of the pills and tossed them back in her throat.

"Do you know what you're doing?"

"Short-acting benzodiazepine, a central nervous system depressant with sedative and muscle relaxant properties. In this pediatric dosage, it will just take the sharp edge off my day. I've been in and out of clinics and treatment my whole life, so, just shut up and leave me alone."

She found a box of condoms, rainbow colored, ribbed and lubricated.

"You're intruding on my privacy, young lady."

"Are you so afraid of intimacy, Mr. Thomas? I would find that... disappointing. If you learned anything from my files, you'll know that dealing with disappointment is not one of my strengths. Work with me here, won't you please?" she asked sweetly.

Barton licked his lips. Holly shifted her hips and the hem of her dress hitched up her thighs another inch. His knuckles were white on the steering wheel. She looked carefully at a package containing bright yellow pills.

"Tadalafil? Is this what I think it is? The weekend party pill for men?"

Barton nodded.

"Then you'd better have two, I think."

"That's a lot," Barton commented.

"Trust me," Holly said, "you'll need two. Melt them under your tongue and they'll kick in quicker."

She pressed the pills into his mouth.

"Tastes like poop."

"Shut up. Won't this land yacht go any faster?" Holly suggested.

Barton pressed the accelerator and the big V8 responded smoothly.

"That's more like it," Holly commented as she tossed the rest of the pills in the back seat. She leaned against Barton and put her hand on his thigh. "I feel ripe and ready for the plucking," she whispered.

The three stories of Casa Thomas loomed over a canal filled with lime green water. The house looked baked to a golden brown in the steamy and humid afternoon sunlight. Barton's housekeeper, wearing an apron and a suspicious expression, was quickly dismissed. Apparently, in spite of Barton's fevered explanation, Holly did not look like a young patient in need of private counseling. As soon as the door slammed shut, Holly dropped her plastic bag, shrugged off her dress and wriggled out of her panties. She walked from room-to-room turning on every television and radio she found. On a Bose Wave Radio, she pressed buttons until she found a salsa station. Dancing, she twirled and shook like an otter. Torn between staring at Holly's nakedness and averting his gaze in shame and embarrassment, Barton offered her a glass of wine. Holly took a sip and carried the glass around the room. She took pleasure in flicking blood red drops from her fingers onto the rich pale cream of the carpets and upholstery. Barton wanted to scream at her, but instead wrapped her in his arms and began kissing her neck. She wriggled free.

"Let's not be getting grabby, Mister."

She turned on a gas fireplace with a remote control and then cranked up the air conditioning as far as it would go. This made her giggle. She crossed her legs and pointed at Barton.

"Let's see your equipment," she said curtly.

Barton tore off his shirt and tie. He wore a tank top t-shirt which exposed a thick mat of gray chest hair. He pulled off his shoes and stood in front of her wearing only the t-shirt and his boxer shorts.

"All of it," Holly hissed.

Barton stripped to the flesh. His skin was white and covered with snaky varicose veins. His cock, fully engorged and vibrating, was thick, but short and terminated with an angry purple glans like a little fist.

"I'm not sure about this," Holly commented thoughtfully. "If this is what I have to deal with, then I think — I'd like to have some ice cream first."

She padded toward the kitchen and found a half-gallon container of Rocky Road behind some frozen pizzas in a brushed steel freezer compartment. She went through the drawers and found a heavy flat-bladed knife. She stared at her reflection in the blade for a moment.

"Heaven or hell?" she whispered.

Carrying her treats, she skipped back into the living room. She made Barton lay on the floor on his back.

"Close your eyes, baby."

She cut the top off the ice cream container and hacked out a serving. She placed this globule on his chest.

"Hey, that's cold."

"Just shut up, you're going to like this, I guarantee it."

She dished out more ice cream and made a trail across his belly, then tucked the last splotch under his prick. She ran her finger up his shaft and pressed the head into the melting mound. Barton groaned and his hips strained.

"Keep your eyes closed, Mister Barton, because here it comes," she commanded.

The housekeeper found Barton Thomas's body 36 hours later. His lifeless eyes stared upward at the ceiling as he lay on the floor of his living room with puddles of molten ice cream on his abdomen and with the handle of the kitchen knife protruding from his left temple. Ants had discovered the ice cream and made a trail across the carpeting. At the instant of this discovery, Holly was cruising south in Barton's Lexus, wondering if it was time to change vehicles or if simply changing plates would carry her a while longer. She drove in the fast lane with her dress unbuttoned and her feet on the dash, letting the cruise control do its job while she weaved through traffic and scanned the radio stations for songs she knew. She found a hiphop station and adjusted the bass to the max. She smiled and her perfect white teeth gleamed in the Floridian sun.

Moshi

As Moshi was pulling the lace of her sneaker tight, it snapped. She sat and stared at the broken lace while hot tears welled and overflowed. She'd been crying a lot lately. The tears would cascade if she broke a fingernail or if a cute puppy appeared on a TV commercial. She worked at the laces until there was enough length on both sides to tie a knot. Sitting on the bed, she waited for Erik to come out of the bathroom down the hall. He'd been in there a long time; she hoped he was simply reading a magazine and not nodded off from the heroin he'd been shooting. They lived in a band house and their room was in the back overlooking an alley. There were honeysuckle bushes outside their window and the scent drifted in and helped hide the stale smell of damp clothes strewn on the floor. Moshi usually kept the clothes picked up, but she'd been too tired lately. She picked up a framed picture. It showed Moshi and Erik at their Senior Prom just before they both dropped out of high school. Erik looked grand in his tuxedo and Moshi luscious in her borrowed gown. She believed that was the last time she had been genuinely and completely happy. Later that night, on a dirty mattress in the back room of the band practice pad, she had granted Erik her virginity and, as far as she knew, it was the first time he had injected heroin. Prior, he'd just been snorting. She worried about him, but he claimed he could handle it and got angry when she suggested he enroll in a program and kick.

Erik came out. His eyes were droopy and he was moving smoothly and slowly. There was a drop of blood at the inside of his elbow.

"I've been ready," Moshi said.

"Look baby, we're going to be practicing late, you should stay home tonight."

"I want to hear the new song you guys are working on."

Erik played bass for a thrashy death-metal band. The most recent name they assumed was Toxic Shock Syndrome, but at various times they had also called themselves Right Wing Hate Speech, Lung Cancer and Bloodclot. The band was surprisingly good in spite of the bitter arguments between the players and the fact that they got high and partied more than they really practiced. The guitar player, main singer, and songwriter was a bright young kid named David Smith, but his stage name was Rusty 'Raz' Razorblade and he looked a lot like a young Johnny Depp. Raz was very talented and, in addition to electric guitar, he could play violin, clarinet, and accordion. He taught the other players all their parts and ranted and broke things when they didn't play exactly what he taught them. The band members hated it, but the result was good. They had a won several battle-of-the-band concerts and their home-made demo CD had attracted the attention of A&R[2] people from

---

[2] Artist and Repertoire. Basically talent scouts, they discover and develop talent for record companies.

three international labels. They had a contract offer from a small label but they were holding out for more money from a major.

"Not tonight. It's going to be an all-nighter."

Moshi had suspicions about these all night rehearsals. The band had been generating buzz in the local music scene and there were plenty of girls wearing spike heels, leather miniskirts and bustiers hanging around trying to catch themselves a cheap ride to the big time. Raz got the best girls, but Moshi knew that Erik had his pick of the remnants. The willing girls too chubby to be wearing their bare midriff blouses. The dull girls with home bleach jobs and part time jobs at Wal-Mart or Wendy's. This train of thought needed to be shoved down deep and covered up well. She knew that whining was unattractive, but she could not help herself.

"We used to do everything together," she said with her chin quivering.

"After the show on Friday we'll get some breakfast and it will be like old times. I just gotta work tonight, okay, baby?" He pulled out his wallet. It was stuffed with cash and Moshi wondered where he got the money. This was a dishonest thought because she knew that he was dealing crank and horse again. She wanted to ask why, if he had cash, was the phone still disconnected, but she didn't want to start another fight. She was too tired. "Here's ten bucks, order yourself a pizza."

She wanted to scream. *The phone doesn't work, you fool. How can I order a pizza? Besides, ten dollars doesn't cover a pizza bill. I didn't give you a lousy ten bucks when your amp blew up and needed repair. I didn't give you ten bucks when you wanted a BC Rich bass like Gene Simmons played in Kiss. I gave you everything I had and I charged the rest on my Visa card when I still had one with available credit.* She remembered when the phone worked that she was hounded by bill collectors, so the silence was a blessing. Still, she missed talking to the college kids selling magazine subscriptions. Some days they were her only human contact.

While she was lost in thought, Erik slipped out the door. She could hear him grinding the starter on their old van. Against her hope, eventually the engine caught and he drove away. She rolled a joint that was mostly twigs and seeds; garbage left over from a plastic bag she found in one of Eric's jacket pockets. She took a drag deep into her lungs and turned on the TV. They didn't have cable but they could get a couple of channels with the rabbit ear antenna. She'd have to tell Erik later that she was pretty sure she was pregnant.

Lester Mike

A bitter wind swirled a few lonely snowflakes between Lester Mike and Harold as they trudged towards their airstrip with a springtime cold snap temperature hovering at twenty-something below. The frigid air was aided and abetted by a stiff breeze funneling down the towering Alaska Range to the west and the closer foothills of the Chugach Mountains to the east.

"It'd be okay with me if you helped pull this damn sled," Harold said, glaring at Lester.

Lester stopped until he could fall in behind the sled and push, but not very hard. Lester had supplied the cases of liquor on the sled and they usually used his battered old Polaris snowmobile to drag the sled to their tiny airstrip. The fact that Lester's snow-go had overheated and seized, while driven by Harold, while attempting an uphill tow of Harold's plane, while Lester was in town and had in no way authorized any plane-towing operation, was the root cause of Lester's dangerous hostility.

"I oughta just gut-shoot you right here," grunted Lester, "and leave you for the bears."

"The bears are still sleeping," Harold said, panting. He hesitated and the sled ran up on the heels of his boots. "Ouch. Aren't they?"

"Keep moving." Lester wanted to keep their momentum. "Wolves, then. There are plenty of hungry wolves around." Lester hadn't seen a wolf around the place in a year or two, but this was among the many things that Harold didn't know about the wild. After all, he was a naïve lower-48-er.

Harold Busman was a six-foot-four, 160 pound former Okie roustabout, fired from a Slope job for failing a random drug test in two consecutive rotations. Harold's (probably valid) concern regarding the random nature of the second drug test didn't change the fact he'd pissed into a bottle the morning after a night that started at Chilkoot Charlie's, deteriorated into a couple of hours at The Bush Company stuffing dollar bills into G-strings, and wound up at some scraggly stripper's drafty shack on Spenard Avenue drinking tequila and snorting a mystery powder the whore assured him was 100% herbal and completely legal. Since the urinalysis lab stubbornly identified the substance as refined heroin (doctored with significant portions of rat poison and talcum powder), Harold now flew an ancient Super Cub into remote areas of the

21

Yukon-Kuskokwim Delta, and sometimes even into Bethel, ferrying loads of bootleg liquor for Lester Mike. Lester sold him the plane for $5,000 and threw in an afternoon of flight instruction. Harold perfected his landing technique in such a fog of Canadian whiskey that for months afterward he had trouble landing the plane while sober. More than one of Lester's hunting clients were startled to see their pilot drag a flask from beneath the seat and pull off half a pint or so on the final approach to some half-submerged sand bar. Lester himself refused to be in the same plane with Harold unless Harold was passed out or strapped into the back seat, preferably both.

Lester Mike was Yup'ik. He and his two sisters were raised by his grandmother after their mother died birthing a brother who was tangled in the umbilical. Depending on who was asked, his father either drank himself to death or accidentally drove his snow machine through thin ice into the Yukon. Looking back now, years later, Lester figured it was some of both, since he'd noted that the people he knew who drove their snow machines into rivers tended to be more than half lit at the time. Lester stood tall for a Native, almost six-feet, with a sturdy build and slightly lighter coloring he'd inherited from his mother. Village rumors held that grandmamma may have befriended a Russian trader in her youth. Lester never questioned his grandmother about the issue, partly out of an innate cultural respect for an elder, and partly because the old woman had been married to an *angalkuk* — a shaman — and the eldest Yup'iks claimed the old woman had twice the orneriness and three times the magic of the old man. Lester Mike loved his grandmother dearly and saw no reason to piss her off.

The sled cleared a small rise some forty yards from the plane. With the wind sharpened into icy daggers, both men hastened to reach the Piper and the relative shelter of the fuselage.

"Goddam, Lester," Harold gasped. "You think this fucker'll start? It's frigging cold this morning." He opened the cargo door to the plane and started shoving boxes of liquor into the back. Lester removed the warming blanket from the cowling and tossed it onto the back of the sled. He pulled out a propane bottle with weed burner attachment and ignited the business end with a kitchen match when his butane lighter refused to function. There should be an Olympic event that included lighting a match with a thumbnail in gusting winds. He waved the burner in the general direction of the exposed engine and exhaust.

"Get in and give her a try," Lester instructed while stepping away from the propeller.

The engine sputtered and popped for a few minutes before settling into a ragged idle. Harold gave Lester a grinning thumbs-up through the frosted windshield. Lester came around to Harold's open door and stuck his head inside to escape the painfully frigid blast from the propeller. "Okay!" he yelled, "you don't unload 'til they pay up for last time!" He reached into a pocket of his Carhartt jacket and pulled out a battered but functional revolver and offered it to Harold butt-first. Their eyes met for a moment and then Harold frowned down at the gun. Lester sighed and placed it on the Cub's dash. "Just leave it where they can see it, at least." Harold nodded, then grinned and slammed the door, giving Lester another jaunty thumbs-up before bending to fiddle with the fuel-mixture controls. Lester sighed again and headed toward an opening in the brush that marked the trail to the house, a different trail than the one that led to the shed, the shed where Lester Mike, grandson of a revered *angalkuk*, stored his bootleg liquor.

Lester Mike stomped the snow off his mukluks and hung his parka on a nail by the door. He examined his domain; the Caribou horns that towered over the air-tight woodstove, the 30-06 that shared a gun rack with his fly pole, the newspaper that was stuffed into the cracks in the log walls and the dreamcatcher that hung in front of the only window that was not shuttered for winter. He poured a tin cup of coffee from a pot that sat on the woodstove. He took a sip and scowled, then splashed in Canadian Club until he could stomach the oily brew. Lester Mike did not really drink anymore, but a few ounces of whiskey in his coffee when the wind howled so fiercely outside did not count. *I'm getting too old for this shit*, he thought sourly. He unfurled newspapers stuffed between his down jacket and long johns to protect them from the weather, lighted the lantern that hung over his rocker, and settled down to read the week-old news Harold had delivered. Lester had his share of adventures around the state and was making good money but he felt strongly like he needed a change. *There has to be more to life than pissing into a coffee can and waiting forever for Spring*, he thought as he dried his feet by the stove and leafed through the paper.

Glen

I quit my job and I'm moving to Alaska to run for US Congress. The arrogance! The audacity! The insanity! Who the hell do I think I am? Do I think this will be easy? A crazy idea lodges in my head and I go after it with wild abandon. What possible reason do I have for thinking I can win? Playing politics on a national scale is big league. The political machines chew up people like me and spit out the barren bones. Again, who the hell do I think I am to attempt such a project?

Don't I believe the laws apply to me? How can I expect to murder and cheat without consequence? The fact is, there is more than one system and I choose not to play the common man's game. Think of OJ Simpson and all the murderous dictators that died peacefully in their soft beds. What about Senator Theodore Kennedy and his lovely boiler room girl, Mary Joe?

I have a confession. I believe that I have been selected for greatness. In clinical terms, this can be a form of paranoid schizophrenia. Delusions of grandeur. I'm special, a man who is going places and will make a mark on the world. I've been beaten. I've been hacked and left for dead. Still, I persevere. I'm not just a man, I'm an unstoppable force of nature.

I could be wrong. I may be destined for failure, obscurity and despair. Just another washed-out never-was loser in a long string of the same. In the grand scheme, aren't we just ants crawling in and out of our hill? Nameless and faceless nonentities? Pull back far enough and look at the scale of space and time, 100 years, 1000, years, a million years? I know this is the stuff of madness, but really, what difference does it make? Every sociopath believes this thing. That the world revolves around them and that others are inconsequential. A few are consumed while we assuage our egos and our many appetites. So what?

But, to my core, I don't believe I will fail. That's right, things will align my way and I will overcome. Knock me down and I will get back up. My enemies will be vanquished and I will live to spit on their cooling bodies. Literally and figuratively. Wager against me if you wish. However, if you will accept some small advice, try to get odds. Something like ten to one should be sufficient. Line up at the window where the man with his face hidden in shadow will take your money. Cash only, no credit cards or checks. Step right up and lay down your bet.

The American, if he has a spark of national feeling, will be humiliated by the very prospect of a foreigner's visit to Congress—these, for the most part, illiterate hacks whose fancy vests are spotted with gravy, and whose speeches, hypocritical, unctuous, and slovenly, are spotted also with the gravy of political patronage, these persons are a reflection on the democratic process rather than of it; they expose it in its underwear.

- Mary McCarthy

CHAPTER 1

The Election Team

Every time Glen made a grand gesture, coffee sloshed out of his cup and splashed onto the hotel carpet. His election team was gathered in their makeshift command headquarters in the Presidential Suite at the Downtown Marriott Anchorage. The dining room table had been pulled into the living room and the team was scattered around it. Glen had hired some installers who, in the background, were rigging a free space optic high-speed voice and data link pointing out the window. A wireless LAN was already set up with nodes for a printer, FAX machine, and PBX telephone system. Everyone on the team had been issued a laptop computer and RF-linked PDA.

"I want to dispense with the foreplay as much as possible," he said. "You were all chosen because you're the best at what ever it is that you do. I don't want to waste a lot of time on introduction, but you're bound to be curious." Glen pointed a rolled up sheaf of paperwork at Murphy who reclined on a couch with her arm around Elke. "Murphy is a retired Florida State Bull, she is in charge of enforcement, security, and she's designated as arm candy."

"I don't want to throw you off track, Glen," Murphy asked, "but why am I the arm candy? Angela is awfully pretty, she could do it."

"I don't generally want to answer every question that comes up, the SOP[3] will be to just trust me. That doesn't mean you shouldn't argue with me if I'm screwing up. Anyway, in regard to your query, you are in charge of security, this means you take down anyone that comes at me. Bodyguard, if you will, and hanging around as my girlfriend is perfect

---

[3] Standard Operating Procedure

cover for staying near me at all times. An additional reason is that my polling shows having an older wife or girlfriend is worth about 2.3 percentage points, and it's more like 3.1 percent if she's a motherly-looking filly like you. Angela is just a little too young. Okay?"

Murphy nodded reluctantly.

"Elke is our accountant because she's German, she can count, and she's joined at the hip with Murphy. They are a couple. If anyone has a problem with that, speak up now."

All were quiet, though Bennie looked at Murphy and Elke curiously.

"Bennie Jackson is our computer whiz," Glen continued. "He's just a little guy, but he's as smart and as good with computers as anyone I've ever met, and that's saying something. Bennie will be doing statistics and handling the online part of the campaign. Walter Crawley used to be known as Doctor Zalooq and you may have seen his shows on HBO. Don't let the Hollywood bullshit fool you, Walt has some diseased ideas housed in that cranium that we're going to need. He's in charge of propaganda, media and manipulating the public masses."

"Why did you pick Alaska instead of someplace civilized like California?" Elke asked.

"Because we're going to pull some serious mind fuck to win this election. The parties don't spend much time thinking about Alaska. There are only six hundred thousand and some-odd citizens up here and we're way off the map as far as the political power structure is concerned. By the time they figure out what we're up to, I believe it will be too late for them to do anything about us. We're going to operate in the stealth mode as long as possible. We're going to run on private cash, this takes us out of the rules for contributed money. What is our starting bankroll, Elke?"

Elke consulted some printouts. "You started with just over eight-hundred grand. I deposited the Hong Kong dollars and sold the gold, that added 1.3 mil. You get a few additional deposits now and then, can we count on a few more of those?" Glen nodded. "Good, the balance right now is a few nickels over 2.5 million."

"We have enough money to buy this election, but we're going to split the remainder as a post-election bonus, so spend what you need, but don't go ape shit. All expenses will be paid, just submit receipts and invoices to Elke." Glen distributed credit cards to all. "Try to use these AMEX cards as much as possible. You are all being paid on a contract basis and anyone who wants a job after I win is welcome to stay on board. I want you all to bias toward action, in other words if you have to choose between doing something or not, pick the active course. Any questions?"

"Yes, Glen," Walter said while spinning his AMEX card in his fingers. "Why exactly are we doing this?"

"What do you mean?" Glen asked.

"Why exactly do you want to be elected to the House of Representatives? Do you have a political objective? Are you trying to repay the country for all the bounty you have received? It can't just be the paltry salary or the small amount of political power that motivates you. And I'm not buying any bullshit about serving the good of the common people or anything like that."

"The main reason is because I'm bored and because I can. Secondarily, I want the lifestyle: sleeping in late and working, if you want to call it that, about 80 days a year. The real reason is the perks, the unlimited expense account, the staff, and all the people who will kiss my ass to get what they want," Glen said dreamily, "and the bushel barrels of tax money I can influence. Okay?"

Walter nodded. "I get it," he said.

"Later, I'd like to meet with you all individually and talk about specific assignments. If there are no more questions, get to work, dammit. Like the Japanese farmer I used to work for always said, I just want to see assholes and elbows, everyone, assholes and elbows."

ALASKA INSTANT POLL

June 1

Alaska Daily News Survey of likely Voters (plus or minus 4% error)
36% Undecided
26% Sanders – REP
12% Van Doren – DEM
3% Other
3% Walters – GREEN
2% Gray – LIBERT
2% Patterson - DEM
1% Onkiak – AK IND
0% Wilson - DM

Glen and Elke

Glen gestured for the waitress to refill his coffee cup. He and Elke sat by a window in the hotel coffee shop. Elke was drinking hot tea and nibbling on a slice of cheesecake. It was mid-afternoon and the place was mostly deserted, though there were a few business people around reading their newspapers and waiting for the airport shuttle.

"I want to thank you, Glen," Elke said quietly. "Two years ago I was going nowhere, it was either Prozac or a Marilyn Monroe cocktail. I was bored and lonely. Now between you and Murphy..."

"You were wasting yourself working for that semiconductor company. Let me ask you, if it all went down the toilet tomorrow, would you have any regrets?"

"None," Elke replied, "I wouldn't change a thing."

"Good," Glen said, "you can't win unless you're willing to lose, that's Wilson's Law. Now, about the money, let me know if we get down to a few hundred grand, it's my job to make sure we don't run out. We're going to do a lot of transactions in cash, so make sure you have a hundred grand or so in mixed bills available at all times. We're going to start a PAC so we can deal with some semi-official money, but most of our initial campaign contributions will be passed on to either the Green candidate or the Libertarian candidate, we won't keep any of it."

"Can I ask why we're going to fund our competitors?"

"I don't want to get in the habit of answering questions because there simply won't be time once we get busy, but we're in no hurry today. The answer is, since it will be too expensive to win with a majority, we're going to split the vote. The Greens take votes primarily from Democrats and the Libertarians take votes primarily from Republicans though you'll see some D's cross over. We'll use them as necessary to steer votes we don't feel are available to us. However, the initial strategy is that we'll be manipulating which party candidates get elected in the primary, then we'll tweak the final vote with the minor parties later. I think we'll end up on the Democratic ticket, but to start with, I want you to file the paperwork to get us on the primary ballot with the Democratic Environment Movement party name, no, use the Democratic Majority, I like that better."

"What's the idea with this name?"

"We're running a crossover campaign. Unless the polling and election simulation says otherwise, we're going to be pro-business, pro-gun, and pro-life Democrats. Besides, with those initials we get a few freebie votes from the knee-jerk liberals who would be confused and vote for a caribou if it had a big DM after its name on the ballot. As I said, I don't think it's going to matter, once we can't hide the polling any more, I think the Dems will come and make a deal with us."

Glen consulted a notepad to see if he'd forgotten anything.

"Murphy and I are going to be spending a lot of time together," he said.

"Yeah, I know."

"I just want you to know now that if she and I do end up having sex a few times, it won't really mean anything. I know her heart will still belong to you."

Elke patted his hand.

"I don't own her. If you want to take a shot, have at it. That said, I don't know how much luck you'll have."

Glen cleaned a fingernail with his salad fork.

"You haven't seen the full force of the Glen Wilson charm or you'd have no doubt."

"Right. I'll burn that bridge when I get to it." Elke looked out the window. There were flowers in a window box and beyond that, shiny SUVs and pickups streamed by on the street and reflected the mid-summer sunshine.

"This doesn't seem to be such a bad place when the sun is out," she said, draining her teacup.

"It won All-American City of the year four times in the last 50 years. Of course, Detroit won too in 1966, so I guess we shouldn't be too impressed. I'm told that in a good year, this place can be quite livable during June. If you're a frigging moose!"

Elke patted his hand. "Now Glen, you're not going to win many votes if you insult these people's home. Be nice."

"I didn't get to where I am today by being nice," Glen grumbled. "You just make sure we don't run out of cash and beer. Let's get back to work, we have an election to buy."

Glen and Bennie

Glen and Bennie were playing a racing game on an Xbox360 and a large plasma display. They were sitting next to each other on a couch, but they still talked to each other only via their headsets.

"I don't know much about kids," Glen said as he maneuvered around a moving van that was weaving on the autobahn. "Do you have a bed time? Is there some type of vitamins we should be buying? Is your mom going to freak out if you don't get your naps or something?"

"I'm just like a real person, only smaller. Just treat me normally."

"Do I need to teach you about sex or anything?"

"I learned all that from cable TV and the Internet. I'll get your website set up. Just let me know what other things you want me to do. I want this job and your money, I didn't come out here looking for a father."

"Good. To start with, I want you to work with Murphy, we need to do a deep background investigation on me. I've had a colorful life, but I think most of the data has been deleted or sanitized. On the other hand I don't want to be surprised by something a background check will turn up. Murphy can help you with the law enforcement databases and the crew in Bombay will help with crypto and hacking."

"Okay, what else?"

"I need state-of-the-art statistical analysis, evaluation of polling data, deep number-crunching of issues and positions. You know anything about SimCity?"

"I hacked that when I was seven," Bennie said while whipping his NSX through a construction zone at 85 MPH.

"Set up an election simulation. Trends, demographics and issue analysis. Put in everything you can think of. You'll be running the campaign for all practical purposes. I want judgments on the color of my tie, the kind of car I should be driving around in, how Murphy should wear her hair, the tint of my contact lens, everything. Will I get more votes by kissing babies in Juneau or cutting construction ribbons in Fairbanks? Where is our money most effectively spent? Is it better to wave a bible in Kodiak or sling hash at a food bank in Ketchikan? Can you handle it?"

"I can handle all that and still have time to beat your lame ass on the race course," Bennie said, running his car across the finish line. He tossed down his steering wheel controller as women with large breasts kissed his driver on the plasma screen. "Perhaps you'll show me some respect before this is over and hand me a real challenge."

"Screw you, kid," Glen said. His car was stuck in a swamp. Mud flew, but the car just kept digging in deeper. "This game sucks," he said, heaving his controller at the screen.

Glen and Walter

Glen and Walter were smoking Costa Rican cigars and sharing a bottle of Glenfiddich. They took small sips and passed the bottle back and forth. They were in one of the hotel suite's bedrooms; the bed had been dismantled and leaned against the wall. They lolled in beanbag chairs in their stocking feet. Angela snored softly on her own beanbag in the corner; the strap of her dress had fallen and a slice of aureole was winking. This was tough for Glen to ignore so he didn't. He accepted the bottle from Walter.

"You seem familiar to me, but I can't put my finger on it exactly. I know I've seen you in the papers, but I think it's more than that. Were you in 'Nam?"

"No."

"I'm good with faces..."

"Everybody looks like somebody."

"Yeah, I guess. I caught your show at the Luxor last year," Glen said, "and I was very impressed. In particular, there was an illusion where you were speaking with the dead and the voices appeared to be in the center of my head. How did you pull that one off?"

"We do quite a lot with limbic rhythms, lights pulsing at hypnotic frequencies, and some phased-array speaker systems. We pump a mild euphoric into the cooling system that suspends skepticism and makes you more open to suggestion. In addition, I think some of this stuff is actually real, the mind has untapped resources that we unlock to some extent. It's state-of-the-art and immensely illegal now, but in five years it will be used to sell Big Macs and Toyotas to Joe-Sixpack."

For a few minutes they watched the purple sunlight creep down the wall as the sun set.

"I need to ask you, what exactly is the story with you and Angela? To be frank, if I don't find someplace to stick my dick, I'm going to go nucking futs, if you catch my drift."

"Angela is a good kid, she caught my eye swinging on a ribbon at one of those Cirque du Soleil shows. She goes off the deep end on occasion, but basically she's simple and sweet and I'd like to keep her that way as long as possible. Great figure, low IQ, she's almost perfect. I don't expect to marry her or anything, but I'd really appreciate it if you'd keep your hands off, go find your own squeeze, okay?"

"I suppose." Glen was tired and was having trouble keeping his eyes open. "For the campaign, some of the things I need you to do are mundane. Work with Bennie to create a campaign sign theme. Mom,

31

apple pie, God bless America and Glen Wilson will save your soul, those sorts of things. Wilson rocks for the kids, Wilson worships with the bible-thumpers, Wilson supports living wages for the union crowd, Wilson wants free pills for the AARP, Wilson nukes terror, and whatever else you can think of. You will be stage manager for our rallies. We'll bus in Native Americans, retired folks, Americorp volunteers and college kids. We'll make these into real hoedowns. You can coordinate the signs, the t-shirts, the flags, and the campaign buttons. Fish tacos for everyone! We'll need a lot of belief suspended. This campaign will be 90% style and zero percent content and it's your job to make sure the bozos eat it up and ask for more."

"Do you mind if I mix in a little Aleutian shamanism? Some of that is quite interesting."

Glen was drifting off and Walter had to rescue the Glenfiddich before it spilled. He took Glen's cigar and quenched it in a glass of water.

"I don't care if you shit in a sauce pan and call it soup," Glen said dreamily, "as long as the sheeple[4] mark my name on the ballot and I get to be congressman for the great state of Arkansas."

"Alaska," Walter corrected.

"Shit, sorry, I meant Alaska," Glen said as he faded completely into unconsciousness. Walter turned out the light as he exited the room and left Glen and Angela to their slumbers.

Glen and Murphy

The next morning, Glen sipped coffee in the kitchenette. Murphy wandered in. Her hair was uncombed and she wore a hotel bathrobe and slippers. She poured coffee into a foam cup and picked up a stale donut from a Dunkin Donut box and started nibbling it.

"Not exactly a morning person, eh Murphy?" Glen asked rhetorically.

"Fuck you, boss," Murphy said absently as she picked up the newspaper's sports page from the floor.

Glen tugged the newspaper from her hands and tossed it aside.

"You're in charge of intelligence and security," Glen said. "Find some goons, outfit them in suits, headsets, blackjacks, all the usual crowd control stuff. I want at least two around whenever I'm in public. You stay by my side at all times. Before we get rolling, I want a dossier

---

[4] Insulting contraction of sheep and people.

on all the other candidates with deep background checks. Bennie will help you with the computer parts of that data mining. We're going to steer the Republicans to offering up a Christian conservative and we're going to get the Democrats to go with some radical lefty. These candidates look good at first and have initial support from the base voters, but it's easy to demonize and marginalize them later. We want to support the best Green and Libertarian candidates we can find, we'll build them up and then discard the one we don't need. They can't win, but they can act as great spoilers. I want to operate under the radar for as long as possible. The candidates may be stupid, but the party bosses aren't, so I want to make sure that time works against them as much as possible. Okay?"

"Yeah, I got it. Anything else?"

"Yes, actually there is. I think the electorate is very sensitive to personal chemistry. They are going to instinctively know whether you and I are lovers. We're going to want to get kinky a few times before we start appearing in public." He untangled and smoothed out a lock of her hair. "The sooner the better, I think. Perhaps we should get officially married just to make everything look good."

"Don't take this personally, but if it was a choice between jumping off a cliff onto jagged lava and marrying you, I would take the leap. If required to choose between slicing my own face off with a hedge trimmer and sleeping with you, I would face the trimmer. If it was a choice between..."

"I'm sensing the theme here, Murphy. I'm just trying to win this election, aren't you a team player?"

"You're going to have to figure out a way to win and keep your boner to yourself. A smart guy like you should be able to handle that."

"I'm good in the sack. I can give you some references."

"Look, its not you, I'm just not that interested in guys, alright?"

"Well, if you change your mind..."

"You'll be very nearly the first to know."

"Okay, look, what if Elke and I go at it a few times just to take the edge off? Would you mind?"

"I'll empty my .357 up your hairy ass." Murphy said quietly.

"Alright, Murphy, just checking, you don't have to blow a gasket. Geez."

Glen picked up the sports page and handed it back to Murphy. He wandered morosely through the suite before plopping himself on the living room couch and clicking the TV onto Fox news. "Nobody is any fucking fun around here," he muttered to himself.

Holly

Holly was naked underneath her flower-print dress. A few drops of dried blood were splattered on the front, but were barely noticeable in the garish floral pattern. The huge dress had been hanging in Chairman Benton Thomas' closet and either belonged to Benton's long deceased mother or he had an additional latent kink that simmered beneath his three-piece suits. A safer kink compared to his desire to bed his pretty young psychopathic patient. She drove the Lexus barefoot with her hair blowing in the white-hot slipstream that poured through the windows. She'd found some Ray-Ban sunglasses in a handy eyeglass compartment and felt like a movie star behind the wheel of her personal limo. The Lexus definitely aced her old truck in creature comforts but she doubted it would make much of a swamp buggy. She missed the heavy rumble and vibration of a glass pack exhaust that made her all soft and squishy inside.

The thin cotton dress was the first piece of real clothing she'd worn since her initial arrest; too bad it wasn't her style. She headed for the freeway but inspiration, in the form of a strip mall anchored by a regional clothing chain, appeared and she aimed the heavy sedan into the parking lot. It was a busy shopping day but she managed to find two handicap slots by the front door so she angled in to take up both. This gave her more room for opening her door. She vaguely wondered why, with all the fools who crammed their station wagons into compact car spaces, no one else took advantage of such opportunities. She assumed the others were too stupid or perhaps, the spot had been provided for her by divine design. Holly held a hazy concept of God as a creator of her Universe who stepped in from time to time at His leisure, to help or hinder according to some Plan he held for her. A grand plan that created all other humans to serve under her. Personally, she felt He had screwed up a few times, but things were finally getting back on track. *Who really knew his way?* She was halfway to the front door when she went back to remove the keys from the unlocked car. God might be busy jacking off and let some cracker jackass steal her car.

She headed straight for the women's clothing section and selected a pair of size-two store-brand jeans and a satiny 32B halter top before heading for the shoes. The women's sizes were all too big and she ended up in the children's section where she found a cheap pair of white deck shoes that felt right when she slipped them on. In the changing room she ripped the tags off her new clothes. She admired her bare body in the mirror and removed a smudge of dried blood from her cheek with

34

a moistened finger. The floral dress was left wadded up in the corner. Walking briskly, she was back in the Lexus and had the key in the ignition by the time the security guard appeared at her open window.

He gripped the door frame with two large hands and leaned in to stare at her through mirrored sunglasses.

"Excuse me, Miss. Do you have a receipt for the clothes you're wearing?"

Holly turned the key and the fuel-injected engine purred to life. The security man frowned and reached across the steering wheel for the key. Holly promptly sank her teeth into the man's forearm, clenching harder when she found she had a good bite. He cursed and jerked away, dragging Holly halfway through the window when she refused to release her grip. He slapped her with his free hand and Holly finally let go. She pulled herself back into the car with a trickle of vivid blood dripping from her chin. The store security man stared at his arm in disbelief for a moment, and then looked up at the young girl who had just taken a chunk out of his arm. Holly offered him a bloody smile before spitting a gory wad to the sidewalk and slapping the car into reverse. He started to reach through the window again and their eyes locked for the briefest of moments. Holly put her finger on the switch and prepared to crush his arms with the power window.

The burly Officer Kanes took the strip mall security guard gig to augment his pension check. He retired after twenty years as Florida State Patrolman and through his work with rapists and murderers had seen what he thought was the worst humanity had to offer. He was now stopped cold by the tiny sparks of death that flashed from Holly's eyes. Tangling with this grinning demon would leave his wife a widow and his three kids without a father. He knew that. He would be dragged, slammed into a guardrail, run over... the exact means of his death were irrelevant compared to the shock of the simple fact he would soon be dead at the hands of this beautiful child. He withdrew his hands and instinctively raised them in surrender. Holly hesitated, then blew him a kiss and floored the accelerator. The car gave a satisfying surge and she turned her attention to guiding it through the slalom course of parked cars that led to the street and escape. Officer Kanes watched with relief as she sped away, too stunned by what had just taken place to note the license number, which surprised the responding officers almost as much as their former colleague's insistence that a baby-blonde angel with death flashing from her eyes was on the loose in South Florida....

Moshi

The band scored a paying gig opening for The Rain Gods at the Showbox. They got $400 for the performance. The Rain Gods had won a Grammy in the Heavy Metal category and had sold two million copies of their latest release so the Showbox was sold out and packed with pierced and tattooed kids all expressing their identical individuality. A grinning teenager flicked and waggled his tongue at Moshi. It was split in half like a reptile. She suppressed an urge to vomit. Raz was playing well, he was both manic and calm. Apparently he had dosed himself with an effective mixture of heroin, crank, and alcohol. His eyes glowed satanically from under his lank hair. He wore blood-red contacts and had streaked his face with black paint. His guitar emitted slick hyperactive glissando runs, squealing feedback and crushing power chords. Erik rocked back and forth and beat on his bass guitar like he was pounding veal with a hammer. For their last song, Raz exchanged his expensive Gibson for a Samick knock-off because they couldn't afford to smash expensive guitars yet. Raz was screaming at the crowd and nicking his flesh with a box cutter. Trickles of blood and sweat ran down his arms and chest. At the finale, Raz smashed his guitar on the stage and threw himself into the crowd where he floated for almost a minute on a sea of hands while his amp died in a howl of digital delay and feedback. Moshi watched with horror as Erik jumped up and down on his bass, a decent black Ibanez for which Moshi had saved a month to scrape together the down payment. He threw the pieces into the crowd and walked off the stage waving the devil sign and pumping his fists.

Moshi worked her way through the crowd toward the backstage. She had trouble getting by security; all she had was a backstage pass from an earlier show. However, one of the sound crew recognized her and let her through. The green room was covered with bumper stickers and graffiti. The Rain Gods were huddled in a corner doing a group prayer and getting mentally prepared for their show. They were older guys who'd cleaned themselves up after three of their founding members had died respectively of an overdose, choking on vomit in a drunken stupor, and a high speed sports car accident. When forced to choose between a clean life and an untimely death, sometimes people chose life. Even the most addled might eventually notice that the fit survive.

Erik was drinking from a bottle of Jack Daniels. His hair was sodden and he had a Filipino girl on his lap who was whispering in his ear and giggling. Moshi pinched the girl hard to get her attention.

"Fuck off, bitch," the girl hissed.

"Tell her to get lost, Erik," Moshi commanded.

Erik wiped his mouth with his sleeve and tried to focus.

"It's okay, baby," he said. He lifted the girl off his lap and patted her on the butt. "I'll catch up with you later."

The girl gave Moshi a black look as she wandered off. The drummer was smoking a joint and telling a story, so she ambled in that direction. Moshi sat beside Erik, took the bottle from his hand, stole a small sip for herself then put the bottle on the floor out of Erik's reach.

"Wasn't that the most fucking awesome show? We really kicked some ass and showed the old men some new tricks."

Overhearing, the keyboard player for The Rain Gods looked over and emitted a thin smile. He was 26 and had spent six month in physical therapy after a motorcycle accident. He remembered being young and feeling immortal. Raz entered the room with a girl on each arm. His clothes were in shreds and he wore a crooked smile. He wiped his body with a towel and exchanged complicated handshakes with his bass player and drummer. He showed them a tooth he chipped on someone's ring during the stage dive. Moshi couldn't help herself, in her head she added up all the costs. The chipped tooth would cost a couple hundred to fix, the Korean guitar was two hundred bucks and hopefully the bass guitar could be repaired for a hundred or so. It was a great show, but how could they afford it? The power in the band house was in danger of being cut off and the rent was past due. Moshi picked up the bottle and choked down a swallow. Someone she didn't know was walking out the back door with Raz's Marshall amplifier. If he didn't care, then Moshi guessed she didn't care either. She took another drink. They sat around and talked past each other for a while until drowned out by the pounding industrial noise-rock that erupted when the Rain Gods took the stage.

"Catch a ride home with Mari and I'll see you later," Erik screamed in her ear.

Mari was the drummer's dim-witted girlfriend and the mother of three of his kids. Moshi liked Mari well enough, but felt sorry for her kids who spent most of their time with Mari's widowed mother.

"I thought we were going to get some breakfast?"

"I'll have to take a raincheck on that. We have a band meeting with the East-West A&R guy. This could be our break. They want to underwrite a tour in Japan."

"I could come with."

"There is no room in the van. Besides, you'll be bored. I'll see you at home. Don't wait up, okay?"

Moshi noticed there was apparently room in the van for Raz's friends and the Filipino girl. The doors slammed shut and the van roared off. Mari took Moshi's hand as they watched the van disappear around a corner.

"I have some Ben and Jerry's ice cream," Mari said cheerfully.

Moshi's guts churned. She made it to the edge of the building before the whiskey and macaroni and cheese box dinner erupted from her stomach.

Lester Mike

In summer, the path to Lester's house weaved through stunted spruce and muskeg, over rotting logs he'd placed at the sloppiest sections — occasionally dragging in another log or two when the old ones inevitably sank from sight — and finally opened into a small clearing where it cut straight through a patch of Devil's Club to Lester's back door. The summer vegetation currently lay under about three feet of dwindling snow pack and the path was a bobsled run paved with ice where overflow from the nameless creek and some intermittent springs overwhelmed Lester's half-hearted bridges.

Temperatures of twenty or thirty below didn't bother Lester too much, but if it got much colder he'd be forced to heat the shed as he'd done for much of December and all of January. He hoped he was through with all that for the year. Lester didn't heat the shed to keep the booze from freezing. The 80 proof liquor still flowed like syrup at -70 or so, but more than one local drunk rasped through damaged vocal cords from guzzling super-chilled whiskey and Lester knew of at least one guy over on the Kuskokwim who died. Whether that was attributable to binge drinking at -40 degrees or an epic blood alcohol level was a matter for some debate. Either way, there are worse ways to die, but for some unexplained reason Lester didn't feel this was to be his destiny.

Tom, the old pirate who delivered Lester's fuel oil, often wondered aloud why a man would need to heat a shed, implying Lester was either stupid or growing some illicit plants.

"Whatcha got in that shed, Lester?" he'd ask. "Tomato plants?"

Lester would laugh. "Why not, Tom? Priced tomatoes lately?" then tip him the ten bucks which bought his silence.

The truth was, Lester, like roughly ten percent of the local residents, had at one-time grown a little pot there, but when people began losing homes and vehicles ostensibly purchased with the ill-gotten gains from a dozen scraggly pot plants in the basement, Lester strayed into safer pursuits. A fifth of cheap whiskey or half-decent vodka (there was still lingering Russian influence in this area so the really bad vodka had no market) could fetch $150 on delivery to a dry village. In addition, an endless stream of out-of-state hunters were willing to part with thousands of dollars to bag a big grizzly or bull moose. In 13 years, only one client, a retired Army officer from the Midwest, had asked about his guide's license. When Lester pretended he hadn't understood the question, the client politely pretended he hadn't asked it.

Now that he had Harold to fly clients in and out of the hunting camps, Lester mostly handled logistics and finances. There were, of course, occasional important clients or even minor celebrities that Lester flew himself. After all, Harold was an idiot who would someday bend the plane around a tree or auger it into a glacier and Lester couldn't afford the publicity that would accompany killing someone famous.

The sun finally eased over the rim of the Chugach as Lester neared the house. The Chugach "foothills" were massive upthrusts of granite and dolomite, glacier-carved and wind-eroded to postcard perfection. The occasionally-inspired Lester snapped 20 or 30 photographs and had some blown up to poster size, the best of which he either crowded onto the walls of his shack or had Harold hustle to the 4th Avenue tourists in Anchorage. Sometimes he just wished the peaks would melt and stop blocking the low winter sun. In darkest winter it was almost noon before attenuated sunrays reached the log shamble that Lester called home. Within an hour those rays would dim and disappear again.

He'd built himself an arctic entry at the back door where he kicked off his Army surplus bunny boots before carrying them into the kitchen. Lester pretty much lived in his kitchen. The rest of the place was mostly taken up by projects in various states of incompletion. For example, one of his snowmobile engines sat on a crate in the living room with the cylinder head removed. Broken snowshoes, rifles laying around waiting to be cleaned, leg-hold traps, leaky kerosene heaters, old car parts and plumbing supplies lay scattered throughout the house like avante garde decor. The walls showcased Lester's photographs and some dusty caribou antlers. The pictures included a sunset over the icepack off Kotzebue Sound, polar bears at Barrow, the sheer cliffs of the Brooks Range, the Chugach peaks outside his door, the Harding ice field of the Kenai Peninsula and glaciers of the Southeast, Lester bow-hunting with Ted Nugent, a super model, and a funny photo with a grinning OJ Simpson skinning a bloody lynx with a large hunting knife. Also, there were snapshots of other smiling clients and their trophies; moose, caribou, grizzlies, and mountain goats. An aged black and white of his grandmother's shack at the edge of a windblown and mosquito-laden tundra town sixty miles down the Kuskokwim river from Bethel reminded him of what he was never going back to.

That shack was gone now, replaced by a new modular home built at Point McKenzie (across Knik Arm from Anchorage) and barged, along with nineteen identical federally subsidized homes, down the Aleutian Peninsula and across Bristol Bay and up the river to be placed on stilts above the permafrost to confront the unceasing grit-laden Western Alaska wind with vinyl siding and triple-paned glass and R31 insulation. At least the paint wouldn't be sandblasted to slivers in a year and the wind wouldn't claw its way through any cracks in the plywood. The new flush toilet might even function as advertised if the engineers and their above-the-ground sewage system weren't as crazy as the villagers assumed. Maybe his grandmother could afford to heat the place properly with subsidized heating oil barged in from Anchorage and keep the lights on at night with power provided at subsidized rates from huge diesel generators floated in from Anchorage. The other villagers could deliver her groceries, flown or shipped in from Anchorage to the new Alaska Commercial Store built over the summer with material floated in from Anchorage. If the people in Anchorage would just leave the villagers alone to hunt and fish as much as they needed, life would be pretty good.

Lester wasn't going back to that village except to visit his grandmother once in a while and to deliver a dozen or so cases of bootleg liquor to the guys that met him at the airstrip with ATVs or snowmobiles, depending on the season. Western Alaska held millions of acres of flat and treeless tundra with life concentrated on the rivers, where the fish and game were plentiful and one might at least scrounge enough dead shrubwood to start a fire. There were moose and caribou to be had, but Lester found his clients were enamored as much with the scenery of the interior as with the thrill of the hunt, so he flew his hunters into camps along the Susitna watershed and the slopes of the Alaska Range, into areas so remote the Fish and Game authorities were unable or unwilling to patrol. The 'Fish Cops' were highly unpopular in rural Alaska and usually traveled in armed pairs or in larger groups within the villages to deter hostile action by disgruntled locals. Lester had enough close calls in his youth to make him wary, once sweating nervously thirty feet from a mostly-dead twitching and steaming cow moose riddled with sixteen .22 bullets and four .30-.30 slugs while a Fish Cop lectured Lester and his friend about the lack of personal flotation devices in their skiff.

Lester thought back. He'd left his village at the age of seventeen and spent his first year in Bethel as an unlicensed taxi driver. Half the vehicles in Bethel were taxis, had been taxis, or would be taxis, as the local climate and road conditions made individual vehicle ownership an expensive and troublesome proposition. Bad people end up in Hell and bad vehicles end up in Bethel serving as taxis. The taxi company charged five dollars to go anywhere you wanted (which more or less meant the general store, the commercial area along the river, the hospital, or the airport) and nobody tipped, mainly because nobody had any money. After a year of not-quite-making-ends-meet Lester decided to work his way to Anchorage via The Alaska Commercial Company.

The AC stores offered just about anything you could possibly need or want, besting Wal-Mart in diversity if not quantity throughout the Alaskan Bush region. From Dutch Harbor in the Aleutians and the Pribilof Islands with their beleaguered fur seal pups to the northernmost reaches at Point Barrow, the AC stores supplied Alaska. You could buy shotguns, ATVs, snowmobiles, a bedroom set, lettuce and tuna and chicken wings, Levis and Carhartts, DVD players and stereos, snowshoes or a cordless drill... but no Jack Daniels. Until Lester came along, that is. He started as stock boy and after two years of spotty performance was in danger of re-embracing unemployment when he was approached by a freight handler from Anchorage who needed an unscrupulous fellow on the Bethel end.

"You look like a smart fella, they paying you what you're worth?" he was asked. Lester had spent the last two years working precisely as little as he could and still get paid, but he didn't mention that.

Six months later they were supplying all of Bethel and most of the surrounding villages with enough cut-rate liquor to raise the homicide rate by 30 percent. All was well until the local newspaper started screaming for an investigation. Since one of the 47 people that knew Lester was involved took the reward money, Lester did 60 days in the county lockup and wound up outside the Anchorage jail one fine winter morning in 1978; 20 years old, wearing a thin windbreaker and carrying a hand drawn map to the local homeless shelter.

The oil pipeline needed labor and Lester needed money. While most of the skilled labor flew in from Texas, Oklahoma or California, the wage Lester made as a cook's helper was three times what he'd made at the AC store. He worked 10 hour days seven days a week, lived in a doublewide Atco trailer with 40 other guys and learned to hate Texans. He was scraping pots and pans at Prospect Creek the morning they registered -73 and he was peeling potatoes at Cold Foot when a mob attacked the airfield and set fire to the company helicopter. After that, armed guards patrolled the camp and rooms were randomly searched for alcohol. Booze was forbidden by law north of the Yukon and smugglers doubled their money just crossing the Yukon River bridge. Lester, who saw an opportunity that didn't involve scraping plates, quit his job and bought a flatbed truck with his savings. He prowled the Pipeline Haul Road for five years, unloading through the back windows of warehouses, under the flaps of canvas tents, at truck stops and rest stops and turnarounds from the Yukon to Prudhoe Bay. After five years he paid cash for his first airplane and a couple of years later he bought ten acres north of Palmer and a surplus Atco doublewide from the Alyeska Pipeline Company. By then the 80's were in full swing and a wave of cocaine swept through Alaska like a tsunami from the '64 earthquake. Fishermen from Bristol Bay to Ketchikan and oil workers from Valdez to the Slope were chopping lines on every bar and table in the state. Lester started out flying the occasional ounce or two from Anchorage to Dillingham and within three months was using a quarter ounce or more a week himself. In the winter of '87 he sold his plane to pay off his debts (it came to that or trying to fly the plane with broken knees) and took a legitimate job at the hardware store in Palmer while his brain recovered from a two-year deep freeze. He'd lost thirty pounds and his hands shook so badly he had trouble making change, but the owner got a tax credit from the state for hiring him and he showed up every day, until his brain thawed completely and he slowly realized what had happened. He started back gradually by mailing booze to relatives in Bethel and the village, but discovered that uninsured packages rarely made it through. Insured packages made it through but left a paper trail, so he took a second mortgage on his acreage and bought his second plane in the summer of '89.

He'd only had the plane a few hours when the former owner passed him a job which consisted of dropping a couple of Microsoft executives at a remote cabin. The job was originally booked by Big John, a licensed big game guide notorious for bar brawling and bear baiting. Big John failed to meet the plane because he was occupied with a baited bear who arrived to take the bait before the trap was in place. A last-second snap-shot with a .44 Magnum blew a three inch hole through the bear's heart, but with a pulse rate of 25, the ursine monster didn't take note of that for the several seconds it took to stamp paid to Big John's brawling days. Two weeks later a local trapper stumbled across the scene and lifted the .44 and the bear's gall bladder. Three more weeks passed before John's long-suffering wife reported him missing on the off chance he hadn't just gone to Hawaii without her again.

Lester hadn't felt comfortable leaving such obvious cheechakos[5] to fend for themselves and ended up 'guiding' them to a big bull moose who'd started to feed at the pond in front of the cabin and then to a foolish young brown bear who arrived that afternoon to dine on the discarded guts of the dead moose.

The executives paid Lester a nice tip, so all-in-all he cleared a tidy sum on the deal. He invested the money at the Army surplus store buying canvas tents, small woodstoves, assorted cooking gear, cots and bedding and lanterns and mosquito netting. This consumed all the money but Lester knew a sweet racket when he saw one. He'd set up a couple of camps where the moose were thick from a mild winter and a lack of predation, then a call came from his new friend, Tom, one of Microsoft's hundreds of Assistant Vice Presidents of Product Development, who the week before had removed a bloody moose bladder with a Gerber knife and his bare hands. Lester offered him a twenty percent referral fee for any hunting clients he sent north. In addition, Lester suggested under-the-table discretion to avoid bothersome tax paperwork and their relationship flourished. Thirteen years later Tom continued to act as Lester's agent, even though he had long ago cashed in his MSFT stock options, divorced his wife, and moved to Mercer Island where he spent most of his considerable spare time living off the interest, promoting local grunge bands and bedding their cute teenage groupies.

A Web site existed, Lester knew that much. He'd never seen it as his wheezing Compaq 286 was barely sufficient for email, exasperating Harold almost to the point of apoplexy.

"Get a real goddamned computer, Lester!" he'd say.

"No," or "Why?" or "Don't need one," Lester would reply, while struggling with a broken snowblower, digging his truck out of the driveway snowdrifts, or taking potshots at the three or four million rabbits that dodged around the treeline. He had plenty to do already and too many rabbit-fur hats already so he just left the rabbits where they fell, which also bothered Harold.

"What happens to all them dead rabbits?" he'd once asked.

"Snow snakes drag 'em off," Lester had replied, "they're our anacondas of Alaska, so watch where you're walking." It was mostly ravens the size of Rottweilers that carried the rabbits off, but Lester still chuckled at the memory of Harold prancing around the place until he'd

---

[5] A clueless newcomer to the wilds of Alaska. Grizzly bears love the taste.

learned there were no snakes of any type in Alaska and no such thing as giant carnivorous snow snakes anywhere in the world.

"Sonuvabitch," he grumbled, "they about laughed me out of the bar."

Lester kept his hunting operation small and discrete, providing his clients with food, shelter, booze and legal targets, figuring he was pushing his luck enough by guiding without doing his five years apprenticeship; he didn't need to draw attention by flying and shooting the same day, baiting bears, taking undersize game or hunting out of season. The setup seemed so above board that most of clients never suspected anything illegal was going on, even when they strayed outside prescribed boundaries. Lester saved his money and in the fall of 1992 he bought a late model Cessna 172, running the Cessna out of Merrill Field in east Anchorage while the Piper mildewed underneath a blue tarp behind his shed, until Harold came along a few years later. The Merrill Field location lent a greater air of legitimacy to his operation and Tom, acting as his agent in Seattle, promptly raised Lester's fee, though he neglected to mention it to Lester. He got away with it for one entire moose season before a client, primarily upset about the primitive conditions at the hunting camp, felt the need to discuss Lester's prices.

"The fucking mosquitoes are eating me alive," she complained, "and for the amount of money we're paying one would think something could be done about it." She stared pointedly at Lester, who'd put up with mosquito assaults every summer of his life and was only vaguely aware there were people who didn't.

"We charge below-market rates," Lester said, stalling for time while he decided how to handle this development. She seemed annoyed by the comment.

"Oh well," she airily replied, "seven hundred for air fare, your three thousand and Tom's fifteen hundred don't seem all that 'below-market' to me." Lester covered his dismay by setting up several citronella candles, which smelled nice but really did nothing for the mosquitoes, and smothering the young lady in 100% DEET, which did repel mosquitoes, but smelled like paint thinner and somehow aroused the woman to the point where Lester got laid without paying for it for the first time in six years. When her husband returned from scouting along the creek she'd raved about Lester's secret mosquito repellent, which he'd bought at Wal-Mart the day before. All Lester could think about was how Tom, the Microsoft shyster, was skimming cash. Lester stuttered through some excuse about flying back home to pick up supplies. He considered his options concerning Tom's actions during the flight. He didn't really need Tom any longer, but it was convenient having customers lined up without having to do any marketing or advertising. He arrived at home and powered up the antique computer, not trusting the intermittent cellular reception, and emailed Tom for clarification.

THE RECORDS I MAY OR MAY NOT GIVE TO THE IRS SAY I PAY YOU $600 PER CLIENT NOT $1500 SHOUD I FLY TO SEATLE TO STRAITEN THIS UP?

Lester didn't care which letters should be capitalized; he left the capslock key on at all times because he thought he was sending a telegram and that's the way telegrams look. He also found punctuation and precise spelling to be unnecessary and best left to experts.

Tom agreed to a flat $200 cut. It was shortly after this that Tom booked the supermodel and her boyfriend. Lester didn't get laid, but he did get to apply a substance known to the State of California to cause cancer in laboratory animals to her arms and legs, which was almost as good. He taught her how to snag salmon in the Little Susitna river and both of them had a great time.

Lester figured life was pretty good. He owned his home and acreage outright, had a nice plane, made great money during the fall hunting seasons and shuttled enough whiskey during the off-season to pay his bills with a bit left over. He met interesting people that respected him for his knowledge of game and backcountry lore, and he was something of a celebrity in his birth village, where he was considered to be both rich and respectable.

Still, he was basically an outlaw who lived on the outer fringe of society. He had no close friends except for the questionable Harold, and late at night when the wind howled outside the windows and he sat alone and fed the woodstove, he wished for something more.

Scott Steele

Mr. Terrence McOlive
Democratic National Committee
430 S. Capitol St. SE
Washington, DC 20003

Subject: Alaska Election Analysis

Hi Terry.

The prognosis for our party in the fall election is not very good, I'm sorry to report. I narrowed the list of viable candidates to two, these are the only candidates that have raised more than $100,000, which I view as the absolute minimum to run any sort of credible campaign.

Jim Van Doren
Age 43
Born in Ketchikan

Graduated from UAS with a BA in Business and teaching certificate. Former school teacher, vice-principal, and one-term Alaska NEA President.
Married twice with three children living at home.

Jim is a popular union leader and school administrator. He is a strong campaigner. He looks good and speaks well.

Police Record He has two minor car accidents and has a misdemeanor marijuana conviction in 1972 and a DUI in 1974. No military service. No felonies. No bankruptcies or defaults.

Personal His current wife was pregnant when he divorced his first wife. He had a sexual harassment suit settled out of court in 1983. A child from his first marriage is currently serving a six-year sentence in state prison for rape.

Financial He claims to have $375K in cash, but his campaign bank account is currently at $188K. He has good support from the teacher's union and other union support. He won the Alaska NEA president race with a 59% majority and did not seek reelection.

Julia Patterson
Age 36
Born in Los Angeles, CA

Graduated from UC Berkley with a BA in Women's Studies.
Former cook and Sierra Club grant writer.
Lesbian

Julia is a fairly typical pro-choice environmental activist. She does not speak well in public and is easily flustered. She is over-weight and not particularly attractive, not at all a lipstick lesbian.

Police Record She has four traffic accidents (one resulting in a manslaughter conviction in 1996) and has many misdemeanor marijuana convictions, trespassing, and protest arrests (she was arrested most recently at the WTO riots in Seattle). She was implicated but not charged in an ALF[6] fire at UA in 2002. No military service. No felonies. No bankruptcies or defaults.

Personal An assault charge against a former girlfriend was dismissed. She had an abortion in high school. She doesn't bath very regularly and is very against fur and scents (perfumes and the like) and frankly sprays a lot of saliva when she speaks in public. She is a militant Marxist lesbian but is smart enough not to rub people's faces in it. Her Che Guevara posters are mostly packed away and hidden from sight.

Financial She claims to have $105K in cash, but her campaign bank account is currently at $8K. She has good support from the environmental groups. She has never held an elected office.

In conclusion, our prospects are poor for either candidate. In the Republican candidate, Bill Sanders, we have a popular natural GOP successor to Don Young's seat. He is popular and well-funded (over $1M). On our side, though Jim's prospects are slim, he is a good candidate and he may have a political future beyond this race, so some token DNC support might be a good investment. Julia is a train-wreck

---

[6] Animal Liberation Front

and will probably end up on the Green ticket. She has no chance of winning the Democratic primary.

I wish the news was better, but it isn't. I will make sure to watch any other candidates that pop up, but this is almost certainly a GOP win this fall. Sorry about that. Let me know if you want to come up for some fishing, as we can get some special permits from the Governor.

Best regards

Scott Steele

Scott Steele
Alaska Democratic Party Chairman

I just received the following wire from my generous Daddy—"Dear Jack, Don't buy a single vote more than is necessary. I'll be damned if I'm going to pay for a landslide."

- John F. Kennedy

CHAPTER 2

The Election Team

The team gathered in a meeting room at the Marriott to hear the initial draft of Glen's first speech. As Glen stood before a podium, Bennie was playing with a Gameboy and Murphy was in the back whispering into a cell phone headset, otherwise the team was mostly paying attention.

"To get things tweaked, we're going to start with some throw-away appearances," Glen said. "Things like small-town Rotary Clubs and community meetings. This first speech will be the one we give to old people at retirement homes and the like. That reminds me, do any of you know anything about photography?" The group was silent. "Okay, Murphy, would you make a note to find a newsie flack to follow us around and take some pictures?"

Murphy looked up, nodded, and scribbled in a spiral-bound notebook.

"Alright, I'll get started. Ladies and gentlemen of the great state of Alaska..."

"Speak into the microphone," Walter said.

"What?"

"Speak directly into the microphone and don't bend down to it like you see those morons do on the Academy awards. The mike will pick you up, just make sure you're speaking right at it."

"I read you," Glen said, annoyed. "Ladies and gentlemen of the great state of Alaska. I stand before you to talk about some old ideas that have gone out of fashion with the political elite. Respect for elders. Care for our senior citizens. Recognition of all your generation's achievements and the acknowledgement that the freedoms we enjoy were purchased with your blood and the blood of your sons on far-away battlefields. Let me ask some questions. What do you think of a political system that says it's good to make seniors choose between food and medicine? What do you think of a government leader who says you should only get one pill when your doctor says you will die unless you take four? The Republican candidate, Bill Sanders, says we should spend your tax money on tax cuts for the rich instead of medical care for the elderly. If you agree, then go ahead and cast your vote for Bill. Do we want a system of the drug companies, by the drug companies, and for the drug companies?"

"Slow down a little bit, Glen," said Walter, "and give the people a chance to respond. We'll have plants in the audience that will speak up. Also, make eye contact with people. Don't read the speech. You can glance at it, but speak with your eyes on the audience. Keep your hands out of your pockets and make sure someone carries your keys and pocket change so you won't play with the stuff in your pockets. Don't rock back and forth, just lean forward a little toward the audience."

Glen glared at Walter, but continued.

"What is Mister Sanders' plan for controlling skyrocketing prescription drug prices? What is Mister Sanders' plan for reining in drug company corporate welfare in the form of exploitive patent protections? I will work with my every breath to protect older Americans from the greed of corporate dictatorships. That's the Glen Wilson plan.

Let's now speak for a moment about your Social Security. Did you pay into this system during your entire working life? Weren't you promised a retirement with independence, dignity, and safety while you were paying into the system? What happened to those promises now that it's your turn to collect? We need leaders who will protect your Social Security, not waste those benefits on pork barrel projects on the continent. They say the Social Security system is going broke. Is that your fault? Did you raid the trust fund and spend the money on wild women, fast cars, and cheap highs?"

"Glen," Walter interrupted.

"What?"

"Go real easy on the ad libbing."

"Okay, I'm just trying to have a little fun. "Where was I? Did you raid the trust fund to spend the money on congressional pay raises? If Mister Sanders is elected, you might as well pack your clothes in a paper bag because Sanders wants to cast you out in the street. He doesn't care if you freeze or starve. Bill Sanders wants to raise the retirement age so there will be more chance for you to die before you ever get a Social Security check. Bill Sanders wants to tax your benefits. What sense does that make? Instead of cutting your benefits, the feds are going to subtract part of what they're paying you and call it a tax? What do we say to Bill Sanders? That's right, we say 'no way, Bill, you take your grimy hands off my check'. We say it loud and proud, 'no way, Bill'. I appeal to the better angels of your nature to defeat the enemies of the elderly. We can do better if you cast your vote for Wilson. We will do better, you have my word as a gentleman and friend of Alaskan seniors. Now, let's enjoy some cookies and tea."

"Pancakes," Bennie said, looking up from his Gameboy.

"What?" Glen asked.

"Pancakes. Our analysis says old folks want pancakes. They'll vote for a guy who gives them pancakes."

"How are we going to make hot pancakes at all these stupid old-folks homes?"

"They don't care if they are good as long as there are plenty of them."

"Pancakes it is." Glen sighed. "Grab your walkers, fish your teeth out of the soaking glass and dig into Glen Wilson flapjacks, there's plenty for everyone."

"Take it easy, Glen. Stick to the script," Walter warned.

"Just shut up and eat your damned pancakes," Glen grumbled.

Murphy and Igor

Murphy took off her sunglasses and peered into the early afternoon darkness of Darwin's Theory bar on G Street. She stood by the bar and spoke to the bartender who was presiding over a blender full of Daiquiris. The bartender pointed at a man at the very end of the bar who was nursing a whiskey, smoking a cigarette, and working on a crossword puzzle. Murphy stood over the man who ignored her.

"Igor Khorochev?" she asked?

"What's a five-letter word for fuck off?" he replied.

Murphy pulled the vinyl-covered stool away from the bar and sat down beside him. She picked up his glass and smelled it.

"Bring us a couple fresh Jim Beam's," she called out to the bartender.

"Make them Martell's," Igor said defiantly.

The bartender looked at her questioningly and Murphy nodded 'okay'. The bartender had to climb on a stool to pull down the whiskey which he then poured. He placed the glasses in front of them.

"And one for yourself," Murphy told the bartender. He produced a buck-toothed grin, poured himself one, and made himself busy at the other end of the bar. Murphy and Igor sipped in silence for a few minutes. Igor set his crossword aside and swiveled his chair to look at her. She was wearing wool slacks, black shoes with gold buckles, and her hair was pulled back in a bun.

"You got my attention, so what do you want?" Igor asked.

"I'm told you are the man to talk to if a person is looking for a photographer. Also, that you can arrange to get photographs printed in the paper."

"Who told you this?"

Murphy sipped her drink and picked at the paint on her fingernails.

"I'm not even going to speak to you unless I know who you've been talking to," Igor said.

"A fellow named Ben sent me," Murphy replied. She opened her purse and pulled out a bank envelope, from which she pulled two hundred dollar bills. She smoothed them out on the counter. "A certain Mister Ben Franklin," she said calmly.

Igor's fingers twitched.

"You a cop?" he asked.

"I used to be, but no more," she replied.

Igor hesitated, then picked up the bills and slipped them into his shirt pocket.

"Is it safe to assume that there are more Mister Franklin's where these came from?"

"Yes."

"Okay, so talk to me, what do you want?"

"I work for a fellow named Glen Wilson. He's running a congressional campaign and he's looking for some friendly press coverage."

"Never heard of him, House or Senate?"

"House."

"That position is pretty well set to pass from Young to Sanders, so competing is going to be a tough sell around here, I'm afraid. I thought the Democrats were running Jim Van Doren."

"We're starting our run as a third party though we're open to a deal later with the Republicrats, we're easy."

"You can't win with a third party around here."

"That's our problem. Your problem is to get Glen's face in the paper helping grandma across the street and chasing druggies out of the park."

"I get it. When do I start?"

"You started the instant you tucked my greenbacks into your pocket. We want to get on the right side of the local issues. Do you have any suggestions?"

"Sure, let's see. Raise the Permanent Fund Dividend, yes on drilling in the ANWR, kill the damn beetles, let us cut down dead beetle trees for firewood, put a $500 bounty on wolves, and just let us drive our fucking snowmobiles where we want. These are all things that would be immensely popular but will probably never happen. I don't suppose this Mister Wilson is a real crusader for the people...?"

"Nope, sorry, he just wants to win the damn election."

"Oh well."

Murphy pushed her stool back and drained her drink. She put another $100 on the bar and gestured for the bartender to come get it.

"We're in the Prez suite at the Marriott, grab your gear and get over there as soon as you can. Also, how about 'scram'?"

"Scram?"

"Try that for a five-letter word for fuck off."

Murphy tossed her bag over her shoulder and left the bar without a single glance backward. Igor drained his glass and picked up his crossword puzzle. He motioned for the bartender to give him a refill.

"Another shot of Martell's?" the bartender asked.

"No, switch me back to Jim Beam," he said sadly, "Money doesn't exactly grow on trees around here."

Holly

Holly had an urgent need to relieve herself, so she pulled off Hwy 27 at Sebring where she drained her bladder at the Bizzy Bee Buffet. Having not looked into Barton's wallet yet, she didn't know if she had any money. As she sat on the toilet, she inventoried the contents and found that the reliable Barton carried over four hundred dollars in cash and a bundle of credit cards. She didn't know if she dared use the cards, but kept them anyway after burying the wallet in the used paper towels in the bathroom trash bin. She irritated the Q-tips[7] in the cashier's line by slapping a twenty on the counter instead of standing in line. Then she walked around the buffet picking food out and eating it with her fingers. She ate so much that her belly poked out like she was slightly preggers. She'd had an abortion, so she knew the feeling. This train-of-thought made her laugh, which made the old folks look up from their fried chicken. She made an ugly face back and stuck out her tongue, but

---

[7] Q-tip is a derogatory term for old folks in Florida. From the back, while driving their huge sedans, their gray heads, riding on their spindly necks, look like cotton swabs.

quickly lost interest in giving them a reason to remember their day. She wrapped up some donuts in a wad of napkins. The manager scowled at her, but didn't say anything as she left with her purloined take-out.

Making a snap-decision to dump the car, she drove through Sebring and found a teenager washing a TrailBlazer at a used-car outfit. She parked on the street and leaned against the front quarter-panel of the Lexus until she caught the eye of the soapy kid. It took about thirty seconds. As he walked over, he left foamy tennis shoe footprints.

"What's your name, kid?"

"Harold, but every body calls me Harry."

Holly could tell already the kid wasn't quite right in the head. He was older than she first thought, about 25 and he still washed cars at the used-car lot. "What's wholesale on a Lexus like this?" she asked.

He poked his head in and did a quick inventory. "Current model-year, moon roof, sport package, low miles. This thing would go for about thirty-five grand wholesale. You'd get a lot more if you ran an ad in the paper for low bluebook, the snowbirds around here love a bargain."

"Okay, Harry. What are you guys asking for that GMC 4-WD over there by the fence?"

"The sticker says 11 thousand, but," his eyes flicked to her haltered chest, "they'd take seven in cash, but don't tell them I said so. It's been sitting around here for a while and they only have 35 hundred in it."

"How bad does it burn oil?"

"It's clean, doesn't leak or burn much. You won't need to add any oil between changes."

"Don't bullshit me, Harry," she said while flicking some donut sugar off her breast. Harry's mouth seemed very dry to him.

"A quart every 500 miles, just top it off every time you fill up and it will run forever."

"That's what I thought. Here's the deal, Harry. I'm going to give you the keys to this Lexus and a hundred bucks. You're going to go into the office and snag me the keys and the paperwork to the Jimmy and pull up here and leave the engine running. You can slip the Lexus to a chop shop and clear a solid ten grand on the deal."

"Oh, I-I-I can't do that," Harry sputtered.

"I'm not done yet, Harry. Don't interrupt me, okay?"

"Yeah, what else?"

"You get the keys to the Lexus, the hundred bucks, and I'll show you my tits. That's the deal."

Harry looked up and down the street, stole a glance at her chest, and then looked back at the office. "I guess I can tell the boss I'm running it down to Jose's for a front-end alignment." He scratched his head. "Can I get a feel?"

"No touchie, just lookie, got it?"

He ran the deal around in his mind. "Deal," he said and stuck his soggy hand out for a shake.

Holly laughed, but she did shake his hand. It took about three minutes before the GMC was idling (a bit roughly and with a hint of smoke from the tailpipe) at the curb. She climbed into the cab and looked down at Harry.

"Tits," he said plaintively.

"Right." She worked out a folded paper out of the pocket of her jeans and handed it over. She rammed the floor shift into first and roared off leaving Harry staring at the paper while coughing in a cloud of blue exhaust fumes. He unfolded the paper. It was a picture in which she was naked from the waist up and licking a sucker. Barton, who had a very nice digital camera setup, apparently had a thing for topless young ladies and Tootsie Pops.

"Okay, I get it," Harry muttered to himself. He jumped in the Lexus and drove it to a junkyard outside Lake Wales that specialized in Japanese automobiles and wasn't too fussy about where they came from. Harry was a 25-year-old loser who washed cars at the used car lot, but he cleared eight thousand after he paid off his boss for the GMC truck. The picture ended up tacked on the wall by his bed near the Kleenex he kept on his nightstand. Some forms of wealth are not financial; Harry felt like a rich man indeed.

Moshi

Erik stumbled in at 8:30 AM. Moshi was sleeping on their threadbare mattress, she had not gotten undressed. She sat up. Erik dropped his guitar case along the wall. His shirt was fastened with a couple of misaligned buttons. His hair was pulled back into a tangled pony tail and his cheeks were covered with patchy stubble. He reeked of alcohol and marijuana.

"I'm going to get a beer, do you want anything?"

"No, I don't want anything," Moshi replied angrily, "except a man who comes home at night. A sober man who loves his girlfriend. I want that sweet boy I fell in love with five years ago."

"Christ, not this bullshit again."

Erik left the room and came back a minute later with a can of Busch Lite.

"Light beer. It's like drinking water."

"I need to talk with you, Erik. It's important."

"I hope its not bad news. We're on a roll. East-West is offering a five-figure advance for a five-record deal. They'll loan us money to record in a real studio and tour support. We'll do a run through Japan, then record our first disk, then go on tour with one of the big guys, either Magick or Putrid, somebody like that. This is big, we're on our way."

His words were slurred together. Moshi knew the signs, he was high on crystal. He took off his shirt and his back was covered with deep scratches. Moshi assumed this was a message from the Filipino girl. This sight stirred a rage in her that she pushed back with all her might. Once Erik understood the situation, he would put aside these other girls.

"What happened to your back?" The question slipped out in an ugly tone she did not want. They needed to talk, not to fight. Their family was at stake.

"Look, I don't come home to get cross examined. It was a wild night but now I'm home and I'm tired. I want some tranquility, some peace and quiet. Okay?"

Moshi calmed herself and decided to just blurt our her news.

"Erik, I'm very sure that I'm pregnant again. I missed my period and the test strip turned blue."

"Oh shit, that's just what I need. Did you do this on purpose to fuck up my dreams?"

"No, it's just something that happened. We have to talk about our options."

"Options. What options are there? We've been through this before. Planned Parenthood has a program that doesn't cost nothin'. Raz takes his girlfriends to the clinic out in White Center. They'll fucking scrape you out. Do you want me to take you down there?"

"I was hoping our options might include keeping the baby this time. We could get married. My parents would pay for the wedding. I can get a job."

"That's just fucking grand. Get married? Keep the baby? Are you stupid? I'm too young for this middle-class family bullshit. This will fuck up the tour. Just get rid of it, there will be plenty of time for breeding later. I can't believe how selfish you are."

"I don't want to kill our baby."

"Baby! It's not a baby, you idiot. It's some cells that got together by accident. It's no big deal to go to the family practice clinic and get this taken care of. Bing-bang-boom, you're in, you're out, and we get on with our lives. The sooner the better. How do I even know this one is mine?"

He drained the beer can and threw it against the wall. Moshi covered herself with blankets and turned away from him.

"Of course the baby is yours," she whispered.

"That's great. Now you're going to cry, aren't you? I need to get some sleep and we have a band practice at four. Shit, I should have stayed at Raz's place. Nobody is crying over there. We're signing a contract with a major label, for God's sake. This should be the happiest day of my life and you're fucking with my head. Look, I gotta hit the road and find a place to grab some sleep, alright? Make that appointment, alright?"

Moshi pressed her pillow over her head. Erik grabbed it away.

"You'll make an appointment? If I can't get away to take you down, maybe Mari will drive you. I'm talking, are you listening?"

She sat up and stared at him. She did not want to cry, but tears dripped down her cheeks in torrents. She felt like she was hovering over the scene. Her soul reached out. Her world made a queasy lurch. She felt oily and slimy. She put aside all the doubt that crowded her mind. Erik was right, she was being selfish. He didn't always wear a condom and they didn't have money for the pills. She should have made him cover himself, even if it meant washing and reusing the rubbers. It was her fault. She had no right to deny him his dream.

"I'll make the appointment. But you have to take me down there. Don't make me go by myself."

"I'll try my best."

A tiny thread snapped in her. "No, you bastard." She looked around for something to throw. His favorite onyx bong was handy. She pegged him on the head with it. "That's not good enough. You made this baby too, you can at least take me to the clinic to get rid of it. At least! If nothing else!"

"Stop this," Erik said, rubbing a bump on his head. "I said I'd take you. Don't go psycho on me, I'll take you. But now I gotta go."

He patted her on the head, grabbed his guitar and walked out of the room. Moshi sat on the edge of the mattress and wiped her eyes with the edge of her pillowcase. The tears seemed like they would never cease, like they were coming from somewhere outside her body and pouring through like a waterfall. Eventually she slept and dreamed of hands that were grasping at her and pulling her body into bloody pieces.

Glen and Angela

Glen rolled off Angela and they lay side-by-side staring at the ceiling. After they caught their breath, Angela stripped the sheet off the bed, wrapped it around and sashayed to the bathroom. Her blond hair was a mess and she was flushed pink from head to toe. She turned in the doorway and looked back at Glen.

"You're a lovely girl, Angela," he said. "I like a girl with a little muscle tone."

"You have some juice in you for such an old guy," she said, allowing the sheet to slip and expose one perfect breast. "And such a slick-talker." She curtsied and pulled the door shut behind her. In a few moments Glen heard the shower start.

There it is again. Old guy. Sure, I have some gray hair and my skin is starting to wattle a bit, but I don't really feel that old. I can't drink like I used to and sex a few times a week is enough these days. I have trouble keeping my eyes open after nine PM and I'm useless in the morning until I get the caffeine in my blood up to the right level. What's next? Dinner at 4:30 at the King's Table Buffet? Yellow jumpsuits and arch supports? A copper bracelet and blood pressure medication? One of those 911 medallions so I can page the EMTs when I fall down and I can't get up? Drooling in a wheelchair and telling my same old stories to the interns who could hardly care any less? All I want to do is live fast, die old, and leave a well-fed corpse. All my mom ever cared about was having a pension so she could retire and still live half decently. Now, my biggest worry is avoiding a long-term decline where the pills and fancy machines keep me alive long after I can actually do anything. I want to die with my boots on, with my sword buried deep in one last dragon, and with jealous women weeping over my cooling body.

What is it that keeps the Wilson machine moving? Will I know when its time to bow out and let the next generation run the big show?

Glen clenched his fists and admired the rippling muscles in his forearms. *Not ready to give up yet, baby, not quite yet,* he thought. He realized he was hungry, so he pulled on his clothes, poked his head out the door and looked both ways up and down the hotel hallway. He pulled the door closed behind him and went on a noble quest for lunch.

Glen and Bennie

Glen was foraging for food in the command center suite. The contents of the refrigerator were schizophrenic; there were loaves of wheat bread, a plastic bag of grapes, hot dogs, and dozens of bottles of beer, bottled water and Diet Pepsis. Glen grabbed some hotdogs and a Kokanee beer, clicked on the TV, and settled on the couch in the main room to watch Fox News. Bennie wandered in wearing pajama bottoms with a sleep mask loosened around his neck. He carried a sheaf of wrinkled papers. The kid worked about 20 hours straight, then slept for a few hours then started again. He was running endless regressions and simulations on pirated cycles stolen from a DOE supercomputer.

"What's up, kid?" Glen asked.

Bennie picked up one of Glen's hotdogs and started eating.

"I'm seeing correlations I don't understand," he said with his mouth full.

Glen muted the TV. "Like what?" he asked.

Bennie waved his printouts. "I'm trying to define and evaluate the decisive issues. For example, the abortion topic. This is a serious party differentiator with Democrats defining the issue as one of choice and the Republicans defining the issue in moral terms. There are small groups of people that feel very strongly about this, but most people don't really think about it much at all. Why does this contentious issue get so much press? Very few people are going to change their minds, so all the talk just upsets people. What's the deal?"

Glen laughed. "You're the smartest kid in the world and you can't figure this one out?"

Bennie frowned. "I'm not the smartest in the world, my IQ is in the top .01 percent, but there are many thousands of people smarter than me."

"Yeah, right, whatever. Each party has a core constituency, a vote they can count on, no matter what. The campaign is actually won or lost with a small percentage of middle-of-the-road swing voters. People who study the issues know who they are going to vote for. The people that can be influenced are the ignorant and the stupid, these are the undecided. These people are the target. They make their decisions based on emotion. This is what we want, people who can be influenced by images they see on TV. Their vote will depend on how the candidate looks, what his mate looks like, how smooth the words are, and how often they see the candidate's name in positive settings. It's like picking a jury. You will be disqualified if you listen to talk radio or if you follow a case in the newspaper. The lawyers want the jury to be bozos, the people that can be influenced by the arguments of the lawyers instead of the facts of the case. These are the people who empower the lawyers."

"We're going to win by seducing dumb people?"

"That's not all we will do. We will promise things we can't deliver. We're going to buy some votes with empty words and free hotdogs. We're going to provide phony voter's guides, bus old people and bums to the polling places, and stuff the ballot box where ever we can. Beautiful, eh?"

"Seems kind of ugly to me."

"Il fine giustifica i mezzi."

"It comes down to that? The end justifies the means?"

"Yes, kiddo, it comes down to that. Want to play some Hitman?"

"Yeah," Bennie said brightly, "I'll kick your cold-blooded ass."

"Bring it on, punk," Glen said while strapping on his headset.

Glen and Walter

Walter walked in and watched Bennie and Glen play at their game for a while.

"Excuse me guys," he interrupted, "what do you think about bingo?"

"What about it?" Glen asked as his character crouched behind a burning truck. He was firing RPGs blindly into the wreck of a burning building in an attempt to frag Bennie's assassin.

"This state doesn't have a lottery or casinos, but a lot of the old folks play bingo. I'm thinking we print up some bingo cards with something like '*Glen Wilson thinks gambling is fun*' printed on the back."

"Sounds good to me, run it through Bennie's simulation and make sure there are no gotchas. Anything else?"

"I'm thinking about victory parties in the major cities. It's illegal to offer people compensation for their vote, but I think we could pull off some parties. Tractor pulls, bring in your Glen Wilson voter's guide for a free drink, a cheerleader dance contest, salmon bake, that sort of thing."

"Are you essentially saying that some folks will sell their vote for a hunk of fish and a glimpse up a bouncing teenagers skirt?"

"That's what I'm saying."

"Outstanding, just do it," Glen said. "What else is on your mind?"

"Nothing really. Have you seen Angela?"

"Nope. You can ask the other folks, but I don't think we have her on a mission or running errands. Call her on her cell phone."

"I did, she must have it turned off. Glen, will you help me keep an eye on her? She's not really safe if I leave her at loose ends. We may need to find her something to do to keep her out of trouble."

"I understand completely. You can count on me."

On the plasma TV screen, an armor-piercing cannon shell ripped through Glen's character's chest; it nearly ripped him in half. Glen threw down his controller in disgust. "That was a depleted uranium round? Goes through a car engine and body armor?" Bennie nodded yes. "Where did you get that? That isn't part of the game."

"I bought it off Ebay," Bennie said, smirking. "30mm Gatling cannon."

"This is war, you cheating little shit, but I'll have to kill you later."

"I'll be waiting," Bennie said, hitching up his pajamas and picking up a huge cereal bowl. This was the object of their wager: who would get Glen's heaping bowl of sugary cereal. After an hour of sitting around, the bowl looked like clown vomit. Bennie strutted out of the room with pride, wiggling his ass in his pajama bottoms and munching on the soggy mess of dissolving Froot Loops.

Glen and Murphy

Glen was on the balcony drinking a beer and watching traffic stream by on the street below. Murphy came out and stole a sip from his bottle. Stripes of murky water were visible between the buildings.

"I have one bit of bad news," Murphy said, "the law up here requires that you register by party and you are only allowed a primary vote in your selected party."

"Ah, no cross-voting for an easy-to-beat opponent, too bad. How much does that hurt us?"

"I don't think it will be a problem. The Republican candidate, Bill Sanders, is pretty much a shoo-in for his party's nomination. I've done a background check and he comes up mostly clean, there are a few blemishes on his record, but nothing we can get much mileage out of. We'll put some money into the Libertarian campaign, Peter Gray is a fair candidate, we can pump him up to four or five percent. Things are more interesting on the Democrat side. They have an okay candidate in Jim Van Doren, but he's no powerhouse. Then there is this lady, Julia Patterson, she's a real mess, completely unelectable. It's going to take some doing, but we think we can get her to win the primary. Radical feminist, looks like a Shar-pei's ass, mean as a rabid coon. She's perfect for us. Build her up then let her self-destruct. It will be fun."

"Cool. What else are you working on?"

"I've done most of the background check on you. You're a piece of work yourself, you know."

"Broke the mold when I was born. I should be mostly clean, what did you turn up?"

"You know your DNA archive is completely hosed, there is the Richard Nixon thing and the cross-links are screwed up beyond any hope. You're missing a few years, we may want to plug some things in so it doesn't look so obvious. The 80's, you know."

"Yeah, those were my drug-running years, we'd better bury that gap real good. Anything else?"

"Some databases are better than others, did you know Mossad has a file on you?"

"No shit? What do they have?"

"Some stuff that popped up from some hand-written reports out of Russia."

"Shit, hard-copies, those are the worst. Fires are the most expensive, but if we have to…"

"No, I think we're okay, there are plenty of unlucky Wilson's in the world we can tie them to. Would you care to say anything about Morgan French? I called her and all she would say was you broke her heart. What's the story?"

"I broke her heart, that's what she said?"

"Yes. She asked how you are doing, I told her you're running for Congress and she got a chuckle out of that."

"I call her Pat, I never could get used to Morgan. That was a long time ago. She is a sweet girl."

"I loved her in those commercials."

"Not her finest hour, I'm afraid."

"She's cute, is she gay or bi?"

"Marry me and I'll tell you everything. I'll even introduce you."

"Tempting, but no thanks," Murphy replied.

"Whatever you say," Glen said, draining his beer and tossing the bottle aside.

Let us consider that we are all partially insane. It will explain us to each other; it will unriddle many riddles; it will make clear and simple many things which are involved in haunting and harassing difficulties and obscurities now.

- Mark Twain

CHAPTER 3

Angela

Angela was having trouble with her sunglasses. She'd bought them off the rack at a convenience store a couple of hours earlier to give her eyes and mind a break from the endless daylight and now they were rubbing her ears raw and she was tempted to toss them. However, since they lent her a sense of camouflage she decided to endure the annoyance a bit longer, even though it was now almost midnight and finally dark enough to do without them.

This entire election operation was a really Bad Plan in her estimation. Coming here, beyond the edge of civilization, did not match her definition of a holiday. Starting at the arrival gate at an airport named for some guy who probably invented snowshoes, the wilderness theme throughout the city was tacky and ordinary. She liked the bright lights and nightlife of Las Vegas, celebrity parties in Beverly Hills, and window shopping down Rodeo Drive and Madison Avenue. She'd said as much to Walter, when he could be torn away from his damned brainstorming long enough to talk to her.

"Walter, this is *not* my idea of a vacation," she'd said. He'd chuckled and walked her to the door, tucking $100 into her cleavage and slapping her on the ass before shutting the door behind her. She didn't need $100. She'd been skimming the gate, cooking the account books, and salting away petty change for as long as she'd been with Walter. Sometimes she thought Walter must know, he really was kind of spooky sometimes, but as time passed with no repercussions she began to believe he either didn't know or didn't care. As long as she was discrete, maybe, and not too greedy.

Lately though, the balances in her primary accounts had begun to dwindle as her entertainment expenditures increased. This could be trouble and Walter should be smart enough not to let her get this bored.

Angela liked to entertain the hell the out of things, and had lately begun to spend a considerable amount of Walter's money on her newest discovery, cocaine. The coke opened her mind, released her inhibitions, helped her to make important decisions, and gave her the energy to carry out her cocaine-inspired plans. She could see priorities more clearly: what was vital and what was trivial. She knew some people were weak and couldn't handle it, but she herself was strong-willed and simply needed the diversion. Not to mention the sexual side effects. Sure, the street variety of Coke was nothing like the stuff that Walter cooked up, but his stash was expensive and served up only on very-very special occasions. Angela needed a high more often and cocaine was the answer. It was Glen and Walter's fault; it was those two assholes who dragged her up here to the edge of creation. Glen — Head Asshole — was pretty good in the sack and had the morals of a sex-starved goat, but would never cough up any money to support her cocaine habit and her cocaine stash was running perilously low. Dangerously low. Cataclysmically low. Not that she really needed it. But that was why she was currently having trouble with her ten dollar sunglasses while seated by herself at a corner table in a fairly typical twenties-something meat market bar on 6th Avenue.

It looked like a lot of other college-town bars she'd seen, except for the huge stuffed fish over the doorway, and that same annoying outdoorsy-wilderness theme the whole state had going on. A girl played guitar and sang at a small stage by the door, and though she was surprisingly good Angela didn't expect to see her in Vegas anytime soon. Thinking of Vegas made her flush with anger. In Vegas she had connections. If none of them came through she could approach a doorman, an elevator operator, a bellboy, or cruise a casino floor until she spotted someone, or more likely, someone spotted her. Here she was like the big fish over the doorway — dead. At least here in a bar there was some semblance of normalcy, some vibe she could pick up on and gain some sense of belonging.

She wore a thin, black, snugly-fitted sleeveless top with a plunging neckline guaranteed to attract the attention of males and the envy of females. The design of the seam-testing tautness of her low-cut slacks was meant to inspire gymnastics after they were removed, certainly not while they were being worn. Unfortunately, she was forced to wear a light jacket which diluted the effect a smidge. Though it seemed the locals felt a fifty degree evening was shirt-sleeve and sandal weather, she herself didn't even start to thaw until the temperature reached at least seventy-five.

She'd cruised through a couple of other joints earlier in the evening, generating a lot of appreciative stares and a few invitations, but not from the type of people she was trolling for. Here she spied a table by the stage that looked promising. Not college boys, who rarely had the kind of money or connections she needed, but three young professionals. Not dot-bombers because it looked like they still had some cash. They were talking fast with expansive gestures and with faces flushed with power and invincibility. They took turns paying brief visits outside singly or in pairs — one of the three always staying behind to save their table — to what Angela assumed was the parking lot... Angela waited impatiently for twenty minutes. She nursed a drink and fended off a college kid with more hormones than sense until the singer ended her set and two of her three prospects promptly rose and headed outside. She felt a moment of indecision as to whether she should approach the pair in the parking lot or the fellow at the table; she'd waited for them to split up primarily because she knew from Walter that three was a powerful number she didn't want to tackle. Some of Walter's shtick was a scam, some of it wasn't, and not even Angela was always sure where the division occurred. Opting for the simplicity of a one-on-one, she grabbed her jacket and the dregs of her drink and headed across the room, slipping an extra radian of swivel into her hips and angling to approach from her best side. He noticed her coming from ten feet away and leaned back in his chair to appraise the view, worked up a smile, and indicated an unused fourth chair at the table with the glass in his hand. *Awfully cool*, she thought with her confidence drooping, then bolstered herself by remembering she was in a hick town, surrounded by hicks, and she made her living helping Walter separate hicks from their money. She sat in the chair he'd indicated and leaned forward just far enough to give him an extended glimpse of her firm breasts. She set her drink on the table and looked him in the eye.

"This is empty," she said.

"Why, yes it is," he agreed. He set his own glass, also empty, next to hers and waved at a waitress. Up close she could see that he was younger than she'd expected, in his mid-twenties, dressed in casual slacks and a polo shirt, no wedding ring, average height and a bit thin, with salon hair and probably wearing tinted contacts. He was one of the few men in the room that was clean-shaven. She read people for a living and figured she was looking at junior management, on the fast track to middle management where he'd marry likewise, bog down with 2.2 children and a mortgage, then either start drinking and divorce at 40 or settle down to the 'honey-do' list and remember, with sad regret, the night Angela walked away from his table.

"I haven't seen any snow in this town and I've been here a week," she opened.

His brow furrowed and he leaned forward a bit with his eyes flickering to her breasts for the briefest instant.

"It's summer," he said. "We won't see snow again until October, maybe November."

Oh God, he's an idiot, she thought, feeling her smile stiffen. She had a bad moment when a scene from two weeks prior flashed into her head. She'd spent ten minutes sweet-talking a small-time Vegas hood into a better deal only to discover she'd had lipstick on her teeth the whole time. The end result was she was forced to pay retail. She snapped back to the present, looked over the guy's shoulder and widened her eyes. When he turned to see what had grabbed her attention she hurriedly brushed her front teeth with a forefinger and dropped her hand back to the table just as he turned back around. Angela confidently hit him with her sexiest smile, proven to stop angry bouncers in their tracks, generate torn-up traffic tickets, produce insider stock tips, and melt suspicious yuppie cokeheads. "That's not the kind of snow I'm looking for," she purred. She saw the realization hit him. *It's not my animal magnetism, my stylish coolness, or my fifty-dollar haircut; this babe just wants to get high.* She watched his inner turmoil last perhaps a second, long enough for another brief glance at her breasts before he achieved reconciliation. He glanced towards the door leading to the parking lot and leaned forward.

"I'm not really into that," he said, with his eyes shiny from whatever it was he *was* into. "What exactly are you looking for?" In response Angela laid a finger alongside her nose, then lowered her sunglasses to look over the top, a move she'd practiced in front of a mirror.

"So, can you help a girl out?" she asked. "I know you guys are doing something." He stared into her eyes for a moment, then seemed to reach some monumental decision and leaned back. Angela replaced her sunglasses, inwardly wincing as they rubbed the tender spots behind her ears.

"Look, it's not coke, it's pharmaceutical." He gave her a lopsided grin. "You up for some of that?" Angela wasn't sure if she was or not, she needed, no, wanted some cocaine, dammit. "What's it like?" she asked. He shrugged. "It's a pretty good rush," he assured her. "OxyCodone, you crush them up and do them as lines." Angela wrinkled her nose in distaste.

"What's that? Some kind of pill?" she asked. "Don't you guys have any rock up here?" He narrowed his eyes and leaned closer, resting his elbows on the table.

"How do I know you're not a cop?" he asked, imitating a B-movie script.

Angela grinned with real humor. "Do I look like I've been wasting my time in public service? Can you picture me in a squad car?" She leaned forward until their eyes were inches apart. "I *create* domestic disturbance, baby." Her perfume wafted across and he felt a little light-headed. He started to reply just as the waitress arrived with their drinks, smiling.

"Christy moved your tab over, ma'am."

"Fine, thank you," Angela replied, not wasting a smile in return. Waitresses couldn't afford good coke. She turned back to — "What's your name, again?" she asked. "Walter Morrison," he replied, holding his hand out for a shake. "Really?" Angela grinned. "Imagine that. Another Walter. Well, frankly, that won't do. What's your middle name?"

"Richard," he replied.

She paused and looked him up and down. "Dull. You look like a Julio to me. I'll call you Julio and you can call me Angela. Let's go see what you've got out there, Julio." Walter-Julio Morrison wasn't sure how his friends would react, but he wasn't too worried about it either. They were small time users, not dealers, and Sergeant Walter Richard Morrison — Anchorage Unified Drug Enforcement Team — figured he might be able to just follow this cocaine queenie around while she did his job and tracked down, or up, some real action. He palmed a ten dollar bill to their waitress to hold the table.

Angela discovered that Julio was right, Oxy-C was not quite as good as a line of nearly pure coke, but it hit the spot nicely. It was better than a lot of so-called coke bought off the street. Morrison was in deep cover, so he was able to smoke what he wanted, snort what he wanted and enjoy the pleasures of the dope-culture girls as much as he wanted. It wasn't the small fry they were after, the big prizes were in the tall buildings downtown, drove around in leased stretch Land Rover limos, and flew into Stevens Airport on private jets.

Morrison had the use of a third-floor condo with a reasonable peek-a-boo view of the mountains. Fortunately, it was within walking distance of the bar, so Angela did not get a glimpse of his car which would have given him away; he spent all his money on clothes and a hair styling. He looked good but did not have the bank balance to back it up. Yet. Morrison could smell the big deal that would allow him to cut loose of the law, hire the wired-in lawyer he needed, and give up this life for good. The condo showed well; there were nice prints on the walls, a pellet-stove fireplace and a bear skin rug. Angela shrugged out of her jacket as Morrison fired up the stove with a remote control. He made up a pair of Scotch on the rocks and handed her one.

"Here's the way the game works," she said. She set down the drink and peeled off her top. Her bra was a deep maroon lacy number from the Victoria's Secret store. "You give me something and I give you something," she said, handing him the blouse. He draped it over the back of a dining room chair. "No," she scolded, "fold it up nice."

Morrison liked the look of this game. "I got the fire going real nice," he said.

Angela looked at him for a moment, then nodded. She pulled off one of her shoes, held it up for him to examine, and then placed it on the floor by the chair that held her carefully-folded top. Morrison turned on the sound system. It was a Bose system and it filled the room with some mellow saxophone jazz. Angela slowly took off her other shoe and placed it carefully next to its mate.

"That Oxy-C was sure nice," Morrison said.

"Yes, it was," Angela replied. She pulled off a silky short sock and arranged it on her shoes.

"It was a pretty night for a walk."

Angela frowned. "I don't like walking."

"Oh," Morrison said, thinking furiously. He noticed that her glass was not quite full, so he added an ice cube and another splash of Scotch.

She nodded and took off her other sock.

Morrison was running out of ideas and was painfully aware of some uncomfortable tenting in his slacks. He remembered that there was some pot in a canister in the kitchen. He rolled a large joint and placed it carefully in her lips. Angela was smiling serenely. She unsnapped her pants and slowly eased down the zipper. Morrison helped her shuck them. Unless she counted jewelry, it looked like all that was left was the bra and matching panties. Morrison found a silver Zippo and gallantly held a flame to the joint. Angela took a deep and practiced hit and then neatly unsnapped the convenient frontal clasp on her bra. Morrison almost tossed it aside, but after a brief stormy look from Angela, he laid it carefully on the chair with her top. Morrison's nervous eyes were divided between Angela's lovely breasts and anything else that might be of use in the room. He couldn't think of anything. Angela was smiling and smoking and clearly enjoying Morrison's dilemma. Then he noticed the ash was growing precariously long. Grinning from ear-to-ear, he found a crystal ashtray and held it out with a grand flourish. She tapped the ash and lifted her hips so Morrison could work off her panties. She reclined on the bear rug and enjoyed the mellow mix of the acoustic bass solo coming from the stereo, the sweet mix of the Oxy-C, the Scotch, the pot, and the reasonable skill Morrison showed in paying attention to the disparate parts of her body, not just the holy troika of boobs and pussy. One of the few useful lessons her momma had taught her was: if you make them work for it, they'll enjoy it more and so will you. *If for nothing else, thank you for that, mom,* Angela thought, as she lost herself beyond the dreamy gates of passion.

Glen and Wal-Mart Employees

Glen sat in the limousine and took deep cleansing breaths which he exhaled slowly. Elke straightened his tie and brushed his hair behind his ears. He riffled though the pages of his first public speech. Murphy whispered to the security people and they tested their headsets. Igor, the photographer, was taking some snapshots inside the car with his Nikon, he also had a Minolta with a long lens around his neck. Walter was looking through his brochures and had a swag box filled with plastic Alaska flags and campaign buttons. They had decided on a minimalist theme to start; the buttons just said Wilson and had a graphic of the Big Dipper/North Star like the state flag.

"Are you nervous?" Elke asked.

"A little, I guess," Glen replied.

"We're on in a few minutes," Murphy said. "We're going in through the employee entrance and down the hall to the cafeteria. We have about 20 minutes to address the crew before their shift starts. I have some plants from the University of Alaska that will pose for some pictures and ask some friendly questions afterwards, two or three questions is all we will do today. Everyone ready?"

The crew nodded. The limo driver opened the doors and the crew piled out. Murphy herded them to the employee entrance. One of the store managers held the door open and shook Glen's hand.

"Welcome to our store," he said.

"I'm honored to be here," Glen replied.

In the cafeteria, Glen posed for a couple of quick pictures with a pair of attractive college students followed by some shots with a little girl; a toddler with pigtails, snow boots, and a parka with fur-lined hood. The cafeteria had a high ceiling and cold florescent lighting. They took a position in a corner by a bulletin board. There were about 30 people in the room and the plants were obvious because they did not wear Wal-Mart name tags. The security team took their positions on either side. There was scattered applause as the store manager introduced Glen.

"Hello folks, thanks for taking a few minutes to listen to our speaker," the manager consulted his notes, "Glen Wilson." He politely clapped a few times as he stepped aside.

"Thank you," Glen said. "I know you'd rather clock in and get to work, so I appreciate you giving me a chance to speak to you today. First of all, I hope you'll forgive me for not being a professional politician, I've been in the business world the last 25 years or so. I just reached a point where I felt like I should give something back to the people, so I've decided to enter public service. You folks know something about customer service, wouldn't it be nice if there were a real sense of providing service by elected officials? That would be refreshing and that's something I'd like to bring to our state. One thing the politicians seem to forget as soon as they get to Juneau is just who it is that pays their salaries.

Alaska has some challenges as it faces the future. For example, if you ask your current congressman, he'll tell you that we have a budget problem that can only be solved by raising taxes. I have a different idea, like how about trimming state spending by cutting out the pork, the fraud, and the waste instead of increasing the burden on working taxpayers? How about if the government gets out of the way so our natural resources can be used effectively? I'm not talking about raping the environment; we can harvest timber, open up our fishing season and create new mining jobs in an intelligent and environmentally-friendly manner by using modern technology and scientifically valid safety measures. Doesn't this make more sense than shutting down the sawmills, the fishing fleets and the mines?

Your current leaders would like to cut your PFD[8] money while increasing their take. This money should go to the people, instead it goes to finance hare-brained schemes thought up by the lunk heads down in Juneau. Is that a good fiscal policy?

You need someone to represent you that understands the pressure you're under. Tax money does not grow on trees, it is produced by hard-working folks like you. You're underpaid, you have inadequate health benefits and limited retirement security. You need to send someone to Washington DC that will help you with these problems, not pile on more taxes and drive you to the poor house. I'm for tax breaks for

---

[8] Permanent Fund Dividend, payments made to Alaska citizens from pooled oil revenues.

college tuition and I'm against tax give-aways to the rich. I'm for tax-free investment in your retirement savings and I'm against bail-outs for crooked corporate executives. I don't think your kids should have to choose between dinners or medicine and I don't think you should have to choose between paying taxes and paying for your heating bill. Let's try a new direction in Alaska. Please give me your vote when you go into the polling place this November." There was some polite applause.

Walter stood and addressed the audience. "Are there any questions for Mister Wilson? He pointed at one of the fresh-faced students. "Yes, ma-am, please go ahead."

"That was very refreshing, Mister Wilson, thank you so much. I'd like to ask a quick question, if you will. Are you more of a business-friendly or a labor-friendly politician?"

"Thank you, that is an insightful question. This is exactly the dilemma I have been rejecting. I believe that we can strike an intelligent and fair balance between labor and management. One does not have to be the enemy of the other. You can't run a business without people and you can't reward hard-working people without a solid management team. Let's throw down the sword and start working together to create and share wealth. Thank you."

"We have time for one or two more..." Walter said.

A large lady in her billowing blue smock strolled down the center aisle between the lunch tables. Murphy and the security people watched her nervously.

"Yeah, Wilson, what are you going to do about the thugs and gangs ruining the school system?"

"Another outstanding question," Glen said as he gestured for Walter and Murphy to relax. "One of the problems with our government schools, is, like our government itself, the inmates are running the asylum. Here's one thing we can do. With parental permission, I'd reinstate spanking and corporal punishment. I'm not a big bible thumper, but there is wisdom in quotes like this one from Proverbs: *Foolishness is bound in the heart of a child; but the rod of correction shall drive it far from him.* From my own experience, I can tell you that the lessons I remember best from school were the ones administered by the gym teacher's board of education."

The large lady stood with her mouth open. "God bless you sir," she sputtered.

"One more," Walter said while shooting Glen (who was looking pleased with himself) a dirty look. The mother with the toddler in her arms raised her hand.

"Can you comment a little more about your stance on corporate welfare?"

"Yes, I could talk about this all night, if you could stand it." There were a few chuckles from the audience. "Corporate welfare is not just a waste of taxpayer money, it distracts from the business that management should be minding. Instead of lobbying for freebies handed out in the form of loopholes in legislation, I'd rather see business people run their business based on opportunities and sensible economics. I'm for free markets and competition, not for government selling our liberty in exchange for campaign contributions. Thank you so much for taking time today, now all of you can get to work."

There was patchy applause. Glen shook some hands and got a kiss on the cheek from Murphy which was photographed by Igor. On the way to the limousine, he mopped his forehead with his handkerchief. The crew climbed in and the driver pointed the car toward the hotel.

"That went pretty well, I think." Glen said, accepting a bottle of beer from Elke and twisting off the top.

"It was okay," Walter said, "but what was that ad libbing about whipping kids in school?"

"Yeah, I just made that up, they loved it."

"In the future, please stick to the script. We need to run stuff like that through the simulations and focus groups. You're going to muck things up."

Glen looked at his crew questioningly. Murphy nodded yes and Elke just stared out the window.

"I'm just trying to have a little fun."

"Well, knock it off, okay? Whipping kids and thumping bibles won't get us elected to anything."

"Okay, dad." Glen said, pouting. He sipped his beer and watched the buildings flow by the window.

Holly

As she roared down Hwy 27, Holly wondered why she loved these old Detroit battleships so much. The GMC was getting seven miles per gallon and the engine had started clicking like crazy after about 50 miles, long enough to burn off whatever goop Harry's boss used to quiet the lifters. STP would have been nice, at least that lasts for a while, but spraying some shit on the lifters while the valve covers were off saved a few dollars. In no way was this old truck worth seven thousand, and certainly not worth a look at her tits, but this was the one she wanted and this is the one she got. On the plus side, she liked the vibration from the drive train coming through the seat, it made her feel all warm and squishy. Or, maybe it was the Percodan she lifted from Barton's medicine cabinet, she didn't know.

She was headed south as fast as she could push the truck. Unfortunately, it was geared low and she could just barely get past the speed limit. This relieved the traffic cop problem, but the truck was so noisy she had to really crank up the stereo to hear anything. After 75 miles, her ears were ringing like a Sunday morning in Saint Mark's Square. Her mind was a little fuzzy around the edges, but she knew the general plan. First, acquire some sort of firearm. Second, find that run-down gas station and liberate those black rocks that were gathering dust in the window. She didn't exactly know the place, but she had a general idea and that was good enough for now. *Larry's or Leonid's or Leopard's or some damn thing*. Whatever. She cut over on 80 to Fort Myers and drove around until she found a pawn shop that looked familiar. The pawn shop clerk, with severe acne scars decorating his face, still looked like the pop star Seal, but he had put on some weight. He stared at her for a minute until the memory clicked in his brain.

"It's the golden girl," he said.

"Yeah, I'm back."

"Did you bring me more black rocks?"

"I'm working on that, right now I need some heat."

He looked at her appraisingly. He made a decision and locked the front door and turned the sign so it said CLOSED.

"Okay, we can deal. First of all, handgun or shotgun?"

"Handgun."

"Revolver or auto?"

"Auto."

"Fine. I have .25, .32, .38..."

"Fuck you, I want a .45 and not a little one either. Something that looks like a bazooka."

"That will cost, little girlie. I have a stainless steel Springfield Armory Trophy Match long-slide 1911-A1, it holds seven in the clip and one in the barrel." He unlocked the display case and pulled out the gun. He checked the clip and pulled back the slide to make sure it was clear before he handed it to her. She weighed it in her hand and looked down the sights. She liked it and she wanted it.

"How much?"

"Two thousand."

"No paperwork."

"Three thousand."

"On a stolen credit card."

"Four thousand."

"With a couple of boxes of ammo."

"Five thousand."

"Bullshit, now you're getting silly. You throw in the ammo, a leather holster, and a cleaning kit for four thousand."

The clerk chewed on his lip for a few seconds. "Deal. I can't do a no-paperwork deal, can we fill in data from the credit card holder?"

"Sure, his name's Barton and he won't be complaining."

"I'll call this one in, I don't want to run it through my credit card terminal. Give me ten minutes? Alone?"

"Sure." She sorted through Barton's cards. "How about a gold AMEX?"

"I'd rather take the platinum Visa," he said, pointing.

"Shred it when you're done, okay?"

"Got it."

The clerk unlocked the door and let Holly out, then locked the door behind her again. She checked the oil in her truck and squeezed the radiator hoses to see if they would hold. She decided they'd be okay. She sat in the cab and searched in vain for a radio station she could stand. It took about 20 minutes before the clerk waved her back in.

"All is good?" she asked.

"No problemo. You load the gun outside, right? And don't come back here looking for trouble."

She blinked her eyes innocently. "Trouble? Me? We're not quite done. Can you believe my ride has an 8-track deck in it? I need some tunes."

The clerk laughed as he handed her a plastic bag with her loot. "Sure, I can spare some, help yourself. I have Boston, Allman Brothers, ZZ Top, and Charlie Daniels Band, go ahead and take them all, they've been hanging around here for almost 20 years. Dust them off and have a ball."

"You should pay me for taking the Boston." she said.

"More than a feeling," he sang, "that's the shit."

"You got that right," she muttered.

Outside, in the cab of her truck, she popped in Allman Brothers Live at Fillmore East, and the Statesboro Blues cranked up. She loaded the .45 clip, jacked one into the chamber, sprung the clip, and loaded that last cartridge. She made sure the safety was engaged, then stuffed the gun into her waistband; it felt warm and alive. The truck exhaust rumbled, Dickie and Duane's guitars soared, and the moment was perfect. She thought the dinosaur rock was crap compared to her beloved hiphop, but she had to admit, at this instant, with her truck idling, the bass drums kicking her through the seat, and with Greg Allman growling out the blues, things could not be better. She unwrapped her buffet donuts and took a big bite out of a chocolate one with sprinkles as she backed up. She found Hwy 42 and pointed the truck southbound. This surely beat the hell out of being locked down in the Institute of Mental Health. She just needed to load up on black rocks and pop a few holes into a stupid white dog and the universe would be completely in balance.

Moshi

"Okay Mosh, I have it figured out," Erik said, while looking over his menu. Erik had invited her to dinner at Denny's, it was the first time they had been on something that could be called a date in almost a year. His pupils were constricted to pinpoints and he had immense black circles around his eyes. He slurped strawberry milkshake directly from the stainless steel mixing cup. Moshi was dressed in her best blouse and skirt, all washed the best she could with Woolite in a sink full of cold water back at the band house. She hadn't seen Erik much in the last week, he was busy practicing and making plans with Raz. "I have some good news for you."

Moshi knew better than to let her spirits rise on his words. Still, there was a fluttering inside as her soul grasped at hope. To distract herself from over-eagerness, she focused on picking up her glass of water. Condensation beaded on the cold glass. There was a slight tang of chlorine on the back of her tongue and a frigid trail of fluid down her throat.

"First of all, would you like to see my newest tattoo?" Moshi had noticed the patch on his forearm, but he had so many tattoos she didn't pay any attention to them anymore. "You'll be the first to see it. Well, except for the tattoo guy. And Raz helped me pick it out. Other than that, you'll be the first."

"Okay," Moshi shrugged.

Erik plucked off the bandage and waved his arm in front of her face. The tattoo said 'Fuck You!' in ornate red lettering.

"Pretty cool, eh? My mom is going to freak, I can't wait to show her."

"Yes Erik, that is very nice, congratulations."

Erik flexed the stringy muscles of his forearm and admired how the lettering crawled and wriggled. The waitress took Erik's double order of bacon burgers and fries. The thought of all that grease made Moshi's stomach churn, but she did not object to Erik ordering for her. She focused on her water. *Water. Cold water is a miracle. It cleanses and refreshes. The first time she saw Erik, he was smoking a cigarette under the bleachers with his friends while Moshi practiced steps with the junior high school dance team. Even then, he was cool. He could have picked any of the girls in his class, but he picked Moshi. His parents were Microsoft millionaires and lived in a yurt in the Cascade foothills. He was a magician with a skateboard and endlessly practiced jumps and tricks. He earned a third place ribbon at an MTV contest before a smash-up involving a telephone company truck left him with three steel pins in his lower leg. So, he switched to playing bass guitar. At first, the older kids tolerated his fumbling only because his parents bought him a huge PA system, but eventually he could play well enough to hold his own. Under the long oily hair and piercings, there was still a smart and sweet kid who chose shy Moshi over all the other girls in the seventh grade. A kid with a sense of humor and potential. A kid with heart.* Lifting her glass left a small perfect circle gleaming on the table. The waitress placed the steaming plate of food over it.

"What did you want to tell me?"

"Oh," Erik said while stuffing French fries into his mouth. "Man, I'm hungry. I don't think I've eaten for a while." He slid a small medicine vial and a foil packet across the table.

"What's this?" Moshi asked.

"You don't have to go to the clinic. This is some cool stuff Raz got from the record company guy."

The bottle held some clear fluid. Methotrexate. The foil held some waxy lozenges.

"What is all this stuff?"

"The foil things are suppositories. You stick them up, you know? French stuff for abortion. Shoot up the stuff in the bottle and you're done. No clinic, no doctors, no papers, no stupid questions. Awesome, eh? I also have some morning-after pills in case the condom ever breaks while we're fucking, you know, getting jiggy on it." The look on Moshi's face made him think for an instant. "Making love?"

Moshi pushed her plate away. She ran the tip of her finger across the top of her water glass and picked up a drop of water. She stared at the drop; she could see her fingerprint magnified in it.

"Want to hear something else that's cool? We were working on one of Raz's new songs, its call Plague of Fools, and it's in E, right? I came up with a little riff that goes up to B and then C. Raz really likes it and he might give me partial song-writing credit."

Water is made of oxygen and hydrogen atoms. Atoms are made of electrons, protons, and neutrons, all spinning and somehow sliding around each other. Electrons are made of quarks and strings or something; her recollection of high school physics got fuzzy at this point. But mostly, they were made of space. Empty space.

She touched the drop to her tongue and she could taste the empty space. It filled her or emptied her, the feelings seemed linked somehow. Yin and yang, perhaps.

"You gonna eat those fries?" Erik asked. "For some reason, I'm really hungry."

The Election Team

Glen reached over with his fork and speared one of Bennie's sausage links. Bennie opened his mouth to protest, but filled it with a bite of strawberry waffle instead.

"Don't look at me that way, these things will kill you," Glen said as he jiggled the sausage onto his plate. "They are made of floor-sweepings and ground-up snouts and lips. Beside the nitrates, the hormones and fat, they say mad cow disease in the US of A will first show up in sausage."

Murphy and Elke sat on each side of Bennie. With sour expressions, they both scraped their sausages onto Glen's plate. He speared one and waved it. "I'll take these for the good of the team," he said with a self-satisfied look.

They were in a Mom and Pop diner downtown, walking distance from the Marriott, discussing strategy over a hot breakfast before taking Bennie to see some of the Anchorage tourist attractions and get some fresh air.

"Bennie's been staring at that monitor so long he's getting pale," Murphy had complained. Glen approved the trek to the restaurant but teased her about her latent motherly instincts.

"You should adopt him, move to Vermont and bake apple pies." Murphy attacked her hash browns with a grim expression and pointedly ignored him. "I'm serious," he continued, "you could invite the ladies' club over and compare recipes."

This thought immediately cheered Murphy. She leaned over and whispered "If Martha Stewart came over we'd spend our time in the bedroom going at it like a couple of minks."

Glen blinked uncomfortably and looked away. After a few seconds he muttered, "Now, that's just wrong."

Murphy liked the changed dynamic of power.

"I'll bet she has the most perfect creamy thighs. I can only imagine the precision of her bushy trim job. And those breasts..."

Murphy glanced at Elke to see how she was taking these comments. Elke shrugged.

"I like her too."

Glen squirmed. "You shouldn't say such things in front on a child."

Bennie laughed. "I read worse things at the library when I was five." Turning to Murphy, but flicking his eyes to enjoy Glen's reaction, he said "Imagine the flavors she keeps in her nightstand. Monday is mango and perhaps you'd enjoy some parsley sprinkles with that."

Glen threw down his fork. "I should fire all your asses and start over with rent-a-temps. Maybe then I could at least enjoy my breakfast."

As he stomped out, his election team gleefully reclaimed their sausages off his plate.

Scott Steele and Jim Van Doren (DEM)

Scott Steele parked his BMW M5 SUV in the parking garage and took the elevator to the lobby. He bought a latté and a bear claw which he chewed and sipped as he waited for the elevator. The small office of Jim Van Doren, the leading Democratic candidate for the open congressional seat, was on the third floor. Steele pushed through and put his coffee down so he could give Cecilia, Van Doren's office admin, a hug. She was a Kenaitze Indian and wore her gray hair in braids.

"Is the big guy in?" Steele asked.

"Yes, he's on the phone, go ahead and go on in. I'm starving, can I have a piece of your bear claw? That looks good."

Steele broke her off some and walked into Van Doren's cluttered office; he put his drink on the desk and cleared himself a spot on the guest chair. Van Doren shook Steele's hand and gave him a two minute gesture.

"You have my word that the Anchorage to Canada railway will be a top priority in my office. We absolutely need this connection to the lower 48, this project will mean a lot to everyone. So, you're in? I can count on your support for our fund-raiser on the 29th? Thank you so much. Bye-bye."

"Sorry Scott, the job never ends." He spoke to Cecelia through the open door. "Hold my calls while I'm chatting with Scott, thanks."

"How are things going, Jim?" Steele asked.

"We're doing just fine, the money is coming in slowly, but it is coming in. I wouldn't trade places with any of the other candidates, that's a good feeling for a change. I can sure use some help from the DNC."

"It's a bit early to commit our money yet. We have our eye on Barton and Dolliver."

"I've heard from a good source that Dolliver is going to hold off and run for the Senate seat and Barton is going to take a lobbyist job over at Philips. That just leaves me here to carry the party. It's June, for God's sake. Let's not still be talking about this in October. I'm not asking for a big bankroll right now, just a five or ten thousand dollar love note from HQ. My polling shows me at 18%, there's no one else that's going to pull numbers like that at this point in the race. It's time to slice me off a little piece of funding."

"The bosses think it's too soon, so it's too soon. Sorry. What's your read on Patterson?"

"Patterson? Why do you even bring her up? She's not even a player."

"We show her at two points and rising."

"Give her another year and she can get up to three points, big deal. Don't give me any of this Patterson crapola. I'm your candidate so let's stop horsing around. Loosen up your ass cheeks and poop me out some cash."

"Jim, you know I like you and if I could, I would open up the pipeline, but the bosses say it's too early. Just hang tight and we'll take care of you."

"What you're really saying is the elections look good on the mainland and they don't think they need us up here. They don't give a shit if Sanders walks away with a seat we could easily win."

"Now Jim, be realistic. Sanders numbers come in at almost 30 percent, you can't really think we have a shot?"

"You're damn right we do, just free up a few dollars and watch us go!"

"Just hang in there, Jim, the reinforcements are coming."

"That's what the Russians at Old Sitka were told back in 1802 before the natives bashed in their heads."

"Don't be melodramatic. You have money in the bank and your message is getting out. We'll kick in when the time is right, don't you worry about that. Say 'hi' to the wife and kids, okay?"

"Sure Scott, will do. Thanks for stopping by."

They shook hands and Steele walked out. He winked at Cecelia and she blew him a kiss. He looked at his watch and was happy to see it was almost lunchtime.

Murphy and Julia Patterson

It took some driving around, but Murphy found the office for the Julia Patterson for Congress campaign on Eide Street. After parking her rental car, she walked into the office, which looked deserted, but a toilet flushed and a woman soon appeared. Her hair was raked into beaded corn-rows; she wore a peasant skirt and open-toed sandals. She had wide hips, thin lips and wore an assortment of hemp bracelets and necklaces.

"Can I help you?" Julia asked while seating herself behind a card table.

"I'm here to learn a little bit about your campaign for Congress," Murphy said.

"I am on a quest for equality, equality between men and women, between Native Americans and the domineering European usurpers, between black and white and between workers and the oppressive capitalist class. I believe in mother Earth and that all humans deserve a certain dignity and support. I believe that women have a destiny beyond being enslaved by the penis. I believe the environment should be protected, not raped. I believe health care is a right, not a privilege for the rich. I believe working families deserve a living wage and that AIDS is not a crime. I support diversity and believe that all people deserve the right to have their marriages recognized and nurtured by the state. I believe..."

"Okay, I get the picture. You're perfect. I'm here to help."

"Who are you?"

"I represent a small company called Urban Dynamics and we're on your side 100%."

"I will not accept help from the dominant corporate power structure. I will not allow myself to be bought or sold by the monopoly of special interests or multinational corporate plantation owners."

"Down, girl. We're a progressive company with a benefit package for same-sex partners, we're unionized, and we're green. We are not the enemy."

Murphy pulled a bundle out of her purse. She unwrapped it and began peeling off hundred dollar bills. We're donating the maximum to your campaign directly, we have thousand dollar donations from each of our thirty employees, and we're donating money to your PAC, that's the Democrats for Equality, am I right?"

Julia looked with wonder at the bills as they piled up.

"Here is the paperwork for your accountant. Everything is in order. There are a few strings attached, however."

"Strings? What strings," Julia asked suspiciously.

"Nothing sinister. We insist that you work with a media consultant and we urge you use Marcus Phillips who is expecting your call. There is more money where this came from if you follow his advice, that's all. We want you to win the primary and we're going to help you do it."

"I don't know how to thank you."

You could start with a soapy shower, shaving your pits, and getting those teeth looked at, Murphy thought. But she did not say this. "Just get out there and kick the male-dominated power structure in the ass." She left Julia counting the money and eying the papers with a happy gleam in her eye.

Glen and Bennie

Glen was trying to sleep, but even though he had pillows piled on his head and the covers pulled up, he was being pelted with ping pong balls and they were annoying.

"Goddam it Bennie, who gave you those fricking balls?"

"I bought them myself at the Wal-Mart. I wanted to buy a paint ball gun but they wouldn't sell one to me."

"Thank God for small favors. Why are you bothering me? It's not even nine o'clock yet. Shit."

"Coefficient of correlation. Correlativity, anti-reciprocal and causal relationships. Interconnection and interdependence. Central clusters. Physiological psychology."

"Shut up, Bennie. You're giving me a headache. Why don't you take your balls and go play in the street?"

"I'm serious, Glen. For example, I understand why some religions promote large families, they are simply manufacturing their continued customer base. But, tell me why the left is so set on supporting abortions when they're simply killing their future constituents?"

Glen sat up in bed. "Did you get Walter to show you how to make a coin disappear and how to pick a pocket?" Bennie nodded yes. "Then you know the idea is to distract you with the left hand while the right hand palms the coin or grabs the wallet. It doesn't matter what the left hand does as long as it absorbs your attention. When you get hung up on these artificial conflicts, you're looking at the left hand. You're trying to analyze the noise when you should be analyzing the signal. The noise is random, that's why it's called noise, it doesn't matter, forget it. Watch the right hand. Actually look at what is being done by the parties and the groups. Ignore the word play and look at their achievements. These issues don't make sense because they can do their job without making sense. That's all. Now get the hell out of here before I take a hanger to your ass, I need some sleep."

"Okay boss."

Glen swept several ping pong balls off the bed and pulled the blankets over his head.

"Correlation," he muttered bitterly as he tried to get some sleep. After ten minutes or so he gave up and padded to the kitchenette in his shorts and bare feet. He gave Bennie a deadly glare as he grabbed Bennie's box of Count Choculas cereal and poured himself a heaping bowlful. Bennie grinned a chocolaty grin and pushed a carton of milk in Glen's direction.

"There's going to be some correlation between my palm and your ass," Glen said darkly as he wiped off a spoon and started eating.

"I probably wouldn't bother you so much if you'd let me get a dog," Bennie said.

"Shut up, I'm eating," Glen replied.

Scott Steele and Julia Patterson

Steele happened to be driving by Julia Patterson's 'headquarters' and was surprised to see some activity. A truck was unloading some furniture and there were some large banners in the window. "Patterson, the Future of Progressive Democracy," they said. Steele was particularly surprised by some poster-photographs of Julia; her hair was coifed and it looked like she might actually be sporting some lipstick and make-up. All this puzzled Steele, so he parked the car and wandered over.

Inside the office, the phones were ringing, there was a receptionist who looked like a black transvestite (it's very difficult to do anything about the protruding Adam's apple) manning (so to speak) an actual PBX system. The last time Steele visited this office it reeked of patchouli and reefer, now the place smelled like money. There were several people dressed in business suits milling around. Steele recognized one, a local political player named Anthony Andrews.

"Hey Ant, what's going on around here?"

"Isn't this something? Julia decided she wants to actually win this election. She's actually getting a manicure over at Studio 419."

"All this stuff costs big dollars…"

"Yeah, she's being sponsored by some company. She even hired Marcus Phillips and he talked her into the make-over. I hate to see her sell her soul to the devil, but it's awfully exciting to be on a team that has an honest chance, I must confess."

"Phillips? Shit, no kidding. I need to talk to her about her financing. When will she be back?"

"She's speaking over at the U of A later today, so I'm not sure if she'll be back in the office today or not. I should warn you, she's not talking about the money. You may have to wait for the election commission forms to be filed. There's plenty of money, though. She even got a line of credit at Northrim with this company's co-signature, I saw the papers on that. Van Doren is going to shit his pants when he gets wind of this. There is a big article coming out in the Alaska Daily News next week. The photographer just left."

Steele rubbed his eyes. He did not like surprises and he did not like the look of this situation at all. Rules were being broken. McOlive was going to come unglued. Steele walked back to his car trying to figure out whether this could possibly be real and how he was going to spin the news to his bosses back in DC.

The Election Team

Glen looked around the room at his people. Walter and Angela were nuzzling and whispering to each other, Bennie was (as always) playing with his Gameboy, Murphy was reading the Anchorage Daily News, and Elke was painting her fingernails a garish shade of rose.

"I have some ideas you're going to like," Glen said. Everyone kept doing what they were doing. "To start, I want to hire some stand-ins to do some of my speeches. We can win this election here in Anchorage, but I still want coverage in the outlying areas, but I don't really want to go to places like Barrow, Kodiak, Nome.... I happen to know that Sitka means 'freeze your balls off' in Tlingit." There was no reaction from his crew. "That was a joke, okay?" Still no response. "What about the stand-in idea? I don't mind making the hop to Fairbanks and Juneau, but I don't necessarily want to ride those tiny little planes to hell and gone when I could be sitting by the fire and drinking brandy."

"Forget it, Glen," Murphy said, looking up from her paper. "You could probably get away with hiring an imposter, but if the word got out, it would hurt the campaign. If the place is worth visiting, then you're going to have to do it yourself."

"Alright," Glen said, hurt, "but make sure you get me a pilot that knows what-the-hell he's doing." Glen looked at a list of Alaskan towns. "If I have to go, then I want to visit Annette Island, Buckland, Deadhorse, Homer, Kake, Sleetmute, Tin City..."

"Wait a minute," Murphy said. "We're going to visit places that have strategic value, photo ops and key pockets of votes. We're not going to pick places just because you like the names."

"I hate you guys. Okay, here's another idea, we hire a crew of punks to put bumper stickers on cars at the mall, we hit the place like a blitzkrieg, the team gets in and gets out in an hour before the cops catch on."

"That's a dumb idea, you'll just piss people off. Maybe it would be better if we did the thinking around here." Walter said.

"That's the point, we don't do our bumper stickers, we do Van Doren's. We pay some high school kids $100 each through some cut-out so it can't be traced back to us."

Walter and Murphy looked at each other and laughed.

"Oh, that's a nasty, evil and delicious idea. It will work, I'll set it up," Murphy said.

Glen looked pleased with himself. "Finally, I think we should have a ball."

"What's a ball?" Bennie asked.

"Just a fancy name for a party. I'm guessing you're talking about sort of a debutante ball, a coming out party, black tie, expensive food, that sort of thing?" Walter asked. Glen nodded his head eagerly. "That's got to be the dumbest idea you've had so far. I'll get right on it."

"Great!" Glen said. "Now who wants to join me for a burger at the Tastee Freez, my treat?"

Glen was forced to take a taxi to the burger joint by himself. He grumbled to the driver the whole way but two Double Country Burgers made him feel a lot better.

Here... more than anywhere else that I know of or have heard of, the daily panorama of human existence, of private and communal folly — the unending procession of governmental extortions and chicaneries, of commercial brigandages and throat-slittings, of theological buffooneries, of aesthetic ribaldries, of legal swindles and harlotries, of miscellaneous rogueries, villainies, imbecilities, grotesqueries, and extravagances — is so inordinately gross and preposterous, so brought up to the highest conceivable amperage, so steadily enriched with an almost fabulous daring and originality, that only the man who was born with a petrified diaphragm can fail to laugh himself to sleep every night, and to awake every morning with all the eager, unflagging expectation of a Sunday-school superintendent touring the Paris peep-shows.

- H. L. Mencken, as related in the article *The Sage of Baltimore* by Jonathan Yardley in the December 2002 edition of The Atlantic Monthly

CHAPTER 4

Angela and Julio

Sergeant Walter Morrison — AKA Julio — parked his '87 Blazer in the loading zone in front of the Marriott. He wasn't exactly worried about parking tickets, though it would seriously piss him off to get towed again. The Parking Authority Nazis in Anchorage were notoriously trigger-happy and had already towed three of his vehicles to an impound yard; one of those vehicles was his personal SUV he'd left blocking the dumpster in front of his condo. The citizenry responded to the Parking Authority's zeal with the Anchorage Parking Fairy, a non-existent entity comprised of Alaskans with a typical lack of respect for central authority, who simply (and illegally) dropped coins into any expired parking meter they came across. City officials eventually surrendered after a period of threats and bluster. They restricted the scope of the Parking Authority and consigned parking tickets back to the police department, which was less than thrilled and much less exuberant in their prosecution of the task. The Parking Fairy remained a bit of local lore.

Morrison's Blazer was rusting through the wheel wells, the windshield was cracked and pitted from too many miles on Alaska roads, but it was his assigned vehicle for the next couple of months. They'd confiscated the Blazer from a marijuana growing operation up in the Valley. This growing operation consisted of a middle-aged couple with a Conex box buried in their backyard, halogen lights, a generator, a hydroponics drip system; the works. They'd still be in business, with the wife collecting disability for chronic lower back pain and the husband working as a seasonal carpenter, with the real money growing out back in the Conex box, except they didn't enjoy each other's company very much and one Saturday night the wife put a .22 long rifle slug through her husband's left foot. The investigating officers took note of the plethora of gardening equipment and the lack of a garden. They subpoenaed power company records and investigated their pattern of bank deposits. The result was a search warrant and that led to Morrison's rusty ride. The Blazer would eventually be auctioned off to bolster the department's budget and Morrison sincerely hoped the new owner would strip it for parts and tow the carcass to Jim Creek to be burned and used as target practice by the local vandals. He'd like to stop by someday and urinate on the smoldering remains almost as badly as the locals would like to see something done about the Jim Creek vandals. For now he left the key in the ignition at all times in the hope somebody would steal it. So far nobody had bothered.

Angela burst through the revolving front door of the Marriott and strode to the curb. She snatched open the passenger door — perpetually unlocked to expedite the hoped-for car theft — and glared at Morrison.

"You're late," she snapped with her hair falling into her eyes. She tossed her head to flip her hair back and whacked her head on the top of the door jamb. Enraged, she kicked at the Blazer and her foot penetrated the rusty quarter panel and lodged there. She lost her balance and fell back with her foot popping free as her butt hit the bricks of the Marriott's valet parking area. She slowly got to her feet and assessed the damage to her white, semi-transparent slacks that now sported a large dirty splotch across the rear. She turned to Morrison, sitting somewhat stunned in the driver's seat, then wordlessly climbed in, slammed the door and stared ahead through the windshield.

"Your car attacked me," she accused.

"Yeah," Morrison replied while dropping the Blazer into gear. "Kicked your ass, too."

Angela turned and glared at him some more. She'd expected some kind of apology.

"Do you know how much these pants cost?"

"No, and I bet you don't either," he countered, pulling onto 7th Avenue.

"And what's that supposed to mean?" she asked, softly, dangerously. Morrison ignored the question. They drove in silence for several blocks until he turned south onto C Street.

"This is one of the main drags through town," he informed her.

"Great," Angela sighed, fluffing her hair into shape with the aid of the Blazer's visor mirror. "Some towns I've been in, guys still open the door for a girl."

"This town, you're lucky I showed up close-to-sober and alone," Morrison replied. Angela slammed the visor up.

"What exactly is your problem?" she asked, exasperated.

Morrison tightened his grip on the wheel and shook his head.

"Nothing, I'm fine." He sat up straighter. "I'm fine, you're fine, every-fucking-thing's just really fucking fine." He pulled a right turn onto Northern Lights Boulevard and headed for Spenard Avenue and a place he knew. "Let's go get you some blow." He threw her a glance. "You got the money, right? This guy's not real big on fronting stuff."

"Yeah," Angela said, sitting back in her seat. "Yeah, I've got money."

"Well, give it to me, you're not going in."

"The hell I'm not."

"Exactly," said Morrison. Angela frowned, glaring at him out of the corner of her eye once, then twice, while replaying the conversation back in her head.

"So I'm going in, right?" she asked. Morrison laughed.

"No, you're going to stay, and uh... guard the car."

"Guard the car?" She popped the glove box open and peered inside. Empty. She left it open and pulled the ashtray out. She plucked out a cigarette butt and used it to stir the contents around.

"What are you doing?" asked Morrison.

"Looking for butts with lipstick." She closed the ashtray and leaned into the back seat, inspected left, right, moved his coat and shuffled some magazines while glancing at the titles. "Guns and Ammo? Alaska Outdoors? Oh, here's a winner, Maxim." She flopped back into her seat and held the cover under her chin. "Do you really think her boobs are better than mine?" She turned the magazine and looked at the cover critically. "Those can't be real." She tossed the magazine into the back and reached for the center console. Morrison saw it coming and slapped her hand. He was starting to worry because he didn't want her finding the .38 revolver he kept under his seat. "Hey!" Angela looked hurt, then grinned. "So, whatcha got in there?" She settled back, crossing her arms, then sprang for the console and flipped it open. Some papers, registration, insurance — she shuffled through them while Morrison gritted his teeth. "These aren't in your name, Julio," she noted.

"Old owner, I just bought this rig," he lied. Angela stared at him blankly.

"Just bought it? On purpose?" She raised up to look out at the surface rust on the hood. "I figured you found it or something, or maybe adopted it from the impound yard." She dropped the papers back into the console and leaned closer. "So, what do you do for a living?"

Morrison rolled his eyes, then braked and swerved to miss a red-light runner, a constant hazard in Anchorage.

"Jesus!" Angela gasped as she was flung against her door. "Where's a cop when you need one?" Morrison inwardly winced.

"Just remember to look both ways, even if your light's green."

"Yeah, right. Like I have, or will ever need, a driver's license," Angela said. "Anyway," she leaned back in, "we were discussing your income tax bracket." Morrison turned left onto Spenard Avenue, an older and seedier part of Anchorage. Some newer construction was evident, but the side streets and alleys were still no place to walk at night, unless you belonged there.

"What is this?" he asked. "You wanna just go through my wallet?"

"Sure," she replied, holding out her hand.

He gave her a dirty look.

"Look," Angela said while pointing a finger at him. "When you have a relationship with a woman, you lose all right to privacy and she gets to be superior to you forever, that's part of the rules."

"What?" Morrison was so unnerved he ran a red light himself. A security company van slid past three inches from their rear bumper. The driver flipped Morrison the finger.

"Hey, he was cute," Angela said, craning her neck.

"What?" Morrison repeated. "I don't recall having a relationship and I think I would."

"Damn right you would, but that's not the point. The point is we're *going* to have one, and it's best you're aware of the rules." She sighed heavily and then perked up. "I just saved us a lot of trouble. A man is a slave to his dick. If a woman owns the dick, she owns the man. Even Abraham Lincoln couldn't do a thing about it with his Emasculation Proclamation."

Morrison pulled into an alley between Spenard and Minnesota Avenue where one side consisted of new multi-family Section-8 construction and the other dwellings from Anchorage's past. Some of the old buildings were actually built from logs with their roofs covered with moss. Angela noticed the log homes had tidier yards and appeared to be more carefully maintained than the newer homes.

"Good God, 'George Washington Slept Here'?" she asked. Morrison laughed.

"No, not nearly that old. Turn of the century at the oldest." He didn't really know how old they were, and was now thoroughly distracted by the shape of Angela's various body parts. Even her throat now seemed immensely female and sexy. And she was beautiful, and... pert. Maybe he could find some way to spare her from the fallout of whatever resulted from this investigation. If anything. Morrison was a fairly junior member of the interagency task force and was mostly just collecting raw data: names, dates, places, trends, quantity and quality. It would be up to senior officers to put together the plan and the indictments. Surely an omission of Angela's involvement wouldn't be a big deal, even though he was counting on her personality and looks to open doors.

He stopped in front of a small apartment building and turned to Angela.

"Money-honey," he said, almost making it one word. She sat still for a moment, then pulled an envelope from under her shirt and handed it over.

"How do I know you're not going to just leave me here..." She surveyed the surroundings with distaste, "at the mercy of the locals?" Morrison flipped through the bills in the envelope.

"For five hundred bucks?" he grinned. "I wouldn't do that to these people." He removed the money, folded it and stuffed it into a front pocket. "Do me a favor," he said. Angela raised an eyebrow. "In about five minutes, get out and smoke a cigarette." Angela slowly smiled.

"Oooooh," she breathed. "Julio's playing games!" She clapped her hands in glee. "Should I undo some buttons? Bend over several times? Wait." She turned in her seat and grabbed the magazine from the back seat, flipped it open. "Let me study some poses." Morrison grabbed the magazine and threw it back.

"Look," he said, "I'm just trying to get you a better deal, okay?"

"Sure Jules, whatever you say," she said, winking. Morrison shook his head, slammed the car door and headed up the sidewalk.

In five minutes Angela was leaning over the hood of the Blazer, pretending to smoke one of Morrison's cigarettes. In six minutes she was inside the apartment being introduced to a small time Anchorage drug dealer. By the time they left she'd been invited to a party, and if she had to bring Morrison along... well, guess that'd be okay. And they got a nice discount, an extra tenth for free.

Back in the Blazer, Angela dug into the quarter-ounce bag of coke with a tiny spoon she'd produced from somewhere. She held it up to a nostril and inhaled sharply.

"This is shit," she complained. Morrison glanced over.

"Christ, keep that out of sight, this isn't LA."

"I can get better stuff from Walter's stash," she continued. That perked Morrison's ears up.

"Walter's stash? Who's Walter?" he asked, trying to remember if he'd left anything incriminating lying about his condo. Angela was annoyingly snoopy.

"Oh, Julio. I told you about them. Glen and Walter. Walter and Glen," she chanted, digging for another spoonful of shit. "Glen's running for office on the Asshole ticket, and Walter's brainwashing the voters into thinking they're voting for JFK-reborn." She giggled as the cocaine reached in and stroked her brain. "He'll do it, too."

"Come again?" Morrison wasn't sure what she was talking about, but he didn't like the sound of it.

"The election, stupid." Angela gave up on the spoon and stuffed a small silver straw directly into the bag. "This really is shit, you know."

"Yeah, I can see that. Maybe we should complain, did you keep your receipt?" he asked dryly. Inexplicably, Angela found that comment amusing and snorted into the bag, blowing a small amount of powder into the air.

"Fuck!" She wet a finger and blotted up some stray powder. She licked it with a grimace. "They cut it with Vitamin B," she said.

"You know your stuff," he admitted. "So you can get better?" he asked casually. Angela hesitated, unsure, with her train of thought derailed by alkaloids.

"Oh, that," she finally said, "its not coke." She gave him a sly grin. "Ol' Walter's a doctor, a magician, a chemical version of Bill Gates," she said, raising her hands and closing her eyes, "a voodoo priest, a warlock, a student of the Gods and a God of the students." She opened her eyes and looked directly at Morrison. "Don't fuck with Walter, li'l Julio. Things happen to people who fuck with Walter." She reached over and pinched his cheek, "and that would be a shame because you're so *cute*." She slid her sunglasses down her nose and turned to watch the scenery, which consisted of strip malls and endless traffic. Morrison wondered where she'd kept the sunglasses and her other stuff. It surely wasn't in those pants. "I can get you a taste of his stuff if you want." She looked at him from behind the dark lenses, her expression unreadable. "It's kinda different. Expensive, though." She lowered her sunglasses. "Money-honey?" she asked, and then grinned at him, displaying her small, white, and perfect teeth.

Morrison swung onto Minnesota Drive and headed for South Anchorage and his condo, with Angela's smile influencing his priorities. He'd find out more about this election business, and Angela's sugar daddy and his stash, after he took care of some personal interests. All in the line of duty, he told himself.

ALASKA INSTANT POLL

June 15

ADN[9] Survey of likely Voters (plus or minus 4% error)
25% Undecided
29% Sanders – REP
13% Van Doren – DEM
9% Patterson - DEM
3% Other
3% Walters – GREEN
2% Gray – LIBERT
1% Onkiak – AK IND
0% Wilson – DM

Scott Steele and Jim Van Doren

Jim Van Doren walked into Scott Steele's office and slammed down a copy of the ADN.

"You fucking prick!" he said hotly.

"Jim, hold on a minute, what's on your mind?"

"Have you seen these numbers?"

"Yes, I saw them before they were published, of course. What's the problem?"

Steele knew exactly what the problem was, but he wanted to play this one cool.

"It's that bitch Patterson, she's up to nine points. Nine goddam points."

"You have a comfortable lead and your number is up. Just relax."

"Don't bullshit me, Steele. If you think you can play me, you are mistaken." Jim turned the paper to page six. This page had a picture of Julia Patterson cleaning oil off some gulls. Jim flipped through the pages. On page nine, there was a quarter-page ad which featured a grinning Julia Patterson with the president of the Alaska chapter of the AFL-CIO. "She has money! Someone has given her a make-over. She is showing

---

[9] Alaska Daily News

cleavage. Someone is advising her. Her nipples are sticking out in this picture, for Christ's sake. You fuckers are giving her money."

"She hasn't received a dime from us. You know me, Jim, I'm as surprised as you are. This is just an anomaly. The next poll will have her back in the dirt where she belongs."

"Where is she getting her money?"

"She has a private corporate sponsor. She's not saying who it is, so we won't know until she files her FEC paperwork next month."

"You gotta help me out here, I'm losing my mind."

"I know," Steele said soothingly, "we're kicking something in, don't worry." Steele opened his file cabinet and pulled out an envelope, which he handed over. "This will get you started."

Jim tore open the envelope and looked at the check. "Ten grand? You're giving me ten grand? One fucking series of radio spots is more than ten grand. I need some real help, not chump change."

"If you don't want it…" Steele said, holding out his hand.

"No, I want it alright, but I can't do much with this, you know that." Jim said, visibly calming himself.

"Of course. But suddenly, the DNC is having some problems in California and Massachusetts. Loose-cannon Kennedy's, you've read the Drudge Report. We have to watch our money. Don't worry, we'll feed you some more as soon as we can. You can't tell me you're broke, your fund-raisers are going pretty well and you made some money off that Tipper Gore dinner."

"These elections are expensive. I'm the leading contender, I shouldn't be walking around with a cardboard sign begging for handouts."

"You show me the plan that beats Sanders and I'll get you more money."

"How can I beat Sanders if I can't afford saturation advertising? Give me the money and I'll win this race."

"The polls don't show that. Give me something to work with and it will be easier for the DNC to justify the spending."

"You're going to fuck me, aren't you?"

"No, I'm not going to fuck you. We just don't have the money to throw around. Raise money yourself, show us some hope, and we'll be there for you."

Jim got up and picked up his newspaper from Steele's desk. "Alright, I get it. See ya." He put his hand on the doorknob.

"And Jim?" Steele said.

"Yeah," Jim said, looking over his shoulder.

"You're up a point. That's good. Keep it up, okay?"

"Prick," Jim muttered in reply as he left the room.

Glen and Walter

Glen was in the living room watching a Fox News show. Walter threw one of Jim Van Doren's campaign signs onto the conference table. Glen looked at it and then shrugged his shoulders. The sign had Jim's smiling face hovering over a flag graphic. He clicked the remote to mute the TV.

"Dull, the usual. So?" Glen said.

Walter handed Glen another poster. It looked identical.

"What do you think of this one?" Walter asked.

"It looks the same. I don't get it."

Walter walked across the room, got as far from Glen as he could, then turned and displayed the sign. Another image seemed to hover over Jim's face. Glen could not make it out. Walter walked back.

"That's a bit too close to get the full effect. We are creating a sort of moiré effect. At a distance, Jim's face gets overlaid by a pig face. Bennie cooked this up for me with Photoshop. It's subtle, but there is a definite subconscious effect. I talked to the printer, if we pay him ten thousand in cash, he will substitute our graphic."

"I like it, Elke will give you the cash."

"We're working on an even better one for Julia Patterson, but it's too soon to say if we can pull it off."

"Is it evil, low, and dirty?"

"Absolutely."

"Cool, then just do it." Glen un-muted the TV returned his attention to the blonde talking-head.

Moshi

Moshi stared at the ceiling. It was 11 in the morning. Erik was naked and sleeping with his head on her stomach. She did not want to disturb him, but he was pressing on her bladder and she would need to walk down the hall to the toilet soon. Their clothes, strewn around the room, were mixed with the debris from the previous night's party. The room was an endless landscape of dirty socks, KFC boxes, empty beer cans and overflowing ashtrays. From outside, thick clouds alternately covered the sun and darkened the room or drifted away and let the room fill with blinding brilliance. Rays of sunlight illuminated a bottle of Beefeater Gin. It was about 2/3's full and the contents glowed. She couldn't reach the bottle, but felt that a stiff drink would chase the cobwebs from her mind and cut the awful taste in her mouth. She held out her hand and willed the bottle to cross space and come to her. *Float to me,* she wished.

Giving up, she focused on a large pimple on Erik's back. It was swollen like an angry little red volcano. She had not told him yet that she was not going to abort their baby. In a week, they were on their way to Japan in a chartered jet with an intermediate stop in Anchorage. Erik joked about burning the rental house to the ground instead of trying to find a place to store their stuff. She hoped he was just kidding around, but sometimes she did not know her man. The record company check had come, but Raz was careful with his money and was not giving much to the band. Erik got an allowance from his parents and made additional money selling Ecstasy to high school kids, so he didn't care. Moshi knew exactly how much money she had. Just over six dollars in her little purse, forty dollars stuffed in the toe of a shoe and crushed aluminum cans in overflowing plastic bags hidden in the basement that could be sold at the recycling center for 10 or 12 dollars. All together, enough to get Erik a new set of bass guitar strings for his coming-soon birthday.

She eased herself out from under him. She noticed a blister on his cock. She hoped it was nothing that she could catch. *Or if it's contagious, at least that it won't hurt the baby.* She sent this thought skyward as a little prayer. *Please, God.* She picked up the bottle of gin and looked through it at her room. The carnage was even uglier when viewed through the distortion of the bottle's content. She unscrewed the top and smelled the liquor. It both repelled her and woke a craving that gnawed at her gut. *Sorry baby,* she thought as she raised the heavy bottle to her lips.

Erik stirred. "Hey Mosh, I'm dying here, could you see if there is any cold beer in the fridge?"

Moshi put the bottle down. *You stay right there until I come back for you,* was the thought she aimed at it.

"Yes my dear, I'll see what we have."

She wrapped herself in one of his shirts and walked to the kitchen where she found a partial quart bottle of Miller High Life and brought it back. He was sitting up and absently scratching his crotch.

"Thanks, babe," he said.

She walked to the bathroom to relieve herself. After she finished, she noticed the toilet paper she dabbed herself with had some pink streaks. Her stomach had been hurting for days. She wondered if this was normal and this thought led her to thinking about the bottle of gin. Her cells cried for a drink. She hurried back to the room to fill this need the only way she knew.

Holly

By the time Holly reached Carnestown, she'd looped around the Allman Brothers tape and listened to *In Memory of Elizabeth Reed* four times. She didn't know what to think of it the first time, but now she thought it was the funkiest and most beautiful piece of music she'd ever heard. *Add a little bit of scratch and maybe some synth loops and it would be perfect,* she thought.

There weren't many main roads near the Everglades in this part of southern Florida, but she took more than one pass through Jerome, Ochobee, and Copeland before she found the gas station she was looking for. She kept missing it because Leonard's Lunch-N-Lube looked completely different. A few years prior, it was rundown and forlorn; now it was freshly painted and busy. There was a new auto repair facility, a restaurant, and something called a gator petting zoo. Holly parked on the shoulder a hundred yards away and watched the traffic with wonder. *What happened?* She had a hundred rounds for her pistol, but with the traffic and the customers, the .45 was not enough weaponry. With an automatic rifle and a scope she could probably do the job, but there was enough traffic going in and out, even that would be dodgy. She'd need time, a crew and a plan and she had none of the above. She pulled into the restaurant parking area and tried to decide what to do. Her belly grumbled and it occurred to her to go in and get a meal.

She sat at the bar and ordered something called a Gator-burger, some onion rings, and a hand-dipped strawberry shake. Holly chatted with the waitress, a gray-haired woman with wide hips, a blonde mustache, and a nametag that read Paula.

"What happened to this place, the last time I was here it was a dump."

"The owners came by some money and fixed it up, hon. Business got better and this place is a goldmine now. They may open one in Naples and maybe even another in Immokalee if the permits come through. There's enough cash flowing though here now that I'm guessing the permits will be approved, if you know what I mean." Paula winked.

"Is the owner around?"

"Yeah. Leonard! Some one wants to talk to you!" she shouted in the direction of the kitchen. Holly tried to stop her, but she was too slow.

Leonard, dressed in clean overalls decorated with the Lunch-N-Lube logo, pushed through the bat-wing doors from the kitchen. Holly didn't really recognize him and hoped he wouldn't recognize her either.

"Can I help you, Miss?" he asked.

"Uh—," Holly replied, "wasn't there a dog around here?" It was the only thing she could think of.

"Yeah, come on."

He waved for her to follow and they walked through the kitchen and out the back door. Past the gator rodeo and the RV dump station a cross was stabbed in the ground. The cross was inscribed: **Dog, he was a good old boy, RIP**. "He was a good old boy," Leonard said.

"I can see that," Holly said dryly.

"I didn't catch your name, missy?"

"Reed, Lizzie Reed." It was the first name she thought of, so she blurted it out.

"You seem familiar, how do we know you?"

"I get that all the time, I guess I have a familiar face, I'm just rolling through on my way to Miami."

A tow-headed kid, about four, raced by at full speed.

"Stevie, you come over here and say how-do to our guest," Leonard hollered.

Stevie slid to a stop and walked back. He offered a dirty hand for Holly to shake, said "Hey" then took off running again. He wore the same overalls as Leonard, only smaller. He didn't look much like Leonard, but Holly did not comment.

"Come on, let's go say hi to Dee," Leonard said.

They walked to the gas station office and entered. DeeDee was running a credit card through the terminal. She looked at Holly and a cloudy expression crossed her face.

"Who do we have here, Lennie?" she asked.

"Lizzie is passing through on her way to Miami and she wanted to pay her respects to Dog."

"Dog was a good old boy, we miss him around here. Seems like I know you from somewheres..." she said with a question in her voice.

"She gets that a lot because she looks like someone," Leonard said.

"Well, I guess I'd better get my lunch bill and be on my way."

"Lunch is on us, right Dee?"

"Leonard, we can't give a lunch to everyone..."

Holly decided to press her luck.

"Weren't there some black rocks around here?"

DeeDee looked startled. "Black rocks. I know who you are," she said.

"Those stupid black rocks," Leonard interjected, "I keep tripping over the darn things, why don't we just give them to her if she'll take them."

DeeDee nodded slowly. "Perhaps you'd just take those rocks and move it on down the road?"

"That would work for me just fine," Holly replied.

"Okay," DeeDee led Holly into a room in the back of the mechanic's bay. She turned on the light and got on her hands and knees and started pulling some things out from under a workbench. "Grab that box over by the window," DeeDee said.

Holly brought the box over and DeeDee tossed the rocks in. Holly noticed some newspaper clippings tacked to the wall. "Who is this guy, Wilson?"

"We had some excitement a few years ago, which you know quite well... Holly."

"So, you do remember me?"

"How could I forget? Wilson gets his face in the paper now and then. He's running for a political office in Alaska. We tear his picture out of the paper when we see it, for no particular reason. He's just a memorable character, that's all. We have a picture of you around here somewhere too."

A thought popped into Holly's head.

"Is Wilson the wallet-guy Manny told me about?"

"Yeah, that's him. You knew Manny too, that figures."

Holly stood with the heavy box in her hand and stared at a grinning picture of Glen Wilson. She was flushed and could not seem to breathe. "I think he killed my sun and moon, the only guy I ever really loved."

"Yeah, that describes Manny. You have your rocks." DeeDee said pointedly.

"Yes." Holly said.

"So take them out of here and don't come back this way again."

"Okay," Holly said as she tugged the picture of Wilson off the wall. "You won't see me again."

Democracy is two wolves and a lamb voting on what to have for lunch.
Liberty is a well-armed lamb contesting the vote.

- Benjamin Franklin

CHAPTER 5

Glen and Bennie

"Social Security?" Bennie said with a challenging tone.

"What about it?" Glen replied, looking up from the sport's section of the ADN. "I'm trying to read the paper while I have a few minutes."

"Where do I start? This looks like an incredible fraud. It's not a pension or retirement program. If it was, then there would be hard assets to back the future obligation. The average employee pays almost 15% of his wages into the social security system in exchange for nothing except a government promise to pay future benefits. The program started small. In 1950 there were 16 people paying in for each recipient. Now that ratio is 3.4 to 1. In the near future it will be 2:1. In order to sustain the system, payroll taxes will have to be increased, we'll have to dump in huge amounts of other tax money, or benefits will have to be cut. Some combination of all three is inevitable."

"So what?"

"Let me try again. Right now we have more money coming into the system than we are paying out. The excess is used to purchase Treasury bonds."

"You invest the surplus, that's a no-brainer."

"Glen! We're not investing the surplus. We're spending it. It's not spent directly, it's used to pay down the national debt, which was caused by government spending. Where is the money to pay the interest payments on the bonds coming from? Also, when the bond is retired, where does that money come from?"

"From the tax-payers, of course."

"Think about what you're saying. The government takes surplus retirement system payments and spends it, but balances the books with taxes and future tax-payer obligation. U.S. bonds are simultaneously an asset of the trust fund and a liability of all taxpayers."

"I don't see the problem."

"Let me see if I can make this simple for you. I take a dollar from you. I pay seventy-five cents to retirees. That leaves a quarter. I spend the quarter and give you an IOU and a promise to pay interest. Where does the interest come from? From the dollar I get from you next year. When the bond is supposed to be retired and I'm supposed to give you your quarter back, I get another quarter from you. You're just moving the quarter from your left pocket to your right pocket. Even worse, to keep things going, I don't take a dollar next year, I need more."

"So I'm even."

"No, you're not even. You were robbed of the original quarter. It was stolen. Next year you're robbed of thirty cents and more the year after that."

"Whatever. Call a cop. You're boring me with this speech."

"The cop doesn't care. In addition to his Social Security tax (which you're paying, by the way), he has another retirement system, one that actually has assets. You're paying for that one too. Your congressmen and government employees also have this sweet retirement plan in addition to Social Security. It's the largest rip-off ever conceived."

"No one cares about complicated things like this."

"It's not complicated. It couldn't be simpler. All this information is readily available on the government's own Social Security website[10]."

"And your point is…?"

"You're making speeches in support of this system. That makes you part of the problem."

"Old folks vote. You don't win unless you get their vote and you don't get their vote by scaring them. I hired you to run my computer systems. I'll tell you what. You show me a strategy and a simulation that wins me this election with a platform that includes real repair of the Social Security system and I'll do it."

"I did. If we execute perfectly, you'll get eight percent of the vote," Bennie said sadly.

"So make up your mind. I hired you to help me win this election, not to change the world. I want to have a few laughs along the way, not listen to long-winded lectures. We'll win this election by telling people what they want to hear. If you want out, I'll give you a plane ticket back to Florida and enough money to buy yourself a BMW. Or, you can get your black ass back to work and let me read the funnies. What's it going to be?"

Murphy poked her head into the kitchenette.

---

[10] See www.ssa.gov

"Glen, get cleaned up and ready, you have a breakfast meeting with the Democratic Party Chairman in an hour. Chop-chop."

Glen glared at Bennie. "You're the devil."

"Chop-chop," Bennie said, dismissing Glen as he plucked the newspaper out of his hand.

Holly

Holly sat in the parking lot of the pawn shop all night. She dozed off intermittently, but spent a lot of the night looking at Glen Wilson's smiling face and crying. She'd only known Manny Rodriquez for a couple of days, but he was the light of her life, the wind beneath her wings, and all the other sappy clichés she could think of. He had money, he loved guns, he didn't talk down to her and he had a huge purple penis. He was everything she wanted in a man. Manny told her about the stupid wallet-man that followed him from Orlando. Wallet-man was supposed to be dead, but he kept popping up. The newspapers reported that Manny was killed in a gang outbreak in a drug deal gone sour. But, except for some stray bills, the money was missing. The situation did not add up. She believed there was more to the story and she believed wallet-man was the missing piece.

One of the clippings she took from the Lunch-n-Lube was a small announcement of the Glen Wilson candidacy for congress in Alaska. She finished her donuts and cried herself to sleep.

The clerk unlocked the back door and entered the pawn shop from the rear entrance. He was not happy to see the GMC truck back and parked outside. He'd made good money the day before and he figured this girlie was done with him. He stuffed a .44 Magnum in his belt at the small of his back and unlocked the front door. He took some deep cleansing breaths before flipping the front-door sign to OPEN.

The traffic on the street woke Holly. She sat up and noticed the pawn shop was open. She emptied the clip of the .45 and ejected the shell in the chamber. She put the shells neatly back in their box. She threw the shells, holster, cleaning kit, the gun, and the 8-track tapes into the box with the black rocks, carried them into the shop, and placed everything on the counter. The clerk watched her carefully while he locked the front door. Her hair was matted and lopsided and her clothes were wrinkled. Returning to the counter, he pointed at the box and she nodded to give him permission to sort through the stuff. He pulled the gun out of its holster, checked the clip and chamber and smelled the barrel. He put the gun out of reach on a shelf behind him. He pulled out the black rocks and arranged them on the counter; he was so excited that his hands were shaking. Holly just watched him passively.

"What kind of moron spraypaints gold nuggets?" he asked.

Holly shrugged.

"I'm going to take these in the back and weigh them, okay?"

Holly nodded.

It was about ten minutes before the clerk returned. He punched some numbers into an adding machine. He tore off the tape and handed it to her.

"There is a 50 percent restocking fee for the gun and accessories. I'm offering 65 thou for the gold, let's call it 68 for the whole package."

"Okay," Holly said. "How about the truck?"

"The truck too, huh? I'll do you a favor and make it 70 including that piece-of-shit truck."

"Careful," Holly hissed.

"Sorry, 70 including that fine old truck."

"Deal," Holly said. "I need some papers, good stuff, not photocopied and laminated shit. Passport, Florida driver's license, birth cert, and a bank account with Visa debit card. Give me a grand in cash and deposit the balance in the bank account. I want this package today."

"No can do. For 20 grand I can get you a package tomorrow, it can't be done quicker."

"Fine. Throw in a concealed carry and prepay a taxi willing to drive me to the Miami Airport tomorrow at two o'clock."

The clerk laughed. "Concealed carry permit, that's a good one." He made some notes. "You're about five-foot four, ninety-five pounds, blond hair, blue eyes, seventeen years old?"

"I'm twenty-one."

"Okay, you're twenty-one. Do you have a name or do you want us to pick one for you?"

"Let's go with Elizabeth Reed."

"Jammin'", the clerk said, strumming a little air guitar. Holly did not look amused, so he quit. In 24 hours he was going to clear almost enough money to buy a houseboat up in Sanibel and spend the rest of his life smoking ganja and watching the sunsets. "Forty-nine in the bank and one in your pocket? One-way to the airport? Two o'clock tomorrow?"

"Deal," Holly said. She held out her hand for a handshake. "See you tomorrow."

Glen and Scott Steele

Glen was dressed in a tailored suit, vest, and silk tie. He shook hands with Scott Steele and they sat at the large table at the Swan House Bed and Breakfast. They selected this location because it was private and was reported to have good buffalo sausage. They asked for the table to be cleared, so the hostess removed the flowers and candles. She poured coffee and disappeared into the kitchen. Murphy was in the sitting room reading a paperback novel.

"So Glen, tell me about this Democratic Majority party," Steele said.

"We're a group of concerned citizens who want to steer the state back toward common sense and middle-class values. We believe that the major parties have drifted away from serving the needs of the elderly, the taxpayers, and the children, in a cost-effective basis."

"Sure, I know. How are you funded?"

"All of our funding comes from private personal resources at this time."

"Can you give me some indication of the magnitude of those resources?"

"It's enough, that's all I care to say right now."

"Do you have any political background? Have you ever been elected to any office?"

"No. We believe the professional political class is part of the problem. We're suggesting a fresh start with a philosophy based on sound principles acquired in the private business sector."

"I see. Do you mind if I speak frankly?"

"Go ahead, Mr. Steele."

"We're an established party in Alaska. Our polling shows us running behind Sanders, though we still think we have an honest chance. I don't understand why a flat-lander like you thinks he can come up here and win an election in our state. Carpet-bagging bullshit can win in New York, but its not going to fly here. You must either be crazy or stupid. Care to give me a clue which it is?"

Murphy looked up from her novel and couldn't stifle a small smile.

"Where do you think you are in the primary?" Glen asked while stirring a teaspoon of sugar into his coffee.

"Our polling shows our lead candidate, Van Doren, at 20 points and climbing. We like our position."

"You're full of shit. Van Doren is at 13 percent and falling like a rock. Patterson wins the primary then flames out and you're sitting with egg on your face, your dick in your hands, and wondering whether you can land a job gutting salmon on a frozen fishing boat for pocket change. Or..."

"Yes?"

"Or, you can ride first class on the Wilson train to Washington, DC."

"You're a funny man, Wilson. The Democratic Party machine will grind you up and spit you out. Why don't you save yourself some pain and just haul your ass back to Buttfuck where you belong?" Steele stood and tossed his napkin on the table. "Good day to you, sir," he said as he walked out of the room.

The hostess watched Steele leave as she placed a platter of pancakes on the table. Glen harpooned a stack, dragged them to his plate and slathered them with butter and warm syrup.

"Hey Murphy, these are good, come over and have some while they're hot."

Murphy sat down and served herself.

"Are you sure it was wise to piss him off like that?" she asked.

"Hey, he started it with that carpet-bagger crap."

"I'm just saying we may need him at some point, what would it hurt to keep the door open?"

"Don't worry about that little worm, he'll be back."

"Whatever," Murphy said, propping her book open. "Now shut up and let me finish this chapter."

"What are you reading?" Glen asked.

"I said shut up," she said sternly while pointing her fork at him, "that means zip it. I'm off duty so leave me alone."

Glen shrugged and stuffed a wad of sausage in his mouth.

"Hmm, that's some fine buffalo," he said.

Moshi

Moshi's belly was swollen and she felt feverish. She had diarrhea and spent the afternoon sitting on the toilet reading an old Rolling Stone magazine. Her head was spinning. A stomach cramp ended with an explosive eruption into the toilet bowl. *That has to be the worst of it,* she thought. *Please God, let it be so.* She wished Erik was there to hold her, but he was recording a new song called I Want to Eat Your Liver. She could send a message to his pager, but he'd ignore it until they were done at the studio. Weak-kneed, she stood up. The bowl was filled with bloody splatters. *Miscarriage* flashed across her mind, but she pushed the evil thought away. She cleaned herself up with a washcloth and refused to look at the pink water swirling in the sink as she rinsed the cloth. She scrubbed spots of watery blood off the sink and the toilet bowl until they gleamed. Then she washed a bloody spot on the floor and noticed how much gross crud came off. As far as she knew, no one had cleaned this room since they moved in. She wrung the washcloth out over and over and scoured until the floor was spotless. Standing, she wiped the mirror and stared at the sad-looking Japanese girl who looked back into her.

Feeling disoriented, she laughed at herself. She could ask Erik to bring home a gallon of milk or a box of Sugar Pops and he would always forget. But if she asked for a little pot or a bottle of booze, he'd almost always remember. Back in their room, there was some weed to smoke and two nearly-full bottles of gin waiting. These would make her feel better until Erik came home. She collapsed on their couch and watched dust motes drift in the sunlight. Gradually, her nerves calmed and she recognized the messy room as a violation of universal harmony. While feeling empty, she moved around the room and tidied up. She folded clothes and stuffed them in drawers or into the closet. Her damp cloth collected dust from the guitars and CD player and she made endless trips down the hall to the bathroom sink to wash it out. Her thoughts drifted back to her childhood.

Her great-grandparents hated the Western world. They called it the metal land. Stones and trees and water carry pieces of the soul of God, but metal and plastic are of the dark land. Moshi washed her hands and rinsed her mouth. On impulse, she poured a mound of bath salt on the floor and stirred serpentine patterns into its surface. *To achieve a pure heart one must follow the way of Kami.* This thought startled her. She could hear her Grandfather's voice as if it was whispered in an echo chamber. The salt contained a fragment of the echo. The water dribbling like a spring from the tap to the drain carried the echo. The hummingbird that hovered at honeysuckle blossoms outside her dirty window held the echo. The sunlight through the trees radiated the echo. The rumble of traffic on the street echoed the echo.

She opened the medicine cabinet and picked up the bottle of Methotrexate. She was supposed to inject this drug to kill her baby. It occurred to her that the best way to kill the baby would be to kill herself. She picked up a metal nail file and examined its edge. There were many easy ways to do the job, but they would leave her out of balance. *In blood and pain I enter the world and that is the way I should leave.* Pressing hard, she was able to cut through the skin of her arm. Blood welled in drops that seemed to inflate as they escaped her body. There can be glory in an honorable death. She searched for any sign that wielding the nail file would please her ancestors. She was slowly filled with knowing. She was going to die soon, but not today. There was some purpose she had yet to fulfill. She felt light as air, like she was the dust floating in the loving sunlight of Kami.

Slowly, she unwrapped the suppositories and placed them at floating quadrants in the toilet bowl. With the nail file, she pried off the metal top of the little bottle of Methotrexate. She carefully poured the fluid directly in the center of the bowl, then sprinkled bath salt on top. She flushed and watched the evil swirl away. Slowly the water stopped flowing and the mirror-like surface became still. Her reflection looked back at her curiously. This girl had lank black hair clumped around her head and tiny nodules of sweat on her forehead and upper lip. Her pale skin was layered with sin and disgrace. Madness. The top of the toilet bowl was clean. She carefully placed the empty bottle in the center. Unconsciously, her hands folded the drug information sheet into a paper bird. This found a resting spot beside the bottle. She scooped up more bath salt and spread it around. She felt like she was almost done. Back in her room, she looked under the cushions of the couch for money. When she had a small collection of nickels and pennies, she walked back to the bathroom and arranged the coins around the bottle. For now, she felt the Shin Tao Gods were appeased. A temporary balance was achieved.

She couldn't let Erik see her in such disarray. Some rouge to color her cheeks and lipstick to gloss her lips would work wonders. She could also do her eyelids, Erik liked it when she did that. She covered her seeping wrist with clean cotton and tape. Feeling like a ghost she drifted back in their room where she sat on the couch and patiently waited for Erik to come home.

Sgt Walter 'Julio' Morrison

Morrison parked his Bronco in the far corner of the parking lot. He hated it when he was summoned to headquarters as there was no telling when he'd run into one the dopers he'd had a hand in busting. With his cover blown, he'd be back on the beat or worse, on traffic patrol or parking enforcement. The cop-shop was a newer brick building on Bragaw Street and he was meeting his boss in an office on the second floor, a throwback named Wallace, an ape of a man with huge hairy arms and a continually sour temperament.

Morrison carried in a box of Dino's donuts which he placed on Detective Wallace's desk. Wallace picked through them and selected a chocolate one with sprinkles.

"The Porter case was tossed on a technicality, there was some kind of chain-of-evidence problem." Wallace said with sprinkles decorating the corners of his mouth.

Porter was caught in a fishing boat with three bales of BC bud. The arrest was based on Morrison's tip, his biggest bust so far.

"The fuckers in the evidence room are smoking the evidence," Morrison complained.

"I won't have this kind of crap from you. Our officers are straight. IA[11] will work this out and until they make a finding, you shut your wide-ass mouth. Got me?"

"Okay, boss."

"You've brought us nothing but shit so far. I'm going to pull you in."

"Come on, Wallace. What about Simpson and Thorvalds? Those were clean."

"You spent over $15,000 of the citizens' money for a couple of rave GHB[12] busts. Your job is to bring down the wholesalers not to save our virgins from being raped by their boyfriends. Besides, all those kids had parents that could afford expensive lawyers. We'll be in court until the Bering Strait freezes over again."

"I'm onto something big."

"Bullshit. You just like wearing civvies and putting bar bills on your expense report. You'll serve the public better directing traffic in Spenard. I've already put the papers in, you're done."

"Listen to me." Morrison pulled out and unfolded a small newspaper article. "Have you heard of this guy running for office? Wilson?"

"Everybody is running for office. Never heard of the guy. What about him?"

---

[11] Internal Affairs

[12] Gamma-HydroxyButyrate, often called a date rape drug. In the right dosage, this drug can make a victim immobile and can cause amnesia. Potential minor side effects include death.

"He's from the lower-48 and he thinks he can buy an election here. He's mixed up in some heavy shipments to pay for his campaign. I'm close to blowing the whole thing open."

"If this is such a big deal, why am I hearing about it now? Are you holding out on me?"

"No, this is brand new, bigger than big."

"If you're fucking with me, you're going to be assigned to Wildlife Officer backup out on the mud flats. Or maybe you'd rather be on gall bladder patrol?"

Morrison paled. Fish cop duty was the most dangerous assignment in Alaska. These guys had odd ways of dying or simply disappearing in the wild.

"Just give me a couple of months, this is going to be a juicy one."

Wallace thought about it.

"Okay," he decided, "a month, let's see what you can do. I want written weekly reports. I swear to the Mother Drum I'll see *your* gall bladder sold to the Chinese if you're fucking me. 10-4?"

"I read you, boss." He closed the donut box and picked them up.

"Leave the donuts, I'll take care of them."

"Sure boss, sorry."

Morrison walked back to his 4x4. He sat behind the wheel and gnawed on a thumbnail. *A month*, he thought. He shivered at the thought of being assigned to the wilderness.

Glen and Ron Swanson

Glen was working on a speech with the remnants of a pencil. The waste basket was overflowing with discarded pages. Murphy tapped on the door and poked her head in.

"I have a Ron Swanson here to see you."

Glen looked at her quizzically. "Does he have an appointment I forgot about?"

"A-F-L-C-I-O", Murphy mouthed. Glen nodded and leaned back in his seat.

Ron was a stocky man with a bulging stomach and ruddy complexion. He wore a leather jacket with a fleece collar, a flannel shirt and he had gray hairs curling from under his black V-necked T-shirt. His arms were covered with sun-bleached hair and faded Navy tattoos. He looked like a throw-back to an earlier era where strikes were settled by fists and baseball bats instead of lawyers and legislators. Glen stood and shook his hand. Ron did his best to break all the sensitive bones in Glen's hand, but Glen just grinned and did not otherwise react.

"Democratic Majority?" Ron said with a question in his tone.

"Yes sir, we're bringing traditional working-man values to the modern world. We're taking up the fight against multinational corporations that export living-wage jobs then import cheap Chinese products built by children and prison labor. We're on the front lines of preserving America for Americans and stopping the flood of undocumented workers that are stealing jobs from our hard-working blue collar work force. We…"

"I'd heard you're slick. You'll have to forgive me for not being as *verbose* as you." Ron said the word 'verbose' as if it was one he'd heard on TV and had practiced saying it in front of a mirror.

"You look like a man who has many important things on his mind. Can I ask what brings you to visit your humble candidate for Congress?"

Ron pulled a rolled magazine from the back pocket of his canvas pants. He tossed it on Glen's desk. Glen unrolled it. The magazine was a cheap black and white publication on smeary newsprint.

"Working Family Magazine?"

"The unofficial mouth-piece of working families in Alaska. We consider it an outreach program for the union HQ. We think a multi-page spread would do your campaign some good. Maybe a four-page insert?"

"How much?"

"Twenty-five thousand bucks," Ron said flatly.

"I see," Glen mused. "How many members are in your affiliated unions and their voting households?"

"Around thirty-five thousand, give or take."

"And you can deliver 40%?"

"No, 55%."

"Bullshit," Glen said, "you can guarantee 40%, that's all. Still, that's fourteen thousand votes." He made a decision. "Okay, I like it, my media consultant will deliver you some copy." He called out to Murphy. "Hey Murphy, would you get Elke to write Mr. Swanson a check for twenty-five thousand make it out to the Working Family Magazine?"

"It would be better if that check was made out to cash," Ron whispered. Glen nodded.

"Just have her make it out to cash."

Murphy shrugged, slipped out and pulled the door closed softly.

"What else can we do for you, Mr. Swanson?"

"You're doing some public appearances? You need transport, setup and A/V techs?"

"Absolutely."

"Then we'll want to make sure these guys have Union cards..."

"I'll have to run that by my media guy as some of his requirements are very specialized."

"That's fine. We can issue temporary cards to your crew if necessary."

"For a price, of course."

"Of course."

"No problem, I understand, and we'll work it out with you. If you don't mind me asking, how do you see this election going for the Democrats?"

"We like Van Doren okay considering he's a spineless weasel. Julia Patterson is a clown. I suppose if anyone thought the Dems had a chance-in-hell against Sanders, we'd get a little more excited about things. As it stands, who gives a rusty fuck? We think Sanders is alright for a right-wing whacko, we can work with him."

"Can I tell you a little secret just between you and I?" Glen asked.

"Sure, pal."

"It's crossed my mind that there might be an opportunity to *Lautenberg*[13] this race? What do you think?"

Swanson looked at Glen appraisingly. "I think there is a small chance maybe you're smarter than you look."

Murphy opened the door about six inches and held out the check. Ron accepted it with a glance and slipped it in the back pocket of his Carhartt painter pants.

"Our get-out-the-vote effort can always use clever and well-connected people who know the lay of the land. Can I get your card and your cell phone number?"

"Right. No card and no cell phone. If you need me, leave a message at Whitekey's Fly-by-Night Club and I'll get back to you sooner or later."

Glen stood. "It was a genuine pleasure doing business with you, Mister Swanson."

---

[13] Frank Lautenberg was the New Jersey Senatorial candidate that illegally stepped into (and won) the 2002 election race after the scandal-ridden Bob Torricelli was forced out by the Democratic Party.

"Likewise, I'm sure," Ron replied. He hitched up his pants and glanced around the room. "Hey, you wouldn't have any of those little bottles in the minibar I can take with me for the road?"

"Help yourself," Glen said, "just leave me the Chivas so I can have a refreshing cocktail when I finish working on this speech."

Ron filled his jacket pockets and left. When Glen checked later, both little bottles of Chivas (and the Ballantine's, Glenlivet and Jack Daniels) were cleaned out. Glen, scowling, had to make do with a cold can of Heinekin.

Mohandas Karamachand 'Mahatma' Gandhi was once asked what he thought about western civilization. His response was: "I think it would be a good idea."

CHAPTER 6

Glen and Angela

Glen let himself into Walter and Angela's suite with his master key card. Walter was doing some work at a chem lab they hired at the University. Glen was sure they would not see him again until the evening. Angela was in the bathroom brushing her teeth. Glen startled her.

"Jesus Glen, don't sneak up on a girl."

"I brought you some Chai tea and croissants."

"Great, just set them down somewhere, I'm brushing my teeth for God's sake."

"Beautiful teeth they are, have I mentioned it?"

"Thanks. They should be beautiful, Walter spent 25 grand on them. Give me a minute, will ya?" She shut the door in Glen's face.

Glen took off his clothes and draped them on a chair. He flopped on the bed and waited. After 20 minutes Angela came out. Her hair was brushed and her make-up was perfected. She had dusted her cheeks with a little glitter and she wore high heels.

"What are you doing? Get your pants on."

"I thought you might have time for a quick one. Nothing serious, just a maintenance screw to take the edge off. What do you say?"

"You're a pig, that's what I say."

"Okay, I'm a pig with a hard on, come to bed, baby."

"No Glen, I got my hair fixed up and I have my face on. Besides, Walter had at me already and I'm sore. I need a rest."

Glen grinned. "I'm easy, would you like a mouth full of congressional candidate?"

"I said no! I'm not a whore."

"I never said you are a whore, you're a lovely, beautiful work of art. Come on, Angela. How about at least a hand job before you go out? I brought croissants."

"I think you have the wrong idea about me. You got me when I was bored out of my mind and it was fine. But now I'm going out and I

112

want you to put your pants on. We had a thing, now it's cooled off. Go find some one else to smooth out your edges."

She slammed the door. Glen sat up and looked around the room. He reached over and grabbed a croissant. He sat, ate, and felt sorry for himself.

Scott Steele and Julia Patterson

Steele waited in the reception area for almost an hour past his appointment time. When the door finally opened, Steele recognized the people that came out; a reporter and photographer from the Anchorage Press. They were all smiles and were carrying a lot of equipment; tape recorder, lighting baffles and tripods. Julia shook Steele's hand firmly and ushered him into her office. Marcus Phillips was sitting in a chair beside Julia's desk. He stood and shook Steele's hand too. Marcus looked a little like Sean Connery and had cultivated a slight Welsh accent to enhance the effect, even though he was born in Nebraska.

"Hello Scott, good to see you," Marcus said.

"Back at ya," Steele replied. "This business never ceases to amaze me, I never thought I'd be meeting you in this office."

"We can speak frankly, Scott. I'm sure DNC headquarters is shitting bricks right now."

"You could say that. Of course, we're delighted that Julia is doing so well."

"Of course," Marcus said with a touch of mild sarcasm.

Steele opened his briefcase and pulled out some papers stapled together. "We're now showing her at a slight advantage. Congratulations. The progress in just a few weeks is quite amazing."

"Thank you," Julia said. The phone rang. "You guys go ahead and chat while I take this."

While talking to Marcus, Steele listened in to Julia's conversation. She seemed to be making a date for Mad Myrna's that evening with someone she called Thunderbear.

"I liked the front page spread in the UAA Northern Light, that was a nice hit."

"That's not all. Walters, the Green party guy, is talking about resigning. If he does, we'll get an endorsement. We're excited about that possibility."

"I'll bet you are. I'm having a little trouble explaining this situation to the brass in DC. They don't like surprises and neither do I.

You did a nice job with Julia's make-over. Are you ready to disclose your financing?"

"The paperwork will be filed on time. Other than that, we're not ready to go public. We're clean, you can be sure of that."

Julia cradled the phone.

"I don't understand why you're being so stubborn." Steele said, "we're not really interested if you can't play nice with the team."

"I got along without you assholes when I was starving for money. Now that we're on a winning roll, you come around here trying to railroad us," Julia said hotly.

Marcus waved at her. "What Julia is suggesting is that we could have used your help earlier, but if you're ready to get on board, we're ready too. Okay? Can we count on some support from the DNC."

"Julia, you're looking great and I love your numbers, but I don't think the state of Alaska is ready to elect a lesbian to Congress. Let's be realistic. We like having you in the primary because it makes us look diverse, but you can't really think you have a chance. Even if you get past Van Doren in the primary, you're going to get your butt handed to you by Sanders, that's just the way it is."

"Listen to me, asshole..."

"Now Julia, let me handle this," Marcus interrupted. Julia sat back in her chair and looked out the window with a bitter expression. "You wouldn't really pull our party affiliation?"

"That's exactly what we're thinking. Work with us or go run under the Socialist Worker's umbrella or something. We want you to keep the lesbian issues private and go easy on the environmental activism and that sort of thing. We want to look at all speeches and press releases before they are public. It's all just common sense for the winning team."

"You can shove it up your ass..."

"Julia! I said I'd handle this. Sit down and let us talk about this."

"I'm going to get some carrot juice." Julia said as she stomped out of the room. She shut the door solidly behind her.

"Are you going to be able to talk some sense into her?" Steele asked.

"I think so, but it will take some time. Van Doren is crapping his pants?"

"Oh yeah, he thinks I'm torpedoing him. I'm more worried about the guys in DC, we're looking like amateurs up here. Any chance you'll switch over or are you locked in for this election cycle."

"Unless the checks start bouncing I'm doing pretty well here. Julia is a pain but she's come a long way in a short time. I'm beginning to think she might do well in November."

"Not well enough to win," Steele said, shocked.

"No, of course not, Palmer is a powerhouse, but we'll land a few blows. I'm not insane, I'm just trying to make a few bucks and enjoy the ride as long as possible."

"Good, you had me worried. A carpet-banger can make it in Berkeley, but isn't going to win shit up here." They sat and looked at each other for a minute.

"What about those Seawolves?"

"We're looking good on the left wing, but we need to get a real goalie."

"I agree, maybe next year we'll have something."

"Yeah."

There was another minute of silence.

"Don't pull out on us," Marcus said.

"Well, try to keep her from getting too embarrassing, okay? If we can survive this election, maybe we can get rolling on something with better odds next time. It was good to see you."

Marcus stood and they shook hands.

"Are you going to the Governor's fundraiser?"

"Sure, do you want me to score you a couple of tickets?"

"That would be great, Shirley loves those things."

"Say hi to her for me, will you?"

"Will do. See ya."

"Yeah, see ya," Marcus replied as Steele exited the office. On the way back to his car, Steele saw an older lady get out of a golf cart and feed coins into his expired parking meter. *Fucking meter fairies,* he thought. He didn't really care, he got his parking tickets thrown out by a friendly magistrate, but the parking meter fairies were really pissing off the city and the police union. The city made a lot of money on parking fines. Their point was that the two-hour limit eased the parking situation for shoppers. Right. Anyway, the people had pretty much run parking enforcement out of business. *Power to the people,* Steele laughed as he got in his SUV and drove away.

Holly

Holly spent the hop from Sea-Tac to Anchorage cheerfully imagining a few of the things that could go wrong with a 737. The engines could fall off, or they could ingest some seagulls and stall, or the pilot could succumb to a death wish, shout praise to Allah and steer them nose-down into the frigid water. The top could peel off and suck out a flight attendant like that plane in Hawaii. The rudder could stick and corkscrew them into a mountain side. They could have a midair collision with a biz jet. The bearded man seated next to her tried a few conversational ploys, but gave up when she ignored him. In a heavy rain, the 737 hit the runway hard, slewed heavily and bounced a couple of times, but pulled up safely to the jetway.

"Thanks for flying with us," the pilot said, smiling as Holly exited the plane.

"Try landing sober next time, asshole," she replied.

In the terminal, she admired some of the mounted game hanging on the walls. She had no idea that moose got so big. This place was like a PETA[14] nightmare. She hailed a taxi and asked for any hotel downtown; the driver ate her up with his eyes. So far, she didn't think she'd have any trouble getting laid. Beards seemed to be standard issue in Alaska, she didn't know if she liked that or not. She supposed a little research into the question was in order. As they rolled through Spenard, they passed A & L Auto Sales and Holly saw something that caught her eye.

She guessed the GMC pickup was a '67, a lifted 4X4 short bed with oversize tires. It was a weird three-tone; black cherry, white and some kind of putrid split-pea green. She pounded on the taxi driver's shoulder and made him turn around and drop her off. She walked around it banging on the sidewalls to get an idea how much road cancer had been body-filled or painted over. Wade, the salesman on duty, came out with a huge umbrella and looked curiously at the soaking-wet waif with a suitcase that was beating on the truck. He couldn't help but notice her tiny nipples erect under her thin sleeveless blouse.

"We have a real nice little Nissan pickup with low miles that a pretty lady like you might like. It's taupe and has a moon roof, mag wheels and an automatic transmission."

"Creeper," she said while popping open the hood.

"Excuse me, miss?"

---

[14] People for the Ethical Treatment of Animals

"Get me a fucking creeper so I can take a look under this thing."

"Uh—, okay." Wade said.

Holly checked the oil and felt the texture with her fingers. As expected, there was some Motor Honey in it, but not too bad. She sniffed it, there was no sign of sawdust. The engine was a 305 long-stroke V6 which suited her just fine. It had a 4-speed floor shift with a ruby-eyed skull shift knob that amused her. She rolled around underneath and spotted the expected minor oil and differential leaks, again not too bad. There was a puff off blue from the tailpipe when she started it. It had glasspack dual exhausts that emitted a satisfying rumble. She threw her suitcase into the cab.

"Write it up," she said.

"Are you looking for a gift for your boyfriend? The engine in this sweetie has been bored out 300 mils over and it has a racing cam. Low miles on the rebuild. It'll smoke most V-8's out there. We're asking four thousand, this is nearly a show truck."

"I said write it up, you've made a sale. I'm paying three thousand cash and that includes tax and license. If you don't have the keys and the paperwork in my hands in five minutes, I'm walking."

Wade swallowed hard. "Yes ma-am," he said. "Right away." Four minutes and twelve seconds later Holly was revving it up, grinning like a maniac, and peeling-out onto Spenard. After she got tired of driving around and scattering pedestrians, she found a Super 8 motel and checked in. She bought an Alaska Daily News from a machine and settled into her room. She put her wet clothes into a dry-cleaning bag and sat on her bed in the nude. She paged through the paper. In the Life section she found a picture of Glen Wilson reading some tots *The Cat in the Hat* at the Loussac library. This was one of the few books that Holly had read. *The sun did not shine. It was too wet to play. How I wish I had something to do!* Something to do with the wallet-man. Just blowing his brains out with a .45 would be too easy. She wasn't going to let him off without making sure he felt some of her pain first. The happiest day of her life had been shooting Manny's guns in a hotel room, then making love with the acrid smell of gunpowder filling her head and Manny's huge cock filling her loins. Wallet-man stole that away from her. He needed to pay. She needed a gun and a plan, but that could wait. She fell asleep, smiling, with the vision of wallet-man doing the delicious double-thump under the huge tires of her new truck.

Moshi

Erik was supposed to pick her up at 2:30. If Moshi believed the clock, it was now 4:00. She didn't really trust the clock because as she watched, sometimes it stopped and sometimes it seemed to skip ahead. The hot June sun poured in the windows and made her feel sweaty and sticky. She had a bottle of gin clasped between her legs and she was pacing herself with small maintenance sips. Between these sips, she chewed ice cubes and gnawed at her fingertips. Their bags were packed. Erik's guitar cases were lined up by the door with some equipment cases. The band logo, Toxic Shock Syndrome, was stenciled on the cases in large red letters. Moshi had created the design and cut the stencils herself with an Exacto knife. As she waited, she listlessly paged through an old Guitar World magazine that was laying around. The words would not register in her head, but over and over she looked at the pictures of guitars and sound processing equipment.

The band was doing a showcase tour in Japan, but they were stopping over for a few days and making a warm-up appearance in Anchorage. The record company had rented a rehearsal studio and set up a gig at Chilkoot Charlie's, a popular nightclub. Moshi had no idea what summers were like in Alaska and she hoped the ice and snow would not be too much problem. She packed her warmest clothes but was only allowed one suitcase; she hoped she would have enough to avoid frostbite.

She was wearing her best head-banger clothes. Black jeans, mechanic's boots, a shredded Marilyn Manson t-shirt and inverted-cross earrings. Under the t-shirt, her stomach felt hot and swollen. If she pressed on her left side, the pain was excruciating, so she tried not to do that.

She heard the van pull up and immediately the horn started blaring. Moshi grabbed her suitcase and Erik's guitar case and staggered to the door. She stumbled when her legs gave out. Crouching, she gasped for air until the spell passed.

"Hurry up, Mosh," Erik called from the back of the van. He took her suitcase and tossed it into the cargo bay. He carefully placed the guitar case on a stack.

With trembling legs and a pounding head, Moshi ran back and forth until the equipment was loaded. When the last bag was stowed, Erik slammed the doors shut and the van lurched forward. Moshi stood on the pavement and watched with a stunned expression. The van skidded to a stop a dozen yards away.

"Come on, Mosh, we're just kidding around. Get your pretty young ass in here."

She ran to the van and Erik helped her aboard. She sat on a transit case and wrapped her arms around Erik's leg and cried until the abandoned feeling faded. Erik passed her a roach and a lighter, a few puffs helped. They struggled through the nasty Seattle traffic to SeaTac Airport in fits and starts. The Alaska Airlines baggage handlers pulled out all the equipment.

In the passenger terminal, the entourage gathered and Raz passed out the tickets. Moshi was surprised at the pack, there were a total of ten people traveling including the Filipino girl who clutched Raz's arm and pointedly ignored Moshi. Mari was holding her two toddlers and was crying and whispering to the drummer. She would not be making this trip because they could not find anyone to watch the babies for the duration of the six week trip. Moshi clenched the ticket to her chest like a lifeline. Her aching belly fluttered like butterflies had been replaced with hummingbirds or sparrows, or worse yet, insane gnawing squirrels seeking escape. These images were absurd and she pushed them away. A snippet of an obscure song drifted through her mind.

Get on that plane, let it take you far away
Try to leave your troubles far behind…

Moshi prayed that she *could* somehow leave her troubles behind. The band had a contract and was starting a mini-tour. All the work, the endless massaging of the songs, the melodrama between band members and the weeks of eating Top Ramen noodles when there was no money for anything else was coming to an end. Their dreams were coming true. But Moshi's head pounded and her stomach hurt. Life shouldn't be this hard or hurt this bad. When Moshi handed her ticket to the attendant, it was crumpled and damp. The attendant looked at her and laughed as she flattened it out.

"Don't be a nervous Nelly," she said.

Moshi nodded solemnly. "I won't." She followed Erik down the gangway and they took their seats in the aircraft.

Glen and Murphy and Lester

Murphy found Glen in the main room. She tugged the USA Today out of his hands.

"I think I've found you a pilot," she said. "The car is waiting. Grab your hat, let's go check this guy out."

"I was reading about the Fur Rendezvous," Glen complained. "They have dog sled races. We missed one hell of a party."

"Stop sniveling. You wanted a pilot and I think we have one. Time to get some work done."

The limo discharged Glen and Murphy at a hangar at the Lake Hood airstrip. Murphy walked around and looked at the small planes as they waited for Lester to arrive. Glen wore the official uniform of Alaska: black Carhartt jeans and a woolen Pendleton shirt. He wanted to appear rugged and outdoorsy. Murphy was dressed in comfortable polyester slacks and a thin sweater. Lester pulled up in his old Chevy truck. He wore old canvas coveralls.

Lester strode forward with a smile and thrust his hand towards Glen. Glen grasped it in a firm grip and studied Lester's eyes. He liked what he saw; basically a good guy, sharp enough, but not above pulling a fast one for a couple of bucks. Just what they needed. Lester's eyes flicked to Glen's mutilated hand, but he did not comment.

Lester turned to Murphy and offered her a smile and a nod. Murphy surprised him by also thrusting her hand out to be shaken. He took it daintily in his work-roughened palm and gave it a gentle squeeze. Murphy laughed.

"I won't break, Mr. Mike."

"Call me Lester," he grinned in return. "Are you folks are ready?"

He extended an arm towards his plane, about fifty yards away, and the three of them started walking toward it.

"Hey, Lester," Glen began, "do you ever do more than just fly tourists around the mountains?"

Lester slowed and glanced at Glen.

"Well, no. I guide hunting trips and carry a little cargo sometimes." He looked at Glen steadily. He'd been told Glen was running for some political office, and he could buy that, but Lester had dealt with a lot of different types over the years, and there was something about the guy... "Also, I've been known to do an odd job or two, for the right price."

Murphy stared at Glen from behind Lester's back and widened her eyes to indicate her disapproval. Glen grinned at her, then at Lester. He started to slap Lester on the back but sensed that would be the wrong thing to do, Lester didn't seem to be a back-slap kind of guy. Instead he kept silent until they reached the plane. Glen whispered to Murphy while Lester walked around and checked the plane.

"I've got a good feeling about this guy, we can trust him," he said.

Murphy turned and spoke out the side of her mouth while watching Lester complete his inspection. "Trust him to do something crooked? Honor among thieves? You guys can spot each other or something? Did I miss the secret handshake?"

Glen grinned at her. "You're still a cop, Murphy. You're telling me this guy isn't a player?"

"Okay," she hesitated, "he'll be a willing pilot for us, I agree."

Glen walked around the aircraft. Something caught his attention.

"Hey Lester, is this a bullet hole?"

"Might have caught a stray somewhere along the way," Lester commented dryly.

Glen grinned. "You'll do, Lester-Mike. Stay tuned. When we're ready, we shall return."

ALASKA INSTANT POLL

June 30

ADN Survey of likely Voters (plus or minus 4% error)
31% Sanders – REP
23% Undecided
10% Patterson - DEM
9% Van Doren – DEM
3% Other
3% Walters – GREEN
2% Gray – LIBERT
2% Wilson – DM
1% Onkiak – AK IND

The Election Team

Glen stood by the window and looked out over the Anchorage skyline. The sky was solid gray and rain hammered the streets below. There were a few pedestrians hiding under their umbrellas. Glen turned and addressed the team.

"Let's start with money. Elke, how are we doing?"

Elke looked up from a notebook. "We're doing fine. We have just over a million in the bank and a hundred thousand or so in cash here in the room. We have some teacher's union contributions coming in that we've been passing onto other candidates. Not a lot. Are we eventually going to start keeping contributions?"

"I'd rather not disclose our bank balance or follow the other election regulations," Glen said. "As long as we are running on private money we can skirt these rules. After the primary and DEM money starts coming in we'll have to change the way we do things, but we'll worry about that later. Bennie, how about our numbers?"

"You've seen the ADN poll. Our own projections shows us kicking ass. The conservative Democrat message is a winner for us. Patterson is pulling good counts. That part of your evil plan looks like it will work. We have things scheduled so you'll start running up Sanders' hind end early in September."

"Good. Murphy?"

"The press is coming along fine, you have an item in the paper every other day or so and a photo once or twice a week. You're getting equal numbers of marriage invitations and death threats which we're taking as good news. You're going to have to start traveling. We need to hit Fairbanks, Juneau and Sitka plus some of the outlying areas. You can fly commercial to the bigger cities and we'll use our bush pilot for the other places."

"Sounds good. Walter?"

"Everything is on track. I have the arrangements for your 'coming-out' ball almost done. We're going to do it in Juneau at the Centennial Hall Ballroom the middle of the month. We have most of the media and political players lined up to attend. Ted Nugent and Emily Saliers are going to play short acoustic sets. We're having some Tlingit dancers. There will be a chemistry experiment with a compound I've been playing with, sort of a designer mood thing. In other activities, we hired a moron to wear a Nazi uniform and heckle Van Doren. 'Heil Van

Doren', that sort of thing. The guy got the crap beat out of him, but we paid him an extra hundred bucks so he's happy. You'll see this hit Van Doren's numbers in the next poll. Basically, he's toast."

"Where's Angela?"

"I don't know, out running errands, I guess."

"Okay. I want to bounce an idea off you guys. I was thinking about the problem with running a railroad down to the states. I think we should annex British Columbia."

"No one wants a fifty-first state, Glen," Murphy said.

"I thought of that, we'll merge North and South Dakota and no one will even notice."

"The Canadians will never stand for it," Murphy said firmly.

"What are they going to do, beat us to death with their back-bacon?"

"Forget it, Glen. If you ever suggest anything stupid like this in public, I'm walking, got it?" Murphy said.

The rest of the team nodded in agreement except for Bennie, who looked intrigued.

"I'll run the numbers just for the heck of it," Bennie said thoughtfully.

"Thank you, Bennie," Glen said, scowling at the rest of the team. "I'm glad someone has some imagination and appreciation for creative thinking around here. Now you assholes get to work, okay?"

Angela and 'Julio' Morrison

Angela and Julio had a table in the corner of Rumrunners Old Towne Bar which they felt was a safe place to meet. Rumrunners was frequented by an odd mix of young professionals and airman from Elmendorf taking advantage of happy hour. Angela was looking resplendent in a tight pair of stretch-denim pants and a silky polo shirt. Her hair was pulled back and she wore drugstore sunglasses even though it was dark and rainy outside and even darker in their corner of the bar. Morrison wore a rugby shirt, blue jeans, and cowboy boots that added almost two inches to his height.

"I need to meet the man," Morrison said, taking a hit off his Dewar's and water.

"Which man? The candidate or the Doctor?"

"Doesn't the candidate get high? I assume he's a big toker."

"I've never seen Glen do any dope, I think he's against that sort of thing. As far as the Doctor, I don't want you to get the wrong idea. He has a lab in Nevada that mixes custom blends for him. I don't think it's exactly illegal; a lot of this stuff doesn't officially exist and some of it is so specialized to the body chemistry that it would be harmless except to the person it was designed for. Is that against the law? I don't understand it. It's not narcotic, it's something else."

Morrison did not like the sound of this. How was he going to get a big bust out of this situation?

"Let's go back to your connection and get some of that Oxy-C," she suggested.

"Not tonight, babe."

Angela pouted. "You're starting to bore me."

Morrison was distracted.

"I did bring a sample from the Doctor's stash," she continued.

"Now you're talking. What is it?"

"I don't know what it is. Walter calls it Love Potion Number 10."

She pulled a small twist of aluminum from her handbag and carefully peeled the foil apart. Inside, there were two tiny yellow dots about the size of grape seeds. Staring into each other's eyes, they popped them. They sat around drinking and waiting for something to happen. They didn't feel anything, but both started noticing the light was prismatic and their color sense seemed to be shifting.

"Do you feel anything?" Morrison asked.

Angel shrugged her shoulders. "Nope. The light looks strange, that's all."

Morrison accidentally brushed Angela's hand when he picked up his drink. The feeling was electrifying. He flushed, the room temperature seemed to be rising. The back of his hand was radiating, it felt as if his skin was on the verge of coming, which is, of course, impossible. They looked at each other curiously and slowly placed their index fingers together. Their flesh was literally throbbing, they could see the pulse in their hands. The waitress looked at them funny as she dropped off another pair of drinks. Morrison pressed some bills into her hand; the touch of her skin did nothing. The drug had created some sort of polarization only between Angela and Morrison. He could feel his clothes constricting him. His skin tingled and wanted to be exposed to the air. He took Angela's hand and tried to stand. The waves of pleasure made his legs weak. His Bronco was parked illegally by a dumpster in the alley. By the time they reached the cab, they were tearing their clothes off. Every place their skin touched was tuned into some sensual overload. It was like their entire bodies had been turned into sex organs. Angela straddled Morrison and he penetrated her. Their brains did not function as thinking engines any more, they were unconscious. There was no stroking or plunging, they just quivered as slow waves overcame them like a tantric dream or a metaphysical earthquake.

They weren't sure how long this lasted, around an hour, though it felt like a hypnotic lifetime. Gradually, Morrison became aware of a tapping on his window. Languidly, in stop-motion time, he turned his head, wiped a spot in the steamy window, and looked into the eyes of the two young boys who were tapping. They pressed their heads on the glass and made grotesque faces at him. Morrison could hardly move, but he cursed them. The boys laughed, then stepped onto their skateboards and rolled away.

Morrison became aware that the areas where their skin touched seemed raw, like a bad sunburn. They separated and got some relief.

"Kind of a hangover to that shit, eh?" Morrison said.

"I guess."

The cab was a mess; the bench seat was slimy with sweat and other fluids. His whole body felt like it had been pressed flat by a steamroller. As they struggled to get their clothes back on, each time they touched it was like a bee sting. A headache crawled up his neck and lodged in the back of his head like a badger in a burrow. He got the truck started and took Angela back to her hotel.

"When you get a chance, I need to meet the Doctor and the candidate."

"Sure," Angela replied.

She got to her room and looked at herself in the mirror. Her hair was tangled and her makeup was smudged. The bright red tint of her skin seemed to be glowing, but that could have been a visual artifact. She took a cool shower then flopped in bed for a 12-hour nap. Walter looked in on her but couldn't get her up for dinner. He sat on the bed, looking. It occurred to him that he didn't know what she did with her days. He figured she'd be smart enough not to screw around knowing that his revenge could be worse than death. He could not fathom that she would betray him but the possibility hovered on the edge of his consciousness like an itch that could not be reached. Leaving the room, he slowly shut the door and went down to dinner by himself.

A core competency of government is the ability to convert a dollar of tax revenue into a dime's worth of benefit to the public.

- Glen Wilson

CHAPTER 7

Glen and Bennie

Glen looked up and down the hall to make sure Murphy was not following him, then slipped into Bennie's room. Bennie was sprawled across his bed sleeping in Spiderman pajamas. Glen shook Bennie's shoulder, he sat up and rubbed his eyes.

"What time is it?" Bennie asked.

"Noon." Glen opened the curtains and let the light stream into the room. The place was a mess of room service trays, chocolate milk containers and computer parts. "What have you been doing in here?"

"I wanted a new video card and I ended up rebuilding my whole PC. I've been working on this thing with British Columbia. I'm convinced this would work. My first projection, without any incentives, showed that 32% of the Canucks would agree to a merge with the United States. They really feel alienated from Ottawa."

"What do we do to double that number? Let's assume we need a two-thirds majority."

"It's not that hard. First of all, we'll allow a thirty-day window to convert all hard assets one to one into US dollars. Basically, it's a bribe, they can increase their cash worth by almost 20% instantly. We'll convert all debts at a discount. We could do some interesting things, like convert the bottom half of Vancouver Island to a free trade zone like Hong Kong. That would get us support from the Asian population. The top half could be converted into a national park. That will get some of the enviros, but we really don't need them anyway. The whole thing could be done in 10 years for a couple hundred billion, that's far less than Germany spent on unification."

"What about the numbering system? Those hosers won't want to change to the US system."

"You're thinking the wrong way. We convert the US to metric or to a dual metric/SI system. We can get 80% support."

"Wow. How do we pay for it?"

"That's one of the beauties of the plan. Generally, one problem of the government is that it doesn't spend money on hard assets that increase in value. If you spent the Social Security surplus on buying British Columbia, that would be a great long term investment, something that actually increases the net worth of the investment dollars for a change."

"There must be a catch?"

"Yes. The problem is where to stop. It wouldn't make sense to annex BC without taking the Yukon Territory. Alberta and Saskatchewan are going to want to get in on this. Then we might as well take The Northwest Territory too. An additional 100 billion dollars would do all that. We might have to take Manitoba too. We can open up homesteading in the Territories then payoff and relocate the hard 20% that won't accept the changes. We can move them all to Newfoundland and Nova Scotia."

"Why don't we just take the whole damn country?"

"Because you don't want Ontario and Quebec, they're too screwed up."

"Okay. The leaders in Ottawa will be steaming mad."

"Screw them, they are a joke. What are they going to do about it?"

"Bennie, don't bullshit me. You're saying this could be done?"

"I'm saying it would be easy."

The door opened and Murphy struck her head in. She had a suspicious look on her face.

"What are you guys doing in here?" she asked.

"Nothing," Glen and Bennie said at the same time.

"We're not going to win this election unless we focus. Focus!"

"Of course, we know that. We're not children."

"Yes you are. I need Bennie to run a research project for me."

"Okay, Murphy," Bennie said. He got out of bed.

"Take a shower first. Come see me after you eat breakfast."

"Okay, Murphy. I'm coming."

Murphy looked pointedly at Glen. "Alright, I have a speech to work on." Glen said. "See you later, Bennie."

Murphy ushered Glen out of the room.

"Glen?" she said and he walked down the hallway.

"Yeah."

"Win the election first, then you can take over the world, okay?"

Glen rolled his eyes. "Sure Mom, I read you."

Holly and Glen

Holly pulled her truck into the parking lot of Chester Creek Park. The parking lot was about half full, but notably there was a KAKM TV 7 truck and several private busses. The stage was set up with red, white and blue bunting and a JBL sound system. According to the newspaper, Glen was supposed to speak at 1:00, Holly arrived early to get the lay of the land. A large BBQ grill was set up. Holly grabbed a free hotdog and Diet Doctor Pepper. College-aged kids were walking around making sure everyone had buttons and little 'Glen Wilson' flags to wave. Holly found an out-of-the-way spot under an alder tree where she could see the stage. She watched the stage crew route some wires and hoses from a tractor trailer rig. Power was routed in from a diesel generator that was set up across the parking lot.

Holly didn't know anything about politics, but this setup seemed more complex and elaborate than she'd expect for a speech in a park for a legislative position. It was like a rock concert, like U2 was playing. U2 was political, so she figured maybe it was the same thing. She sat under the tree and dreamed of what she would do to Wilson, the wallet-man. She could imagine the weight of a .45 in her hand. She would say *Do you remember Manny Rodriquez? Manny was my soul mate, he was the earth to me. You killed him. Do you have anything to say before I blow off your dick? Do you have anything to say before I shoot off your kneecaps? Do you have anything to say...*

"It's quite a set up, isn't it?" Glen asked.

Holly opened her eyes and saw blue jeans and hiking boots. She looked up slowly. It was the candidate. He sat down beside her.

"You wouldn't have a cigarette, would you?"

Holly shook her head no.

"Too bad. I'm trying to quit, but these speeches make me nervous." He held out his hand. "I'm Glen Wilson."

She hesitantly held her hand out for a shake. She damned herself for not buying a gun yet. She looked around for a branch or a shovel she could use to beat him to death, but nothing was available.

"And you, pretty lady, are...?"

"H—, Elizabeth."

"Well H— Elizabeth, are you interested in politics?"

"Sorry, its just Elizabeth, and no I'm not particularly interested in politics, I just didn't have anything better to do."

"Cool," Glen said, "I'm not really interested in politics either. I saw you drive up, that's quite a rig you're driving. Late sixties?"

"Sixty-seven. I call it Manny. Manny is a good ride."

"Manny, that's not bad. Can I ask how old you are?"

"I'm 21, why do you ask?"

"Just curious." His eyes satisfied their curiosity by looking her over from head to toe. His eyes lingered on the flesh exposed by unbuttoned top buttons of her blouse. "21 is good. I have to go soon, I can see my handler is looking for me. I have to change and stuff. I'm going to give you my card which has my private cell phone number. If you want to get together and have a few drinks and some laughs, give me a call."

A middle-aged woman dressed in a business suit had spotted Glen and was calling and waving at him. He got up and brushed the beauty bark off his pants.

"I hope you enjoy this, I'd really like to get your opinion and advice later. Your point of view as a young person would be very helpful. Please give me a call soon."

"Sure thing," Holly said.

Glen walked toward the limousine. About half way there he turned and wiggled the fingers of his mutilated hand at her. She grinned at him through gritted teeth. *He's just another aging pussy hound*, she thought. She had some experience with that. The possibilities were boundless. There was poison, cutting him open with a box cutter, pouring hot oil on him while he was enjoying the afterglow. She could cut off some more of his fingers, that would be a great place to start. She was confident she'd find the right revenge for her Manny. The thought of it warmed her from groin to neck.

She watched as the candidate came out of the limousine dressed in a light gray suit and bright yellow necktie. An uplifting Bruce Springsteen song blasted from the PA system. He waved at her as his entourage escorted him to the stage. She waved back. The speech was forgettable, but Glen seemed to hit all the right buttons to stir up the crowd. There was something weird about the background music and she felt a little light-headed. She oddly felt like she'd vote for Glen if she didn't first plan to kill him first. She sat through the speech and the handshaking, baby-kissing and photography that followed. She watched the kids pile on the busses and drive off and she watched the sound and light crew clean up and pack all the equipment.

After the trucks were gone and the light started to fade (it wasn't going to get completely dark until after midnight) and the air cooled, she got up and stretched the kinks out of her little body. In her hand, she found Glen's card which she tucked into her back pocket. She warmed up the truck and tried to decide what to do. She needed to get a weapon so the next opportunity with Glen would not go wasted. On the way back to the motel, she stopped at a Williams Express store and picked up a Pennysaver newspaper and a quart bottle of malt liquor. The clerk carefully looked at her ID, but she passed scrutiny.

Back at the motel, she drank the liquor and looked at the ads in the Pennysaver. She circled the ones she planned to call in the morning. There were many possibilities and she fell asleep dreaming about shooting Glen with a Remington 30-06 rifle ($550), a .40 caliber Glock ($700), or her favorite, a 1912 Colt .45 automatic ($475).

ALASKA INSTANT POLL

July 15

ADN Survey of likely Voters (plus or minus 4% error)
33% Sanders – REP
20% Undecided
12% Patterson - DEM
8% Van Doren – DEM
3% Other
3% Walters – GREEN
3% Wilson – DM
2% Gray – LIBERT
1% Onkiak – AK IND

The Election Team

Glen addressed the election team in their meeting room. Everyone was in attendance except for Angela. Elke handed out coffee orders from the espresso stand downstairs. Bennie had a hot chocolate while Glen sipped a double latte. Murphy was drinking drip, Elke had mocha, and Walter was drinking spring water from a plastic bottle.

"We need something that will make a big splash." Glen said, "I've been thinking about this. I'd like to win one of those dog sled races. That would be awesome."

"Unfortunately, all the races are in the Winter, ya moron," Murphy said.

"There aren't any Summer races up north? Like in Barrow or something? There's always snow up there."

"No."

"We have to think of something that will impress the roughnecks."

"How about disrupting some terrorists that are trying to blow up the pipeline?" Walter asked. "We can hire some North Koreans pretty cheap."

"I like the sound of that. " Glen said thoughtfully.

"That would cost some real money. Also, I don't think we can slide it into the schedule." Murphy said.

"You could rescue some bald eagles or bear cubs from poachers or something," Bennie suggested.

"That sounds like a Movie of the Week, I don't like it," Glen said. "We need something with zip, something that would look good on the front page. I could pull some virgins out of a burning building?"

"We're not letting you anywhere near any virgins," Murphy said.

"How about rescuing a high school hockey team from a bus wreck? We'd get some media for that," Walter asked.

"Too many people would have to be in on it. We don't want something that could come unraveled before the election, it's too risky." Murphy said.

"I could bust up a bank robbery, that's always good," Glen said.

"No banks, let's not get the FBI on the case if we can help it. You just barely got away with your skin the last time you got involved with the FBI."

"Hey, I had that Florida stuff completely under control." Glen protested.

"Children, stop it. Let's keep things constructive." Walter urged. "What about something to do with that puddle-jumper airplane? You're going to log quite a few hours in one, let's crash it and Glen can save the day."

"I'm not sure about that," Glen said pensively. "It's bad enough I have to ride them, I don't want to mess around. Those things are dangerous without inviting other complications. All the press in the world doesn't help if you've killed your candidate."

"Mel Carnahan's widow won his senate race in Missouri after he was killed in a plane wreck. What do you think Murphy, want to be in Congress?" Walter asked.

"Forget it. I like the plane crash though, you might be onto something, Walter," Murphy said. "I'll let Lester-Mike in on the scheme.

We can pick the scene and the timing. Those planes aren't that expensive, we can afford to crash an old one."

"Can I ride to safety with a dog team somehow?" Glen asked.

"Glen, I'm going to kill you myself if you don't can it. No dog sleds," Murphy said harshly, "you can haul the pilot out of the wreckage before it explodes."

"I'm not doing this unless we can fit a dog sled in somehow."

"Does anyone have any better suggestion?" No one spoke. After a pause, Murphy continued, "It's settled then. Walter can work up some digicam footage and the evening news shows will eat it up. *Congressional candidate saves pilot from fiery plane crash.* That will play."

"Hello, can anybody hear me? I'm not doing this unless you work some dogs into the scenario. No dogs, no Glen, that's that."

"Glen, there are not going to be any dogs, just forget that part. We'll work this out with the pilot, don't you worry your evil little political mind about it." Turning to the team, Murphy continued, "We'll need for them to be lost overnight at least. It would be nice if there was a freak snow storm."

"I'm the boss and I'm saying this does not happen without dogs."

"Just shut up Glen, we're working here. The pilot needs to break a leg or something. Can you fake that, Walter?"

Walter nodded in assent. "How about a big reward? That would get people's attention. We could get a cute native kid to win. That way we can cover the native Alaskan demographic, we've been a little weak there so far."

"You can't offer a reward for a rescue like this. I'm not a lost cat or wallet, for Christ's sake." Glen picked up his coffee then got up and left the room cussing and grumbling. "Jerk-offs," he muttered as he slammed the door on them.

"Well, the native Alaskan rescue angle will play out well. With the digicam footage, we can make this like one of those reality shows. It will be like an instant docudrama. We can stock some food and firewood at some cabin they find in the wild. Or maybe he has to kill a rabbit or catch some fish for dinner, how does that sound?"

"That's too over the top," Elke said, "and we don't want to stir up the animal rights crowd. To get some sympathy, Glen should have some kind of wound, something that won't look too gross on camera."

"We'll just wrap a bloody bandage around his head or something. "

"What's with the boss and the sled dog thing?" Bennie asked.

"He's just an idiot, don't pay any attention. He gets a weird idea in his head and it's almost impossible to make him see reason. Don't you be like that when you grow up," Murphy said, shaking her finger sternly.

"Yes, ma-am," Bennie said. "I won't."

Thus, they solidified the details, assigned the action items and the plane wreck was penciled into the campaign schedule.

Glen and Murphy and Lester

Lester met Glen and Murphy at the Lake Hood Airstrip. Lester wore a fur hat with the ear covers turned up and leather boots that were run down at the heels. The plane was a Cessna 172 Skyhawk. The paint was chipped and faded and the engine cowling did not quite fit. It looked like some extra hardware had been attached to the engine. Lester looked at Glen critically.

"You're kind of a big piece of meat, what do you weigh?" he asked.

"Two hundred, give or take." Glen replied.

"Right. Two-twenty-five?"

"Yeah, alright."

"Well, layoff the pasta and take a dump before we fly and we'll be okay. We'll have to limit the cargo to about 30 pounds."

"I changed my mind. I want something bigger. How about a Lear or a Gulfstream?"

"Just shut up and let us worry about the details."

Lester finished his preflight check.

"There's something I wanted to mention. I don't exactly have my pilot's license anymore," Lester confessed. Murphy made a small choking sound and both men turned to look.

"Nothing," she said, trying to stifle a knowing smile.

"Hey Lester," Glen said, "a license isn't a major problem with us, we're not real big on paperwork and tax forms, if you catch my drift. We've got some connections, might even be able to get you that license." Murphy emitted another sound but both men ignored it this time. Lester studied Glen's face for a moment before turning back to cleaning the windscreen.

"Why would you do that? Not that I wouldn't appreciate it," he hastily added. Glen shrugged.

"I've put quite a team a together, talented misfits mostly" — surprisingly, Murphy let this small slander pass — "but I don't have anybody local yet." Glen paused to formulate his thoughts.

"Not that you're a misfit," Murphy snickered, "before the silver-tongued-devil talked me into coming up here, I was sitting on a beach and drinking Pina Coladas with my lover."

Lester indicated Murphy with a nod. "So, you two aren't, uh..." he made a vaguely descriptive hand gesture. He'd already suspected as much. The two of them seemed to like each other too much to be a couple.

"No," Glen replied, "I have standards."

"Yeah," Murphy interrupted, "Glen needs a woman he can outrun."

"Murphy!" Glen sounded hurt.

"Personally," Murphy continued, "I carry a gun."

"That does rather dampen the mood," Glen admitted.

"Okay," said Lester, "you guys seem like you're okay. Let's do it."

"Great," said Glen. "I get the impression that operating in this state definitely requires air travel. And commercial flights are visible, I may not always want to be tracked." He produced a thermos and filled coffee cups for the three of them. "I assume flying without a flight plan wouldn't be a problem?" He looked at Lester with a raised eyebrow. He pretty much suspected how Lester paid his bills. Lester read the look correctly.

"Not a problem," Lester assured him, straight-faced. "As a matter of fact, there's nothing filed for this flight, which is a good thing, because I'm thinking of a little clearing that might be a good spot for us to set down."

"A little clearing? I don't think I like the sound of that," Glen said pensively.

Lester flashed a reassuring grin. "The landing is easy. Taking off again is the tricky part. The clearing is maybe six miles from Petersville and the country's mostly safe. Glen should be able to walk that in three hours or so without getting lost or eaten. There's a trapper's cabin nearby if we need it."

"Is there a trail?"

"Sure," Lester nodded, "too many, in fact." He turned to Glen. "I'll give you my compass. Stick to the well-traveled routes and head directly east. If all else fails you'll cut the highway and somebody will pick you up." Murphy and Glen exchanged a look.

"Uh, Lester," Glen said. "This is kind of a dry run to see if you'd be up for this, we don't really have a firm plan in place."

"We're thinking that the heroic congressional candidate pulls you out of the plane," Murphy proposed, "he starts a fire, fends off wolves and generally saves the day. A day missing in the wild followed by a rescue operation. We think we'll get some good press out of this deal."

Lester smiled. "I see. Okay, whatever. I'll have to charge you extra, of course." They fell silent. Lester sipped his coffee and watched the reaction of Glen and Murphy. Then Lester smacked Glen in the upper arm with the back of his hand. "Just kidding. Besides, I haven't looked in the shop manual to see what to charge for pulling a scam like this."

"Uh-uh," Murphy said. "I have, it's five thousand in off-the-books cash plus any damages and documented expenses."

"Kind of a sweet little thing, isn't she?" Lester asked Glen. "Well, we can fly over the clearing before we decide for sure."

"The only thing left is we need to figure out how to work a dogsled into the story. I think a front-page picture of me with a whip and a dog team would play well."

Murphy snorted.

"Uh—," Lester said hesitantly, "it's June? You're just going to look like a flatlander if you have a dogsled and no snow."

"Oh, the many burdens of genius I carry," Glen lamented, "to be a man of vision among the unworthy, to be a shining light over the pathetic masses who are not capable of fathoming the brilliant strategy and art of..."

"Just shut up, Glen," Murphy interrupted, "we've already told you a thousand times there is not going to be any dogsled in this scenario."

"Is he like this often?" Lester asked Murphy. "Dealing with someone stubborn will cost extra." Lester turned to Glen. "We might be able to work a whip and an Indiana Jones hat into the plan, how's that sound?"

"Great," said Glen, "now, let's talk about this little clearing thing."

Walter Crawley

Walter was looking over the copy for the ADN ad he was preparing.

Volunteers Needed for Clinical Trial
21 to 35 year old candidates will be considered. Must pass drug screening (blood and urine). Healthy men and women only (pregnancy test required). No users of Prozac, Zoloft, or other psychotropic agents will be accepted. Screened candidates will receive $1,000 for a four hour commitment.
Reply to ad 1744.

This should be interesting, he thought as he pressed the email 'send' key.

Moshi

The Filipino girl from Seattle sat as far from Moshi as she could and still reach the pipe they were passing around. The other girls were locals and there seemed to be a uniformity of piercings, torn net stockings, tattoos, and leather miniskirts. They were sitting on folding chairs in the back of the old theater that the band was using as a rehearsal studio. The walls were covered with sound-deadening egg cartons. Cables and fast food wrappers formed an unavoidable hazard underfoot. The girls were passing around an onyx hash pipe and lighter. Moshi's eyes were inflamed from the smoke and she felt increasingly detached from the scene.

Raz was trying to get Erik to hit some accents on his bass at key sections of a long guitar solo. Erik was trying, but he could not seem to keep the notes straight. The music was an echoic rumble as they ran over the parts again and again. Moshi could see the right pattern on the fretboard and she would usually help Erik, but he had screamed at her earlier and she was afraid to approach the stage. She prayed that he'd move his hand to the fifth fret and play the inversion, but he kept trying an awkward fingering at the nut. The record label guy smoked a cigarette and watched for a while from behind the sound board.

Rousing from her reverie, she heard Erik shouting her name. He was calling her. *He needed her.* Her heart soared and she could not help a satisfied look at the Filipino girl as she weaved toward the stage. The groupies twittered.

"Hey Mosh, go get us a case of Kokanie beer, we're getting thirsty up here."

Beer? Go get some beer? She wanted to tear out her hair. *Play a chromatic run starting with E on the seventh fret. Hold the D-flat while Raz plays his ultra-fast Myxolydian pattern. The passing tones and the unresolved dissonance would be very dramatic and cool.*

Instead, she said: "I don't have any money."

"What happened to the money I gave you yesterday?"

He didn't give her any money yesterday or the day before either, but Moshi just shrugged. Erik scowled and looked through his pockets. He found some wadded bills and handed them to her.

"Get the beer from the back of the cooler so it will be colder when you get back here."

With slow dignity, Moshi found the backstage door and exited into an alley. She leaned against the bricks and sobbed until she could get a grip on her emotions. Her stomach hurt and her head was throbbing from the marijuana and the pounding music. She breathed fresh air in gulps until she had the strength to walk. Strolling to the convenience store, she avoided making eye contact with the other pedestrians. In a small act of disobedience, she took the beer from the front of the case.

There were two more girls loitering by the backstage door smoking cigarettes. They looked young to Moshi, perhaps even high school girls skipping their math classes or something.

"Are you with Toxic Shock?" one of the girls asked breathlessly.

Moshi nodded as she pounded on the door.

"They're so awesome," the girl said.

Awesome. Yes, they are immensely awesome.

The roadie manning the door threw it open. He looked intently at the young girls necklines, before allowing them to slip in behind Moshi. She placed the beer on the stage. Erik was playing with the knobs of his rack system and didn't see her. She paced back to her chair and ignored the smug look the Filipino girl was throwing her way.

Glen and Dan Swifte

Glen breezed in the door of the Marriott Anchorage Downtown. Murphy took a sweep through the lobby and the cocktail lounge. Everything looked quiet so she grabbed a free Wall Street Journal and sat on a bench near the reception desk. Glen walked into the lounge and let his eyes adjust to the dim light. A man dressed in a dark suit waved him over. Glen examined him as they shook hands. The man, Dan Swifte, was lean and well-groomed. He looked like a runner; rail thin with straight white teeth, his suit was expertly tailored.

"I have to confess that the FAX you sent was intriguing. Your numbers show us running ahead more than our own research shows."

Dan had FAXed over a poll that showed Glen at 7% with a bullet. The only other thing on the FAX was Dan's name and the words: Meet me at the bar, Marriott, 2:30.

"We've had good luck with our own poll team. Even more interesting is I think we've figured out what you're up to."

"Who is this *we* you mention?"

"Myself and my associates."

"What business are you in?"

"We're campaign consultants. Sometimes we're troubleshooters, sometimes we're nursemaids and sometimes we're a clean up crew. Whatever the job requires. Today, I'd guess you could call us messenger boys."

"Bringing a message from...?"

"The Gods."

"Ah, I expected this would happen sooner or later." The waiter hovered a respectful ten feet from their table. Glen waved him over and ordered a Pellegrino mineral water with a lime twist. "What is the message?"

"Ah, you want to get right to the point. I like that. Very well, the message is that we want you to pack up your bags and go home."

"I see." Glen's drink was placed on the table. He took a sip and looked at Dan carefully. "I didn't think you guys would get this scared until after the Primary."

"We're not scared. Look Wilson, you have a nice little state down there in Washington. You could win a nice rural state seat for yourself and work your way up the ladder. Play by the rules and the system will reward you all in good time. You're going to spend a lot of money and lose up here anyway. We're suggesting you take the easy road."

There's that easy road again. I spent two years in Viet Nam, muled dope out of Bolivia and had two fingers hacked off. I've been stabbed, shot and cursed in twelve languages by beautiful women around the world. I was probably the last person slapped around by the Nazi Butcher of Lyon which I hope was a fond memory for the old man as he rotted in his French jail cell. I certainly did not get to where I am today by taking the easy road. I spit on the easy road. The easy road is for pussies.

"Are you willing to sweeten the deal to get rid of me?"

"What do you have in mind?"

"Something like ten million would begin to pique my interest."

Dan laughed. "Ten million, that's rich. Let's stop living in the clouds and get real. I suppose we could lay our hands on something like two million to buy your mailing lists and donor database. We'd want you out of the state by the end of the week."

"I have a better idea. Why don't you come work for me and see what a winning team looks like for a change?"

"I'm not sure you grasp the seriousness of our offer."

"Oh, I grasp it alright. You think I'm a clown, but you're uncertain enough to spend two million dollars to get rid of me. You know what? I am a clown. Just a bumbling moron up here causing trouble for the ruling class. You just can't decide how serious a contender I am, so you're hedging your bet. I'll tell you something, Mister Dan Swifte, if you offered me twenty million, I'd still tell you shove it up your ass."

"Please reconsider, Wilson. We don't want to get rough with you, we prefer to work this out like professionals."

"Well, there's a difference between you and I. I do want to get rough. Bring it on."

Glen caught Murphy's eye and waved her over. She leaned over the table. "Let's cuff this sweet-talking piece of shit and throw him into the dumpster."

Murphy raised her eyebrows. "Are you sure?" she whispered.

"Do it," Glen said.

Murphy scooted into their booth. She pressed her .357 into Dan's chest.

"What are you doing? Stop this immediately," Dan said sharply.

"Put your hands behind your back and turn so I can see them." She jammed the gun into his ribs hard. Dan was sputtering, but did as he was told. Murphy slipped some Flex Cuffs onto his wrists and cinched them up tight. She yanked up on the cuffs and Dan gasped. She hauled him out of the booth. They escorted him through the kitchen and out the back door into an alley. She stuffed a napkin in his mouth to quiet his screeching, engaged another pair of Felx Cuffs on his legs and threw back the lid of the Dumpster. The interior was filled with table scrapings and slimy brown produce. Glen and Murphy lifted him off his feet.

"Okay, that's enough, I think," Glen said. They lowered him back to the pavement. Glen slammed the lid. "Go ahead and cut him loose." Murphy produced a Buck knife and cut off the Flex Cuffs. Dan shook himself free of their grip. He was red-faced and couldn't seem to speak, he just sputtered. He gave them an evil look and walked quickly to the end of the alley. As he turned to take a last look at them, Glen waggled his fingers and said "Ta-ta."

Members of the Asian kitchen crew had followed them out the back door and watched the operation. On the way back to the lounge, Glen waved hundred dollar bills and handed one to each person who shook their head when he suggested they didn't see anything.

Back at their booth, Glen tossed a pair of hundreds on the table and finished his mineral water.

"Are you sure that was wise?" Murphy asked.

"I'm sure it wasn't, but it sure felt good. He offered two million for us to pack up and go home. They wouldn't do that unless they're worried about their election."

"Wow, two million, that's a lot more than I thought they'd offer."

"Think he'll tell his boss or will he be too embarrassed?"

Murphy thought for a moment. She shrugged. "I think he'll just say we turned down his generous offer. However, you're going to have to start watching your back."

"That's what I hired you to do, Murphy. What you really mean is you're going to have to start earning your money for a change."

"Yeah, whatever," Murphy replied.

Political campaigns are the graveyard of real ideas and the birthplace of
empty promises.

- Maria Teresa Thierstein Simoes-Ferreira Heinz Kerry

CHAPTER 8

Glen and Bennie

Glen rubbed his eyes and sat up in bed. "Damn it, Bennie, what time is
it?"

Bennie sat on Glen's bed and sorted through some printouts.
Glen turned his clock around so he could read it. "Five AM, give me a
break." He flopped back down and covered his head with his pillow.

"I ran simulations all night."

"Okay Bennie, tell me what you are talking about." Glen
mumbled through the pillow.

"You told me to run some simulations based on modifications to
automobiles. You asked me to model taking out the seatbelts and
installing six-inch spikes on the steering wheel."

"I was drunk, don't do anything I tell you to do when I'm
drunk."

"No, you were right. I figured it out."

Glen tossed aside the pillow and sat up again. "Fine Bennie, tell
me what you're talking about."

"You were right."

"Don't act so surprised."

"If we install lethal devices on steering wheels, over the first two
years, auto fatalities go up, then level off, then go down dramatically.
You were right, kill off the small percentage of really bad drivers, get
them off the road and you can save thousands of lives a year. After five
years, you break even, after that, things get a lot better. It's cruel, but it's
true. In addition, it looks like people drive more carefully when you
remove the safety equipment."

"Of course. So what conclusion do you draw from our safety
regulations and traffic laws?"

"They don't work. They must exist for other reasons."

"Yes, it's a full employment program for legislators, cops,
courts, lawyers, case workers and emergency personnel."

"We're killing people in the name of trying to save people. It doesn't make sense."

"Welcome to the real world. Now get out of here, I need another couple of hours of sleep."

Bennie hopped off the bed and stood by the door. "Do you want me to write up a policy statement for this?"

"Are you crazy? We'd get massacred. We're trying to win an election here."

"If you're not part of the solution, you're part of the problem."

"Out!" Glen threw his pillow at Bennie, but Bennie was fast and escaped through the door. Glen flopped down and pulled the blankets up over his head.

Glen and Murphy and Angela and 'Julio' Morrison

Later that morning, Murphy was doing her Tai Chi exercises in a corner while Glen sipped coffee and read the ADN. Angela tapped on the door and entered with Walter 'Julio' Morrison in tow.

"Hi guys," Angela said. "I want you to meet Julio Morrison. He works for the Anchorage Press weekly. He asked to meet the candidate."

Morrison extended his hand and Glen shook it. Murphy wiped her head with a towel and flopped on the couch.

"Do you have time for an informal interview?" Morrison asked.

"I've been reading that liberal rag and I haven't seen your byline. What do you write?" Glen asked.

"We're pretty loosey-goosey over there. Usually I write about hockey, but sometimes I get a political assignment. Do you mind?" Glen shook his head no. Morrison removed a voice recorder from his jacket and placed it on the coffee table. He placed a notepad on his knee and looked at Glen expectantly. Angela went to the kitchen and got herself a Diet Pepsi.

"Can we start with your stand on environmental issues?"

"I'm completely in favor of protecting the environment in a fiscally responsible way."

"So you oppose drilling in the Artic Refuge?"

"No, I think we can use modern technology to protect the habitat while doing some small-footprint drilling."

"You're in favor of corporate exploitation of the last vestiges of protected areas?"

"I'm in favor of extracting natural resources in desolate areas using environmentally friendly methods. I haven't been up there to visit the area yet, but I've seen pictures and I'm told that area is harsh and nearly devoid of wildlife. I'm for protecting the environment, but I'm not in favor of being stupid about it."

"I was hoping you'd be more sensitive to environmental issues."

"And I'm hoping, that as an objective journalist, you will report my positions without coloring them with your biased political agenda."

"Fair enough. Can I get your position on illegal drugs?"

"Sure."

"What is your position on marijuana?"

"I think it should be decriminalized, regulated and taxed like hell to pay for treatment programs for the few people who abuse and ruin themselves with it."

"What about harder drugs like cocaine and heroin?"

"I would pursue the same strategy with all illicit drugs."

"What about the social and health costs of addiction?"

"I think it's interesting how the government involves itself in providing health care, then, when the system inevitably goes bankrupt, tries to restrict people's freedom in order to control the costs. I don't see why a doper who kills himself with heroin is a taxpayer problem."

"What about the addicts? They will kill and steal to maintain their habit."

"If the stuff was legal, it wouldn't be as expensive. And the money that feeds organized crime would dry up. Overall, with legalization I think society would be safer and the cost to the public would be much lower."

"Have you ever inhaled?"

Murphy looked at Glen intently. This was an area they had not rehearsed.

"Oh yes. When I was younger, I inhaled, snorted, and injected everything I could get my hands on. I've been clean for a long time, but there was a time when I did it all."

Morrison sat with his pad and stared at Glen incredulously.

"You're saying that you're completely clean now?"

"I'm so clean, I could get good money selling my urine to someone trying to beat a drug test. Like baby's piss. Like artesian spring water."

"You have some unusual ideas for a politician," Morrison said.

"I'm just getting warmed up," Glen replied.

Morrison shot a glance at his wristwatch. "Well, I have to get going. Deadlines, you know." Morrison stood and picked up his recorder.

He opened the suite door and let Angela exit first. He waved at Glen and Murphy and closed the door behind him.

Glen and Murphy looked at each other. "Cop," they said simultaneously.

"What is Angela getting herself into?" Glen asked.

Murphy shrugged. "Can I assume your answers would have been different if Morrison was really a reporter and actually turned his recorder on?"

"Of course, Murphy," Glen answered with his trademark toothy grin.

"Good," Murphy replied. She tossed aside the towel and resumed her Tai Chi. Glen clicked on the TV and watched the end of an old episode of Buffy the Vampire Slayer.

"That Sarah Gellar is one hot tamale," he muttered to himself.

Walter Crawley

Walter Crawley had once been a young professor at the University of California at San Diego. He had a promising future except for the one small problem that always plagued his work: human trial subjects. In spite of long legal and medical releases, some of the surviving subjects complained and even worse, found sympathetic lawyers. Millions of people died of disease and accidents each year and people got excited about a few clinical trials gone wrong. It did not make sense. Walter was an artist and some of his research in the world of biochemistry and altered states of consciousness should have easily earned him a Nobel Prize. Instead, he was wanted for questioning in three states. The state of Massachusetts actually issued a warrant for his arrest. Clearly, that particular state had no sense of humor at all.

Walter blinked in the dim light of the Pioneer Bar. He watched a sallow young man nodding off over the dregs of a schooner of beer. The only other patrons nearby were a couple playing a video game. The drowsy kid had festering tracks on his arms and wiped his running nose on the sleeve of his sweatshirt. Walter slid onto the adjoining bar stool.

"A can of Rainier beer please," he told the bartender, "and bring a fresh one for my friend."

The kid's eyes were intermittently focused but he found the beer and chugged half. Walter sipped his beer and watched a hockey game playing on a dusty TV hanging in the corner.

"What's your name, kid?" Walter asked.

The kid looked suspicious, but muttered "Tommy," in a barely audible voice.

"Get Tommy another one," Walter called out to the bartender. To Tommy he said, "You can call me Doctor or Doc, as you prefer."

The hockey game concluded and ESPN switched to coverage of a bowling tournament. The lunch customers flowed in and out like the tide, but the core drinkers hunched over their beers and talked slowly between themselves about the weather. They drank slowly because it was several days before their next welfare checks would come.

"You want to get high?" Walter asked.

"I ain't no faggot," Tommy replied.

Walter chuckled. "This isn't that sort of thing. I have some stuff I want you to try, that's all. You look like a man who knows his dope."

"I'm clean," Tommy said.

"Sure you are. If you're not interested, that's cool."

They sat in silence.

"Didn't say I wasn't interested."

"That's right, you didn't."

They walked down Spenard to the Qupqugiaq Motel where Walter rented a room. The clerk did his best not to look at them as Walter filled out the form with the name Tom Smith. The room was plain but clean. Walter made sure the curtains were pulled and turned on the TV. He adjusted the volume until it was moderately loud and tossed the remote to Tommy. Tommy switched the channels until he found Scooby Doo on the Cartoon Network. Walter set up a DVR camera to record the scene. He adjusted it until he was happy that Tommy, in center frame, was in focus. Walter opened his fanny pack and pulled out a syringe and some small bottles. He spoke soothingly.

"First I'm going to give you something to perk you up a bit. I need you to be able to talk to me." He filled the syringe with a quarter cc of clear fluid. He handed Tommy a length of rubber tubing. Tommy tied off his arm expertly and injected himself. Walter spoke for the sake of the camera.

"Subject: Tommy. 1450 hours, injected Sulfuracone 27."

Walter pulled over a chair and watched Tommy intently as he loosened the tubing. Tommy watched the TV and slowly seemed to become more conscious.

After five minutes, Walter spoke. "How do you feel, Tommy?"

Tommy rolled his head on his shoulders. "I feel very well," he said precisely. "My arms itch and I have a low grade headache. My stomach is queasy. I don't think I've eaten since yesterday."

"That's good Tommy, I think you're almost ready. The S27 is temporarily aiding some of your synapses. You should feel clear-headed. Your IQ has been enhanced by about 25% and you are able to articulate your thoughts more explicitly, you're doing very well."

"I feel good, Doc."

"That's outstanding, Tommy. You're a good boy."

"Can you make me feel this way permanently?"

"No, Tommy, that's not possible, your brain is far too damaged. This effect is temporary, I'm sorry to say. I'm going to give you a dosage of G111 and I want you to tell me how it makes you feel. Are you ready?"

"Yes, Doc, I'm ready."

Walter carefully filled a syringe with a cc of an emerald green fluid.

Tommy watched the process with obvious fascination. "I was enrolled at ACC. I played guitar and I was taking some computer science classes. My girlfriend got pregnant and wanted to keep the kid, but I made her go in for an abortion." Tears dribbled down Tommy's face. "She didn't stop bleeding and she died. I stopped going to class and spent my PFD on heroin. It was the only way I could sleep. I'm so sorry."

"I know you are, Tommy," Walter said sympathetically, "so far, none of my patients have survived the dosage I'm going to give you. It's almost certainly fatal, do you understand what I'm saying?"

Tommy nodded.

"So you take this of your own free will?" Walter continued.

Tommy answered by tying off the tubing again and reaching for the syringe. He quickly found the vein and shot up the green liquid. He handed the syringe back and loosened the tubing. Walter repacked his little bottles back into his fanny pack.

"Oh," Tommy said dreamily. "Eigenvalues…"

"Talk to me, Tommy. What are you thinking?"

"We were studying Eigenvalues in my Engineering Mathematics class. I understand them now. Equipollent systems of vectors. Eigenvectors of mass times velocity-squared. This is so elegant and beautiful."

Tommy's eyes rolled up in his head and he fell back so he was laying on the bed.

"Keep talking, Tommy," Walter insisted.

"'Not until a machine can write a sonnet or compose a concerto because of thoughts and emotions felt, and not by the chance fall of symbols, could we agree that machine equals brain — that is, not only write it but know that it had written it.' I read that in the college library on the afternoon of December 14th in a paper written by Alan Turing. I remember everything."

"Go back to before you were born and after you die, tell me what you see and what you know," Walter whispered urgently.

"I see everything and nothing, chaos and filters, gravity and particles and waves. It's ripe in its perfection."

"Do you see why?"

"Yes," Tommy said as he died.

"Fuck!" Walter cursed in anguish. He kicked over the camera tripod. Taking deep breaths until he was finally calm, he stood by the door and looked back at Tommy's body. *The same goddam thing every single goddam time,* he thought bitterly. He packed up his equipment and looked around the room to make sure he left nothing behind. After one last scan of the room, he pulled the door closed gently behind him.

Angela and 'Julio' Morrison

Angela and Julio sat at their usual stools at Darwin's Theory bar. They were nursing Bacardi and Diet Cokes and staring into the mirror at themselves.

"That was really intense," Julio said.

"You've used the word intense three times today. You don't get to use that word anymore, once a day is your limit."

"What are you talking about?"

"I'm saying I get tired of hearing you say the word 'intense', so stop it."

"Alright, you don't have to jump down my throat. Your boss and his girlfriend are really... sharp-edged. Focused. I felt like they were looking through me. I don't like that."

"You're a doper, you should be used to being treated like shit."

Julio looked around to see if anyone was within earshot. "I'm not a doper. I'm a professional, a small businessman."

"Fine, whatever you say. Besides, Murphy is not his girlfriend, she's a lesbian."

"Really? Maybe you and her could get together and I could take some pictures?"

"Can't you at least try not to be such a prick? Is that asking too much?"

"It was just an idea. No big deal. We can talk about something else."

"I'm sick of this wilderness village. I want to go back to Las Vegas where my friends are. LA, New York, Miami, I don't care. This place is boring. What do people do up here?"

"Its summertime, there's a ton of things to do. We could go fishing, I have a friend that has a boat. We could get some crab."

"I don't want to go fishing, you idiot. I want to eat in a revolving restaurant at the top of a skyscraper. I want to snort some coke, drink champagne and dance until three in the morning. I want to take a limo to a Hollywood party. I want to shop on Rodeo Drive, get my hair done and sip an espresso with people you've only seen on TV. I want to have some fun for a change. Get it?"

"I have an idea. Maybe if we burn Wilson to the narcs, he'll shut down his campaign? Maybe Walter would take you to Rome or Paris?"

"Yes! I've never been to Paris, that would be awesome. But, if Glen is clean, how do you get the cops on his ass?"

"You can help me plant some horse on him."

"That sounds scary. I'm not sure you want to mess with him, I think he can be dangerous."

"In France, they fill the hotel bathtubs with champagne and bake little cakes with real gold in the frosting."

"And they have those cute accents."

"You'd be like a queen over there."

"I have to get out of this backwater town somehow, I don't think I can take another week. I will only be young and beautiful for another ten years or so. I'm wasting away here. But double crossing Glen? I'll have to think about it."

"Fine, you think on it. In the meantime, want to go up to my place and smoke some weed?"

"Okay."

Julio threw some bills on the bar. Outside, they were blinded by the sun. Simultaneously, they slipped on their sunglasses and walked unsteadily toward Julio's old Bronco.

ALASKA INSTANT POLL

July 22

ADN Survey of likely Voters (plus or minus 4% error)
35% Sanders – REP
16% Undecided
14% Patterson – DEM
6% Wilson – DM
5% Van Doren – DEM
3% Other
3% Walters – GREEN
2% Gray – LIBERT
1% Onkiak – AK IND

Moshi

The rehearsal had degenerated into a screaming session. Raz was angry with Erik for refusing to play a line. Moshi knew that Erik simply could not play it; a furious flurry of eighth notes. Erik threw his bass off the stage. It landed on its neck and snapped in two. The sound system shrieked with feedback. A roadie silenced the amp by pulling its plug and gathered up the guitar pieces. Erik stalked backstage toward the green room and Moshi got up to follow. Raz stopped her.

"Hey Mosh, you play some keys, don't you?"

Moshi stopped and stared at the floor. Almost imperceptibly, she nodded her head yes.

"Can you do some left hand bass lines?"

Moshi tried to read his intent. "I can play quarter-notes if the tempo is not too fast."

"There is a keyboard plugged into the mixer." Raz jumped back on stage and waved at the sound man to bring up the sound again. He pointed at the keyboard and impatiently waved at Moshi to play it. It was a Kurzweil. Moshi fingered a few chords and the digitally-sampled grand piano sounds came through the PA system with brilliant clarity. Raz motioned at the drummer to get his attention.

"From the bridge," he shouted and the drummer clicked his sticks and counted them in. Moshi played the patterns she had been hearing in her head throughout the endless rehearsal sessions. She tried to focus on the bass notes and not play high notes with her right hand, but a few could not be resisted. After the bridge section was complete Raz made a throat cutting motion and the room was silent.

"Fuck, that was cool," he said. "Mosh, go ahead and do more right-hand stuff this time. Let's take it again."

She played the same bass line, but added in some Bach-like counterpoint with her right hand. When the section was complete, again the room was silent. Raz put his guitar on a stand and jumped off the stage. He pointed his finger at the tour manager and said "Are you thinking what I'm thinking?"

"Use keyboards instead of bass guitar? It's unusual, but it might work. Chicks are cool on stage."

"Hell yes!"

Erik, carrying a bottle of Jack Daniels, emerged from behind the stage to see what was going on. He stomped toward Moshi. He raised his hand. Moshi put her arms along her sides and faced him with a shamed look on her face. Erik slapped her hard and she sank to her knees.

Raz motioned for the roadies to approach. Raz, glaring at Erik, helped her to her feet.

"It's your call, Moshi. If you want in, you're in."

Moshi wiped tears from her cheeks and stood up straight.

"I —," she said. "I can't go against Erik."

Raz looked at her for several beats.

"Okay everyone, take a ten-minute break." To Erik, he said: "Work out your lines or I'll find someone else to play them, got me?"

"I'll play them," Erik said. He gave Moshi an evil look and pushed her back toward the groupie gallery. He stomped back to the stage to get another bass tuned up.

The Election Team

Murphy gathered the team for a late night meeting. Murphy and Elke were wearing hotel bathrobes, Walter wore sweat pants and a t-shirt, and Bennie wore a pair of Bugs Bunny pajama bottoms. It was almost midnight. Elke squirted coffee into a paper cup from an insulated urn.

"Are we sure Glen is out?" Walter asked.

"He nodded off about nine after a few drinks. He's out of it," Murphy assured them. "The situation is getting serious. So far, we've been operating around the fringe of things. We're reaching the point of no return. To be honest, I've been wondering about our candidate. Is he the right man for the job? What do we really know about him?"

"Is this a coup?" Walter asked.

"No, not at all. I don't want to be a politician, I have too much self respect. My mind is a muddle of worry. I'm nervous about how things are going. He might actually win. Before the events of the last few days, I didn't really believe that was possible. Along the way, we're making enemies. We're playing in a national arena and this is serious business to some powerful forces. While we're rising in the polls, these weird things he latches onto bother me. Like the stupid dogsled idea. Is he serious or just a goof? I'd really like to know."

"Are you thinking of bailing out?"

"No. I just want to compare notes about our guy. We haven't really talked about him among ourselves. I'll go first. I initially heard of him when I was drafted into an FBI and DEA tiger team which was tracking some disruptions in the cocaine distribution network in Florida. I worked with a DEA guy named Stephens who knew Glen back in Viet Nam. He didn't like Glen much. That whole situation was strange, I could never tell if we were supposed to arrest Glen or not. It was like Glen was beating the bushes and we were watching what flew out. There were some deaths and the cocaine trade was upset for a while. That might have been the point. Perhaps Stephens was simply using Glen as a tool against the dealers. The whole time I felt like Glen was playing us. It was an odd scene."

"I met Glen at a computer trade show," Elke said thoughtfully, sipping her coffee. "I was having a bad time with my life and my career. I can't explain this, but I think Glen saved me. I'm not sure what he did exactly, but I have not been bored or depressed since Glen started stirring things up. I feel alive again. It wasn't just Glen, of course." She smiled shyly at Murphy and ran her bare foot over Murphy's. Bennie blushed as much as a young black kid could manage. "I've never actually seen him do anything, but he seems to get things done somehow. It's odd how he does that, he sends an email or makes a cell phone call and things happen. Every time I start to think he's just an empty-suit bullshitter, he comes up with some queer scheme that works out in the end."

"He contacted me out of the blue while I was doing my show in Las Vegas," Walter said thoughtfully. "I was looking for a new gig and he came along at just the right moment. It sounded like fun so I signed on. I don't really know anything about him. He has money and shakes things up, that's all I know. That's enough for me."

"I was walking down the street in my hood in Orlando," Bennie said in his quiet voice. "Glen had his computer hooked up to a dataport on a payphone. We played a computer game. He was pretty good, but no match for me. I'm inspired at playing those things. I remember his exact words. He gave me one of his cards and told me to contact him when I got serious. I didn't know what he meant exactly, but one day I decided to call his office. He gave me some advise on some tests to take and some technology I should study. The next thing I knew, I was on a plane."

"Okay. We don't know much about this guy and we're running his congressional campaign thousands of miles from home. We don't know if he's Bozo the clown or the reincarnation of Adolph Hitler."

"Attila the chump?" Bennie suggested.

They sat and looked at each other for a minute.

"He does have the uncanny ability to be at the right place at the right time. Is that an accident or some bizarre sort of talent?" Elke asked.

Bennie got up and stood in the center of the room. "Let's look at this in terms of the second law of thermodynamics. All closed systems tend toward disorder or chaos. This is the way of the universe. It takes intelligence and work to reverse entropy."

"Bennie, with all due respect, "Walter interjected, "we know you're a goddam genius, but what the hell are you talking about?"

"Look at this team. Murphy is tough and street smart. Elke is beautiful, good with accounting, and she makes Murphy happy. Walter is a genius at manipulating the public. I'm adequate in math and statistics and inspired with exploiting computers and networks."

"And humble too."

"I'm just a punk kid, I know that. But I played an online game of chess with Steve Jobs and I beat him, okay?"

"I'm just kidding you, Bennie. We know you're smart."

"Who is Steve Jobs?" Murphy asked. The team ignored her.

"Here's what I'm trying say," Bennie continued, "look at us. We fit together and augment each other. That's called synergy. Together, we're extraordinary. According to thermodynamics, a team like this can't be an accident, it can only be the result of a higher intelligence."

"Now you're saying Glen is the Supreme Being?" Walter scoffed.

"I think I'm following what Bennie is saying," Murphy said thoughtfully.

"You mean we can measure Glen by the team he assembled?"

"Thank you Murphy, that is exactly what I'm trying to say. We can measure Glen by what he built. I'm not going to hide under any false modesty. Glen has proven a curious sort of genius by assembling such an effective team. I say we ride this out. If we lose the election and go home, then so be it."

The rest of the team seemed convinced. At that moment, Glen walked in.

"Aha, I found you guys. Are we having a team meeting? What's up?" Glen asked.

After an instant of stunned silence, Walter spoke. "We're trying to work up a plane crash scenario that includes the dogsled idea."

There was murmured agreement, though Murphy had a disgusted look on her face. "It's not coming together," she said.

"Outstanding! Keep working on it, you'll figure it out. They use whips, don't they? Make a note, Elke. We have to find a bullwhip I can practice with." Glen said as he pumped some coffee from the urn. "Do we have any Baileys to sweeten this swill?" he asked.

Glen and Murphy and Lester

The next morning, Murphy sipped her coffee and grimaced in Glen's general direction.

"It's insanely early and I deserve good coffee. This sucks."

They'd left Anchorage shortly after 4:00 AM and driven a rental car up the Glen Highway to Lester's alternate home airfield north of Palmer. Now they watched as Lester completed a cursory preflight check of the plane.

"I didn't brew it, go bitch at Lester," Glen replied. He was having second and third thoughts about this whole idea. "You know, we could save a lot of time by just saying we crashed. Just drop me off a quarter mile down the road from some joint and I walk in from there."

Murphy shook her head. "Stop. It would definitely blow the election to get caught at this," she said.

"Did we run the numbers on you hiking out instead of me?" Glen asked. Actually, Bennie had. Glen would be ruined but she could make a serious run at Lieutenant Governor. She didn't want to mention this scenario.

"No, because that would be stupid," she replied. Side-by-side, they leaned against the front fender and watched Lester approach their car. He surveyed them with a quick and professional glances and waved them toward the plane.

"I see you dressed for the occasion," he commented. Glen and Murphy both wore comfortable khaki slacks and Pendleton shirts,

Murphy in sneakers and Glen wore lightweight hiking boots. Murphy carried a small purse and Glen packed a small canvas backpack. "What's in the bag?" Lester asked.

"A gun and feminine napkins," Murphy replied. "'Lightdays' if you really want to know."

Lester coughed and looked at Glen.

"I'm carrying some medicinal whiskey."

Lester nodded approvingly. "Okay, let's do it," he said. "Who's flying co-pilot?"

An hour later they watched gloomily as a solid bank of clouds appeared in the west. They were still several hours short of their intended landing site.

"Hasn't been a cloud in the sky for a week," said Lester. "I should have known this would happen."

"Don't you pilot type guys check this stuff out?" Murphy asked.

"Yeah," Lester admitted. "But sometimes we screw up." He leaned to the side and checked the ground below. "I recommend we either turn back or set down somewhere closer to the highway."

"It's just some clouds," Glen said. "They're just made of water vapor, right? Can't we fly under them, or around them, or something?" Glen didn't appreciate a change in plans at this point of the operation.

"Well, it looks more like a storm front moving in," Lester replied. "May not be much trouble. We'll at least take a swing around Denali before we abort."

They approached the massive bulk of the mountain (still labeled as Mt. McKinley on most maps but now more commonly called Denali) from the east. An endless swath of muscular, snow-covered peaks stretched to the northern and southern horizons. Lester pointed out a few landmarks, the Don Sheldon Amphitheater and the granite cliffs of the east face. By the time they swung into shadow on the west side of the mountain — at 20,000 feet, far higher than Lester's plane would fly — the wind was buffeting the plane at regular intervals as the approaching front loomed to their west.

"That's enough of the scenery, Lester," Glen broke the silence. "This weather wasn't in the brochure. I think we'd better plan on doing this another day."

"No way," said Murphy. "Your schedule is packed." She reached forward and tapped Lester on the shoulder. "Just set this bastard down a couple of miles from the highway. It won't hurt the candidate to get a little wet on his walk." Glen glowered at Murphy but didn't deign to reply. He knew his schedule was tight.

Lester nodded agreement and pointed the plane toward a pass south of the mountain. A few wispy cirrus clouds had already formed above them and the wind continued to rock the plane, now bouncing them roughly as they neared the shoulder of the mountain. The wind tore at the top of the peaks around them, trailed streamers of snow and created ugly weather out of blue sky. Clouds began to take shape around them and Lester was suddenly worried. Their clear sky dimmed as fog began to condense from the moisture of the front. Visibility shrank from unlimited to five miles, then two, then one. Lester had never seen anything like it.

"Shit, Lester!" Murphy exclaimed. "What's going on?" Lester, struggling to keep the plane level and hoping he was still in the middle of the pass, shook his head and muttered something unintelligible. Glen, sitting beside Lester, took note of the grim face of the pilot and understood they were in trouble. For some perverse reason this cheered him immensely. He turned to face Murphy in the back.

"Well, Margaret, you wanted a plane crash." He flashed her a wicked grin. "Hey Lester, does a real plane crash cost extra?"

Lester grunted something in reply and applied more power in an effort to combat the powerful downdrafts. A sheer granite cliff appeared out of the fog on the right side of the airplane and Lester grunted again, this time in recognition. He pulled the plane closer to the wall, which brought a "Lester!" of complaint from the back seat, but the air was calmer there and everyone relaxed somewhat, until they rounded the pillar and the standing wave of wind that had piled up there, invisible and deadly, pounded the plane downward a thousand feet in a few seconds. Loose papers and objects flew into the air and Glen, who had finally been in the process of donning his seat harness, bounced off the roof of the cabin and sailed into the back of the plane. Murphy yelped in dismay as Glen slammed into her, instinctively gripping him to prevent him flailing and inflicting more damage. Lester fought controls that suddenly seemed meaningless. Nothing he did made the slightest difference as the plane plummeted toward the ground. He turned to check the situation in back as he reached for the radio and then found he was laying on his back under an overcast sky, with the wind cold on his face, and Murphy, sporting a swelling eye and looking a bit rough in his opinion, leaning over him.

"Hey, sport," she said, giving him a smile.

"Hey," he replied. He studied the sky behind her, sensing it shouldn't be this way. He started to roll to one side and Murphy held him firmly in place.

"Hold on there, buddy." He relaxed, conceding to the authority in her voice. "Can you wiggle your fingers?" He could. "And toes?" He could. "How many fingers?" She held three fingers in front of his eyes.

"Several?" Lester asked. Murphy grinned.

"Close enough." She eased her hand off his chest and eyed him critically. "I already checked for broken limbs and I think you're okay, but take it a little slow at first."

Lester rolled to one side and pain stabbed through his chest and he knew he'd cracked some ribs. He moved more slowly and managed to get to his knees. He was on a rough shale slope. An airplane door lay nearby. He looked up the slope and spotted the fuselage of his plane fifty yards away and tilting to one side. The wings had been ripped completely free. A debris trail led across the slope to the point of impact a good quarter mile away. They'd apparently struck at an angle and slid, then maybe rolled a few times from the looks of the fuselage. He noticed some seats mixed in with the trail of wreckage.

"Glen?" he asked.

"He's okay, concussion I think. Skull's too thick to fracture. I left him in the plane. You were thrown clear." Lester struggled to his feet and noticed he was standing in his socks.

"My boots?" he asked.

Murphy looked down at his feet, then shrugged. "I have no idea."

They looked at each other and broke into laughter. Lester looked closely at Murphy for the first time. Her hair had torn free of its bun and blew loosely in the wind. Along with her black eye, she sported a fat lower lip and was definitely favoring her left side as they limped slowly back to the plane.

"How about you?" Lester asked. "You okay?"

Murphy nodded. "More or less." She gently prodded her swollen lip. "Banged up a knee."

They reached the plane and Lester carefully leaned over to look inside. Glen lay in the back where the seats had been. He looked pale but his eyes were open and clear.

"Lester, you fly like shit," Glen grinned. Then he grimaced as a spasm of pain lanced through his skull. Glen figured they were in big trouble and there was no sense in being rude, even though Lester had probably killed them. "What are our chances?"

Glen could see Lester pondering, and wondered whether he was considering the odds or preparing to lie to them the bad news. Lester looked Glen in the eye for a moment, then indicated Murphy with a questioning nod. Glen risked another grin. "She's probably tougher than both of us and already has a plan." He winked at Murphy. "Right, Murph?"

Murphy stared at Glen for a moment and then shook her head. No. "I don't know," she said. She looked at Lester. "Does your plane have an ELT?"

Lester hesitated. "No," he finally replied. "Me and the FAA aren't exactly on speaking terms."

Murphy's head sagged, she then banged it on the side of the plane several times.

"Well, fuck!" she yelled. "It's not like you'd ever use it, except for something like this!"

Lester looked confused, and shrank away from her. "They say — they say the FAA can track those things, even if they're off."

Murphy stared at him in disbelief. "And you believe that paranoid bullshit?"

She stepped toward Lester with her hands clenched.

"Murphy!" Glen snapped, wincing from the pain in his head. "Stand down, girl. Besides, he's right, they can track them if they want to." He closed his eyes and rested his head back against the fuselage. "You knew we were hiring an outlaw, don't act so damned shocked." Murphy stared at Glen in surprise.

"Since when did you become a real politician?" she asked. Glen smiled with his eyes closed.

"Now that was below the belt, Murph," he murmured, before passing out.

From the Anchorage Daily News website:

October 8, 2003 (Bloomberg) — A California author and filmmaker who garnered national media attention for his films of close encounters with brown bears was killed and partially eaten by his subjects, the Anchorage Daily News reported.

A bear, or bears, killed Timothy Treadwell, 46, and girlfriend Amie Huguenard, 37, this week near Kaflia Bay on the Alaskan coast, the newspaper said, citing Alaska State Troopers and National Park Service officials. The couple had gone there to live among the bears that were the subject of Treadwell's 1997 book, "Among Grizzlies."

Treadwell, a self-proclaimed "eco-warrior," had developed a cult following among bear lovers. He appeared on David Letterman's show, "The Rosie O'Donnell Show" and "Dateline NBC," to talk about bears, the paper said.

The bodies of Treadwell and Huguenard were discovered Monday by the pilot of a Kodiak air taxi that was to pick them up and return them from the wilderness. It isn't known when the attack happened or what led to it, the paper reported. The couple's tent was flattened and bears had buried their remains, the Daily News said.

Darwinism according to Microsoft Bookshelf 2000:

A theory of biological evolution developed by Charles Darwin and others, stating that all species of organisms arise and develop through the natural selection of small, inherited variations that increase the individual's ability to compete, survive, and reproduce. Also called *Darwinian theory.*

CHAPTER 9

Holly

Girdwood was a sleepy little town with single-story buildings scattered amongst the trees at the end of the Turnagain Arm. It lies forty miles south of Anchorage and is populated by ex-hippies, tree-huggers, Democrats, Subaru Station Wagons and ski bums. The ski bums hang out there because Alaska's premier ski resort, anchored by the Alyeska Prince Hotel and the attendant and stunning scenery, lies only a mile or so uphill. The local color, mainly a peace/love/hemp crowd, augmented their PFD checks by catering to the big crowds that swarmed to their yearly festivals. Tension and strife packed up and moved to Anchorage since none of the locals could summon the energy to support them. Wine and weed were the vices of choice in this neighborhood.

Holly rumbled into town on a warm and wet Saturday afternoon. The steady drizzle was a function of the bizarre micro-climate created at the cul-de-sac of salt water and towering mountains. The area, though only a few miles south of the Anchorage Bowl, received three to four times the precipitation, much of it arriving as winter snowfall. The moisture was funneled in from the Prince William Sound on the other side of the mountain barrier. The clouds were wrung dry by the time they reached Anchorage. Prince William Sound, incidentally, achieved infamy by hosting the site of the Exxon Valdez oil spill when Captain Joseph Hazelton's wayward tanker breached her hull on the rocks. To Holly, it was just a dreary fucking day in a town that looked like something from a child's book of depressing fairy tales.

A '67 GMC requires constant fueling and she'd neglected to fill the tank before leaving Anchorage. Her baby needed gas. A service station sat at the turnoff to the town. The gas pumps were a hive of activity at one end while civilization stretched toward the mountain in a mad mélange of donut shops, pizza joints, Laundromats, and the ever-present gift shops offering semi-authentic Alaskan merchandise. Holly locked the wheels at the turnoff and judiciously applied brake and throttle to slide the truck to a stop at the pump closest to the front door, scattering a covey of tourists. She took note of the 'Prepay For Gas' sign with disgust and strolled into the station. The tourists gawked and made rude comments, but Holly ignored them. A middle-aged fellow holding a toddler's hand appeared about to say something directly to her but she silenced him with a feral smile and a wave of her index finger. She burst through the doors and presented herself to the smiling young doper behind the counter.

"Nice truck," he offered, "but if you'd clipped those pumps we'd have a heck of a mess to clean up. Blackened tourists. You might want to take it a little easier next time."

"If I ever come back to this hopeless burg it'll be to burn the place to ground. Gimme twenty bucks worth of premium and help me find this guy." She drew a matchbook from a shirt pocket and tossed it onto the counter, staring at the clerk insolently. The slacker stared back at her, aghast. Rudeness simply didn't happen in Girdwood where even the police were polite. Numbly following orders, he picked up the matchbook and noticed the name and address scribbled on the back.

"You don't want —" he managed before his eyes rose to meet Holly's and he reversed his thought, "uh, maybe you do." He pointed up the road. "Joshua is up about a mile. Dirt road to the left. Keep going until you see a bunch of shot-up cars and old shacks." Holly reached over and plucked the matchbook from his fingers and dropped a twenty dollar bill on the counter with her other hand. She left without saying another word. The clerk watched nervously until she'd pumped the gas and drove off into the rain. The truck's rumbling exhaust was audible long after she was out of sight.

Holly spotted the clearing full of junked cars first, it was a graveyard of Detroit and Japanese relics with shattered windows and side panels peppered with bullet holes. Most of the holes were ringed by rust, but others looked fresh. She stopped and rolled down her window to survey the damage. Looked like mostly small caliber stuff, some stitched together from what looked like full-automatic bursts. She noted some larger holes created by heavier calibers and grunted approvingly. A mossy sign was nailed to a Spruce tree. She was able to read it by squinting. Brotherhood Church, Jesus is God. *Lovely*, she thought. She pointed the truck down a muddy driveway that led to a compound of shacks at the back of the clearing. They appeared to be single-room plywood cabins with sagging roofs. The buildings were unpainted and weathered to a neutral gray color by the interminable rain and snow. The nearer sprouted a rusty metal pipe which emitted a thin trail of smoke that wavered skyward. She rolled to a stop ten feet from the door and cut the engine. Jamming the gearshift into low held the truck on the slope. She tapped her fingers on her teeth and contemplated the situation before deciding to try the horn. The truck emitted a low buzzing sound and she slapped the steering wheel in disgust. She popped open the door and jumped to the ground, splashing muddy water with her Keds. She reached the door and raised a hand to knock as it flew open.

A heavily-built man of indeterminate age glared down at her. He was bearded, dirty, wearing overalls spotted with grease and dirt and what looked like — alert — blood. She slid back a step without thinking to give herself more room for fight or flight. The guy towered over her.

"I'm looking for Josh," she said, defiantly. The slovenly giant peered at her from beneath bushy brows, ran his thumbs up under his suspenders and spat into the mud.

"I'll be Reverend Joshua," he rumbled. He looked past her at the truck. "Big truck for a little girl." He puckered and spat another brown stream that left a few glistening droplets in his beard. "What are you wanting with Joshua?" Holly stared at the drops in his beard, wishing he would wipe them away. She fumbled the matchbook cover from a shirt pocket and offered it to him as a token of goodwill and fellowship.

"Guy in town said you could help me with some hardware with no questions." She tried a smile. It felt weak and out of place so she replaced it with a more comfortable cold stare. He glanced briefly at the book of matches and then regarded her thoughtfully. He nodded shortly. A drop of snoose shook free of his beard and Holly watched in fascination as it fell to the ground. He took the matches between a finger and thumb, carefully avoided touching her hand, and backed through the doorway, scanning the road and tree line as he went.

"Maybe Joshua can help, but you must come inside." He disappeared into the dark interior. Holly leaned over and peeked inside. Her craving for weaponry won out against common sense, so she followed him into the gloom.

Her eyes adjusted slowly to the darkness and her nostrils flared to the scent of tanning hides, spoiling meat, gunpowder, burnt metal, wood smoke, sweat, dirty socks and some mixture of organic stenches she couldn't identify. Her eyes watered from the olfactory assault. She spotted her man in the center of the room with his back turned toward her, bent on one knee. She could see where he'd flipped back an animal hide to reveal a trap door. He lifted the heavy door with a grunt. Ignoring Holly, he swung his legs into the hole and climbed down, moving easily for such a large man. His voice echoed from below.

"Is the little girl coming?" Light flooded the room from the opening and Holly moved to the edge of the hole and looked down. In contrast to the weathered shack, the smooth concrete tunnel walls were covered with fresh paint. The ladder was well-built and solid and the lighting was bright and steady. She grasped the edge of the opening and lowered herself onto the ladder, climbed down, then hopped lightly to the cement floor. She discovered Joshua standing nearby, uncomfortably close. He pulled on a rope and the trap door slammed shut with a meaty *thunk*. Her attention was immediately drawn to the scene behind him.

Lining the cement walls of the tunnel were racks of weaponry: M1s, AR-15s, M-16s, AK-47s, Winchester Defender and Mossberg Mariner assault shotguns, machine pistols and assorted handguns, slide semis, and revolvers. Farther down the hallway she could see crates labeled with military stencils, partially covered with moth-eaten canvas tarps. She slid past Joshua to behold the assortment. She was enraptured and enchanted. A pegboard was covered with a dozen Model 1911 .45s. She ran her hands over them all, and then flew to the next display. Shotguns, she marveled at their well-oiled sheen. She tugged a glittery silver Mariner free and pumped the action, snapped it to her shoulder, and squinted down the barrel over the fiber-optic front sight.

"Kaboom," she whispered. She held it at arm's length, admired it for a moment, then placed it back on the rack and moved along the wall. She dimly heard Joshua chuckle somewhere behind her as she dropped to her knees in front of an open crate and gasped at the ammo boxes inside. Military issue. Tracers, incendiary and explosive rounds and depleted Uranium shells. She struggled to remove one and was taken aback by its weight as Joshua clamped a huge arm around her waist.

"The little girl likes Joshua's collection?"

"Oh yeah," she mumbled, trying simultaneously to tug free of Joshua and remove the ammo box from the crate, "the little girl likes your guns just fine, it's — this — fucking — box," she grunted as it popped free of the crate and slammed onto the floor, "that is pissing me off." He released her. She popped the latch on the box and smiled gleefully at the belts of ammunition.

"Joshua, I think we can deal. I'll need that Mariner, a full-auto AR-15, cases of ammo for both, and I'll need a hide. You got a .22 or a .25 semi I can slip in my sock?" After several seconds passed with no sound from Joshua, she looked up. He stood with his back to the light which outlined his enormous bulk and bushy beard.

"Little girl knows her guns," he rumbled. A bear-like paw reached down to finger a lock of her hair. "And so pretty."

"Yeah, well," Holly muttered, discomforted. The penis people were all the same although this one was much larger than usual. For an instant she wondered if all his parts were proportionate, but she pushed the thought aside. She slapped his hand away from her hair and stood up, suddenly aware of how his massive frame filled the hallway. "Maybe we can play later," she said, almost gagging at the thought, "but right now we need to do some business." He looked at her intently, as if gauging her character, then slowly nodded.

"Do you resist the New World Order? I've been looking for breeding stock." he said, turning back down the corridor to stop in front of the shotguns. He watched over his shoulder as Holly followed.

"Um, right, of course." she answered. "How much for the hardware?" She watched as he gazed at the shotguns thoughtfully.

"You should stay here with Joshua," he replied, softly, without looking at her. "You're not weak like the others. You appear worthy. We will reproduce the master race. Joshua has food, water, sour mash, everything. I think Joshua will have to insist."

"How much for just the shotgun?" she asked, pointing.

"I think Joshua would like to breed first and then talk about weaponry."

Patience was not one of Holly's virtues. As Joshua directed his gaze backward, Holly lifted a bayonet from the wall. Before he could speak again she drove the bayonet into his back, to the hilt, aiming like a surgeon for his left kidney. He grunted with the impact and fell into the rack of shotguns, swiping a massive arm that caught Holly full across the face and knocked her across the tunnel. She lunged back at him with her hair in her eyes and her head ringing from his blow. She plunged the bayonet into his chest. Their eyes met; his were filled with wonder and disbelief, Holly's were calm and detached. The blade bounced off his sternum and skittered along the ribcage. He swung at her head and caught her on the shoulder. The force spun her across the hallway and sprawled her into the cement. She came off the wall low and stabbed into his groin, digging for the femoral artery. He clubbed across her back and she fell to her knees, losing her grip on the bayonet. It clattered on the floor and he kicked it down the hallway. Holly scrambled after it. When she reached it, she turned to see him dragging a Thompson .50 from a hook on the wall. The moment was frozen. She hurled the bayonet with all her strength and in a one-in-a-thousand nothing-but-net moment, it slammed into his throat. His eyes widened in horror as he clamped his hand onto the knife. Watching his eyes, she saw realization turn into resignation. He collapsed against the wall, glaring at Holly who crouched in front of him on her hands and knees.

"You fucking harlot," he rasped, "you've killed Joshua."

Blood dribbled out of his mouth as he slid down the wall. He realized that he still held Thompson submachine gun. The click of the safety lever was deafening in the silence. Holly dived behind a crate as the gun spat lightning. Joshua lived long enough to empty the drum and fill the air with cordite, concrete grit and thunder.

Holly peeked. When Joshua's bowels and bladder loosened, she gained her feet and gingerly stepped around the blood and pried the weapon from Joshua's grip. She set the Tommygun on a workbench and looked over all the weapons before deciding on a 9mm Uzi. She ratcheted the slide and fired the full clip into Joshua's head. Only then did she feel safe.

She spent a long time admiring the Brotherhood Church's armory. She wanted it all. In the end, she decided to exercise discipline. She selected a Springfield Armory 1911 .45 with rosewood grips and 100 rounds of ammo. She tucked the hand cannon into the waistband of her jeans and climbed the ladder. It took twenty minutes of strain and a crowbar to lever the massive trap door open. By the time she was back in daylight, she was sweating and her mellow feeling of goodwill had dissipated. On the back porch, she found four jerry cans of kerosene. She spilled them into the basement and threw in a road flare. While the fire was catching hold, she found the kitchen and explored the refrigerator. It was filled with white-paper-wrapped mystery-meat and Miller High Life Beer. This confirmed her decision that Joshua had to die. In the back, she found a solitary bottle of Snapple Peach Iced Tea and the harmony of the universe was re-established.

The GMC started right away. As she pulled onto the highway, the first tendrils of smoke were visible. Later, there would be an interesting fireworks show. Holly felt a twinge of regret that she'd miss it. Her thoughts turned to the comfort of the .45 pressed into her back and the various ways scum like Glen Wilson could be killed with it. Kneecaps, groin, and a finishing headshot would be the classic dispatch, but Holly felt something more creative could be done. These thoughts occupied her as she made the drive back to Anchorage through a torrential downpour.

Moshi

At the main bar at Chilkoot Charlie's, Moshi spread her last two dollars on the damp bar. No matter how she massaged them, there were still just the two. A shot of gin was five bucks. She went through all of her pockets and found a dime which she carefully placed on top of the bills. The bartender knew she was with the band but was not dispensing any free drinks. With an impenetrable look on his face, he finally took her money and served her one last oily shot. Her face was swollen and despite heavy makeup, the bruises from Erik's blows were still plainly visible. The PA system was blasting out classic Metallica songs at ear-splitting volume while the crowd on the dance floor writhed and undulated. The record company had done a good job promoting the show and the place was packed from wall-to-wall. Her glass was suddenly empty, how had that happened? She ran her finger around the inside and got one last unsatisfying taste.

The music faded and a local radio DJ introduced the band.

"From Seattle, Megaton Records latest talent, Toxic Shock Syndrome!"

The lights dimmed as the band took the stage. With a roar of raging guitar and thunderous drums, the band launched into their set. Raz looked messianic in the bright spotlight as he wrung riffs and feedback from his guitar. Erik was a blur of long hair, a black figure in his trench coat and heavy boots. The sound was so loud that the song could not be clearly discerned; the bass guitar was a subsonic rumble mixed with the drums. Moshi could not tell if Erik was hitting notes accurately, but it didn't matter, the music was like an earthquake splitting the continent. Raz was inspired, he improvised long guitar solos and sang as if his soul was on the line. Moshi imagined synthesizer accompaniment, accents and harmonies and, unbidden, her left hand played intricate bass patterns on the sodden bar.

The bartender was giving her angry looks, so she abandoned the bar and found a spot to rest against the wall. The crowd demanded and received two encores. Finally, a long jam based on Nirvana's Lithium mesmerized and satiated the mob. An hour after the show, the bar was still half full. Moshi made her way backstage, but a duo of burly security staffers didn't know her and would not let her into the green room. The door opened and closed and Moshi could see Erik snorting lines of coke but could not get his attention. Bouncing off patrons like a pinball, she wandered through the Chilkoot Charlie's complex. In one of the quieter bars, several contestants from the All Alaska Arm Wrestling Championship were drinking energy drinks and flexing their biceps for the bar girls. Moshi finally found the rear stage door. There were about 20 kids smoking and hanging out, mostly girls dressed in leather and spandex. A passenger van idled in the alley and the driver, with a petite underage girl wriggling on his lap, was chatting up two girls who looked like twins, but it was hard to tell under their identical makeup. After a few minutes, the driver opened the door and the girls slipped in to join a small crowd collecting in the back. Moshi sucked desperately on a joint that was being passed around. The joint was laced with something because soon all the streetlights grew coronas and the fog drifting along the pavement tugged at her legs with ghostly tendrils.

The backstage doors flew open and the band swept out. The small crowd surged and the chatter increased in intensity. Moshi felt welded to the brick wall where she leaned. She wanted to call out to Erik, but her vocal cords were frozen. In seconds, they piled into the van and were gone. Moshi had a vague idea where the band house was, but had no energy to dream of walking there. Gradually the alley throng dissipated until there were just a pair of teenaged boys left. They glanced at her and worked up their courage. Eventually, they approached her. The older boy looked like he was about 15, they both wore straggly mustaches and bore filaments of hair on their chins.

"Toxic Shock are insanely awesome, aren't they? We couldn't get into the show, but we could hear them out here. We have their CD and a bunch of MP3's."

Moshi still could not speak, but she nodded. *Yes, Toxic Shock are cool, the hottest new death-metal band and the carefully engineered buzz around the band is undeniable.* Moshi was tired of the whole scene and really just tired of everything. She liked it better when the band was playing high school and battle-of-the-band gigs for little or no money and scrabbling for survival. Scraping by, writing songs and dreaming of making the big time. So this was the big time, freezing in an alley with abused ears ringing, swollen face throbbing, belly hurting and nowhere to sleep.

"You can crash with us if you if don't have anywhere else..."

Moshi nodded. "I can't move," she whispered.

The boys exchanged unreadable glances and shrugged.

"I'll bring the car around," the older one said.

Walter and Elke

Walter stood before a lectern and looked over his audience. There were 43 people in attendance. They were young and mainly dressed in colorful parkas and light-weight hiking boots. The room was near the Cook Inlet and housed in an abandoned fish processing building. The room was freshly painted, filled with rental furniture and the windows had been masked with newspaper. Arrays of Bose speakers were mounted on all four walls and gentle Andean pipe music was playing at the lower limit of perception. The crowd had been told they were part of an experiment, but this was not exactly true. Walter knew exactly what the effect would be on over 85% of his participants. He was proud of his work but was chagrined that most of his best stuff could never be made public.

"Thank you all for coming. Has everyone been paid?" There was an affirming murmur. "And everyone has their tea or coffee? I think we're ready then. We're going to start a multimedia presentation that will take about three hours. When the presentation is done, you are free to go. Are there any questions before we start?"

"What is the experiment?" someone asked.

"Good question. We're going to plant some engrams into your brain. It's a sort of brainwashing technique. Have you folks seen the Jehovah Witnesses on their bicycles going from door-to-door preaching their brand of the gospel? I did a study and figured out why they do that. There is a cross-connection between the pleasure centers and the analytical parts of the brain. I'm going to turn you into proselytes like those JW's except you'll be spreading the word about your congressional candidate Glen Wilson instead of God. Any other questions?"

"What is an engram?"

"Its like a memory, except its implanted. Simple engrams are used to sell cars and beer, they create artificial links between satisfaction or pleasure and commercial products. You'll find my technique is a bit more radical and effective."

"You're Doctor Zalooq. You're just one of those fake magicians on TV."

A smile flitted across Walter's lips. "Indeed, 'tis I," he said. He glanced at his watch. "If we don't get started, we won't get you out of here by three. Just relax and enjoy the show."

He stepped down from the lectern and Elke started the program. A slight mist emerged from the ventilation system and a projector system displayed faint images on a screen. Walter ushered Elke out and they closed the door and sealed the seams with duct tape.

"I can't get used to that. Are you sure they won't remember what you tell them?" she asked.

"Not a single bit of it. It won't work on all of them. The resistant will wake up with a headache, but that's all. None will have any memory of what I told them."

"Robots selling our candidate door-to-door. It's kind of creepy."

"No it isn't. One day these techniques will be used to create a whole world of perfect little consumers. We're just ahead of the curve a decade or so. Trix is for kids. Cuckoo for Cocoa Puffs. We are driven. Like a rock. Pepsi generation. These are all crude engrams."

"Is there any way to stop it?"

"You can kill your television, stop reading magazines and stay off the Internet, otherwise, forget it. Commercialism is the new opiate of the masses."

"What are we going to do until the program is over?"

"I have an idea." Walter brought out a cribbage board and a deck of cards. "Penny a point?"

Elke pulled over a chair. "You're on," she said, rubbing her hands together.

Bennie

"Will it be the usual, little man?" Celeste wore a plaid jumper and lacy apron. She worked at L'Aroma Bakery on 13th. The usual was a hot chocolate and a macaroon. Bennie nodded and fished some crumbled bills from his jeans which he exchanged for a white paper bag. Bennie liked candy like any other twelve-year-old, but by far, these chocolate-dipped coconut cookies were his favorite.

He skipped through traffic and sat on a bus bench. As the busses came by, he waved them off while he ate. He noticed a slim round-faced girl staring at him. She was dressed in high-top moccasins and a leather jacket with fringes. She wore her hair in tight braids. Her young eyes glowed with an awareness of the world that Bennie rarely saw in the people he watched on the street.

"Are you a Negro?" the girl asked solemnly.

Bennie laughed. "Haven't you seen a black person before?"

The girl shook her head no. "Only on TV. Does it hurt?"

"No it doesn't hurt. Your skin is brown, my skin is black, it's no big deal."

"That cookie looks good."

"It is."

"Can I have a bite?"

Bennie started. It had not occurred to him to offer her some. He broke off a section and handed it over. As he watched her nibble it, he felt something unfamiliar. His skin was flushed and tingling, he felt magnetized.

"Are you an Eskimo?"

"Yes, I'm full-blooded Tlinget. My daddy is a chief. What's your name?"

"Benjamin Franklin Jackson Junior."

"I guess I'll call you Bennie."

Bennie shrugged. "Everyone else does."

A group of three boys raced up on razor scooters. They spilled the scooters onto the sidewalk. The largest, a plump Eskimo dressed all in black, stood between Bennie and the girl. He wore a bandanna on his head and a shark's tooth on a leather cord around his neck.

"Is this jigaboo bugging you, Emma?"

"Just leave him alone, Ira. We're just talking."

"Don't you know better than bothering people, jig?"

Bennie stood up. Ira was a few inches taller and weighed about 20 pounds more. "I'm not doing anything."

"That's right, nigger. You're not doing anything and you're going to get out of here."

"There is no need to be impolite," Bennie protested.

"Emma is a princess."

Bennie didn't see the blow coming. His world filled with crimson pain. His cup flew through the air spewing a muddy arc. He banged his head against the bench and fell hard to the sidewalk. He heard the boys laughing. The bus pulled up and Emma and the boys filed on. Bennie sat up and felt the back of his head. It was bleeding. His lip was swollen and split. He saw Emma looking at him through the window. "I'm sorry," she mouthed as the bus pulled away.

Glen and Murphy and Lester

Glen floated in a black pool under a sky studded with twinkling stars. Warm and comfortable, he bobbed gently along without worry or concern, completely content.

"Glen?"

The stars brightened and blazed in the sky. Pain replaced comfort and a numbing chill overcame the warmth.

"Glen! Can you hear me?" Murphy.

"Goddammit, Murphy," grumbled Glen. "Go away and let me die in peace." Murphy smiled grimly. Glen opened one eye. "Damn, Murphy. You look like hell." He opened the other eye. That didn't help. "I hope you shot somebody for that."

"Well, there's you or Lester. Tough call."

"Maybe, but I sign your paychecks." He raised himself up on one elbow. The throbbing in his skull marched alongside his pulse. "What time is it?"

"Around noon. Lester's scrounging." She sat down beside him, easing one leg out straight. "We're kinda screwed here, Glen. We're at least a hundred miles from our planned landing site and our trusty guide has perfected the art of *not* being located." She offered him a steaming metal cup filled with a thick black liquid. "How do you feel?"

"Better. Is that coffee?"

"Sort of. Lester found his thermos." Glen used the bitter coffee to wash down the four aspirin Murphy produced, then pulled himself up to sit beside her. He looked around the wreckage with amazement. The rear of the plane had torn away at the start of the baggage compartment. The sun slanted through the ragged hole that had been the right side of the passenger cabin and the co-pilot's seat looked lonely, deserted by its fellows. A tangle of wires and electronics dangled from the dash and the windshield above it was shattered in a spiderweb of glass with what might be an imprint of someone's head. "We need to get out of here, preferably in time to make your next speaking engagement." She slowly got to her feet. "You might ponder our little problem while I give Lester a hand. He's got some broken ribs, I think."

Glen noticed she limped as she walked down the slope. She'd found his backpack and left it beside him; as soon as she was out of sight he dug into it and poured a generous shot of whiskey into his coffee, then leaned back against the cabin wall. *We're all busted up, miles from where we're supposed to be, and nobody's going to start looking for us any time soon.*

It was enough to give a man a headache.

Murphy found Lester dragging an Army surplus duffle up the slope. He'd found his boots earlier, still lying in the cockpit of the plane, fully laced. He gave Murphy a grateful grunt when she grabbed the other end of the bag.

"What's in this thing, car batteries?" Murphy asked.

"Camping gear, mostly. A tent, sleeping bags, food, water, some hardware."

"Hardware?"

"Shotgun, flare gun, emergency radio —"

"Radio?" Murphy interrupted.

"Yeah, but don't get your hopes up," Lester cautioned. He indicated the bare walls of granite around them. "Not a great location. I already tried the radio in the plane. Got nothing but static."

"It looked pretty messed up, maybe it's broken," Murphy suggested.

"Maybe."

"Hey, Lester."

"Yeah?"

"It wasn't your fault." Lester avoided her eyes and shrugged.

"Pilot error, that's what they'll call it," he replied.

"Lester. The wings were torn off before we hit the ground. That downdraft, windshear or whatever, ripped us apart in midair." Lester stopped and turned to look at her. Murphy, forced to stop with him, appreciated the break. Her knee wasn't enjoying the workout.

"How do you know that?" he asked.

"Look," she said, pointing up the slope to their impact point. "That's where we hit, angling downhill, thank God. A flat impact would've killed us. But over there," she pointed farther up the canyon wall, where Lester could vaguely see a glimmer of red that just might be one of the wings to his plane, "is where one of the wings landed." She motioned for him to grab his end of the duffle again. "That wing was off the plane before we hit and I don't even see the other one." They finished dragging the bag to the plane in silence, both of them collapsing to the ground by the jagged hole at the rear of the plane. Frayed cable ends and shredded aluminum fluttered in the breeze.

"Thanks," Lester said.

"No problem." She sat forward and unzipped the duffel. "Okay! Let's see what you've got in here." She reached in and pulled the tent bag free, setting it aside. "This feels sort of like Christmas, doesn't it?"

"Not really, I already know what's in there," Lester pointed out.

"You're saying you didn't peek at your presents when you were a kid, Lester? I don't believe you."

They pulled two sleeping bags out of a duffle bag. Also, a shotgun wrapped in oilcloth. By the time he turned around, Murphy had the radio out of its case and powered up. She was operating the controls confidently. Lester went over to check the settings and saw that Murphy knew what she was doing.

"General Av?" she asked.

"121.5," replied Lester, unnecessarily. "Probably our best bet, anybody might pick that up." Murphy began a series of Mayday calls while Lester peeked in the back to check on Glen, only to find the plane empty. Puzzled and little worried, he circled around to the front of the plane. He spotted Glen standing at the edge of the slope, looking over the edge at the rugged canyon below.

The plane rested on a wide bench at the summit of the 'pass', which wasn't really recognized as such, in that it wasn't commonly used by the community of Alaska bush pilots. It was more of a slot canyon shortcut Lester used to shuttle loads of booze to McGrath, and they had crashed well above timberline. The nights would be very cold at this elevation, patches of snow and ice still lurked in the shadows. Wind whistled through the canyon, racing down from the mountains, further chilled by the glaciers visible across the way. Glen looked over his shoulder as Lester approached.

"Spectacular view, anyway," Glen said, turning back to gaze across the canyon.

"Yes it is," agreed Lester. They enjoyed the vista in silence for awhile, then started back to the plane together. Murphy met them halfway with a look of disgust on her face.

"You son of a bitch," she snarled. Glen and Lester shared a startled glance.

"Me or him?" Glen finally asked.

"Probably you," Murphy snapped, looking at Glen. "But don't you get cocky," she added to Lester, before turning back to Glen. "Just how did you arrange this?" she asked.

"The plane crash?" Glen pointed at Lester, who stood beside him. "That was Lester." He nudged Lester with an elbow and spoke in a stage whisper loud enough for Murphy to hear.

"Don't worry, *you* she won't shoot."

Lester watched Murphy warily, not nearly as certain.

"Not the plane crash, you jerk," Murphy said, undistracted by Glen's attempt at humor. "The dogs. The goddamned dogs. Tell me you don't know anything about this." She turned, almost falling in her haste as the knee gave out, and jabbed a finger back at the plane. Glen peered over her shoulder and broke into a wide grin.

"Now see, Murphy? This is what clean living and daily prayer has done for me."

A dozen panting dogs lay beside the plane, harnessed to what looked to be a miniature Conestoga wagon with the canvas top rolled back. A scruffy old guy wearing suspenders over a plaid flannel shirt rummaged through the plane's wreckage, looking up guiltily as the three of them approached. One of the plane's seats already lay in the back of the wagon.

"Lester! I was just telling Beau Henry this looked like your plane! What the hell happened?" At the mention of his name the lead dog rose wearily to his feet and sniffed at the three strangers.

"Hi, Harry!" Lester replied, ignoring the man's question. He stepped past the dog and offered his hand. "Man, am I glad to see you." He looked over his shoulder at Glen and Murphy as if to apologize for the quality of their rescue. The two men shook hands for a full minute as Glen and Murphy waited. Lester displayed admirable patience but eventually broke free and walked over to the wagon. He kicked one of the rubber tires and pretended not to see his plane seat. "What's up with this, Harry?" he asked, looking the contraption over, overlooking some of his plane's electronics but casually removing his shotgun and Glen's backpack.

"Training," said Harry, puffing out his chest and appearing oblivious to Lester's actions. "High altitude, and I'm starting early. That ringer from Montana trains at high altitude and this year I'm gonna kick his ass." He frowned and moved closer to Lester. "Uh, you don't need to say nothing about this, don't want nobody stealing the idea." He lowered his voice to a whisper and continued talking to Lester, who occasionally nodded and replied. Lester finally returned to Glen and Murphy while the old dog musher sidled over to inspect more of the plane wreckage, muttering to himself.

"Harry's okay," Lester informed them with a grin. "He's been running in the Iditarod sled dog race since the late seventies. Usually comes in at the back of the pack somewhere. This year he's got yet another secret plan, something to do with that Montana musher who won three or four times. First Outsider to ever win, annoyed the hell out people like Harry."

"And this is pure coincidence?" asked Murphy. "He just shows up here and now?"

"As far as I can tell," Lester shrugged. "Unless Glen controls the weather and knows a crazy old dog musher from Kotzebue."

"Hmmph," said Murphy. "Glen might know the devil and Bill Gates but the weather is currently beyond him, I believe."

"That's a shame," said Lester. "That'd be worth a lot of votes up here." Silence reigned for a few moments. "The weather, I mean." Murphy and Glen looked at Lester, then at each other.

"Murphy! Lester made a joke!" Glen hooted. "Things must be looking up." He grabbed Lester by the arm and dragged him toward the plane and Harry. "Now, here's what Murphy's thinking," he said softly, "she's thinking we all ride this thing down to a road or trail, and then I take it on into town by myself. Do you think your buddy will go for that?" Lester looked back at Murphy, who watched them suspiciously.

"Murphy thinks that's what we should do?" he asked.

"Yes," Glen nodded emphatically. Lester looked doubtful.

"Well, I can ask him," he said. He started towards the plane, then turned as if to call to Murphy. Glen quickly stepped in front of him.

"Come on, Lester! Just ask him," Glen urged.

Lester sighed and dragged his feet toward the plane, where Harry was prodding one of Lester's flattened tundra tires with evident disappointment. Murphy moved up to stand beside Glen.

"What did you just do to me?" she asked.

"What? Why?"

"Glen..."

"Murphy, you have trust issues," Glen admonished.

"Yes, and with good reason," Murphy pointed out. They watched as Lester and Harry conducted an animated debate, punctuated by Harry throwing his hands into the air at irregular intervals. After a few minutes of this Murphy turned to Glen, "This involves you somehow."

"And how do you know that?" asked Glen, genuinely curious.

"Lester's nervous, the old guy's outraged, and you're far too happy." She headed toward the discussion. "That means you're up to something, and somebody should be worried." Glen laughed aloud at Murphy's analysis.

"And when you start laughing, *everyone* should be worried," she added.

The ultimate result of shielding men from the effects of folly is to fill the world with fools.

- Herbert Spencer

CHAPTER 10

Bennie

Bennie sat on the curb and watched the Anchorage Dojo until the last student climbed into a minivan and disappeared. Inside, the proprietor, a squat Korean named Taji, was rolling up exercise mats. Taji noticed Bennie standing in the doorway.

"I'm closing," he said with a thick Asian accent.

Bennie stepped into the room. Taji noticed Bennie's swollen lip.

"What happened to you, little guy?" he asked.

"My name is Bennie and I need you to teach me some moves."

"No problem, I can sign you up for one of my junior classes. We meet twice a week."

"No, I need you to teach me now." Bennie pulled a wad of damp hundred-dollar bills from his blue jean pocket. He arranged six of them on a table and looked at Taji expectantly. "Show me how to fight dirty."

Taji licked his lips. He looked at the money and calculated how short he was of making his overdue rent. "Offense or defense?"

"Both."

"Kill or immobilize?"

"Yes," Bennie replied solemnly.

It is impossible to teach martial arts without training the body over time, but Taji noticed that, in spite of Bennie's lack of coordination, he did not forget anything that Taji told him. Taji kept it simple, knees, hip joints, genitals, eyes and Adam's apple. Show no fear, watch your opponent's eyes and strike first. Several hours later, he watched Bennie walk away down the sidewalk carrying some instructions for strength exercises and a Tae Kwon Do DVD. Taji shook his head ruefully. He hoped his ancestors would forgive him, but he needed the money.

Walter and Elke

"Is any of this stuff you're doing FDA approved?" Elke asked. She and Walter were sharing a pitcher of Midtown Brown Ale and a halibut pizza at the Moose's Tooth Pub. The sun hovered behind a layer of clouds and did not appear to move.

"FDA? That's a joke. Most people think the FDA protects them, but the truth is that it is a first line of defense for the pharmaceutical companies. 'Our crap killed your kid? You can't sue us because we're FDA approved'. Most people have no idea. We're on the verge of an incredible revolution, more significant than the information revolution and probably at least equal to the industrial revolution. Biotech. Neuroscience. There are chemical and genetic breakthroughs that will change life as we know it. There is no way the FDA can keep up."

"This work you're doing for Glen is amazing, I had no idea."

"That's kid's stuff compared to the state of the art."

"What the hell are you talking about?"

"From the biochemical side of things, Prozac, Paxil, Luvox, Zoloft, Serzone and all the others were just the beginning. We're working with chemicals that go way beyond Venlafaxine, Nefazodone, Nortriptyline, Clomipramine, Flouxetine…"

"Excuse me, Walter, but I don't understand a word you're saying."

Walter drained his beer and refilled their glasses. "Okay, let me put it this way. The science of neurochemistry is crossing with bioinformatics and genomics and we're approaching a nearly complete biometric cartography."

"I swear to God if you don't start speaking English I'm going to beat you to death with this pitcher."

Walter sat back in his chair. "You're being a bit testy. Partly, this is caused by external stimulus that includes the background noise in this room, the effect of the alcohol in the beer and the carbs in the pizza, and frustration with my complex terminology. Partly this is caused by the programming of the neural pathways in your brain as influenced by your experiences and your innate cognitive transfer functions. We're understanding this more and we can manipulate this transfer function."

"If I'm following you, you're talking about the designer personality. Mood and response alteration."

"That's the root of it but it goes way beyond that. I can take a sample of your DNA and a magneto-spectragraph of your brain and define a chemical and sensory immersion program that will have a predictable result. Here's an example. If I wanted to kill a world leader, I could kidnap his wife for a day, analyze her genetic and chemical state and program her so the next time she sees her husband, she goes into a manic state and kills him. I can do this with a dog or just about any mammal that has a higher brain function. I could do it with a gerbil, but the result would not be very impressive."

"That's scary."

"Yes, but it's not very practical. The analytical lab and the chemical synthesis equipment is very expensive, it would be cheaper just to hire a thug to put a bullet in the leader's head. What are more interesting are the cost-effective things that can be done. For example, the most instantly addictive substance I know of is a exotic chemical called Octanone-36."

"What does it do?"

"Besides being addictive, nothing. But the withdrawal is about 97% fatal. Suppose I invent a soft drink with Octanone-36. If I can get you to drink one bottle, then I own you. You will have to drink this stuff daily for the rest of your life."

"If I don't?"

"Then you die in excruciating pain."

"Wow."

"Who do you suppose owns the patent for this one?"

Elke shrugged.

"I can't tell you out loud, but I can whisper it to you." He leaned over and breathed the name into her ear.

"No shit?" Elke asked.

"No shit," Walter replied. "But it really doesn't matter because there is almost an infinite series of these types of drugs and we add more to the list every day. A personal interest for me is the temporal-psychotropic drugs. You know how the way time passes is subjective? If you're sleeping, ten hours can go by quickly, if you have a toothache, ten minutes can seem like hours? I started out with some doses that you can take during the work week to make time go fast, then you slow down your time perception over the weekend when you're having fun. My crowning glory is a drug that can make an orgasm last a couple of hours. I can actually kill you with that one. The orgasm is so intense you go away and you don't come back."

"Holy crap."

177

"Yeah. I can do things like bond a couple together. You know how heteros respond to members of the opposite sex and the homos respond to their same sex? I was able to isolate and refine the biochemistry so the sexual response is narrowed down to one specific person. If I don't like you, I can tune you so there isn't a person you respond to. You'll crave the connection, but it will not be found."

"You're screwing with the things that make us human."

"I think you're starting to get it. The human organism is on the verge of a huge evolutionary step. There is nothing the government can do to stop it. Any bright student with 100 square feet and one hundred thousand dollars can get in. The proverbial cat is out of the metaphysical bag. Here is something I find interesting. I think you are programmed for a certain amount of pleasure and pain. If I synthesize your pleasure response, after so much of a dosage, your brain stops working unless we balance it with ratiometric pain. This ratio is different for each person, some people were born to experience more pain than pleasure and vice versa. This is embedded in the underlying brain infrastructure, I have not figured out how to hack that part yet. It may not be possible, I don't know. The interesting part is we're all pleasure seekers and it is much more efficient to give you your pleasure quota in a lab in a few hours. You will have your full life's worth of bliss, then you are gone. The universe seems to evolve toward a minimum energy state, it may be that we are supposed live fast and intense, then move aside for the next generation. I can compress the whole life cycle into almost nothing. Maybe that's the way it's supposed to be, I don't know. The ethics of this are infinitely complex. For example, how about a welfare case? Does society owe this person anything other than his quota of pleasure? What if someone wants to get on with it? Does society have a right to ration his or her life experience?"

"I don't like science fiction."

"Well, you better hold onto your hat because the pace is accelerating. The genome mapping project has identified some odd snippets of DNA that we can activate. The result was so disturbing that I don't even want to talk about it."

"How about a hint?"

"Mutations, hybrids and what might be the next evolutionary version of man."

They drank beer in silence, both lost in the vector of their thoughts.

"We're going to win this election?"

"I think so. In about a decade, the election model will be obsolete. Free will itself might become obsolete."

"You're freaking me."

"That just means you're catching on. Don't be afraid. In fact, I have taken the liberty of creating a small gift for you." He slid over a twist of tin foil. Elke looked inside to see two BB-sized blue pellets. "When you want to have a special evening with Murphy, take these. Make sure you don't have to be anywhere for a couple of hours and be sure you lock your doors so no one walks in on you. Oh, I should warn you that this is a once-only. The crypto-synaptic interconnection can't be repeated."

"Should I be scared?"

"No, I assure that you'll like this. I just don't want you coming back for more. And don't lose them, they cost about $400,000 to synthesize."

"Hmmm," Elke said.

Holly

Bored, bored, bored. This was a thought rolling around Holly's head that she could not evict. The television was on, but muted because she could not stand the constant yammering of the afternoon talk shows. She was field stripping and reassembling her .45. She could start from complete disassembly, put it together, load the seven cartridges, jam in the clip, cock, eject the clip, load in the eighth cartridge, and be ready to fire again in 55 seconds. The room reeked of the odor of Bubba's Gun Lube, she had even bought a spray can of Pledge and some cotton swabs to meticulously polish the hardwood handles. The gun gleamed with intimate loving care. When she pointed it at the television, it felt like an organic extension of her body. It was simply a common stainless steel Springfield Armory .45 ACP with tritium sighting, but it was a classic beauty.

As she paged through Pennywise ads she decided to take a run up to Birchwood to fire her new friend at the Izaak Walton Recreational Shooting Range. She bundled up in boots, wool sweater, and down parka. The day was misty and cold, she was used to the heat and humidity of Florida in June. She jumped in her GMC and drove up the Glenn Highway, the scenery was almost enough to distract her from her feeling of lassitude and despair. The ride took about 45 minutes which included the obligatory top-off of the GMC fuel tank.

She pulled into the gravel parking lot of the shooting range and strolled inside. The shop was typical of rustic Alaska; a squat cedar-sided building with a full assortment of muddy American-made pickup trucks equipped with a canine chained up in the bed as required by state statute. She wrinkled her nose upon entry, apparently the civilized no-smoking rules had not drifted this far north yet. She smelled a mix of cigar and pipe smoke, wet clothing, gun oil, and intermittently-washed bodies. She bought a stack of Osama Bin Laden targets and strolled to the outdoor range. She had already attracted an entourage, she stared each in the eye as she poked foam plugs in her ears, neatly loaded her 1911 and took her stance. She looked like a cuddly bear bundled up in her parka. She clicked off the safety and held the gun casually at an angle. From 40 yards, she fired deliberately at the target, catching and pocketing the brass as it ejected into the air and fell into her palm. Eight rounds, eight catches, 16 seconds, all slugs slamming within the periphery of OBL's turban. The guys watching took a step back and murmured among themselves. Weapons were common in the Alaskan wilderness, but apparently 90 pound girls who looked like they were 15 who could clearly handle a large-bore weapon like the .45 ACP were unusual. She reloaded and fired until her 100 rounds were gone. Her hands felt like ground meat, her hair was torn from her ponytail by the wind, and her spirits were soaring. The smell of cordite and the satisfaction of shooting was exactly what she needed. It was a poor substitute for sending Glen Wilson into oblivion, but for now she was happy.

She put her gun back in its holster and was headed back to her truck when the air split open with the rending of an automatic weapon. The shock waves were almost visible and the earth trembled. She stopped and looked at the edge of the range where a pair of WW2-aged old timers were feeding and firing a machine gun. She was drawn to the scene with a force akin to magnetism. She had the foam plugs in her ears, but the sound of the Browning was still deafening.

The firing team had to be in their late seventies and they wore military fatigues and metal helmets. Both had more hair growing out of their noses than they had on their heads and their skin was wattled and sagging. Holly generally despised old people (to her this would describe any one over 40), but she was oddly impressed by the military ribbons and medals that these geezers wore. She noticed their nametags, the man firing was Watson and the man feeding was Oligant.

Watson noticed her and spoke first.

"Hello honey, we were watching you shoot. Most kids your age don't know which end the fire comes out of. You're good."

"Thanks," she said, blushing to her toes. She didn't care what anyone thought of her, but there was something warming about being praised by a man with a machine gun who wore a pair of purple hearts on his chest.

"You've probably never seen one of these before?" Oligant commented.

"M1917, 30 caliber, water-cooled, fully automatic, recoil-operated, firing 600 rounds a minute with an effective range of 1000 meters. I've never seen one, but I've read about them in my dad's magazines."

"Your dad served?"

"Viet Nam, 65-67, then he was a cop."

"You must be proud of him?" Watson commented.

"He was a complete prick and I've never been as happy as the day he died. He wanted a son and got me."

"Sorry to hear that," Oligant said. There was an uncomfortable silence while Holly stared them down.

"Look, would you care to try her?" Oligant asked.

Holly tried to stay angry, but a smile snuck out.

"May I?"

They nodded. Watson stepped back. Oligant popped the latch and fed in a fresh fabric belt. He closed the flap and pointed at the release. Holly sighted down the barrel, they were firing at Korean uniforms stuffed with straw 150 yards away. She pulled the release, squeezed the trigger and unleashed devil's fire into the world. When the belt was complete, she was shaking and coughing. She felt like she'd been running a jackhammer all day, her bowels were loose, her arms were rubber, and her mind was shattered. She felt the satisfaction that must compare with giving birth. On shaky legs, she stood and wrapped her arms around both the old guys and gave them kisses on their gray-whiskered cheeks.

"Thanks," she whispered.

She walked back to the shop and bought a hundred cartridges for her .45. Her plan included heading back to the room, ordering in some cashew chicken, and getting some sleep, but she passed the bar in Birchwood and realized that she could use a beer. She should have known better, but she didn't.

Moshi

Something big was crawling on her. She woke with a start and sat up. Her head was filled with steel wool and her mouth tasted like dead fish.

She was not being attacked by a giant bug, one of the boys had his hand under the blanket that covered her. Feeling panic surge in her, she desperately tried to figure out where she was. Swiveling her hips, she sat up. The boy was on his knees with a shamed look on his face. She was on a couch in a messy living room. Dim light leaked through gaps in the curtains.

"I'm sorry, but I don't think you should be here when my parents get up," the kid whispered.

Slowly, recollection of the concert the night before seeped into her mind. She vaguely remembered the boys fondling her in the car, but they were young and inexperienced. Moshi didn't feel like she had been overly violated. She did an inventory. Her face hurt, her stomach was in knots, her head ached, but beyond that, everything seemed normal. She was still dressed, though the buttons on her blouse were misaligned and her bra was unhooked. She did not want to think about this so she didn't.

"Jordan, who are you talking to?" a voice shouted from the back of the house.

"No one, mom," Jordan shouted back. "Hurry," he hissed to Moshi.

Moshi shrugged off the blanket and slipped her feet into her boots. Tripping over loose bootlaces and game console cables strewn across the floor, she made it all the way to the front door.

"Who is this girl, Jordan?" a lady asked with an accusing voice.

Turning, Moshi stood quietly while Jordan's mother stood angrily before her with arms on her hips. "Jesus-shit, Jordan, were you guys in a car wreck?"

"She's just a friend from the concert. We didn't wreck the car, we found her like this."

Jordan's mom lifted Moshi's chin and examined her bruises.

"Man problems?"

Moshi nodded slowly. "I gotta go."

"Yes, you do need to go. But we can at least get some coffee and breakfast in you first. Go sit in the kitchen and I'll cook something. Lord knows, I've seen more than my share of man problems myself," she said gently. She shot a brief harsh look at Jordan that said much. *How dare you stay out all night with your worthless friends drinking and smoking dope and bringing home street trash while your Dad works hard all day changing the oil in diesel engines and your grades go down the toilet?* To Moshi she said "The bathroom is on the right if you want to clean yourself up."

In the bathroom and under the harsh lighting, Moshi was shocked by what she saw. Her lipstick and mascara were smudged across her face. There was an open wound on her temple that was seeping and her hair was matted and lumpy. She brushed her teeth with toothpaste and an index finger and rinsed out her mouth. This helped a little. There was a bottle of Advil and she helped herself to three or four. Making sure the door was secure and feeling a twinge of guilt, she slipped the bottle into her jacket pocket. Her need was great. She decided to take a shower and peeled off her clothes. Under the hot water, she began to feel almost human. As the Advil kicked in, she felt detached from the pain in her head and her stomach. What she really needed was a drink, but she dared not dream of it. She rinsed her panties out in the sink and put them back on though they were damp and clammy. There was no makeup in this bathroom, so she couldn't do anything to cover the purple welts on her face. She ran a comb through her hair and laced up her boots. The door hinges squealed as she eased the door open. The odor of fresh coffee and bacon almost made her retch, but after the initial shock Moshi realized she was hungry. Very hungry. The family was seated at the table watching her. Jordan's mom gestured to a folding chair and timidly, Moshi sidled to it and sat down. She tried to make herself as small as possible, but all attention at the table was on her. Even the cat, peeking around a corner, openly stared at her.

"I'm Mister Brown and this is Missus Brown. I think you already know our useless sons Jordan and Jack." There was a pointed silence. "And you are?"

"Moshi."

"Is that a first name or a last name? I suppose it doesn't matter."

Mister Brown was a large man with huge hands. Embedded black grime collected under his fingernails beyond where a nail file could reach. His hair was thinning and he had a large belly that extended a long distance over his belt. The end of his fleshy nose took a sharp turn to the left; he looked like he might have been a not-particularly-successful boxer in his youth.

"The boys tell me that you were at the concert last night. I don't approve of the boys hanging around bars. They're in enough trouble at school already with the police coming around for tagging and skateboarding and drinking and smoking dope with their loser friends."

He said this as if it was a question, but Moshi could not think of anything to respond to. Mister Brown sighed.

"I suppose we should just eat." He speared a sheaf of bacon and spooned scrambled eggs onto his plate. Once Moshi began eating, she did not think she would be able to stop. Coffee, bacon, eggs, toast and jam were not enough, she even ate most of a bowl of leftover mashed potatoes Mrs. Brown found in the refrigerator. The Browns were amazed that Moshi ate everything put on her plate.

Mister Brown pushed back his chair. "I'll run you where ever you want to go on my way to work."

Jordan and Jack instantly protested.

"I'll take her, Dad," Jordan said.

His dad looked at him suspiciously, then glanced at his watch. "I'm running a little late. If I catch you skipping class today I'm going to kick your ass from here to tomorrow," he warned. He bent over for a kiss on the cheek from Mrs. Brown, grabbed his lunch pail and, after casting one last glance over his shoulder at Moshi, exited his house. The boys ran around and gathered up their books and backpacks. They herded Moshi to Jordan's old Honda Civic, well-decorated with Coldplay and Linkin Park stickers, and drove off in a scud of blue smoke.

Moshi could almost remember where the band house was located beyond where Third Street turned into Commercial and near the Eagle Glen Golf Course. After driving in circles for twenty minutes they found the bus, which the boys recognized.

"Hey, that's the band bus," Jack exclaimed. "Do you know the band?"

"Erik is my boyfriend."

"Erik Olsen?"

Moshi nodded.

"Jesus crap!" Jordan shouted. Moshi winced. Jordan and Jack looked at each other with a dawning realization. The girl they picked up at the concert was connected with the hot new band Toxic Shock Syndrome. The potential of this situation slowly sank in.

"Take us in and introduce us. Jack plays a little guitar and I'm going to play bass as soon I can get dad to buy me one. I played one at the music store and it was awesome. This could be our big break. Wouldn't it be cool to open for TSS? We could party every night."

Moshi cradled her head in her hands. Her headache was creeping up the back of her neck.

"Alright, you can come in," she whispered.

The front door was not quite closed. Moshi pushed it open and the trio entered and filled their eyes with the scene. Cans and bottles and several bongs were the main part of the debris. Lumps of bodies were scattered around draped in blankets and sleeping bags. Raz was sitting in a corner wearing headphones and noodling acoustically on his electric guitar. He grinned at Moshi and nodded toward a back room. The boys followed into a bedroom. Erik was naked among several other naked forms; male and female and unknown. Jack and Jordan were bug-eyed. They made gang signs at each other then clasped their hands.

"Long live rock and roll," Jack said.

"Word up," Jordan replied.

Erik blinked his eyes. He sat up and cradled his head in his hands.

"Shit Mosh, where have you been?" he asked with a slow thick voice while scratching at his crotch. "Nevermind. I'm really thirsty. Could you see if you can find me a Pepsi or some coffee or something? I would even take water if that's all you can find."

Moshi nodded and walked to the kitchen.

Erik, crawling around on his hands and knees, looked for his pants. Jack and Jordan tried to think of something to say.

"We're your biggest fans in Alaska, we have MOV files of your videos and MP3's of your music. You're a most-awesome bass player."

"That's nice. Maybe you guys will *buy* something sometime. Who are you, anyway?"

"I'm Jack and I play some guitar. We're going to start a band called Toxic Rock Syndrome. Get it? Rock Syndrome instead of Shock Syndrome?"

"Great, very original," Erik replied acidly. He proffered a shoe. "Could you boys see if you can find a mate to this?"

Jordan and Jack looked around the room. The idea of searching among the naked girls appealed to them greatly. They started rooting around. Erik staggered to his feet and walked to the door.

"Can we feel up your groupies?" Jordan asked.

"Do what you will, there are no rules in rock-n-roll except chaos and anarchy," Erik muttered.

Jack found the errant shoe being used as a pillow by a petite blond who looked to be about 12. He stood and handed it to Erik subserviently.

"Good job," Erik said, "when you're done in here, see if you can get these girls dressed and get them out of here.

They looked around the room with ravenous eyes.

"Yes, sir," Jack said.

Glen and Murphy and Lester

"Now Murphy," Glen grinned. "You're just jealous because I get to drive the dog team and you have to ride in the wagon like a little girl."

"You're not driving that dog team," Murphy declared flatly.

"Am too!" Glen said angrily. "This is not an accident. This was fated. From the instant we realized that we could win an election in Alaska, I knew that I would drive a dogsled to victory. This was foretold."

"No, " said Murphy, "that is bullshit, not prophesy. As your bodyguard, it's too dangerous, I can't allow it. And, as someone who has to listen to your crap..."

Glen drew himself up another inch and glared down at Murphy. "Once in a while I get to be the boss, dammit, and this is one of those times. I'm mushing these dogs." He stared into the distance and rubbed his chin, "And I'm thinking you should maybe call me by some rugged nickname in front of the old guy, what do you think? He might be able to let it slip to the press."

Murphy's eyelids fluttered and she sagged against him. Glen caught her before she could slide to the ground. "Murphy!" he exclaimed, alarmed. She grasped him tightly and rested her head on his chest. Glen staggered slightly from the unexpected weight.

"Oh, Glen," she whispered. "I just love it when you're all manly and tough." She squeezed his upper arms and shifted her footing. Glen watched her through narrowed eyes.

"If you're thinking of throwing me down and tying me up or something, I might have to blacken your other eye too," Glen said dryly. Murphy froze, then released him and backed away with a guilty gleam in her eye.

"I'm just being practical. You may be rabid and I may have to put you down before you infect others." She placed her hands on her hips and eyed Glen up and down. "Let's say I do give in and let you live this weird Jack London fantasy, are you going to be insufferable about it?"

"Probably."

Murphy knew this was a lost cause. "Okay fine, let's move on to the rugged nickname." She began to slowly circle him. "How about 'Glen-Boy'?" She paused, deep in thought, and began idly chewing on a fingernail, then continued her circling. Glen crossed his arms and rocked back on his heels to wait her out. "Or, 'the Li'l Wanker'?" She gauged his expression, shook her head. "No? Then how about 'Killer', or 'Ace', or 'Slash', or 'Buck', or —"

"Okay! Forget the nickname," Glen broke in, exasperated. "But look, the old guy's already taught me both commands —"

"There's only two?"

"Basically, yes. 'Gee' turns one way and 'haw' turns the other," Glen said.

"Which is which?"

"I forget. If one doesn't work, the other will," he explained. Murphy rolled her eyes.

"Great. And how do you stop?"

"Stop?" Glen looked embarrassed. "Hey, Harry!" The old musher/trapper/poacher/thief looked up from arranging the loot in his wagon.

"What?" he asked, impatiently. He was completely unimpressed by Glen's credentials as a prospective Congressman, but with the promise of a thousand dollars and suspicion eased by Lester's assurances, he had promised a grudging cooperation. With Harry's lifestyle, a thousand bucks, plus his Permanent Fund Dividend, would carry him through the winter, maybe longer.

"How do you make 'em stop?" Glen asked. He sat atop the wagon looking over the dogs, anxious to take a test drive but wishing to appear competent in Murphy's eyes, lest she start up with the objections again.

"Just yell 'stop'," Harry replied, without looking up.

"Yell 'stop'?" muttered Murphy, sitting beside Glen on the wagon seat. She spun to face Harry in the back. "Are you serious?" she asked. Harry gave her an elaborate shrug.

"Well, them other mushers use 'whoa', except those Norwegians, and maybe that other damn foreigner from Montana. But my dogs don't much care. If they're sitting and you yell at 'em, they figure it's time to go, and if they're running and you yell something besides 'gee' or 'haw', they figure it's time to stop." Glen looked ahead to where Lester knelt by Harry's lead dog, Beau Henry. Lester held a tight grip on the dog's harness. The dogs had been fed from a cache of chum salmon in the wagon and were rested and ready to run. The buckets of salmon were sealed but still emitted a rancid odor that permeated the whole wagon, much to Murphy's disgust. "Best to use the brake too, of course," Harry added, pointing to a wooden lever beside Glen's seat. He moved forward to stand behind the front seat. His unwashed ripeness wafted over them and caused Murphy to lean as far away as possible. "We're gonna be plenty heavy with all of us in here. You sure you don't want me and the little lady to walk out and get some help?"

"We're sure," Glen answered before Murphy could contradict. Glen had decided this was a golden opportunity. Murphy was determined to keep Glen on a short leash and it seemed cruel to make Lester wait at the crash site by himself. Harry continued to grumble about the strain the extra weight would mean for the dogs and the wagon but declined to remove any of his assorted cargo, although he didn't say anything when Lester and Glen tossed the plane seat overboard.

"Whenever you're ready," said Harry with a sly grin, "yell 'mush' or 'giddyup'."

"Everybody settled?" Glen shouted, and the dogs leaped up and ran straight for the edge of the cliff, tumbling Murphy into the wagon bed with a startled curse.

Lester held a ten foot lead connected to the harness — Harry's version of training wheels — and the team tangled to a stop short of the edge, though dragging Lester to his knees in the process. He managed to pull the lead dog out of the pile and straighten the harnesses while Harry sat in the wagon and cackled, wiping tears from his eyes. Murphy watched the action nervously, especially since Glen seemed more amused than concerned about the mishap. As soon as Lester had the harnesses somewhat organized he walked Beau Henry to the middle of the bench and aimed him down a barely visible game trail. He moved ahead to the extent of his lead rope would allow and held his hands out to the dog, palms up.

"I'm going to just lead them for a bit, nice and slow," he said. But as soon as he turned his back Harry let out a whoop and the dogs charged ahead down the trail. This time they had a good twenty foot run before they hit the end of Lester's lead; he was jerked completely free of the ground and landed on his side, skidding to a stop with Harry's guffaws in his ears. The fourth rib on his left side, previously cracked, splintered under the impact and a sliver of bone slipped into his right lung before retracting as the rib sprang back into shape. Glen hauled back on the brake lever, locking the wheels so the wagon bucked to a shuddering halt just short of overrunning Lester. The dogs strained at their traces momentarily before settling down.

Murphy spun and backhanded Harry across the face, releasing a whole day of frustration into the blow, then leaped to the ground and ran to Lester's side. Stunned, Lester lay on the jagged shale at the edge of the trail, gritting his teeth against the pain but unaware of the extent of his injury. Glen locked the brake in place and dropped to the ground, reaching Lester right behind Murphy. The two of them helped him to his feet. Glen dusted him off while Murphy inspected several new cuts on his face and hands. None were severe enough to warrant immediate concern.

"That's it," Murphy said, through clenched teeth. "That drunk old bastard's going to get somebody killed." She watched as the old musher clambered awkwardly over the side of the wagon with his lip swollen and bloody. Murphy smiled grimly at the sight.

"You guys are just going to have wait here while I go with Harry." She braced herself for Glen's protests and was surprised when none came. She looked up to see if he'd heard her proposition and saw he was staring intently at Lester, who was now bent over with his hands on his knees with his breath coming fast and shallow.

"Hey, Lester," Glen said softly, gripping his shoulder, "You okay there, guy?"

Lester nodded his head and started to reply. He gave up in favor of dropping to one knee to concentrate on catching his breath. He coughed with a ragged and wet sound and blood splattered on the ground.

"Oh shit," said Murphy, horrified.

The wagon bed was barely long enough for Lester to stretch out and the blood pooling in his lung soon drove him to lean up against the back to keep from gagging. Glen and Murphy squeezed in on either side of him but did little more than take turns asking how he was doing. They all knew Lester was riding a fine line, though Murphy had considerably more experience with trauma cases than the others. If the air building up in Lester's chest cavity bled over to the other side, the undamaged lung might be affected as well, or the delicate feedback mechanism that drives the respiratory process could very well shut down — resulting in respiratory arrest.

"How long?" she asked Harry, who was running the dogs as fast as he dared over the rough trail. Harry rode the brake to keep the heavy wagon from running over the dogs on the downhill sections and yelled coarse encouragement to his team on the flats. His wounded passengers bounced from one side of the wagon bed to the other. They were still above timberline but a forest of spruce and alder spread out below them. Harry claimed the trail smoothed out considerably once they reached the trees where actual topsoil replaced the jagged shale and karst of the mountainside. Then the greatest danger would be becoming mired in muskeg if they strayed from the path.

"Four, maybe five hours," Harry answered. Glen held Lester as steadily as he could, aware that he'd played no small part in the current crisis and wishing he'd listened to Murphy's nagging for once. Lester panted weakly, slowly suffocating in the thin mountain air.

"He's not going to last that long," she told Glen.

"What do we do?" he asked, feeling helpless.

"We've got to get the air out of his chest cavity," Murphy replied.

Glen looked at her. "How?" he asked, fearing what she might be intending.

"Just hold him steady," she replied, easing forward to the front of the wagon bed. She dug through the pile of parts, tools, and junk Harry had amassed and returned with two sections of fuel line and a big glass jar.

"I saw this demonstrated one time in a trauma class," she said with nervous waver in her voice. Lester watched uneasily as she dug Glen's whiskey from the pack and quickly rinsed the fuel line by taking a swig and squirting a stream through the line. She swallowed some before handing the bottle to Glen and nodded toward Lester. Glen took a shot himself and held the bottle for Lester, who grinned weakly.

"Since. I'm. Not. Driving," he managed say between gasps. He pulled long and hard on the whiskey, spilling some down his chest as the wagon lurched over a rock.

Murphy pulled a roll of duct tape from the pack with astonishment. Glen grinned at her.

"Don't leave home without it," he said.

Murphy shrugged. She filled the jar half full of water from Harry's jug, sealed the top with tape and poked both sections of fuel line through, pushing one all the way to the bottom and leaving one end at the top of the jar. She handed the assembly to Glen and moved to sit beside Lester, grabbing the whiskey from Glen on the way.

"Lester, this is going to hurt like hell. Drink," she said, handing him the whiskey.

Lester slugged down another gulp before choking and handing it back. Whiskey and blood dripped onto his shirt. He wiped the back of his hand across his mouth and suddenly spasmed. His body arched off the wagon bed and his hands flailed.

"Hold him, Glen!" Murphy shouted. "He's arresting!"

Glen fell onto Lester's shoulders and pinned him to the wagon bed. Murphy snatched her purse and dumped its contents on the floor. She scrabbled though the debris and came up with a small pocketknife. She yelled for Harry to stop the wagon, then slid over to Lester's side and tore the front of his shirt open, ripping it down to expose the side of his chest. She flipped the blade open and probed beneath Lester's armpit with her free hand, locating a space between the ribs.

"Hold him!" she shouted again, and Glen swore as he fought to control the smaller man.

Murphy screamed over her shoulder again for Harry to stop but the musher assumed she had to go to the bathroom — women were always needing to go to the bathroom, in his experience — and he decided she could damn well wait.

"Okay go!" Glen yelled, unsure how long he could keep Lester pinned. Murphy took a deep breath, held it and made a half-inch slice between Lester's ribs. She pried the cut open and sliced again to deepen it. She bit her lip as blood flowed over hand, belatedly wondering about Lester's lifestyle, then grabbed the fuel line and firmly inserted into the opening as Lester thrashed against Glen's restraint. The jar promptly began bubbling with the water turning pink as Lester gave a huge gasp and started coughing.

"He's expelling it!" Murphy exclaimed. "On his own!"

She held the fuel line in place with one hand and wiped the blood free with the remains of Lester's shirt, wadding it around the tubing. She ripped off a piece of duct tape with her teeth and slapped it over the wound. Lester's manic heaves subsided, allowing Glen to ease up and help her add more tape to seal the gash. Lester gagged and coughed up another wad of foamy blood, then sagged back against the side of the wagon, breathing heavily. Bubbles burst into the jar with every breath. Glen braced the jar between Lester's body and the side of the wagon, then sat back and stared at Murphy.

"Good God, woman," he said in awe. "What the hell did you just do?"

"Hell, Glen," Murphy drawled, wiping the sweat from her brow and leaving a bloody streak, "When I was a kid we did this every Friday night."

They smiled shakily at each other, then Murphy let herself fall back against the wagon, dizzy and faint. Harry finally looked back over his shoulder and saw Lester with his shirt torn off and a fuel line inserted into his side, connected to a glass jar filled with bloody water. He glanced fearfully at Murphy and Glen, then turned back around and shouted at his dogs, bringing the wagon to a final stop with the brake. Murphy and Glen glared at him in unison for awhile while he stared at Lester, aghast.

"What the — " he started.

"Just shut up," Murphy snapped. Harry's face reddened and he swelled himself up to reply but caught himself when he saw the look on Glen's face. He deflated, turning again to stare at Lester in wonder and confusion. Murphy found a clean sanitary napkin that had spilled from her purse — she hadn't lied to Lester about that — and used it to wipe the blood from Lester's face.

"The water acts like a one-way valve," she explained to Glen, who nodded. He'd figured that part out already. "We just need to keep a slight vacuum in that jar." Glen looked at the assembly with distrust. "Don't worry, the water will catch any blood or yucky stuff, you just have to keep enough negative pressure in there to bleed the air from his chest cavity faster than it's leaking in."

"All the way to Petersville?" Glen asked.

"Yes, Nanook, all the way to Petersville," Murphy replied. She saw Lester's eyes twinkle at the 'Nanook' dig, but he made no effort to speak. Glen leaned over to look in Lester's face.

"You're just lucky it ain't your colon, Lester. I'm afraid in that case you just flat wouldn't make it," Glen informed him. At that Lester had to laugh, though it quickly turned into a coughing fit which sent a frenzy of bubbles into the jar.

"Okay." Murphy handed the Glen the loose end of the fuel line. "Glen, you suck."

"Thanks, Murphy. You're a real peach yourself sometimes." He glanced briefly at Harry. "Show's over, Harry. Take it a little easier now."

Harry nodded numbly and eased off the brake, shouting something unintelligible at his dogs, who started off fast but soon slowed when Harry jolted them with the brake a few times.

After twenty minutes or so Murphy took over tending the vacuum line and Glen leaned over to talk to Lester.

"HMO or private plan?" he asked. Lester looked at him blankly. "That's what I thought." He clapped Lester softly on the shoulder. "Don't worry about it, I'm thinking we can pick up this tab," he frowned, "assuming you don't sue my ass for negligent sled driving."

"Oh. No. Can't," Lester gasped. He used one hand to pantomime an airplane flying into the ground. "You. Might. Sue. Me. Back." They shared a grin.

"Hey!" Murphy exclaimed abruptly. "Look! I've got a cell signal!"

"What?!" Glen was shocked.

"I was looking for my gun, but found my phone first." Glen looked, and sure enough, her phone claimed to be receiving a roaming signal. Murphy promptly dialed 911,and then smacked Lester in the leg in glee while waiting for the call to go through. "Where the hell are we?" she asked Harry.

"Roughly twenty miles northwest of Petersville."

"Doesn't matter," Glen spoke up. "Ask them to triangulate." Murphy looked at Glen as if he'd lost his mind. "I'm serious," he insisted. "They can do that up here, I checked for uh... other reasons." Murphy looked askance, making a mental note to follow up on that little tidbit. Then the 911 operator picked up the line. It turned out Glen was right, the E911 locating system had been deployed in this part of Alaska.

A National Guard helicopter out of Kulis on a training mission, happened to be the closest flight, and the 911 operator coordinated them to a large clearing only a few minutes way. Murphy climbed in the chopper with Lester's stretcher. The National Guard medic-in-training examined Murphy's jar with disbelief but was hesitant to tamper with it, other than hooking up a small vacuum pump. Glen stayed behind with Harry due to a lack of space, which worked out nicely for Glen.

Three hours later Glen drove the team into Petersville. A crowd lined the street as the story had been 'breaking news' on every radio and TV station in the state. Murphy had ample opportunity to spin the situation in the chopper and at the hospital and managed to contact Glen in Petersville. He was able to follow her story perfectly; luckily, since Channel 2 had rushed camera crews to the town — catching Glen in all his mushing glory — and to Providence Hospital, where Lester was undergoing surgery but Murphy was able to make a statement.

Later that evening Glen and Murphy brought Bennie to meet Lester in his hospital room. Lester smiled when they walked in.

"Thanks," was all Lester could say.

Bennie looked curiously at the bandages Lester sported. He waved a copy of the ADN.

"Lester, you made the front page," he said. Lester almost grabbed the paper before Glen got it. **Candidate Saves Local Pilot**, the headline said. There was indeed a picture of Lester with the makeshift chest pump. However, the picture on top of the fold showed a grinning Glen Wilson wielding a whip and driving the dog team. The picture was cropped so you couldn't tell he was driving a wagon instead of a sled.

"I'd pay good money to watch Swifte's face when he sees this. I'm a fucking superhero. Musher Wilson, Alaskan God-Warrior of the North."

"Oh Christ, here we go," Murphy said, resigned. "We'll never get him to shut up now."

A man sits with a pretty girl for an hour and it seems shorter than a minute. But tell that same man to sit on a hot stove for a minute, it is longer than any hour. That's relativity.

- Albert Einstein

CHAPTER 11

Bennie

Bennie waited at the bus stop. He saw Emma come out of the private school. Her face brightened when she saw him. Without a word, he handed her a macaroon. She touched his lip. It hurt, but he was stoic. They sat and watched traffic stream by and nibbled their cookies. Bennie was hyper-aware of the square inch where their hips lightly touched. He wasn't sure what he was feeling but he liked it. She made him feel clumsy and tongue-tied. They finished their cookies and Emma brushed some stray coconut off his sweatshirt.

"You'd better go before Ira comes." Bennie shook his head no. "He's mean," Emma continued.

"Is he your boyfriend?" Bennie asked.

"No, I hate Ira and I don't have a boyfriend. Besides, I'm only 13 and my dad says I'm too young."

Ira and his friend rolled up. Bennie stood and faced him.

"Hey Sambo, I told you to stay away from Emma," Ira said belligerently.

"Stop it," Emma said plaintively.

Bennie saw Ira's eyes flick and he slid to his right just in time. Ira's friend was swinging his skateboard in a wide arc. It breezed by Bennie's head and slammed into Ira's face. Bennie turned and gave a roundhouse kick to Ira's friend's hip joint. Ira and his friend fell to the sidewalk. Bennie took a defensive crouch and watched as the boys simultaneously crab-walked away from him. Both struggled to their feet. Ira's nose was bleeding. Bennie rolled the scooter toward them and they took it and ran up the street.

"Are you okay?" Emma asked.

Bennie's knees were weak and he felt shaky. "I'm fine, they didn't touch me," he said as he watched the boys disappear around the corner of the next block. "Do you have to get home right away?" he asked.

"Not really," she replied. "Why?"

"I want to introduce you to my friends."

"Okay."

They walked toward the hotel. As they walked, their hands brushed together and Bennie felt the sidewalk sway with each contact. They arrived at the Marriott and the bellboy opened the door for them and said "Hey Bennie."

"Hey back at ya, Bobbie," Bennie replied.

"Do you live here?" Emma asked as he punched the elevator button.

"Yes, for now," Bennie replied.

The door to the master suite was propped open with a telephone book. Bennie led Emma inside. Glen saw them first and shoved the Alaska Daily News in Bennie's face.

"Look Bennie, I'm a hero."

Bennie looked at the picture in the paper then at Glen. Glen wore a bandage on his head.

"Is the bandage real?"

"Yes, it's real. Why does everyone think everything is fake around here? The damn wings came off the plane, for cripe's sake. We crashed in the mountains and I saved our asses. No shit." He noticed Emma. He crouched in front of her. "Have you ever met a real super-hero before?" he asked.

"My dad is a Chief," she replied.

"Whatever you say, little girl. Who are you?"

Elke was applying fresh cotton pads and tape on Murphy's arm. They looked up and noticed Bennie's guest. They came over and led Emma to a couch.

"Who are you, dear?" Elke asked.

"I'm..."

"You're just the cutest little thing, isn't she sweet?" Elke turned to ask Murphy. Glen rolled his eyes. "Let me take your parka, dear."

"What did she say her name is?" Murphy asked.

"I'm..."

"She hasn't said yet. She looks like a perfect little native girl."

"Can we get back to what we're supposed to be doing here, folks? We need to figure out what a super-hero does next. Let's focus, we have an election to win."

"What are you running for?" Emma asked.

Glen sat on the coffee table in front of her and pushed Elke and Murphy apart so he could see her. "I'm running for US Congress and I want to be your state representative." He tapped the newspaper. "This photograph is going to bump us two points. All we have to do is figure out how to milk this for a few more days."

"You can't beat Sanders."

"Wait a minute. Who are you and how do you know I can't beat Sanders?"

"My name is Emma and I hear my dad and my uncles talk about politics all the time. My dad says no one can beat Sanders."

"Who is your dad? Does he know anything about politics?"

"My dad is Chief Eddie. He talks to all the politicians."

"What does he say about Patterson?"

"He says the lesbo doesn't have a chance."

Glen got up and tossed his paper onto the table. "Who is this kid! Did you bring a spy up here, Bennie? What happened to the kids of the world? She should be playing with her Barbies, not spying and eavesdropping on her Uncles."

"Barbie represents oppression. She makes men think of women as objects and presents an impossible idealized figure to drive girls into bulimia, anorexia and despair. Barbie is evil."

"A miniature feminist! Just what we need around here." Glen finally noticed Bennie's wounds. "What happened to you, kid? I leave town for a couple of days and you're getting the crap beat out of you and hanging around with Alice Paul[15]. This is too much, I need to get some sleep." He stomped out of the room.

"Can I get you something, dear?" Elke asked Emma.

"I would love to have a spring water if you have some."

"Absolutely, I'll be right back."

Murphy cupped Bennie's chin and tilted his face up so she could see his lip. "Are you okay?" she asked.

Bennie nodded. "I figured it out," he said.

"Where did you meet your friend?"

"Out on Spenard by the bakery. She knows the word 'existential'."

Murphy nodded knowingly. "I see," she said. "Maybe we can offer her a job helping out around here." Bennie threw his arms around Murphy's neck. After a moment, Murphy got over the small shock and patted him on the back.

"That would be perfect," he whispered into her ear.

Murphy turned to Emma. "Well young lady, we could use some help around here answering phones and stuffing envelopes. Can you help us out after school?"

---

[15] Alice Paul, (1885-1977) was a pioneering American feminist.

"Oh, I'd love that. My dad and mom don't get home until six, usually I just watch TV and that would be great, thank you."

"I'll drive you home and ask your parents. It sounds like I should meet your father anyway. I'll bring the car around and meet you out front in five?"

Bennie nodded.

Elke came back in and handed Emma a bottled water. "I can't get over how cute you are with those braids. You're like a little Indian doll. I think a turquoise fingernail paint would go great with your brown eyes. The boys are going to be fighting over you when you get a little older." She glanced at Bennie's swollen lip. "If they aren't already."

Bennie took Emma's hand and helped her from the couch.

"We have to get Emma home," he said.

"You come by later and I'll show you how to weave some Bavarian braids into your hair, dear."

Emma nodded. Bennie held the door open for her and they left. Glen came back in.

"They're so cute." Elke said dreamily.

Glen snapped his fingers. "I need my I-T[16] man sharp, no distractions allowed. We have to focus."

"Too late, I think," Elke whispered to herself.

Glen and Murphy

"In News Radio 1250 traffic news, there is a moose on the Old Seward Highway near Huffman Street, you're going to want to watch for that. You don't want to wear those antlers on your SUV. I'm Dave Tollen and I'm visiting with congressional candidate Glen Wilson, who has joined us in the studio. Mr. Wilson, welcome to the Tollen show on 1250 KENA."

"Thank you Dave, I'm pleased to be with you."

"First of all, you look like you've been through the wringer."

"I sure have, Dave. I've been traveling around the state spreading my message and we had a bit of a mishap up in the mountains."

"I think mishap is a misnomer. I have yesterday's copy of the ADN. It says that you saved the pilot's life."

"We don't want to get too carried away with all that. If anything, I'd say the dogs are the real heroes, aren't they magnificent?"

---

[16] Information Technology

"You're right, that is a fine looking team."

"I'm just thankful the pilot's going to be alright. My assistant and I are banged up a little, but we'll be fine. There is nothing that will slow us down when it comes to taking our campaign to the good people of Alaska."

Murphy was visible through the broadcast booth glass. At the word assistant, she looked up and gave Glen a blank look, then returned her attention to the Guns and Ammo magazine she was skimming.

"Very well," Tollen said. "Let's talk a minute about your political party, the Democratic Majority. You've decided to start your own organization instead of tying up with the other parties?"

"I don't want to rule out working with the more established parties if they can accept my platform of support for social programs in a fiscally responsible manner. I can't really accept the callous treatment of minorities and the elderly at the hands of the Republicans and I can't accept the free-spending pork-barrel fiscal policies of the Democrats, so I felt forced to start a new party that would represent the hard-working Alaskans that are left out of the current party discourse. If the R's or D's care to get on my winning team, then I'll listen, I don't want to rule out a future alliance."

"I'm having a little trouble locating you on the political spectrum. Would you describe your philosophy as conservative, liberal, or libertarian, or what exactly?"

"That is an outstanding question. You're right, we're a little hard to locate on the political map. I reject the way the battle lines are drawn. We're not in the conservative camp because I want to make sure the government stays out of my bedroom, I'm not in the liberal camp because I want to make sure the government dips into my wallet as little as possible, and I'm not in the libertarian camp because I don't want school kids to have automatic weapons or free access to crack and heroin."

"That's an unfair way to characterize the Libertarians..."

"You're probably right. I'm not a libertarian, so I'll leave it to them to define and explain their policies. I'm representing my Democratic Majority party and I suppose I should stick to presenting our platform and our core beliefs."

"How about if I run down a list of issues and get your take on each of them?"

"Sure."

"Social Security?"

"We've made a contract with our seniors that must be honored as one of our top priorities. I'm for reasonable cost of living adjustments and removing the taxation of these benefits."

"A state income tax?"

"That is a state, not a national issue, but my opinion is that Permanent Fund assets can be managed in a more rational way. I don't think a state income tax is needed. We can fill our budget gaps with cost controls and more aggressive fund management."

"Subsistence hunting and fishing?"

"One of the tenets of our great country is that all are created with equal rights. I support subsistence hunting and fishing, but I don't think this policy should apply only to our friends in the Native American community."

"Drilling in Arctic National Wildlife Refuge?"

"Our caribou herds are currently in great shape due to the stewardship of the environmental groups and their work with the energy industry. I think that high technology, in partnership with the habitat preservation groups, can allow us to drill in a responsible manner. I don't see this as a win-lose situation. With intelligent cooperation, I think the people of Alaska can win, the energy consumers of our nation can win, and the wildlife of the great northern wilderness can also win."

"How about prescription drug benefits for retired folks?"

"Generally I'm against expensive government programs, but cost-effective assistance to distressed groups, like our senior citizens, makes sense to me. I have not looked at all the proposed programs, but I am in favor of putting our heads together and defining a prescription drug benefit program that helps those who need it but doesn't over-burden the long-suffering taxpayer."

"Thank you. I'm speaking with Glen Wilson, candidate for US Congress. We're going to take a break, then come back and take your calls for Glen Wilson."

Tollen took off his headphones and gestured at the darkened on-air lamp.

"You're pretty smooth."

"Thank you."

"Do you really believe this stuff or are you just trying to win the election? It seems like you're for everything. It certainly sounds good, but how can you promise the voters all the goodies they want and lower taxes at the same time?"

Murphy sat up on her stool and looked intently at Tollen. Glen waved at her to relax.

"I'm in this race to win."

"I don't appreciate your dumping on the Libertarians. Personally, I lean that way."

"I don't mean any offense, but regardless of how many views we hold in common, aligning with them is the kiss of death. The Losertarians[17] are not even getting one percent of the national presidential vote anymore."

"You can't be serious about your chances. The Republicans have this state sewn up unless Sanders is found in bed with a mountain goat or something."

"You're right, that might do it, thanks for the suggestion."

At that, Tollen gave Glen a puzzled look. The show producer gave him a sign through the control room glass. Tollen put his headphones back on and watched for the on-air light to illuminate.

"Welcome back to the Dave Tollen show. I'm speaking with Glen Wilson, Congressional hopeful for the coming election. Shall we take some calls from our listening audience, Glen?"

"I'd be delighted."

"Phil is calling in from Ocean View. What is your question for Mister Wilson please?"

"Hi Dave. Hi Mister Wilson. Can you tell me your views on Japanese drift nets?"

"Hi Phil, thanks for that question. When I was in my 20's, I spent a summer on an Alaskan fishing boat, so I certainly understand how hard this job can be. I have immense respect for the fishery workers and their families. To address your question, if it were up to me, I'd extend our territorial waters to 400 miles and use our submarines to tear up and remove the illegal nets. Due to the partisan political atmosphere in DC, this isn't something I can promise, but it would certainly be something high on my list of things to do for the good folks of Alaska."

Tollen looked at Glen with horror. "Wouldn't that be viewed as an act of war by the world community?" he asked.

"We're the world's last superpower, what good does it do us if we're not willing to exercise that power in the interest of our citizens?"

"All right, I guess, though that seems a bit extreme to me. Let's go to Zora who is calling on her cell phone from Eagle River. Go ahead Zora."

"Hi Dave, how are you? Oh, I forgot I'm not supposed to ask that. Uh, Wilson, aren't you a carpetbagger? You're not from Alaska, what gives you the right to come up here and enter our politics?"

---

[17] Rude name coined by social commentator and radio talk show host Michael Medved to describe members of the Libertarian Party.

"That's a great question, Zora. I think there are two parts I'd like to talk about. First of all, I have the right as a United States citizen and current resident to run for office up here. The secondary part of your question is the more interesting one, I think. I was born in Oregon and lived most recently in Washington State. Why am I running in Alaska? If you'll accept a flippant answer, I wanted to move north and the Canadians wouldn't have me." Tollen chuckled. "But seriously, I felt a strong need to get away from the corruption and pollution of the cities down south. I'm here for the same reason you are, because this is the last frontier and I want to build a life for myself where the air is clean and the people are real. I believe I have good plans and policies. If the voters don't like my message and my vision for Alaska, then they certainly have the right to vote for one of the other candidates. I think that's the best answer for whether I should run for office in Alaska, let's let the voters decide."

"Let's hear from Sammy calling in from Palmer. Sammy, what is your question for Glen Wilson, Democratic Majority party nominee for US Congress?"

"I like most of the things you're saying, Mister Wilson. Can you comment about your competitors?"

"Sure, Sammy. Bill Sanders is a strong candidate for the Republicans. I know he has something like 35% support in our polling, he's going to be tough to beat. That said, I wonder how well his attempts to gut social security and his support of tax cuts for the rich will resonate with voters as we get closer to the elections in November. We'll just have to get our message out and see what happens."

"What about Julia Patterson?"

"Julia is a bit too fond of granola and hemp for my taste. If you'll forgive me for being blunt, I don't think her socialist message is the right one for Alaska. Honestly, if you'll allow a politician to use such a word, it doesn't matter what I think, the voters will decide which agenda and vision of the future to support."

"Let's go over to Chet in Soldotna. What's on your mind, Chet?"

"The big oil and timber companies have banned hemp because it doesn't line their pockets with money. Hemp is the world's strongest fiber, you can make rope and clothes and paper out of it. It takes a tree 20 years to grow, you can grow a hemp plant in a couple of months. Hitler had a car that was made of hemp and used hemp fuel, it got 200 miles per gallon."

"Chet is one of our regulars. Do you have a question for our candidate?"

201

"Yeah, what's this fascist going to do about the hemp prohibition that is killing our country? The original Old Glory was made of hemp."

"Where do you fall on the hemp situation, Mister Wilson?" Tollen asked.

"I think Chet has been smoking a bit too much of his rope. I'm just kidding. If Chet's question is whether I think elementary school kids should be able to smoke dope, then the answer is absolutely not. If Chet is asking if I support decriminalization and regulation of marijuana, then the answer is yes. I would be a poor politician if I allowed a perfectly good source of tax dollars to get by me. If Chet is asking if I believe that free use of hemp fiber is a wonder that will turn the world into an earthly paradise, then I'd say: nope."

"I'm wearing hemp boxer shorts!" Chet interjected.

"That's nice Chet. Your bong is going out, you'd better run," Glen said dryly. Tollen chuckled.

"That's about all the time we have today. Do you want to leave our listeners with any parting thoughts, Mister Wilson?"

"Yes, thank you, Dave. In November, the voters will have a choice to make. They can choose to go backwards into failed policies or they can put their check by my name and help direct Alaska into the future. I'm confident the voters will make the right choice and I would like to thank each and every one of them in advance."

"Thank you. That was Glen Wilson, he's running for Congress on the Democratic Majority ticket. When we come back from the break, we'll be speaking with Arnie Platt who will demonstrate his championship duck calls. We'll be right quack, I mean back."

Tollen took off his headphones. He shook Glen's hand.

"Please excuse me, I have to pee bad. Thanks for coming by, come see us closer to the election?"

"You can count on it," Glen replied. Tollen walked away quickly. Glen nodded at the duck call guy. He picked up one of the calls.

"This is nice, can I have one?" Glen asked.

"That one is cocobola. You can have one of the plastic ones." Arnie said.

Glen shrugged and held the door for Murphy. As they walked down the hallway together, Glen was squawking with his new toy.

"Tollen didn't use any of our callers," Murphy said, grimacing at the racket.

"I think it went alright, we didn't need them."

"I guess. That hemp guy was a character."

"See if you can find me some hemp underwear, will you? We can silkscreen my name on them and win the doper vote."

"No."

"What happened to your sense of humor, Murphy? Was that part of your brain injured in the plane crash?"

"Bite me. Move your ass, we have a speech to give to an assembly at the Chinook Elementary school in twenty minutes."

"Good, I'll show them my duck call."

"No you won't, give me that thing," she said, holding out her hand.

Glen handed it over with a disgusted look on his face.

Holly

That which passed for a bar in Birchwood was an old cabin converted from a 1930-something homestead into a tavern with neon beer logos in the windows and a hand-painted sign that did little to mask its decrepit ancestry. To Holly, the whole area felt remote and unsettled — the road ahead was as deserted and empty as the view in her mirrors. The rustic old bar was the only man-made structure visible in any direction. The sign said draft beer was available and it didn't look like a place that would question her out-of-state ID, so she decided to stop.

She braked, then jammed the GMC in reverse, chirping the tires and roaring backwards into the gravel and mud parking lot. A half-dozen gunk-splattered pickups were carelessly parked in more or less random formations.

Holly maneuvered neatly between the other trucks — still in reverse — and slid to a stop near the door with the truck's front end aimed at the road for a quick exit. Just in case. She hopped to the ground, leaving the key in the ignition, and — after a closer look at the place — reached under the seat and tucked her .45 into an inner coat pocket. It didn't fit well and the butt jabbed her in the boob, but she felt better having it there. If she needed a weapon it wouldn't do to have the gun sitting out in the truck.

As she stepped onto the weathered wooden porch she heard some god-awful country or western or hillbilly music from inside and almost turned around on the spot, but now she'd worked herself into the mood for a beer and she didn't recall seeing any other likely places on the trip up from Anchorage. Maybe she could pick up a couple of cold ones to go.

The heavy wooden door didn't seem to have a doorknob or handle and didn't budge when she pushed. She was looking around for another entrance — feeling slightly stupid and about ready to give up on the whole idea — when the door opened from the inside. A guy stuck his head through the doorway and grinned at her. He looked to be about her age, tall with curly black hair and dimples, but dressed in dirty bib overalls and missing a tooth or two. He held the door open and winked at her, grinning cheerfully.

"Howdy!" he said. "This here door's kinda tricky, ain't it? Saw you pull in, that was some slick driving. You a pool player? We don't get many women in here. Except for Kirby's wife and she don't shoot pool and there is some argument about whether she's actually female, if you catch my drift. You coming in? You can come in. We don't bite. We're just playing a little —"

"PAUL!" A voice bellowed from inside the bar. "Would you shut the hell up!" The grin on the curly-haired guy wilted. He stood back, abashed, and let Holly pass through the doorway.

"I'm Paul," he confided, while standing beside her as her eyes adjusted to the dimly-lighted and smoke-filled room. "That's my buddy Hank over there at the bar, Bob and Bob, that's Big Bob and Little Bob, they got the table right now, you gotta put a quarter up to challenge, Kirby he owns the place, what's your name?" Holly eyes were adjusted well enough to see the guy he'd called Hank drop his head to the bar and pretend to pound it several times. The scarred wooden bar started a few feet from the door and ran the length of the room. The pool table was adorned with green felt that was worn through to bare wood in places. A pair of dart boards and a gawdy jukebox filled with 45 RPM records completed the entertainment options. Hank stood up and walked over to where Paul and Holly stood. He gave Holly a friendly smile and held out his hand.

"Hi, I'm Hank. You gotta forgive my friend as we haven't seen a real woman in here for a while," he tossed the last part over his shoulder and Paul waved a hand in dismissal, "since somebody stole the Bud Girls calendar." Holly rewarded Hank with a smile and reached over to shake the proffered hand. Though his grasp was gentle his hand was rough and calloused, hardened by work; she could sense the controlled strength and felt a faint stir of interest, the first genuine little itch-that-needs-occasional-scratching she'd experienced in some time. She checked him out as he led her to the bar; a six-footer, dirty blonde with a trimmed beard and blue eyes — not bad looking, actually. Paul the Talking Fool, as Holly thought of him, trailed along, suddenly subdued.

Kirby, the Bartender-Owner-Proprietor, set a thick mug of a dark, golden beer on the counter and pushed it towards Holly.

"I'd say the odds of you buying your own drinks tonight would be slim-to-none," he observed.

He looked pointedly at the two men who flanked her at the bar. Paul scrambled to dig his wallet from a rear pocket but Hank quickly slipped a five dollar bill out of his shirt pocket and slapped it on the bar with a grin. Paul stood awkwardly with his wallet in hand, then pulled a ten dollar bill free and waved it at Kirby.

"Well, I've got the next one, I sure do. Maybe the next two. That's Alaskan Amber you're drinking there, the best beer in the world. I got paid yesterday and this was a good week for me. Monday I worked overtime, and Tuesday we started early —"

"So!" Kirby shouted, making Holly jump, "you guys want to shut up for a minute? The poor girl hasn't been able to squeeze a word out since she got here and probably thinks we're a bunch of lunatics." He smiled at Holly in a fatherly way. He was easily old enough to be her father, too. But Holly didn't let that fool her; she'd met a few old guys who were just as randy as the young studs, if not more so, and behind the smile this old guy's eyes were plenty lively as they scanned her from top to bottom. He rested his elbows on the bar and leaned closer. Holly caught a whiff of hard liquor on his breath. "What brings you into my humble establishment, Miss...?"

"Lizzie," Holly replied. Hank and Paul both nodded and made appreciative sounds, as if she'd just provided the Meaning of Life. "Lizzie Reed, from... down south."

Kirby nodded sagely. "Ahhh, from the Lower 48 then. Well, how do you like Alaska so far, Lizzie?" he asked as he started wiping the counter with a filthy rag, for the first time in quite a while, as it looked. She decided they could wait while she took a long pull off her beer. She wiped the rich foam off her upper lip with a sigh. She belched, a petite little burp, and the men chuckled.

"ExCUSE me," she said. "My goodness." She waved a hand in front of her face, daintily. Holly wished she could blush on demand, that would be useful. She cleared her throat and leaned back to more easily address all three men at once. "I just LOVE Alaska," she gushed. "It's so untamed and wild, and... lawless." The two younger men nodded enthusiastically — she could've spoken Latin to them with the same result — but the more-alert Kirby blinked a few times in response. Holly backpedaled. "I don't mean lawless in a bad way, of course. I mean there's such freedom here. It's like, you guys are so rugged and independent." She took another long pull at her beer. It was achingly cold. She took her time and checked the room while she drank. Other than the guys shooting pool there were a couple of biker types hunched over a table by the jukebox. All were staring at her.

"Did you know the Eskimos have 610 words for snow?" Paul asked.

"We call them Inuits now, asshole, do you want the lady to think you're ignorant?" Hank asked while slapping Paul with his hat.

"I ain't ignorant, I've been to California and you ain't even been south of Ketchikan your whole life," Paul sputtered.

Holly decided she needed some elbow room. She slapped the empty mug on the bar and pulled out her .45. She dropped it next to the mug and looked pointedly at Kirby. "The amber is okay, I guess, but I'd rather have Bud Light, if you please."

Kirby's eyes flicked to the gun as Paul and Hank stepped one-half-step back.

"I don't have it on tap, is long-neck alright?"

Holly nodded. Kirby did a practiced spin, a flip of the cooler handle, an extraction of the beer and completed the twirl while twisting off the bottle cap. He set the vaporous Bud next to Holly's mug with a flourish. Holly pushed the mug away and drained half the bottle with a single draught.

"Nice piece," Kirby observed. "Springfield?" Holly nodded. Kirby moved some dusty bottles so Holly could read a wooden sign on the wall. **An armed society is a polite society**, it said. "Heinlein."

"Who?" Holly asked.

"Stranger in a Strange Land? The Moon is a Harsh Mistress? Have Space Suit—Will Travel?"

Holly shook her head.

"Starship Troopers?"

A flood of recognition. "Yes! That was a great movie. Which character did Heinlein play? Sergeant Zim?"

"Shit," Kirby muttered under his breath as he placed a fresh Bud Light in front of her.

"We got squirrels out back," Paul mentioned.

Holly turned to him. "I'm curious. Why do you think I would even be microscopically interested in squirrels?"

Paul was uncomfortable. "Uh —, I just thought you might wanna shoot at them with your pistol."

Holly was able to hold her stern expression for a few seconds before she burst out laughing. "Let's go see what you have."

There was a rough-cut door at the back of the bar. The foursome pushed through and startled a large man pissing into a bush. The man glanced back at them but finished his business. He took three vigorous shakes, stuffed in his unit and casually rebuttoned his jeans. He nodded at them before wandering out of sight behind the building.

"Some people just aren't comfortable pissing indoors," Kirby commented.

The view from the back of the bar was mostly brambles and evergreens. The lot was cleared for about 100 yards. It took a few moments for them to appear, but indeed there were several squirrels chattering and foraging.

"What's back there?" Holly asked.

"Just Alaska. A whole lot of nothing." Kirby replied.

"I can't hit nothing at that range with my pistol."

Kirby walked back inside and reappeared with a bolt-action .222 Remington with a scope. He handed it to her with a handful of cartridges. "Try this," he said. Holly worked the bolt and loaded a round. With the scope, it looked like she could reach out and touch the squirrels. She squeezed off a round and a squirrel flew off a tree and disappeared in the ground cover. At this range, the other squirrels froze when she fired but did not flee. Seven shots and seven dead rodents. Holly shrugged.

"Okay, that was fun, I guess," she said. She handed the rifle to Kirby. Paul and Hank watched her with their mouths open and wondered whether this little girl could cook.

"I have a .600 Nitro Express Double, if you want to try something with a little more punch. It will kick you into the next time zone."

"Let's see it," Holly said.

Kirby disappeared inside and came back out a few minutes later with a huge rifle. It broke open in the middle like a shotgun and had a cavernous bore. Holly felt weak at the knees. To her core, she felt like bigger is better and too much isn't ever enough.

"Holy shit," she said. Kirby dropped a two-pound cartridge in her palm. Holly weighed it and whistled through her teeth.

"Obviously, this thing is for looking, not for shooting," Kirby said.

"Will it fire both barrels at once?"

"Technically."

"Let's do it," Holly said flatly. Kirby was smart, but he didn't have the will to say no. He passed out foam earplugs and stuffed some bar towels under his jacket to make a large pad. He broke open the rifle and Holly loaded the chamber. She held out her hand and Kirby gave her another cartridge. She noticed his hand was shaking slightly. He jammed the weapon against his shoulder and Holly came around underneath to peer over the barrel. She leaned back into his bulk. Her fingers caressed the trigger. Kirby pulled back the hammers. Holly aimed and held her breath. Paul and Hank stood with their index fingers pressing in their earplugs.

"Wait a minute," she said. She unwound herself from around the cannon. Kirby breathed a sigh of relief.

"Thank God," he said. "The last time I fired this thing it about killed me. This is nothing to mess with. You scared me."

"We're going to fire it, I just want something more fun to shoot at than a tree." She led them back into the bar. She watched the pool players. Holly was not a great player, but there was little else to do back in the Institute of Mental Health. Many days she spent 8-10 hours at the table trying to win Jello-with-whipped-topping desserts from the other inmates. By the end of her tenure, she was eating 10 or 12 of these desserts every day. She never got tired of them because they tasted like victory. She figured she could beat any man in the place. Sipping a fresh beer, she thought about what she might offer in wager. That was easy.

"Listen up!" she shouted. "I want to play a game of pool. The man that can beat me can kiss my boob for ten seconds."

"Which one?" one of the biker-types asked, smirking.

"The left one," she replied without hesitation. All the men in the bar had their hands raised and were waving for attention. "However, if you lose, you're going to let me shoot your truck with Kirby's pea-shooter. Any takers?"

They dropped their hands and looked at each other considering the odds.

"I just bought an F350, I'm not taking that chance," Big Bob muttered as he threw down his cue.

"I'll do it," Little Bob said. Little Bob was the bigger Bob; his belly jutted over his belt like a tidal wave. He wore a Sturgis South Dakota t-shirt and scuffed leather boots.

"Okay Bob, I'll let you break," Holly said. She looked over the selection of cues and picked one that was mostly straight. She chalked the tip carefully as she watched Bob line up his shot. The ball formation exploded and Bob sank two solids and a stripe. He wore a small smile as he stroked in an easy shot into the side pocket. The ball eased into position for another easy side pocket shot. His next shot was harder, the best choice was a moderately difficult bank shot that just missed. However, he left the cue ball flush against the rail. Holly did not have a good shot at anything, but she delicately made a double banker that sank one and left her with a string of easy ones to make. She called and made the 9-ball shot to the middle pocket and the game was over. Little Bob glared at his three lonely balls resting on the table and smashed his cue against the wall. "Crap," he spat.

The patrons of the bar filed into the parking lot.

"Which one is yours, Little Bob," Holly asked sweetly.

He pointed at a classic old restored Chevy pickup. It was chopped with mag wheels and custom-chromed exhaust. The pretty paint job was something like teal. He shot Holly the finger and walked back in the bar. Holly stuffed in her earplugs and tugged Kirby into position as he raised the gun. Holly leaned against him and peered over the barrels. Wearing a small evil smile, she squinted and massaged the trigger. She increased the pressure until the world split open. Kirby fell back and slid almost a yard. Holly was tangled up on top of him and she struggled to regain her feet.

Big Bob was fuming. "You goddam bitch!" The rounds had pierced the old Chevy just behind the firewall. The rounds and shrapnel ripped into the side of the F350. It was sitting on a flat tire with oil and antifreeze pooling underneath it. Both trucks were beyond repair.

"That will teach you to be such a coward," Holly whispered to him as she blew him a kiss.

"At least I'll be seeing those titties," Big Bob shouted as he stalked her.

Holly produced her .45 and pointed it at him.

"I don't think so," she said. "I want to thank everyone for the beer and the fun," she said to the stunned observers. "Hi-ho Silver, I'm away."

She started her GMC and spewed gravel as she popped the clutch and slewed, laughing, back onto the highway.

Glen and Chief Eddie

Glen peeked at the slip of paper in his hand and checked the number on the house before rapping firmly on the door. While he waited he did a quick survey of the street to make sure nobody had followed him; it was becoming increasingly difficult to sneak around without somebody, usually Murphy, catching him. But this particular mission didn't involve sexual release or even a late night back street prowl to clear his head — his I-T man was being distracted and that was unacceptable. Glen was fully aware of how distractions could foul things up; being somewhat distractible himself he couldn't allow those he depended upon for checks and balances to flake out and lose focus. The door opened and Glen's eyes widened in surprise.

The house sat well back from the curb in an upscale neighborhood off Turnagain Arm. The large circular driveway was clean, the yard landscaped, and the house was a solid two-story affair with an overhanging deck and a huge bay window in front. Not exactly what Glen had expected, and the tall, middle-aged Eskimo who opened the door, wearing Dockers, a white dress shirt with a loosened tie and a twinkle in his eye, further shattered Glen's expectations.

They regarded each solemnly for a moment, then Glen reflexively thrust out his hand. The gentleman gave it a friendly shake and looked Glen over. He released Glen's hand and crossed his arms, waiting patiently for Glen to make his pitch with a trace of a smile creasing his face as Glen's discomfort grew.

"Hi, Chief?" Glen tried a grin. "I, uh, think we have a mutual concern I'd like to talk to you about." He offered his hand again. "Glen Wilson, candidate for Congress." The Chief's smile slipped a notch and he glanced at Glen's outstretched hand. He gave it quick, perfunctory shake and stepped aside, indicating Glen could step inside.

"Sure, Mr. Wilson. Please come in." Glen could hear resignation in his voice and realized candidates looking for endorsements from the Native community probably bombarded the guy. Not that Glen would mind an endorsement, but that wasn't a priority at the moment. He followed the Chief through a tiled foyer and past a large living room. Glen had few seconds to register a brightly-lit room decorated with Native artifacts and charcoal drawings. The Chief stopped at the entrance to another room and motioned for Glen to enter. This room was smaller and the lighting was less intense. Books lined one wall from floor to ceiling in a jumble of disorder; Glen realized that these books were not for show for they were clearly read and referenced. They were adorned with sticky notes as bookmarks.

A modest but sturdy desk faced a window that overlooked the dark and silty waters of Turnagain Arm. A phone and fax machine were the only modern accouterments. An old leather couch, fronted by a dusty wooden table covered with another stack of books, was the room's only other furniture. Brass-and-glass lamps that mimicked turn-of-the-century gas fixtures graced the corners of the room and an old banker-style lamp sat on the desk, providing a warm, intimate atmosphere enhanced by the flickering light of a gas fireplace.

"Very nice," Glen said as he inspected the room. He walked to the window to check the view and was rewarded by the sight of a full moon dancing on the racing tide of Turnagain Arm. "Looks like a river," he noted. The Chief moved to stand beside him.

"We have a forty foot tide here, Mr. Wilson. But as an Alaskan congressional candidate you surely know all about that." Glen turned to look directly at the Chief.

"I'm a relative newcomer to the great state of Alaska, sir, but —"

"Yes, I know," the Chief broke in, "political concerns consume a great deal of my time, Mr. Wilson." He fixed Glen with a steely stare. "Unfortunately," he added.

Glen stared back at the older man and noted the straight shoulders and posture. *Crap, ex-military. Undoubtedly an Officer, too.*

"While Native Alaskan issues are of course a primary concern with our campaign, I'm here on a personal matter," Glen said. After a long moment he added, "Sir." He refused to break eye contact. The Chief blinked first.

"Okay," he said, indicating the worn sofa. "Have a seat, Mr. Wilson."

"Please call me Glen." Glen crossed to the couch and seated himself at one end. "You have a daughter, I understand?" The Chief, indeed an ex-Marine Corps Colonel, frowned at the unexpected tangent.

"Several, Mister... Glen," he replied. "Why do you ask?"

Glen leaned forward.

"I have a young employee, more of a protégé actually, who seems to have become enamored of your Emma, sir." The Chief raised his eyebrows and moved to sit on the other end of the couch.

"You can cut the 'sir' as friends and enemies alike call me Eddie. Chief Eddie, actually, but I think we can dispense with the 'Chief' while we're conversing here in private." He offered Glen a wry grin that quickly faded to concern. "I consider Emma a bit young to be involved with boys, Glen. Are you sure you've got the right family?" Glen nodded.

"One thing we're very good at is research, sir... Eddie." Glen felt uncomfortable calling the man 'Eddie'. He didn't look anything like the several 'Eddies' Glen had known in his lifetime. "It's definitely *your* Emma that's distracting *our* Bennie."

"Distracting?" Eddie's brow wrinkled. "That's an interesting choice of words, Glen."

"Bennie is an unusual boy, Eddie. Literally a genius, actually. Brilliant at what he does, and what he does is handle all the information flow and computer modeling for our campaign, a 24-7 job, so you can understand our natural concern."

Chief Eddie stood and walked to the wall behind the door. He pulled a section of paneling to one side and revealed a rack of tilted wine bottles, crystal glasses and a small refrigerator.

"Alcoholism is the bane of my people, Glen." He poured a stiff measure from an unmarked bottle into a large shot glass. "Luckily, I escaped that particular curse." He set the glass down and picked up another. "You look like a Scotch man, Glen." He filled it without waiting for a reply and returned with both glasses, handing one to Glen, who nodded appreciatively. The two men made small talk for a few minutes; Glen rose and inspected the Chief's library, which ranged from an extensive collection of Alaskana to contemporary fiction. Not crap either, some Nelson DeMille, early Gary Jennings and even a well-thumbed copy of Nabokov's Lolita.

Both men freshened their drinks several times and Glen began to feel at ease and relaxed for the first time in days. Eventually Eddie returned to the couch and motioned for Glen to join him. The Chief politely waited for Glen to take a sip of his drink before returning to the awkward subject of Emma and Bennie.

"When discussing Bennie you say 'we' and 'our', is that a figure of speech or do others share your concern?" he asked.

Glen replied immediately. "Oh yes, we're all very worried about this, there's major concern across the board —"

"Because it seems odd that you would handle something like this personally," Eddie interjected before Glen could get fully wound up. "Generally it's some flunky that comes around to do the dirty work."

"Okay, Eddie. Look, the other parties happen to be a couple of women who think the kids are just too cute for words, you know what I mean?" Eddie grinned briefly at that, then set his glass on the table.

"How old is Bennie?" he asked. Glen considered his answer.

"Chronologically he's twelve, intellectually he's much older, emotionally — I have no idea."

"So he's a nerd," the Chief observed dryly. Glen felt slightly stung.

"Hey, Chief. This kid's got college degrees, open offers from major corporations, and an IQ in the top —"

"So he's a super-nerd, mega-nerd, ultra-nerd, uber-nerd..." Eddie broke in, "nerd, nerd, nerd." Glen drained half his glass and swirled the remainder.

"You always interrupt people like this, or is it just me?"

Eddie looked startled. "Sorry, bad habit. Drove my last wife nuts," he confessed, sipping his drink.

"How's the current wife feel about it?" Glen asked with a grin. Eddie coughed on his whiskey.

"She gives me hell for it." He rose and crossed to the wet bar, returning with the bottle of Scotch. He filled Glen's glass and then his own. "You married, Glen?"

"Not at the moment, but I've been there. Left to see the world."

"Any kids," Eddie asked, then smiled slyly, "that you know of?" It was Glen's turn to cough, as the remark caught him mid-drink. He regained his composure and considered Eddie with appreciation.

"You're a smart man, Ed. But I'm running for office here, so the answer is no, without qualification." They grinned at each other and lifted their glasses in a silent toast, savoring the moment. The Chief held his glass up to the light and swirled the amber liquid.

"My Emma's smart too, Glen. I don't know, maybe not as smart as your Bennie or maybe she's smarter. Regardless, I don't think she's ready to elope with a twelve-year-old whiteboy." The remark startled Glen. He felt a flush of anger and reached for the bottle of Scotch, refilling his glass while he counted to ten and reminded himself to be diplomatic. He placed the bottle on the table and regarded the Chief steadily.

"Just so we're on the same page here, Chief, it doesn't matter to me if Emma's white, brown, black, green, polka-dot, or changes her skin every morning, but if it matters to you, Bennie is black, a person of color, African-American." He waited for the other man to react but Chief Eddie merely sat and regarded Glen impassively. "And frankly I don't think of that as his primary defining trait." The Chief finally leaned forward and grasped the bottle, taking his time topping off his drink. He pushed the bottle back towards Glen, then eased back in his seat.

"There are Native villages, some just across the inlet in fact, that don't allow whitemen to spend the night, Glen. Did you know that?" Glen gave a curt shake of his head. *No, he hadn't known that.* "If you were to visit those same villages an elder would be assigned to escort you wherever you went. Would you find that agreeable?" Glen didn't bother indicating his displeasure at the thought; the Chief was no longer seeing him anyway, his eyes were directed out the window. "And if your plane couldn't make it out because of the weather you might be locked overnight in the schoolhouse with a loaded .45 for your own protection." The Chief's focus shifted to Glen's face. "Is that the Alaska you're signing on to represent?" Glen drained his drink and set the glass on the table next to the rapidly-emptying liquor bottle. The whiskey burned all the way to his gut. He was starting to feel the effects of the earlier drinks and he took care to speak clearly.

"I'd say you have some legal issues there, Chief. But frankly I'm not in favor of trying to legislate social attitudes. Maybe there are some underlying factors that could be addressed and that's something we could certainly discuss." The Chief briefly swam out of focus and Glen blinked several times to clear his vision. "Some other time, I'm afraid." He was surprised to see his glass had been filled again. *When had that happened? What the hell?* "Right now we're discussing Emma," he said, "who, I'm sure, is a fine young girl," he hastened to add, "but needs to keep her hooks out of my Bennie, at least until after the election." There, he'd laid it on the line. He sat back to await Chief Eddie's response. The Chief gazed at Glen solemnly.

"I'm not sure if Emma has developed 'hooks' yet, Glen." He held the bottle of Scotch in his hand. He sipped straight from the bottle and grimaced. "You just admitted you're not in favor of legislating social mores, yet you intend to legislate Bennie and Emma's affections? Has that been an effective tactic for you in the past?" He nodded towards Glen's glass and held the bottle at arm's length. Glen dutifully drained his glass and held it out to be refilled. Eddie shook the bottle instead and Glen took the hint. He took the Scotch from Eddie and took a swig. The Chief held his hand out for Glen to return the bottle but Glen held on to it, selfish and oblivious.

"That's pretty damn slick, Chief. Did you set me up for that?" He stared into the open end of the bottle for a moment, then took another swig before noticing the Chief's outstretched hand. He reluctantly handed the bottle to him. "Good sluff, I mean stuff, Eddie."

"Not really," Eddie admitted, "but the parallel is certainly striking." Glen frowned.

"Its not good stuff?" he asked, confused. Eddie frowned in return.

"This?" he asked, indicating the bottle. "This is twelve years old, it's great stuff. I meant I didn't set you up." He took another healthy slug from the bottle, some of it escaping to dribble down his cheek.

"Oh, that's good," Glen replied. "because dirty politics always pisses me off, unless I'm the one doing the dirty." He took the bottle from Eddie and drained the last of it as the Chief lurched to his feet and stumbled back to the bar. "So Chief, what *do* we do about those damn kids?" Eddie, concentrating on reading the labels as he clinked bottles in and out of the rack, missed most of the question.

"Damn kids?" he blurted, selecting another bottle. "Damn all kids," he agreed. "You got any kids, Glen?"

"Uh, no," Glen replied, watching with concern as Eddie weaved back towards the couch. "We covered that already."

"That's right," Eddie agreed, plopping back into his seat. "I remember, none you admit to." He slapped his leg in glee with a crooked smile on his face. "I'm getting shitfaced here, Glen. How about you?"

"Yeah," Glen admitted, "I should slow down a bit."

"Here," Eddie said, passing the bottle to him, "you open it."

"Or not," Glen shrugged, popping the seal.

"I like you, Glen." Eddie said, suddenly serious. Glen swallowed some whiskey and passed the bottle to Eddie.

"I like you too, Chief. But what's this 'whiteman' shit?"

Eddie stared at Glen blankly.

"Oh that. It's nothing personal, and it's not like we hate whitemen in general. It's all your damn laws, regulations, and rules." He stabbed a finger in Glen's direction. "Mostly we're pissed about subsistence hunting and fishing. I hear you're on the wrong side of that." Glen remained perfectly still, aware they were broaching dangerous waters. Eddie peered at Glen, his eyes shiny. "Ever been to a remote village, Glen?" Glen shook his head slightly. "Think about it, it's mid-winter, there's three hundred people and twenty jobs, the freezer's empty, your kids are hungry, and there's an old bull moose down at the creek that probably won't make it through the winter anyway. Enough meat on those bones to carry your whole family until spring." He leaned toward Glen with barely controlled anger. "And if you shoot him they'll take your rifle, your snowmachine, and maybe throw you in jail." He glared at Glen a moment longer before slumping back in his seat. "Better to let the wolves have that damn moose. Wolves are good for the tourist industry, you know."

Glen watched while Chief Eddie regained his composure. He finally flashed Glen a brief and bitter smile before waving a hand in apology. "Sorry, kind of a sore subject," he said. Glen nodded in understanding. He had earlier encountered an Anchorage hunter who could argue the other side of the complex issue just as passionately. That grizzled old hunter was born and raised in Nome so he was a native Alaskan too, had been in Alaska longer than the Chief even if his ancestors hadn't, and who cared about ancient history? This was America, dang it, where all men were created equal, dang it, and the AC stores carried ground beef just like Safeway, dang it...

He had no intention of debating Chief Eddie on such an emotional subject, a subject that Glen knew less about than he apparently should.

"Look, Chief. The subsistence issue will be handled in court. I'm talking about racism. You think my Bennie's not good enough for your Emma, is that it?" Eddie was drinking and couldn't reply right away.

Glen stared in awe at the amount of whiskey the other man drank. "Damn, Chief," he said. "Let me have that." Eddie passed Glen the bottle. Glen pulled off a huge slug himself while Eddie grinned appreciatively. Glen gasped and wiped his mouth, fighting back the urge to gag.

"Glen, I got nuthin' against whitemen, blacks, anybody. Most of my people don't either. Hell, a lot of the village people are intimidated by whites, flankly...I mean, frankly."

"The Village People?" Glen asked. "Oh man!" He broke out in song. "*YMCA! I love to sleep at the...*" he trailed off. "Always hated those guys." He passed the bottle to Eddie. "Now I know I've had too much."

"You sing like a dying moose," Eddie noted. Glen frowned.

"Oh yeah?"

"Yeah. An old bull moose. Maybe I should shoot you."

"I'd rather go down fighting wolves, thank you," Glen replied. Eddie gauged the amount of whiskey left in the second bottle.

"I haven't been this drunk in years. You're a bad influence, Glen."

"I get that a lot," Glen admitted. Eddie held the bottle out, not quite directly at Glen.

"Maybe you could put that back for me," he slurred. "Think I'll just take a little nap here on the couch." Glen got unsteadily to his feet and managed to grab the bottle even though Eddie made it a moving target. He slipped it into an empty slot in the rack, taking three tries to hit the opening, and slid the panel shut with a bang. Eddie jumped.

"What?" he exclaimed. He looked around, dazed.

"Nothing," Glen assured him, "just me."

"Oh. Well." He had a sudden thought. "Hey, you didn't drive, did you?"

"Yes," Glen confessed, "but I think I'll be calling a cab."

"Good idea," Eddie nodded wisely. "Wait, did we decide what to do about those kids?"

"No, but I doubt there's much we can do. Play it by ear, I guess," Glen said. Eddie tipped over on the couch and raised his feet. His eyes closed.

"If Bennie tries anything with my Emma I'll eat your heart, Wilson," he mumbled.

"Huh," Glen snorted. "Pretty tough chewing, old man. Still got your own teeth?" Eddie smiled with his eyes closed.

"You're a mean bastard. Phone's on the desk," he pointed by raising a middle finger. Glen contacted Information and selected Alaska

Cab from the choices the cheery young woman offered. He let the service dial the number for him and wondered how he was going to sneak back into his room, retrieve the rental car, and explain the inevitable hangover. He hung up the phone after providing the address and turned to see Eddie staring at him with one open eye. The Chief raised a hand, held it overhead for a moment and then pointed at Glen.

"You know, Wilson, most politicians up here ignore the Native vote," he murmured.

"That's just politics," Glen said. "We only have to win in Anchorage, Fairbanks and Juneau —"

"You think about it," Eddie interrupted. "I know people. Yup'ik, Athabascan, Aleut, Tlingit... you think about it," he repeated. He lowered his arm and dozed off before Glen could reply.

Glen let himself out of the house. He found a dim corner of the yard and took a long and refreshing piss while waiting for the cab.

Glen and Walter

The room was suddenly filled with painful light. Glen squeezed his eyes shut as much as he could but the sun streaming in the window still found a direct path to his brainstem. Giving up, Glen slowly sat up in bed. He stole a peek to see who was torturing him.

"Damn it Walter, this better be an emergency. I'm dying here."

"You're lucky you threw up most of what you drank. I flushed the toilet for you."

"Thanks, I think."

Walter placed a tumbler of reddish liquid on the nightstand. It was thick and oily. It looked too much like blood for Glen's taste.

"I have a cure for you," Walter said.

"You can cure a hangover? God bless you sir,"

Glen reached for it, but Walter swatted his hand away.

"Before you drink that, I want to talk to you about Angela."

Glen groaned. "What about her?"

"She's been staying out late and coming back with her panties on backwards. She's been showering before she comes to bed. She's been stealing from my stash. I told you I'm fond of her. I told you to stay away from her. Was that too much to ask?"

"Shit, Walter. I admit I made a pass at her, she's too young and delicious to ignore. You can't blame me for that. But, if she's fucking around on you, it hasn't been with me."

217

"If not you, then who?"

Glen rubbed his bleary eyes.

"How the fuck should I know?" Then a thought occurred to him. "What about that cop she's been hanging out with? Julio something?"

"Cop?"

"Yes, cop. Come on Walter, how stupid do you think I am?"

"I'd rather not answer that, if you don't mind."

"You're an amusing man, you should try show business. My head is splitting, let me try your headache cure."

Walter pushed Glen's hand away and picked up the tumbler. He stood up and hovered over Glen.

"You don't want any of this. Try a handful of aspirin and as much water as you can stomach."

"Thanks for nothing, you prick," Glen complained.

Walter stood at the door with his hand on the knob.

"Can I ask you a hypothetical question?"

"No," Glen said with his eyes clenched shut.

"Suppose you had a body to get rid of...?"

"That's easy. Drain the fluids in a random motel bathtub. Seal the body in plastic, put it in a nylon ski bag, and Fedex it to a company I know in Alabama. Wire transfer them ten thousand dollars and they'll take care of the carcass."

"What do they do with it?" Walter asked.

"They take care of it. Dogfood, fertilizer, expensive soap bars, slug bait. Who cares?"

Walter glanced at his watch. "Thanks. It's time to get your ass up, boss. You have a telephone interview at ten," he said over his shoulder.

"Can't you just let me die in peace?" Glen muttered as Walter left the room and let the door click shut behind him.

Scott Steele and Jim Van Doren

Jim Van Doren saw Scott Steele sitting in an easy chair at the Dark Horse Coffee Company. He stood in line and ordered his mocha, then joined Steele. They shook hands.

"How's it going, Jim?" Steele asked.

"You know how it's going. We're tanking. Your sacred cow, Patterson, is running away with this one. You bastards really screwed me."

"Don't be like this. We're not driving Patterson, she's doing this without our help."

"I'm tired of your bullshit. I wanted to talk to you before you read about it in the papers."

"Are you dropping out?"

"No, you back-stabbing piece of shit, I'm switching to the Reform Party. They are kicking in money and Pat Buchanan is coming up here himself to help me raise some more."

"Don't go third on us. This may not be your election, but you never know where we're going to be two or four years down the road. Perhaps we can get you a state position until we're in a better place to win a big one."

"Fuck you, I'm sick of state politics. I'm going national and it's going to be now. I think I have a better chance with the Reform ticket than with you trying to bend me over so you can rape me up the ass."

"Be reasonable. With the presidential coattails, barring a miracle, we don't stand much of a chance anyway. Hang in there and let's see what future election cycles bring us."

"It's done, I've signed."

"So this is it?" Steele said in a resigned voice.

"Yes. Good luck with your lesbian."

"Yeah." Steele folded up his paper and tucked it under his arm. He nodded and walked out. Van Doren sipped his mocha and watched him walk away.

ALASKA INSTANT POLL

July 29

ADN Survey of likely Voters (plus or minus 4% error)
32% Sanders – REP
18% Undecided
15% Patterson – DEM
8% Wilson – DM
4% Other
3% Walters – GREEN
2% Gray – LIBERT
2% Van Doren – REFORM
1% Onkiak – AK IND

The Election Team

Elke poked her head in. Glen was wearing a cell phone headset and doing a telephone interview with a political reporter for the Fairbanks Daily News-Miner. Glen pressed the mute button and looked at Elke questioningly.

"There is a large Eskimo to see you. He seems pissed. Chief Eddie?"

"Oh, shit. Okay, I'll wrap this up and be right out. He's a VIP."

Elke ducked out. Glen unmuted his phone.

"I completely agree that the suicide rate is unacceptable and I will work fulltime in Washington to get some help for your community. I think the main thing we can do is stimulate the economy so our people are working instead of sitting around drinking and getting depressed. We have a civic duty to make sure everyone that wants to work has a chance for a good job. Look, something has come up here and I need to run. I look forward to meeting you in person when we're up that way. Keep your powder dry, okay?"

Glen slipped off the headset and walked into the room they used as a reception area. Chief Eddie was sipping Nestea from a can. He looked troubled and tired. Glen shook his hand.

"How's the head this afternoon, Chief?"

"Not great. I have to stop drinking like a teenager."

"I hear you, Chief. What brings you to campaign central?"

"I'm looking for Emma. She wasn't on the bus."

"I don't think Emma is around here? Elke, have you seen her?"

Elke shrugged and shook her head no.

"If she's with your Bennie, I'm going to twist his head off and boot it down the hallway. Emma's supposed to come straight home after school."

Murphy walked in the room and looked at Chief Eddie curiously.

"This is my security officer, Margaret Murphy, everyone calls her Murphy. Murphy, this is Chief Eddie Kleedehn."

Murphy gave him one of her classic bone-crusher handshakes.

"I've read about you Chief. Retired Colonel? Jarhead? Hoo-wah? CEO of one of the Native American Corporations?"

Chief Eddie flexed his fingers to unkink them and tried to maintain his grumpy expression, but could not manage it.

"Hoo-wah," he replied. "I knew a Murphy in boot. From Florida, looked a little like you."

"Yeah, that was my old man. He took one too many in the line of duty and didn't make it."

"I'm sorry to hear that."

"Well, he was an asshole."

"Some things don't change. I'm looking for my daughter, Emma? Seen her around?"

"Emma is yours? She's cute as a button, we're getting pretty attached to her. I haven't seen her today, though. We can go check with Bennie."

The group walked down the hotel hallway. Murphy tapped on the Bennie's suite door.

"Bennie, you home?"

There was a rustling behind the door. Bennie opened the door and was startled by the group staring at him.

"What?" he asked.

"I'm looking for my daughter," Chief Eddie grumbled. He pushed through the door. Emma was sitting on the bed and playing an Xbox360 game. She jumped up and stood shaking with fear. Bennie slipped between them and grabbed Chief Eddie's huge hand and gave a brisk shake.

"You're Emma's pa? I'm very pleased to meet you, sir. I've been wanting to meet you, but Emma said it was too soon. I want to complement you, sir, for raising such a bright and lovely girl."

Chief Eddie kneeled and looked Bennie directly in the eye.

"I'm hung over and grumpy. Don't blow smoke up my ass, kid. What are you up to?"

"I was helping her with her Economics homework."

"To me, it looks like you're playing a stupid video game."

"We're just taking a break." Bennie picked some papers off the bed and waved them. "Macro-economic theory. Optimum consumption bundles. Profit-maximizing production functions. Cournot oligopolists. She's going to get an A."

"She always gets A's."

"This is a Phoenix University online master's class. I bet her ten bucks she could do it and I'm winning. She picks up things really fast."

"Emma is supposed to ride the bus home after school. I don't approve of her sneaking around."

"Yes, sir. I understand."

Chief Eddie stood and looked around the room. A table held three computer screens that were displaying spreadsheet data. The kids had kicked off their tennis shoes which were heaped on each other in a corner. The coffee table had a bag of trail mix and a couple of paper Starbucks cups. Chief Eddie pointed.

"I don't allow Emma to drink coffee."

"Hot chocolate," Bennie responded.

"How has she been getting home?"

"Taxi."

Chief Eddie deflated slightly. He glared at Bennie, but he didn't seem as intense.

"I don't think I like you," he said.

"I'm sorry to disappoint you, sir," Bennie said, looking at Chief Eddie steadily.

"Alright, you two." He turned slightly and gestured at Emma. "You be home by six. I don't really like this, but if you want to invite Bennie to join us for dinner, you can."

"Okay, daddy."

Chief Eddie ushered all out of the room. He did not speak until they were back in the main campaign room.

"That's one special little guy," Chief Eddie said.

"What you said in there —" Elke interjected.

"I just wanted to give the kid a fighting chance. Parental approval can be the kiss of death. Did you notice how he took the heat without making excuses or trying to blame Emma?" Chief Eddie shook his head. "Wilson, what's your poll number to date?"

"We're running at eight percent and rising."

"You guys really do your homework. I don't have a lot of time to screw around. How does a guy sign on? You need a real Alaskan consultant on board to keep you from saying stupid things about subsistence, development, and environmental issues. If we visit the largest villages, with my help, we can get you ten thousand native community votes. Like it?"

Glen glanced at his team. He grinned.

"Hell yes, we like it a lot. Welcome aboard, Chief."

In any sufficiently robust axiom system for arithmetic there will be statements that are true but which cannot be proven from the axioms of that system.

- Kurt Godel

CHAPTER 12

The Election Team

Chief Eddie was examining a campaign flyer. Across the top it said Bill Sanders for Congress (REP). The bottom had a picture of Bill Sanders' face over a red, white and blue waving-flag graphic. Glen walked in accompanied by Walter.

"Hello Chief, I want to introduce you to another member of our team. Walter Crawley is in charge of events, advertising, propaganda, dirty tricks, fear, uncertainty, doubt, crowds, power, and general magic."

"Please call me Eddie," the Chief said. "Perhaps you can tell me why are you spending your money printing flyers for your competition?"

"Let me show you something. Cover your right eye. I'm going to walk backwards with this poster. Stop me when you see something funny about it. Okay?"

The Chief nodded with a puzzled look on his face. Walter held up the poster and walked backwards slowly until he was about 40 feet away.

"Stop," the Chief said. "Holy crap. Am I seeing what I think I'm seeing? That's really nasty."

Walter walked back.

"Impressive?"

"I'll say. How did you do that?"

"I've been manipulating images and perfecting a more direct connection to the subconscious for decades now. You wouldn't consciously notice that overlay, but it will link with your serial reptilian-mind which is tuned to notice ugly things with big teeth that might be camouflaged in a bush or in a jumble of rocks. The image itself is not that detailed or scary, but it matches with a simple template stored in a primitive part of your brain."

"Does it really work?"

"The intensity of effect depends on the person and the environment. However, for the first time since the polling started, Sanders is down two points."

"Is that legal?"

"Technically, no. On the other hand, I don't know how you'd prove it in a court of law. One interesting fact: it takes a positive immersion of ten times the exposure to reverse the effect. Your mind records and reacts to perceived peril very effectively, it's only natural that your mind is tuned to danger. Instinct. This stuff is genetically imprinted. The only thing you'll consciously notice is a general aversion to Sanders' face and name."

"I think I have seen the face of evil."

"Thank you," Walter said, averting his eyes with false modesty.

"I've only seen one thing stranger than that."

"Oh? Might I ask?"

"My grandmother was full-blood Yup'ik, the only female shaman I've ever heard of for her era. She scared the hell out of me when I was little with an Ap'apaa mask, a human-like mask with a huge mouth and lots of teeth."

"That's a psychic imprint used to keep kids from wondering too far from home."

"Well, it worked."

"Of course it did. Please continue."

"Sure, sorry. I was very young. There was a man who simply would not hunt. He would cook and sew and render blubber, but he would not hunt. In our tradition, a man hunts or he is sentenced to death. My grandmother cast a spell that turned his blood to ice. I watched him die. He was wrapped in skins, sitting by a fire and scraping leather with a flint. Within minutes he turned blue and froze solid. It was definitely some kind of Inuit magic. I would not believe it if I had not seen it my own eyes."

"Is your grandmother still alive?"

"Yes. She is very old now, of course."

"I must see this spell performed." Walter's eyes glowed with a cold intensity.

"Nothing personal, but you're a white guy. She's not going to perform for you."

"You let me worry about that. I must see this. You will introduce me to her."

"Well, okay I guess. I can't join you, but you can take your bush plane out there and see if you can find them, her people move around. I'll give you a talisman for introduction."

"Fine."

The Chief turned to Glen.

"This is an interesting team you've assembled."

"That's one way to put it, I suppose," Glen replied.

Holly and Glen

Holly sat on a folding chair in the back of a conference room in the Quality Inn. *How these politicians can go on and on,* she thought. She tuned into Wilson's speech now and then; Social Security this, Alaska Permanent Fund that, and fill in the gaps with blather about universal medical insurance. *Were people actually interested in this stuff?* She supposed that some must be, there were about 150 people crammed in the room which was humid and stuffy and smelled like soggy dogs. There was an underlying metallic tang to the air which she could taste on the back of her tongue. For some reason, she felt a little dizzy as she listened to Wilson drone on and on. A fat man in a yellow polyester suit was filming the event on a tiny digital video recorder and a few people off to the side were holding microphones and taking notes. Reporters. Holly was bruised and impatient, she had her hand in her knapsack where she clicked the safety on her .45 on and off. She visualized standing up and firing. The crowd would scatter and she should have a clear shot. At 35 yards, chances are she could hit Wilson a couple of times, which may or may not be fatal. She didn't like the odds, but she was impatient. She was in her early twenties, her time was almost up. In all of her visions of the future, growing old was not even a remote possibility.

Holly made eye-contact with a middle-aged woman who shared the small stage with Wilson. This woman was ancient, at least in her 40's. Holly recognized her from the rally in the park. *Cop? Bodyguard? Mistress? Some combination?* She was dressed in a wool business-style suit and held a large leather purse on her lap. Her eyes scanned the crowd and she seemed like a spring ready to be unleashed. Just like Holly felt. The woman seemed to peer into Holly's volcanic soul, but soon her eyes continued on their sweep of the room. When the agenda moved to questions from the audience, Holly tuned into a Wilson non-answer of a question on gun control. The answer seemed to satisfy the questioner, but

225

between the balance of second amendment rights with reasonable restrictions on convicted felons and children, Holly couldn't tell exactly what the Wilson position was. She supposed that was the point.

After the session was over, Holly stayed in the back of the room and watched the reporters pack their bags and the hangers-on shake hands and chat with the candidate. Glen noticed her and motioned for her to meet him by the back door. Holly loitered by the indicated door and tried to figure out if this felt like the night. *Was it time for Glen Wilson to die writhing in agony? Shoot the old woman or Wilson first?* Holly felt like the woman might be armed. Holly could hear the woman and Wilson talking. They weren't exactly arguing, but Holly could tell the woman was exasperated.

"She looks like she's twelve, for God's sake."

"She just looks young, Murphy. We're just going to talk about my platform. I'm a school project for her or something. I'm going to have a lot of groupies before this is over, you need to relax a little."

"Jailbait."

"Bullshit."

Holly was happy to assign a name to the woman. Murphy. Holly watched her as she grabbed a valise, looked at Holly intently, and hauled the bag out of the room. Wilson walked over.

"Handler?" Holly asked.

"Mother hen," Glen replied with a grin. "Elizabeth, am I right? You never did call me so we could talk about my positions on your issues."

Positions. Cute, Holly thought. *This guy is about a suave as coal miner.*

"I've been tied up," Holly said. *Two can play this stupid game. He actually unconsciously licked his lips. What a pig. Of course, all of the penis people were swine, so it was no surprise. Was this the right time? One slug for each kneecap. Leave him as a cripple for life, then run for the fire exit? She could feel Murphy's eyes boring into her from the hallway. Holly made a decision. Not now.*

"We're looking for volunteers to run the phones and autograph my pictures, are you looking for a job? I'd pay you very well. I can tell by looking at you that you're very talented."

Why don't you just drop to your knees and snuffle at my crotch like a dog? That would be subtler.

"No thanks, I'm not looking for a job." She turned and walked toward the exit.

"How can I get in contact with you? Give your I-M[18] sign-in or something," Glen cajoled.

"I'll be around, don't worry," Holly said over her shoulder.

Murphy strolled back in.

"I don't like her," she said. "What kind of girl has blonde hair and dyes it brown?"

"I didn't notice that."

"You didn't notice anything above her neck. She has strawberry blonde eyebrows and blonde roots."

"Makes you wonder, doesn't it. Think she's natural down below?"

"She's not exactly my type."

They strolled together to the limousine that idled in the parking lot.

"Look Murphy, are you sure you won't help me out? Just a quickie in the limo? I'm carrying a load."

"The answer is no and the answer, for future reference, will always be no. Got it?"

"I don't think you're a team player."

"That's what everyone tells me."

They rode silently back to the hotel immersed in their respective thoughts.

Moshi

Jack and Jordan unloaded the last of the guitars and equipment cases onto a series of luggage carts. The band and the entourage, except for Raz, were standing near the security line. Their Korean Air flight to Osaka, with a connection in Seoul, was scheduled for departure in 43 minutes. Raz sat on a bench and was having an intimate conversation with the record company executive. Moshi clung to Erik's arm as if it was a lifeline. The TSA[19] screener motioned for Erik's ticket and Erik produced it. Moshi was watching an old man, quivering from Parkinson's, fumble with removing his shoes at the "additional security" line.

---

[18] Instant Messaging, a near real-time messaging system supported by the Internet.

[19] Transportation Security Administration, the federal agency that that took over airline security after the September 11 terror attacks.

"Ma-am, could I see your ticket and your photo-identification please?"

Pulling away, Erik had already strolled through the X-ray scanner.

"My boyfriend has my ticket," Moshi said as she tried to get around the guard to place her bag on the scanner conveyor belt.

"Excuse me, ma-am, he only showed me one ticket. You can't pass through without a ticket. Could I see your ticket, please?"

Erik was shouting at her from beyond the security station. "Go talk to Raz." On the other side of the security station, Moshi could see the entourage gather their things and start toward the departure gate. The Filipino girl smirked at her and took Erik's arm. Moshi could hardly see through the tears. She stumbled back into the terminal toward the approaching Raz.

"I'll handle this," the record company guy said.

"I'm sorry, Moshi," Raz whispered as he walked around her.

"Could I have my ticket please?" Moshi asked plaintively.

"I'm afraid that we didn't have enough budget to get everyone on the plane. These flights to Asia are very spendy."

"I don't understand."

"We do not have a ticket for you. When we come back through after the tour, you can catch up with us."

"What am I supposed to do?"

"Just hang loose and we'll connect with you after the tour, I'm sure we'll have money to get you back to the lower 48 then. Wait for us."

"Wait? Where?"

"Here in Anchorage."

With that, the record guy patted her arm and walked away quickly. Moshi collapsed on a chair and tried to figure out what had happened. The realization that she'd been ditched slowly became unavoidable. She hoped she was dreaming but the airport scene had a hard edge that felt real. A huge blind native man walked by, led by a Malamute seeing-eye dog. Moshi did not think her imagination could come up with something that surreal. The terminal vibrated with when the jets took off. Jack and Jordan walked over.

"Hey Moshi, I thought you were going?"

She shook her head and wiped at her eyes.

"What are you going to do?" Jack asked.

Moshi couldn't help herself. She laughed.

"My car is in the parking lot, can we give you a lift somewhere?"

"Yes, please," Moshi replied.

Bennie and Emma

"Eddie tells me you're a math whiz?" Mary Kleedehn was a short woman with long gray hair pulled back into a thick braid. She had dark skin and the nearly-Asian features of a Native Alaskan. They were eating a roast beef and mashed potatoes in the Kleedehn dining room.

Bennie chewed his peas and swallowed before answering. "It is one of my interests, but I hardly think of myself as a 'whiz'."

"I had a math minor in college," Mary commented drily. "Which field are you partial to? Vector analysis? Set theory? Linear algebra?"

"I have a fair grasp of all those fundamentals. For the last few days, I have been exploring mathematical philosophy. Take the number pi for example. It can be simply described in words as the ratio between the circumference and the diameter of a circle. If we express pi as an integer, we find it is irrational and that the distribution of its digits is equal. In other words, pi cannot be accurately represented by a ratio of whole numbers. In addition, pardon the pun, the incidence each digit appears in the decimal sequence is almost the same. Fives occur very nearly as often as sevens, for example. All this means that pi, when expressed in decimal form, is a very complicated number. To my thinking, this indicates that pi was not meant to be defined in decimal numbers. What is so special about the base 10 numbering system except that we have ten fingers? Therefore, I have been evaluating pi in non-rational number systems and have determined the real number system of our physics. Based on that approach, I have reworked molecular and atomic-level chemistry along with the periodic table of elements. As an aside, I have found this number system encoded in our DNA."

Emma continued chewing as she pulled over a bowl of mashed potatoes and spooned herself out a heap. Eddie and Mary were frozen with their forks suspended in mid-air. Slowly, they set their forks down and looked at each other.

"Did you follow that?" Eddie asked Mary.

"I think he just said he reinvented chemistry and found God's signature in our genetic structure."

"I was afraid it was something like that," Eddie said. "Bennie, are you the smartest person in the world?"

"Oh no, sir," Bennie replied, "from my analysis, there are 107, give or take two or three, smarter people in North America alone. I haven't bothered to figure it out for the world, but it should be several thousand. Most of them are clinically insane, of course."

Chief Eddie squirmed in his seat. "I'm not sure how to put this diplomatically. Could you please, Bennie, try not to give us this kind of detail about your work? It's very disturbing."

"Yes sir," Bennie said, shrugging while chasing an errant pea around his plate with his fork.

"Mom and Dad, could we be excused to go upstairs to watch a video? I want to show Bennie the anaglyph[20] version of Gilligan's Island I downloaded."

"Sure, kids, go ahead," Chief Eddie said. He pushed his still-loaded plate away. "I need a drink. How about you, Mary?"

"Yes, please," she replied.

Murphy and Elke

Elke gave Murphy a peck on the cheek and said "I'll be right back," while sorting through her papers. She grabbed her purse and fumbled her way out the car door. She looked both ways before crossing K street to the Anchorage Savings and Loan. Murphy sat in the car and paged through a Redbook magazine. She read an article on the joys of teen-age sex and planned a helpful lecture on abstinence for Bennie. The kids were young, but everyone grew up fast in these times. Murphy sighed at the thought.

She looked up when a black BMW, with deeply tinted windows, stopped in front of the bank and parked in the handicapped parking zone. Two men dressed in black trench coats got out of the car and scanned the area. One of the men dropped a box with a conspicuously protruding stubby cell phone antenna outside the door. The men disappeared into the bank. *Oh shit*, Murphy thought. She dialed 911 on her cell phone.

"I'm at the Anchorage Savings and Loan on K street and I believe there is a robbery in progress. Two men entered the building and dropped a suspicious package outside the front door. A black BMW is idling outside. I can't see inside the car but it has at least one person, the driver, in it."

She heard muffled pops. "Shots fired," she shouted into the phone. She closed the phone and pulled out her .357 pistol. She checked

---

[20] A method of creating 3D simulations with two contrasting-color image perspectives superimposed on each other. The images are viewed through colored lens, usually red and blue.

the bullets in the chamber and put the gun down the back of the waistband of her skirt. She slipped a reload into her blazer pocket. As she walked across the street, it occurred to her that this was how her father was killed. He tried to stop a bank robbery before backup was in place. She walked behind the BMW and tried the bank doors. They were locked from the inside. She took a quick step to the car and broke out the passenger window with the butt of her revolver. The driver was fumbling with a MAC-10 when Murphy shot him in the face. She got in the passenger seat, leaned over, pushed open the driver's door and shoved the body out. She worked herself over the bucket seats and settled behind the steering wheel. Fastening her seatbelt and gunning the motor, she reversed, and then drove over the curb and into the glass doors. She put the car in drive and eased out of the entrance. Without a conscious plan, she pressed the button that popped open the trunk. Leaving the car running, she flopped down on the seat and worked her way to the passenger door. Taking a few deep breaths, she gathered her courage. In her mind, she could feel that Elke was already dead. The world was hollow and did not have enough oxygen. She opened the door and crawled out onto the sidewalk. She could hear sirens spooling up in the distance. She threw the bomb into the trunk and slammed the lid. Dropping to the sidewalk and peeking around the corner, she could see a security guard bleeding on the floor. Bank customers were huddling and she could not see Elke. Murphy's ears were ringing and she felt disconnected from her body. One of the burglars crossed her field of view and Murphy did not hesitate. She fired and his head exploded. She pulled back and sat with her back to the wall as automatic fire roared. A black-garbed man ran out of the bank, threw a bag into the BMW and, with tires squealing, raced away.

Murphy slowly stood up and entered the bank. Elke was bleeding from a blow to the face, but she seemed otherwise alright. They hugged. Murphy smoothed Elke's hair, then walked over to the dead robber. She looked through his coat pockets until she found a cell phone. She scanned through his address book until she found a phone number for 'bomb' and pressed the talk button. *Were these robbers really this literal? Morons,* she thought. After a few seconds, a muffled boom rattled the windows. She put the cell phone back in the robber's jacket, then laid her weapon on the floor and stood with her arms raised as the police stormed the building.

After all the questions and the medics bandaged them up, they finally had a chance to talk.

"That was really stupid. Glen is going to be really pissed off," Elke said.

"I had to do something, I don't want to live without you."

"I know," Elke said quietly, "and I love you too."

The Election Team

Glen was fuming. He scanned the room and glared at the members of his team one-by-one. Walter was typing text into his Blackberry messaging device and Bennie was playing an electronic game on his cell phone. Elke and Murphy, wearing various bandages, were cuddling and whispering on the couch.

"This team relies on each and every one of you. We cannot accept unnecessary risks. You have to look at the bigger picture. This was not part of the plan and we don't do anything that is not part of the plan."

"You think I nearly got myself killed on purpose?"

"The cops were on their way, you should have waited. I could have ended up with both of you killed, then where would my campaign be? Swirling down the toilet, that's where. Chewing on the shit-end of the stick. Floating belly–up in a fishbowl of stale piss."

Angela interrupted before Glen could invent more lame homilies by throwing open the door. She walked in with an armful of newspapers.

"You guys made the front page," she announced, handing the papers to Walter. Glen snatched them out of his hands. Above the fold there was a large color shot of Murphy being attended by paramedics. The headline above the fold read **Woman Breaks up Robbery Attempt**. The subhead said **Congressional Candidate Girlfriend and former Police Officer Kills Two, Third Suspect Killed in Explosion**. An inset picture showed Glen at a campaign event.

"Couldn't the photographer use some of the pictures he took after I got there?" Glen complained.

"Hey boss," Bennie said quietly.

"When did we ever decide that Murphy gets to be the hero? The candidate should always be above the fold."

"Boss?" Bennie repeated.

"What is it Bennie? I'm trying to make a point here," Glen said, exasperated.

"I just got overnight numbers on my phone. Your name-recognition and approval ratings are up two points in overnight polling."

"Two points in 24 hours? That's big," Glen said, musing.

"Very big," Bennie said.

"Alright guys," Glen said in a subdued manner while dropping the newspapers. "Keep up the good work." He walked out of the room and eased the door shut carefully.

"What did I miss?" Angela asked.

Walter stood up and started pacing. He waved a rolled newspaper for emphasis. "We're running around like a head with its chicken cut off. The candidate should always appear above the fold. Nobody gets themselves killed without the candidate's advance permission in writing. Unless we can get a two-point bump. Then it's okay."

The election team collapsed in laughter. Tears streamed down their faces. Glen poked his head back in the door. "Don't you fucking fucks have any fucking work to do?"

This comment made them laugh even harder. Glen slammed the door and went downstairs for a sandwich.

CHAPTER 13

Walter

For some reason, the compass was erratic and Walter was not sure how Lester Mike was navigating. The cloud cover was broken, but due to heavy fog, they lost sight of land for extended periods. After flying in the rented plane for a couple of hours, Walter craved the ground. Lester took a couple of passes, and then set the plane down on an island snowfield marked with faint charcoal stripes. The air tasted of salt and the wind bored straight through the layers of clothing the men wore. Lester stopped at a low building and carefully laid down one of his cargo boxes. He pried up a flap and handed Walter a bottle of Canadian Club whiskey. He waved at a building buried in snow a hundred yards away.

"Eddie's grandma will be there, make sure you give her the whiskey before you try to talk to her. It's traditional to offer a gift. Then, if you show her Eddie's talisman, maybe she won't run you off."

Sleet was blowing horizontally and Walter thought he would freeze before he reached the hut. He looked for an entrance and found a window covered with some sort of skin near the leeward side of the roofline. He pulled a section of rope, the window flap raised and he was able to duck inside and climb down a short ladder. The inside was illuminated with oil lamps which cast off the flickering dimness. The place looked deserted, though a small fire was burning behind a cast iron grate. Walter dropped his bundles and stomped his feet in front of the fire. Slowly, his blood thawed and his eyes became accustomed to the lighting. He turned to warm his back side and saw eyes staring at him from under a lump of blankets. Remembering himself, he picked up the whiskey bottle and offered it. A wrinkled hand, covered with blue veins, slowly reached out and took it. Walter tried to remember why this trip seemed so important back in Anchorage. He couldn't pass on the opportunity to meet a shaman, but now he wished he was back in the comfort of his room in the Marriott. The bottle disappeared into the folds of her blankets. Chief Eddie's talisman was a bear's tooth embossed with silver and strung on a leather thong. Walter removed it from his neck and showed it to the old woman. There was no visible response.

Walter decided to show off his demonstration and hurry back to the plane. He could be back in Anchorage and enjoying a flute of champagne and filet mignon by nightfall. He unpacked a small can of sterno and lighted it. He placed a vaporizer on the flame and from a duffel bag, extracted the equipment that implemented his latest trick. The illusion was small. Using high-voltage potentials and aural standing waves, he was able to warp the flame into various shapes, including figures. He did a little pantomime with a puppet. The puppet lived in sin, it had sex with many women and injected drugs. At the end, the puppet was ignited and crumbled away to nothing, leaving behind a plasma hologram figure that represented the soul. The soul writhed in flaming agony until the hand of God came down and saved it. The illusion was nearly perfect and in full color. The folks in Las Vegas were going to be amazed when Walter unveiled the life size version if he could ever afford to build it. When he was done, he sat back on his heels and looked into the eyes in the bundle of cloth. A pair of gnarled hands appeared and clapped slowly in appreciation. Walter nodded and started packing his gear.

The old woman slowly cast off her coverings. She grasped a carved cane and shuffled slowly around the room gathering things. She was short, less than five feet tall and very hunched over. She looked like she was two-hundred-years old. She threw a lump of fat into the fire and the light took on a golden tone. The air filled with an acrid odor similar to cat piss. She took his hands and guided him to a spot before the fire where they kneeled together with clasped hands. Her eyes were buried in wrinkled flesh, but their milky surface reflected flame intermittently. She pressed a tin cup to his lips and Walter drank a bitter concoction.

She whispered to Walter and he could understand most of her accented English.

"The Western way to God is through machines and space," she said gesturing to the sky. "Whether you go out or go in," she said, touching his chest, "it doesn't matter, the destination is the same." She grasped his hands again. "Close your eyes and look in," she said softly.

Walter became aware of a burning in his lungs and queasiness in the pit of his stomach. It reminded him of a vaguely-remembered Peyote ritual in New Mexico. Hand-in-hand, they floated to the ceiling, then out into the cold. The wind tugged at them, but they were weightless and they drifted across the island and black water. Back over land, they approached a pair of polar bears tearing at the flesh of a rotting seal.

The taste of the meat was delicious, it was rank and sloppy and sweet. He crunched on bones and raised his bloody paws into the air. He reared up and felt like he was the largest thing on earth. He decided to run and lumbered across the snow with his mate by his side. They ran and ran until his muscles were molten and breath roared out of his lungs.

They found a sheltering fissure of ice and collapsed. It was not the right season, but while nuzzling and nibbling playfully at his mate, he felt a flame in his groin. She pretended to resist and this inflamed him even more. He mounted her and plunged into her heat. It only took a few strokes before the blood was raging in his ears and his loins exploded. His essence erupted and filled his wife. Still embedded in her, he raised his paws and groaned into the wind. They were king and queen of the world. He collapsed on the snow and she plopped beside him. Slowly their breathing slowed and they slept and dreamed bear dreams of conquest and bloody meat.

Walter's eyes opened. The old woman grinned and touched him on the temples.

"So you see?" she asked.

"Yes, I saw," Walter replied.

The woman got up and then pressed a cup of whiskey into his hand.

"It will always live inside you. You are welcome to come see me again, if you wish."

Walter trudged through the snow and found Lester Mike trading stories with a group of men drinking around a stove made out of a 50-gallon barrel. Lester finished his drink.

"Are you ready to get the hell out of here?"

"Yes, I am," Walter replied.

ALASKA INSTANT POLL
August 5 – Primary Election Day

ADN Survey of likely Voters (plus or minus 4% error)
28% Sanders – REP
18% Undecided
16% Patterson – DEM
12% Wilson – DM
3% Other
3% Walters – GREEN
2% Gray – LIBERT
2% Van Doren – REFORM
1% Onkiak – AK IND

The Election Team

Emma and Bennie were sitting on the floor by the window playing Battleship with their cell phones. Elke and Walter were sitting on a couch munching low-fat popcorn and sipping cans of diet soda. They had three TV's tuned to different channels; they muted and unmuted each in turn to follow the primary election results. The suite door was wedged open with a wad of folded cardboard. Chief Eddie walked in and stood by the sofa until Elke and Walter scooted over. The Chief plopped himself down and excavated a huge fistful of popcorn.

"I don't understand why you guys care so much about the primary, you don't have a stake in it."

Emma piped up. "Geez Dad, I thought you were paying attention. The goals were to promote Patterson, kill Van Doren, and to show some serious weakness in Sanders. This is a test of our influence and to set us up for the election in November."

"We're also calibrating our simulations and electoral modeling," Bennie added.

"Don't forget the cost calculations, this is great data for figuring out how much money we need and how it should be spent," Elke stated.

"The demographics will tell us how effective the mass marketing has been," Walter inserted.

"Is this supposed to make sense to me?" Chief Eddie asked.

"Yes," the whole team said simultaneously.

"Now shut up, the polls are closed and the official results should be coming in," said Elke. She tossed one remote onto Walter's lap and clicked the sound on another. Murphy and Glen walked in. Glen looked tired and Murphy looked frazzled; her hair had escaped from her tight bun and was drifting around her face. She gave Elke a quick peck and sprawled on the floor hugging Elke's legs. Glen went to the kitchenette and came back with an Amstel light. He pulled over a kitchen chair and watched the TV screens.

"Did someone get Eddie in the pool?"

Elke handed over a grid and a pencil, most of the squares were claimed. "It's five bucks a square, just scribble your initials and give me the money," she said absently.

The Chief fished a five out of his pocket and wrote on a random square.

"I'm in," he said.

KAKM had the official count first.

ALASKA PRIMARY RESULT
August 5 – Primary Election Day

Preliminary Counts with 92% of precincts reporting
Republican
83% Sanders (Winner)
11% Write-in (scatter)
6% Other

Democrat
56% Patterson (Winner)
32% Write-in (scatter)
12% Van Doren (write-in)

"Who had 85 and 55?" Glen asked, grabbing for the grid.

Elke held it outside his grasp. "Hang on and I'll declare a winner." She scanned the grid. "Bennie gets it," she declared. Glen groaned. Bennie played his game with one hand and stretched his other palm out. Elke fished the wad of bills out of her pocket and handed it to the Chief who stretched out and dropped the them into Bennie's hand.

"Thank you all very much," Bennie said smugly.

"That's not fair, Bennie got on the grid first," Glen complained.

"He did not, you insisted on getting first pick," Walter responded.

"Well, it's still not fair."

"Shut up," Murphy said.

Glen drained his beer and went into the kitchen area for another. The Chief laboriously got off the couch and joined him. Glen handed him a beer and they sat on stools by the kitchenette breakfast bar.

"I guess I'm behind the curve. What was the strategy? Are we on track?" the Chief asked.

"We nailed it almost perfectly. We wanted Van Doren out because he was too good of a candidate. You notice he got 12 percent of the primary vote even though he dropped off the Democratic ticket. He did real well. We just wanted Sanders to show some vulnerability, he should have easily gotten more than his 83 percent in a race that was virtually uncontested. And we wanted Patterson to be the Democratic candidate. We built her and now we'll destroy her. Once she goes down in flames, who do you think will be standing by and ready to take the reins?"

"Will they really accept you?"

"It's a combination between not having a choice and not caring because they are essentially conceding the race to Sanders anyway. The precedent for entering an election after the primary was set by Lautenberg in New Jersey and Mondale[21] in Wisconsin. The Dems might not like it, but they'll take me on."

"In other words, you really did it?"

"Hey Chief, I didn't come up here because I liked the weather. I came up here to kick some ass." Glen clicked his bottle against the Chief's and took a deep swig. "There is a lot of work to do yet. The stakes get higher and the pressure is going to be on. We've been operating under the radar, but all that will change in a month or so. Hang onto your headdress, the ride is just starting."

The Chief grinned. "I wouldn't miss it for anything."

Julia Patterson

The Aurora Winds Bed and Breakfast was nestled in the trees on the very edge of Anchorage. As soon as the official primary results were in, a cheer rippled through the crowded dining room. Julia stood on a footstool and waited until she had everyone's attention. Camera flashes illuminated the room. Julia was flushed with trickles of perspiration that dribbled down her pink cheeks.

"In case you haven't heard, the results are official. I'm your Democratic candidate for the House of Representatives." The room erupted in applause and cheers. Julia spread her hands to settle everyone down. "This is not just a victory for me, but this is a victory for all of Alaska's gays and lesbians. For those who thought we couldn't do it, well, we did do it!" It took a minute for the crowd to quiet again. "We have a lot of work to do and another election to win, but win it we will. Then we can make progress on critical gay and lesbian issues like gay and gender-confused marriages, adoption rights, and anti-discrimination laws. I'm here to tell you that gay-bashing will soon be a thing of the prehistoric past. My opponent, Jim Van Doren, has graciously sent over his congratulations and some cup cakes. Let's make sure to enjoy them.

---

[21] Walter 'Fritz' Mondale entered the 2002 Minnesota Senatorial race late in October 2002 after incumbent Senator Paul Wellstone was killed in an airplane crash shortly before the November election.

Okay, for the members of the alternative press, please take your final pictures and recordings now, we're going to switch to our private celebration. All done? Please put away your cameras and recorders. We have rented the whole facility for our private party and I must insist that no more pictures or recordings be taken. Everybody understand? The public part of this get-together is over. Okay. Let's party down."

She stepped off the stool and embraced her partner and they enjoyed a long and sloppy kiss. The rules in her community were well-understood, so there were no pictures taken by her followers of the festivities that followed. Unfortunately, they did not notice that the security cameras were active and connected via wireless point-to-point link to a digital recording studio a few miles away. In addition, the cakes were not actually from Jim Van Doren but were from a special Walter Crawley recipe. Within 48 hours, MPEGs of the security system orgy tapes were available on Ebay and on hundreds of Internet porn sites. At one point, their sales were exceeded only by Pamela and Tommy Lee videos, but this popularity did not last. However, sales remained respectable for several months.

The tapes would have probably not been fatal to Julia's campaign except for the specially-trained German shepherds. Apparently, as tolerant as Alaskan voters are, they draw the line at seeing their congressional candidate being mounted by a canine.

ALASKA INSTANT POLL

August 12

ADN Survey of likely Voters (plus or minus 4% error)
35% Sanders – REP
28% Undecided
18% Wilson – DM
6% Van Doren – REFORM
4% Other
3% Walters – GREEN
3% Gray – LIBERT
2% Patterson – DEM
1% Onkiak – AK IND

Walter

Walter could see Angela and her 'friend' Julio having lunch at the Red Robin on Dimond Boulevard. He was watching through some opera glasses from under an awning of a building across the street. They seemed to be having a spat. Angela poured a cup of soda on his lap and walked stiffly away. Walter was good at reading lips but was too far away to practice this craft. Angela came out and Walter turned away so she would not recognize him. When he turned around again, she had disappeared around a corner. As Walter watched, Julio mopped up the mess with a bar towel. He slammed some bills on the table and walked out. Crossing the street, he walked right by Walter while cursing under his breath. Walter slipped his opera glasses into a sport bag and followed.

They came to a squat apartment building and Walter made note of the door that Julio entered. Walter took some deep breaths and built up his courage. He climbed the stairs and tapped on the door. He could hear Julio muttering as he approached.

He threw the door open and was surprised to see Walter. He poked his head out and looked both ways. "What do you want?"

"A minute of your time," Walter replied.

"I know you, you're Angela's boss."

"Is that what she said? Boss? Interesting. Can I come in?"

"Alright, I guess. But I'm on my way out again."

He stood back and followed Walter inside. Walter wrinkled his nose at the mess. Clothes were strewn around and dirty dishes were collecting dust on the table in front of the TV.

"Look, do you get high? I can get you some stuff wholesale. Primo."

"You can dispense with the pretense. I know you're a cop."

Julio got twitchy. "Cop, I ain't no cop. Who told you that?"

"Whatever you say, snitch. Stool pigeon. Narc. Human trash."

"That's horseshit. Who do you think you are?

"I am Doctor Zalooq. And you, my little friend are about to explore life's final mystery."

Walter unzipped his bag and pulled out a bundle. He pushed all the trash off the coffee table and unrolled a velvet pad. The pad was covered with hieroglyphs. He pressed nasal filters into his nostrils. He lit a pellet in a small brass cup which emitted a sweet smoke into the air. He pulled out a metronome and set it to clicking back and forth. All the while, he was speaking quietly. Julio pulled a small revolver from his ankle holster. He waved it at Walter who smiled patiently.

"I'll shoot your ass," Julio threatened.

"You can't shoot me with a beetle," Walter suggested.

"What beetle?"

"The large and rather ugly beetle you are currently holding in your hand," Walter said quietly.

With a look of horror, Julio dropped the gun.

"Jesus! Where did that come from?"

"From a place in your head right about here," Walter said, pointing at his skull above and slightly behind his ear. "Your mind is particularly susceptible to hypnotics, did you know that? Perhaps you'd be more comfortable if you took a seat?" Walter waved his hand slowly and Julio sank into his easy chair. "Before we get too far along, perhaps you'll tell me about your relationship with my Angela?"

"We had a thing. It was fun. We got high, we screwed a few times. I had some drugs but hers were better. She dumped me. She was a very fine piece of ass."

"Yes, I know. How did you find her?"

"She was in a bar looking for a good time. She was frustrated and bored. She hates Alaska. I distracted her from herself for a while."

"I see. Angela is still young and impressionable. I was neglectful and you took advantage of her."

"I suppose I did. I was in the right place at the right time."

"I think it remains to be seen how lucky you will feel in the end. Tell me about your police work."

"I work undercover. I bust dopers."

"But you get high too? How do you justify that?"

"Sometimes you have to get high to gain the confidence of your target."

"But you like it."

"Yes, I like it. I can handle it. I do good work."

"Of course. Now tell me what you were planning for the candidate?"

"I figure he is a big user. I need a big score to keep my boss off my ass."

"But Glen is clean."

"I was going to plant on him, bribe a maid to hide stuff in his room and bust the whole crew. It would have been great."

"Does your boss know the details of this outstanding plan?"

"No, he would have nixed it. I was going to tell him in a few days."

"I think you've told me everything I need to know. I take some responsibility for your fling with my Angela. She likes a more metropolitan lifestyle and my mind has been on other things. It was obvious she was unhappy. If I'd been more attentive, none of this would have happened. So, I would slip you a break. But, I cannot forgive your underhanded plan for the candidate. That was partly my fault too, I need to pay more attention to the details. You are human filth and I'm too earthbound to rise above your betrayal and let you spread more of your evil on the world. Angela might have mentioned my skill as an alchemist? I know you've enjoyed some of my work already. First of all, I'm going to give you some of my new temporal. Time will stretch out like saltwater taffy; a second will become a minute, a minute will become an hour, and an hour will become 60."

Walter opened a small metal box and took out a tiny syringe. He removed a protective cover and handed the needle to Julio.

"Inject yourself with this, don't worry about finding a vein, just any old place will do."

"I don't want to."

"So, you're afraid? That's good, you should be. You don't want to inject yourself, but you will do it now." Walter's eyes bored into Julio's. Slowly Julio pressed the needle into the flesh of his wrist.

"Very well. Let's just relax here for a few moments until that takes hold. You won't be able to speak, so don't bother trying."

Walter watched Julio sink slowly back in his chair.

"Okay Detective, here is the part you will find much more unpleasant, I'm almost sorry to say."

Walter carefully powdered his hands and slipped on some latex gloves. He examined the surfaces carefully to make sure there were no tears. He unscrewed the cap on a small jar and gently placed it on the table.

"I'm not sure if you know what a convulsant is. This comes from the rainforest in Brazil. In that forest there lives a rare wasp and like all wasps, it has a venom. This venom contains a nasty and rather complex chemical which I have isolated and extracted. Several thousand of these bees donated their venom to create a small amount of this particular poison."

Walter extracted a cotton ball. He used a small eyedropper to apply a teardrop of fluid on the cotton ball. He gently put the top back on the jar and stowed the jar back in his bag. He pulled off two inches of medical tape.

"This venom will travel quickly through your bloodstream. As it flows, your muscles will convulse and lock. You will literally be pulled apart as your muscles tear tendons away from the bone and shred themselves. I don't think there is a more intense pain a person can experience. Generally, the brain goes into shock and protects us from intense pain like this, but I think in your case, you'll find the vapor you've been inhaling has quite disabled this protective mechanism. I'm afraid this pain will seem to you to last nearly an eternity. It will stop when your body dies from the dehydration which will only add to your pain as the day wears on. Quite a diabolical fate, I'm afraid. If you're uncertain about the exact lexicality of the word diabolical, it can be defined as appropriate to a devil, especially in degree of wickedness or cruelty. So, you will agree that this is a most pertinent word to describe what I'm doing to you."

Walter placed the cotton ball on the tape and gently applied it to Julio's arm. Instantly, the muscles in Julio's arm flexed and this flexure passed up the arm to the shoulder, to the torso, and into his entire body. Walter carefully removed his gloves and placed them into a zip-locked bag. He rolled up his mat and stored everything away. Some tearing of the muscles was actually audible; they popped and snapped like popcorn kernels. Walter made a sour face as these sounds were unpleasant to hear. Julio's back was flexed and his eyes were straining at their sockets. He was frozen except for some twitching as particular muscles and tendons ripped apart. Walter turned the light out and quietly closed the door behind him.

Bennie and Emma

"Are you sure you are ready for this?"

Bennie and Emma were seated in the back seat of a rented limousine backed into a far corner of the Marriott parking garage. In spite of Bennie's brilliance, this plan had been conceived and implemented by Emma. She hired the limo and scoped out the garage for the best location. They were keeping a watchful eye for other election team members, particularly Murphy who had a knack for turning up at inopportune moments. The security screen between the driver and the passenger compartment was raised and for the first time, Bennie and Emma were truly alone.

"Yes, I believe I'm ready," Bennie said quietly.

"Once we've done this, our lives will never be the same."

"I know, irreversible steps toward adulthood and all that. I'm tired of agonizing over this. Let's just do it and get it over with."

"Well, if that's your attitude, then I'm not sure if I want to."

"I'm sorry, Emma. You have to be feeling at least some of what I'm feeling. It's true that we're too young, but I know there is something special between us and this act will mark us forever. Our first time, together, the way it was meant to be."

"Bennie, are you getting metaphysical? Who would have guessed your big old brain could hold such sentimentality."

"Indeed."

They turned toward each other and embraced. Slowly their faces approached and, after a clumsy alignment of their noses, they kissed each other directly on the lips. The kiss lasted about 10 seconds and for these kids, it was 10 seconds of bliss. They clung to each other and caught their respective breaths.

"That was lovely," Emma said breathlessly.

"Yes, it was," Bennie replied, "but now I have to run because Glen is waiting for a report. Perhaps we can do this again tomorrow?"

"Perhaps we can," Emma replied.

Moshi

The old Honda idled a block from the Brown household. Jordan was dispatched to reconnoiter the house and make sure the way was clear to sneak Moshi in. The boys had been fighting about which room she would sleep in, but Moshi ended the argument by insisting that she would sleep on the couch after the parents were sleeping. Neither boy was satisfied with this solution and they glared at each other with fraternal malice.

"I'll beat the shit out of you."

"I'll tell mom."

Moshi sighed and looked out the window at the neighborhood. Rain drizzled from a solid leaden sky and a sodden newspaper boy walked by throwing plastic-wrapped newspapers listlessly onto wet lawns. A dog barked angrily from a porch, but showed no inclination to come out of his shelter and get wet.

"Look, Moshi. I'm sorry that you were left here with no place to go and whatnot. We should make the best of it. I don't know much about girls, maybe you could help me. Show me what to do and stuff."

"You'd be better with hooking up with someone your own age. You'll figure out what to do when the time comes for you."

"I'm tired of waiting." He leaned over the parking brake and touched her neck. "I don't think you have much choice, do you? You need a place to stay, right? Besides, its no big deal to you, you've slept with a lot of boys."

"Only Erik," Moshi whispered.

"It would mean the world to me. I'm not a virgin or anything, but I could use more experience." He allowed his hand to trail down her neck and to the side of her small breast. Moshi cast her mind out. She visualized an old man with a single chopstick teasing wavy lines into the pebbles of a bonsai garden. Slowly, one-by-one, pebbles were moved into place. The wind that stirred cherry blossoms was the breath of her ancient ancestors.

Jordan jerked open the door.

"No problemo. Mom left a note, she is grocery shopping and Dad isn't home yet. Let's get her in."

Jack pulled the car into the muddy ruts of its parking spot along side of their house. They scurried inside and settled Moshi into Jack's room because it was further away from their parent's room. They turned on the TV to mask any noise. Moshi sat on a pillow in the corner of the darkening room. After a time, Mrs. Brown came home and shouted for the boys to help her put away the groceries. As Jack left, he held his fingers to his lips to remind Moshi to be quiet. It seemed that a lot of shouting accompanied the household routine until Mr. Brown came home and ordered everyone to shut up while he read his paper. The scents of cooking filled the house and Moshi's stomach grumbled. She sat with her eyes closed and tried not to think about how hungry, thirsty and lonely she was. Hours passed slowly. She could not discern order from the mix of voices on TV and could not focus on the stream of images. Her stomach burned, it felt like a flaming coal burned in her midsection. Unnoticed tears streamed down her cheeks. After darkness fell, the only light in the room came from the flickering TV and from intermittent headlights that stroboscopically swept across the room through gaps in the curtains.

Finally, light speared Moshi's eyes as Jack entered the room. He kicked off his shoes and cross-legged, sat facing her. Slowly, as the sounds of the house quieted. Jack lifted her arms and worked her sweater over her head. He reached around her back and pinched and fumbled until her bra came loose.

"Fucking without love is soulless and empty. Cheap. Unworthy of a good man."

"Yeah, whatever," Jack whispered while panting in small breaths. He took off his t-shirt and jeans and sat with his small cock pressing against his jockey shorts. He pointed at his socks and motioned for Moshi to remove them. She shook her head and, exasperated, Jack tugged them off himself and threw them aside. "Get your goddam pants off," he hissed urgently.

"I need something to drink first. Gin, if you have it."

"Crap! Okay, I'll go see what I can find."

He opened the door quietly and tip-toed out. After a few minutes, he came back with a partial bottle of ice-cold vodka. "This is all we have." He took a drink, then, grimacing, handed the bottle to Moshi. She tipped the bottle and drank as much as she could. The liquid traced a flow in her throat that was both frigid and lava-hot. When the searing faded she drank deeply again.

"Don't drink it all," Jack insisted. "I have to refill it with water so Dad won't notice."

"The water will freeze, he'll notice."

"Damn it, you're right." He tugged the bottle from her hands and took another small sip himself. Carefully, he set the bottle down and crawled toward her on his hands and knees. He pulled his shorts down over his skinny hips and waited expectantly for Moshi to get undressed too. As the alcohol kicked in and the pain of the world faded, she unzipped her skirt and worked it off. She let her fingernails creep up his thigh and his penis, small and thin like a finger, stirred and became erect. Her finger trailed over his scrotum and she grasped the shaft. She stroked him for a minute and he squirted onto his thigh. After he caught his breath, he wiped his leg with a sock.

"I know I come too quick," he said defensively, "but, I'll be ready to go again soon and I'll last longer next time." The door opened and Jordan came in.

"Did you start without me?" he asked. "It took a long time for Mom and Dad to go to sleep. I have to listen to them humping. It's gross."

Moshi stretched her arm and snagged the vodka. She drank and tried to close her mind to the degradation and shame that the boys created. It took nearly an hour of groping and coupling before the boys fell asleep. Moshi gathered her clothes, a blanket and a pillow, and made herself a bed on the couch in the living room where she slept like death until morning.

Gradually the sounds of the house increased and Moshi drifted into consciousness. She sat up on the couch and ran a finger around her teeth and tongue to dislodge the gummy gunk that filled her mouth. Surreally, the Brown's were seated at the breakfast table watching and waiting for her. She tried to interpret their expressions. The boys, with disheveled hair, were dressed in odd combinations like they'd just thrown on whatever they picked up off their floors in a hurry. They looked into their bowls with a glum guilt. Mr. Brown was holding in a thinly controlled rage and Mrs. Brown dished out Cream of Wheat cereal with an air of sadness and disappointment. A dish of brown sugar and a plastic jug of milk shared the center of the table with the nearly empty bottle of vodka. Juice glasses with cranberry-flavored drink completed each table setting.

"Good morning, Moshi. Sit down and have some breakfast," Mrs. Brown said quietly.

Spooning in heaps of sugar, Moshi mixed up her mush and tried not to stare at the vodka. Its presence on the table was disturbing. Like Moshi herself, it did not belong. She did not fit in the middle of this family. She drained most of her cranberry juice then deliberately reached for the vodka. She poured until her glass was full and spilled some as she slurped at it. All action at the table stopped as they watched this scene. Mr. Brown's mouth hung open. "Everybody just eat," he was finally able to say. When he was finished, he wiped his mouth with a paper napkin and grabbed his lunch pail. He pointed a thick accusing finger at Moshi and simply said: "You." He walked out heavily and they heard his truck start then drive away.

"Alright boys, get yourselves off to school," Mrs. Brown said. The two women sat and moved mush around their bowls while the boys ran in circles gathering their things. Finally, they kissed their mother on the cheek and dashed out the door. They could hear the Honda starter grind for a while, then the engine caught and they drove off. Mrs. Brown pawed through her purse and found a rumpled package of Virginia Slim cigarettes. She straightened one out and lighted it with a disposable lighter and a shaking hand.

"I quit these things for a while, but the habit keeps coming back." She turned to face Moshi. "I have sympathy for your position, I really do. Once, I was not so different, I was dancing at Charlie's and I did some things I'm not proud of. This family has problems, maybe more than most, I don't know, but we're trying very hard. Do you understand? You are not helping."

She stood and gathered the breakfast dishes and stacked them in the sink. She disappeared into Jack's room and came out with Moshi's bra and panties. She dropped them on the table by the vodka.

"I want to think the best of my boys. I wish they could just slow down and enjoy being children for a while longer, ride their skateboards and play their games, but that's not the way things are for kids these days. It's a damn shame, but it does no good to pretend. I just pray that they don't do something so dumb that it marks them for life."

Moshi could not take her eyes off the vodka bottle. Mrs. Brown sighed and stubbed out her smoke. "Go ahead and finish, I know you want it."

Moshi nodded and drank the last draughts from the bottle. Mrs. Brown reached across the table and grasped Moshi's hands. With their fingers intertwined, Moshi was transfixed by the purple veins and well-chewed cuticles of Mrs. Brown's hands.

"Let's pray for the Lord to show us the way."

Moshi squeezed her eyes shut and really tried. She reached out with her soul, but only emptiness and silence echoed back.

"Lord, guide us and protect us. Please," Mrs. Brown whispered urgently. She sighed and released Moshi's sweaty hands. "Gather your things and I'll run you downtown. I can spare some food and a few dollars, but that's all. You will not come back here, yes?"

Moshi nodded in agreement.

Near the airport, Mrs. Brown pulled over and left the car idling. She drew undecipherable lines in the dust on her dashboard. To Moshi they looked like the wavy lines drawn in pebbles by her imaginary ancestor from the night before. Harmony was trying to reach her, but the wall was too thick and built too high. Mrs. Brown brushed away the dust and wiped her palms on her skirt.

"This is as good a place as any," Mrs. Brown said firmly.

Moshi nodded and gathered her plastic bags. "I think your boys will be fine if you watch them closely," Moshi lied.

"I know and I'm trying," Mrs. Brown replied.

Pulling on the door latch, Moshi stepped out onto the sidewalk. Staring straight ahead, Mrs. Brown merged into traffic and drove away. Moshi watched the car recede until it was gone. She looked around. Jets roared high overhead and the sun peeked through the clouds in blinding patches. An old man with wispy gray hair and stained beard was carefully stuffing chewing gum into the coin slot of a parking meter.

He turned to Moshi and grumbled "Motherfuckers." Then he shambled off, shoving a fresh piece of gum into his mouth and talking to himself. Carried by a burst of wind, his gum wrapper scooted across the sidewalk. Moshi took it as a sign of the direction she should walk and she headed unhurriedly toward the north.

Glen and Scott Steele

The limousine arrived at the Captain Cook Hotel on time, right at noon, but Glen sat in the back and made calls on his cell phone while the car idled in the parking lot. When Steele had been kept waiting for a half hour, Glen and Murphy exited and took the elevator to Fletcher's Restaurant. Steele was dressed elegantly while Glen wore wrinkled Dockers with a necktie tied loosely around his neck. Steele shook hands with both Glen and Murphy and they took their seats. Glen looked at the wine list and selected a bottle of Château L'Église Clinet Pomerol 1997. Glen didn't know anything about wines; he just selected something expensive because he intended to stick Steele with the lunch bill. The waiter smiled and said "Excellent choice, sir." Steele looked pained but did not say anything. Murphy hid behind her menu while Glen and Steele simply looked at each other.

"That's a shame about Julia Patterson. I thought she'd last a few more weeks."

"Funny how fast her money dried up. I guess some of the donation checks bounced. I don't suppose you know anything about that?" Steele said bitterly.

"You suspect something underhanded? Besides, it doesn't matter if you have a billion dollars if there are naughty pictures readily available on the Internet."

"Those pictures are illegal. We're pressing charges."

"Sure you are."

"How about the hecklers in dog masks? Barking while she's making her speech? You don't know anything about them either?"

"Dog masks. That's funny."

The waiter appeared and handed Glen the cork. Glen sniffed it and shrugged. The waiter poured a splash of wine into Glen's glass. Glen swirled and tasted. It was good; a fruity rich flavor with the subtle aftertaste of his enemy's humiliation and despair. Glen nodded and the waiter poured for everyone. Glen ordered a thirty-dollar Kobe beef hamburger and garlic fries. Murphy and Steele ordered grilled salmon.

"I think we got off on the wrong foot, Glen," Steele suggested. "I was a little hasty. If I offended you, then I apologize."

Glen sipped and grinned. "Apology accepted." He stretched his hand across the table and they shook on it.

"I've been sent to extend an olive branch and see if there is any way we can forge a union between us."

"You've been sent because you don't have a candidate. Van Doren has cozied up with Pat Buchanan and your primary winner has gone from victory to complete embarrassment in a week. You don't think you can field a winner, but you assume I'll make the race respectable. I'll save you some rhetoric. Yes, I will run on your ticket."

"Okay, Glen. I just want to go over some ground rules with you..."

"Hold onto that thought, Scott. I'm going to continue doing things my way. The bosses can blow it out their collective asses if they have a problem with that. I don't need your money, all I want is the big fat D by name on the November ballot."

"We don't want to be unreasonable. Can't we just take a relatively low profile and slide through this election without further — uh, perplexity?"

"Perplexity, that's a good one. Let me make one thing clear to you. I am in this race to win."

"Don't be flippant. The polls..."

"I know precisely what the polls say. Support for Sanders is a mile wide and an inch deep. He can be beat and I'm the man that can do it. Unless you're retarded, one thing you should have figured out by now is that I'm not to be trifled with."

The waiter placed the orders on the table. Glen drained his glass and stood up.

"I'm not really hungry. Let's roll, Murphy."

Murphy stood. She frowned at Glen as she leaned over and speared a forkful of the salmon. She shrugged to Steele.

"Let's get together for coffee real soon," Glen said.

Glen and Murphy walked away, leaving Steele staring at the food and looking stricken. He filled his glass and drained it with one swallow. He could feel the eyes of the other patrons boring into him as he sat by himself and picked at his fish.

In the limousine, Glen instructed the driver to take them through the McDonald's drive through. The car was just barely able to make the turn around the building.

"Why did you tweak Steele like that? Was it absolutely necessary?" Murphy asked.

"What good does it do to achieve power if you won't use it to make your life more pleasant? Now what do you want? Are you still in the mood for fish? You could have a filet of fish sandwich."

Murphy rolled her eyes. "Sure, get me one with a Diet Coke," she said sadly.

Glen gave their orders to the driver who relayed them. Glen took out his wallet and peeked inside.

"Shit Murphy, I'm broke. Get this one, will you?"

"Perfect," Murphy muttered.

Walter and Bennie

Walter stood and watched Bennie work. He was wearing headphones and Walter could faintly hear some kind of rock-n-roll fugue seeping out of them. Bennie was running some multi-dimensional plots in Excel, but Walter could not tell what the WXYZ parameters represented. Eventually Bennie noticed him and swiveled in his chair and dragged the headphones down around his neck. He clicked his mouse and the music stopped.

"Sorry Walter, I didn't hear you come in."

"Can I talk to you for a minute?"

"Sure. I've been at this all night, I could use a break."

Walter rolled over a chair. "We haven't had the chance to get to know each other. I'm really impressed with the work you did on the voice stress analysis on the Sanders tape. That guy is wound up tight, we should be able to really hammer him. It's buried deep, but we're starting to figure out what it is about his assignment in Iraq that traumatized him. We think he might have killed some kids or witnessed something like that."

"Funny how the simple stuff gets noticed. That VSA[22] was trivial, but I'm glad it's helpful. The best work I've done so far is the eight-dimensional multi-ethnic regression simulation, but no one said anything."

Walter shrugged. "I know what you mean. I had an illusion that was devilishly difficult to execute, it lasted a few seconds and implanted a false memory of a naked ballerina. I just did it to see if I could. It was insanely beautiful, but no one really noticed. There are a few thousand people who so intensely believe they witnessed something real that they would pass a polygraph test."

"What is on your mind, Walter?"

---

[22] Voice Stress Analysis, an electronic method of truth detection via voice inflections.

"A couple of things. I don't know much about computers, but I have some friends at the UNLV[23] and UCSD[24] that assign their grad students little projects for me. Can you help me with some of my biochemical and genetic simulations?"

"Sure. I assume you mean hacking pharm databases and stealing supercomputer time?" Walter nodded. "With the system Glen set up, that would be child's play. Which is good, since I'm still officially a child, ha-ha."

"The other thing I wanted to suggest is for after the election. Have you thought about what you're going to do?" Bennie shook his head. Walter continued, "The only thing I really have is some aggressiveness in using technology before it's been completely evaluated and approved. Of course, I mix cross-technology science using stuff I steal from Merck, Medtronic, GE, Glaxo, IBM, Pixel Works, and some of the other big guys who would not think of working together. This gives me a window, just couple of years, before the technology enters into the mainstream or is banned by government bioethicists. The bottom line is I'm suggesting we work together after the election."

"I'm intrigued. Can you be more specific?"

"We're on the edge of isolating the mind and the body. Virtual reality is becoming more real than virtual. We're unraveling the biochemical soup of our brain. We're decoding and conquering the genome. We're synthesizing new organs from T-cell cultures. What I'm saying is that we can make billions if we bring immortality to the market under the FDA radar a few years earlier than the monopolies."

When Bennie was really concentrating on something, his hands floated away from his body, as if his focus was so complete that physical body functions were neglected and he became catatonic. This spell lasted for ten seconds while Walter looked on with concern. Bennie refocused and cupped his hands on his lap.

"I'm in," he said.

---

[23] University of Nevada, Las Vegas.
[24] University of California, San Diego.

CHAPTER 14

ALASKA INSTANT POLL

August 19

ADN Survey of likely Voters (plus or minus 4% error)
31% Sanders – REP
26% Undecided
23% Wilson – DEM
7% Van Doren – REFORM
4% Other
4% Walters – GREEN
3% Gray – LIBERT
1% Patterson – DEM
1% Onkiak – AK IND

The Election Team

Glen had purchased a telescoping metal pointer from Office Depot and was marching back and forth with it. He tucked it under his arm like General Westmoreland carried his riding crop and waved it like a conductor's baton to emphasize his points. Murphy was fuming, she had left Glen with Elke for an afternoon. Elke should have known Glen was not safe in an office supply store. She thought they had learned their lesson when, on a previous trip, Glen had returned with a multi-colored laser pointer. Murphy finally had to smash it to pieces with the heel of her shoe to get rid of it.

"We have to decide if we're going to build or destroy." Glen said. "Let's talk about the 'destroy' strategy first." He aimed the pointer at Bennie. "What's your status?"

Bennie looked up from the Fantastic Four comic book he was reading. "We had to hack military tribunal records and his psychologist's files. Some were paper, so this was not easy. In summary, when Sanders was an officer in the first Gulf war, his platoon was first on the scene at a children's hospital. Some National Guard troops were hiding on the top floor and Sanders authorized a mortar attack. Some of the kids died and some of the enemy soldiers were executed. We think Sanders was temporarily deranged."

"How can we use this?"

Walter spoke. "He has some repressed memories that can be activated with some subliminal images on his computer and one of my psychotropic cocktails. It's delicate, but we can disturb him without driving him clinically insane."

"What about the tribunal?"

Murphy handled this part. "The military cleared him. The kids weren't supposed to be there and there was no testimony that he actually pulled the trigger on any of the Iraqi troops."

Glen spun on his heel and waved his pointer like a magic wand. "What else?" he asked.

"One of his kids had an abortion. The father was a married pro hockey player."

"How does this help us?"

"He's on record as pro-life. The daughter was 15 and Sanders called in some favors to bury it. The hockey-guy is a well-known Christian conservative. The scandal is worth something like three points to us."

"What else?"

"A marijuana misdemeanor in college. There is a topless home video of the wife taken by a former boyfriend. One of his dad's wives inherited some money that came out of some shaky real estate deals related to the pipeline. Nothing direct."

"That's all?"

Murphy shrugged.

"I can't believe that's it. This guy is a saint compared to most politicians. I don't care about all of this shit, but if you find anything really ugly, I want to know about it. Let's leak what we have to his handlers and let them know we're sitting on this stuff. If they get too low-down and dirty, we'll leak. Okay, let's talk about the 'build' strategy."

"Our missionaries are starting to have an impact," Walter stated. "We've been manufacturing 40 or 50 new ones each day and they are doorbelling, promoting, and delivering campaign lit. Your name recognition is up to 43% and your approval rating is over 70%. We have flyer teams in Anchorage, Fairbanks, and Juneau plastering your face on telephone poles and walls. We're starting soon in Sitka and Valdez. Your novelty song, *Glen Wilson to the Rescue*, is being played on four stations in regular rotation."

"What's that costing me?"

"Not too much," Elke said. "Just some cash payola, we're in it about 40 grand so far."

"Good," Glen replied. He aimed the pointer back at Walter. "What else?"

"There are some local TV interviews coming up. The dogsled rescue film has been a hit on Channel 3 and the local access stations. The AP picked it up and we got coverage in Omaha, Denver, Atlanta, and Newark."

"I told you guys the dogsled angle would play. I could ride that dogsled to the presidency if you guys were more on the ball. I like the heroic theme. It's cheap and effective. You guys put your heads together and come up with a few. Save a commercial flight from hijackers? Rescue orphans from a sinking fishing boat? Maybe I can help the local cops bust up a meth lab? I'm paying you guys a lot of money, I shouldn't be the only one creating all these outstanding ideas. Get on it."

Murphy rolled her eyes and threw down her notebook. "Presidency? Orphans? Are you out of your mind?"

"I won't be dragged down by niggling negativity and shackled imagination. You'll dampen my creativity and inspiration, right Bennie? That's the way it works?"

"Right, boss," Bennie said without raising his eyes from his comic book.

"That's the spirit," Glen said while tapping his pointer on Bennie's shoulders as if he was bestowing knighthood. "Where were we before Murphy derailed my advanced thinking?"

"The Chief has you scheduled to visit some native villages and you have your Debutante Ball next week in Juneau. There are more interviews for local radio programs and you're giving a speech to the teacher's union. You're introducing Clint Black at the fair and you're introducing a Russian ballet troupe at the civic center."

"Bennie? Our numbers are on track?"

"The Julia Patterson meltdown has us two weeks ahead of schedule. We're in fine shape."

"Elke? How is the money holding up?"

"We're doing good. Just over a million in cash. There were rather large direct deposits from Belize and Thailand. Can we count on a few more of those?" Glen nodded. "We got an huge electronic invoice from a company in the Bahamas?"

"Pay it," Glen said.

"That's a lot of money. Can I ask what we're paying for?"

"No. What else?"

"Now that we're in the Democratic Party, we're going to have to start filling out the FEC forms."

"So, do it."

"We're getting resumes from UA students who want to be interns."

"Interns? I like the sound of that. Just hire the tubby girls who wear berets."

"Glen!" Murphy sputtered.

"I'm making a little joke. Lighten up, will you? I'm not going to diddle the interns. Give me some credit."

"Phht." Murphy made a rude sound with her lips.

"Pay them crap and get them working the phones and stuffing envelopes. Get some accounting students and they can work on the FEC forms. Anything else?"

"Steele wants you to fly back to NYC and meet the DNC and other Democratic leadership."

"If we can work it into the schedule, fine. Otherwise forget it, those guys can come here if they want to see me. Maybe a video conference? Handle it."

"We're getting some speaking requests from churches. What about the religion thing? Where do we stand on that?"

"Crap, I forgot about that. Let's say I'm a lapsed Baptist. No, make that a Pentecostal. Bennie, can you plant some history?" Bennie nodded. "I'm a spiritual, but not particularly religious, man. Let's upload to the Internet some pictures of me carrying a bible. Somebody invite a preacher in here on Sundays, I don't want to attend any church. Our position is that I'd like to go, but the campaign takes all my time so I worship privately. Anyone see a problem with that or have a suggestion? No? Okay."

Glen assumed a fencing position and shuffled back and forth. He touched the point on Murphy's chest. "Touché," he said. Murphy grabbed the pointer, bent it into quarters, and sailed it perfectly into an overflowing wastebasket. As the team got up and left the room, in turn, they patted Murphy on the shoulder.

"Thanks, Murphy."

"Way to go."

"You saved me the trouble."

When they were alone, Glen glared at her. "That was completely unnecessary," he said plaintively.

"Touch me again and I'll break *your* back and stuff *you* in the trash."

"There were some real swords at a little shop at the mall. Sir Glen the Gallant saves an old crone from muggers? Think that would play out?"

"I swear to God, Glen, I can't tell if you're really smart and you play dumb or if you're really dumb and play at being smart. Which is it?"

Glen waggled his eyebrows like a low-budget Groucho Marx. "*It is the dull woman who is always sure, and the sure woman who is always dull.*"

"Will Rogers?"

"No, H. L. Mencken. He actually said man, not woman, but the same sentiment applies, I think."

"Was that an answer to my original question?" Murphy asked.

"I doubt it," Glen replied wearing his trademark smirk. As Murphy pulled the door closed behind her, she could see that he was still wiggling his eyebrows at her.

Moshi

Standing on Spenard near where Lakeshore Drive forks away, Moshi peered in the window of the New Party Time Liquor Store. She carried the plastic bags that held her worldly belongings; Toxic Shock Syndrome t-shirts, the bottle of Advil she stole from the Brown's and a few aluminum cans she hoped to sell at the recycling center. Float planes buzzed overhead as they approached for landing at the Lake Hood Floatplane Base. The liquor store glass was dirty and covered with wrought-iron bars. A steady stream of customers came and went; business-folk, housewives from the housing developments, airmen, bums and other assorted drunks. The Asian clerk glared at her between customers and clearly wished she'd either buy something or go away. Moshi stared at a bottle of Gordon's Gin and willed it, with all she could muster, to float through the air and into her hand. The bottle did not even vibrate when a truck rumbled by, so there was no hope to cling to.

"Excuse me?"

Moshi turned to see who was speaking to her. It was a young man dressed in canvas work pants and rubber boots. He reeked of fish and looked exhausted. One hand was wrapped in a dirty cloth that was gray with grime and stained with blood.

"I have a room down at the Barratt Hotel and I could use some company. What would you charge me for a couple of hours?"

Moshi closed her eyes. She tried to absorb all the energy in the universe to help her with this tipping point. If she went with this man, she would be officially and undeniably a whore. After all she'd been through, she'd still never crossed the line into dirty sex for hire. The only celestial force that came through was the magnetic pull of the gin bottle. She shut down her mind and said "Two bottles of gin."

"Bullshit," the man said. He turned to go.

"I'm sorry," Moshi gushed. "One bottle and I will join you. Just one."

The man hesitated. He weighed the bargain in his head. "Alright. All I can afford for myself is cheap wine so you'd better be worth it. I'm Marvin, by the way."

Moshi watched him enter the store and place his order. He didn't come out with the Gordon's but brought a fifth of cheaper Taaka Extra Dry. He slipped the bottle out of the brown bag and showed her.

"Walk this way," he said.

At the motel, he fumbled with the room key, then pushed his way in. The room was dark. Wet work clothes were draped over the shower curtain rod in the small bathroom. The odor of fish and sweat engulfed the room like an evil fog even though the windows were cracked open.

"Give me the gin now," Moshi insisted.

"Ha! I want to see what I'm buying first," Marvin said.

"Bath first," Moshi said.

"Bah! Okay. I'm tired, you undress me."

He set the bottles on the chest of drawers and held his arms out like a scarecrow. Moshi undid his buttons and zippers and took off the many layers in which he was dressed. There was a woolen sweater under the overcoat, and a sweatshirt under the sweater, and a sodden t-shirt under the sweatshirt. Under the rubber boots were two pairs of wool socks. Under his canvas pants were a pair of jeans and under the jeans were long johns and under the long johns were a soaking pair of briefs. Under all this clothing was a much smaller man than he appeared on the street. His ribs were prominent and his skin was gray and clammy. Moshi toweled him off and pushed him toward the bathroom. His eyes were barely open and he was moving slowly. Clearly he had just finished a long shift on a fishing trawler or something. Moshi ran hot water in the tub and guided him in. She soaped up a washcloth and started by washing his feet. With the feet finished, she got up, opened a partially empty bottle of wine and filled a water glass for him. She looked longingly at the bottle of gin, but did not touch it. With his head leaned back on the tub, Marvin sipped his wine and struggled to stay awake. The hot water became dark with grime as Moshi washed his legs and thighs. She moved to his chest and washed under his arms. She moved downward and rubbed at his groin. His cock stirred and poked above the sooty suds. She washed his testicles gently and stroked the erect shaft. After just a few minutes, his back arched and he ejaculated a thin arc of jism. She got him up and toweled him off. She led him to the double bed and covered him up. He was snoring like a buzz saw almost immediately. Moshi sat on the bed and stared at the bottle of gin. When she could not resist the pull any longer, she opened the bottle and drank deeply. The fire spread in her torso and the pain in her abdomen faded instantly. She could still feel it, but it was remote and almost tolerable. The bottle was gone too soon, but she was able to drift into sleep.

When she awoke, the room was bright with light and a maid was pounding on the door. Marvin was gone and all his clothes were missing. Moshi staggered to her feet, the only things left behind were the two empty bottles and a geologic layer of greasy sediment in the bathtub. There was a five dollar bill under the empty gin bottle. Moshi shoved it into her pocket. She unlatched the door.

"Checkout time was at noon," the maid said. "Are you going to pay for another night? My shift is almost over, I have to clean the room."

Moshi nodded and gathered her plastic bags.

"Sorry," she whispered as she maneuvered around the maid and fled into the hallway.

Bennie

Glen walked into the main room and found three strangers talking to Bennie. The strangers were black and included a small and dapper man wearing a thin mustache and dressed in a white suit, a large man bursting the seams of what looked like a special order suit from the Gargantuan Man Shop, and a conservatively-dressed middle-aged woman who was seated and writing notes.

"Ah'd lack to inderduce ya'll to my white massa, Missa Glen Wilsa," Bennie slurred.

"Ah, Mister Wilson. Allow me to introduce myself," the dapper man said holding his hand out for a shake as the large man scowled and the woman scribbled in her notebook.

"Kurt Zonta-Mackle, Vice President of the Anchorage branch of the NAAPC, representing all of Alaska's people of color."

Glen shook his hand and nodded at the other two.

"I'm please to meet you, Mister Zonta-Mackle. I wasn't aware that there were many black folks in Alaska?"

"We're not playing the numbers game, Mister Wilson. Oppression and discrimination are evil whether it's one incidence or a million. Justice in the fabric of social order, that is our mission and our sociopolitical calling."

"I'm with you one-hundred-percent," Glen replied. "I would be delighted to sign up your volunteers for help with my door-to-door campaign. You will find my progressive program proposals to be a huge benefit to the minority community."

"We're not here today to talk about your campaign. We're investigating a serious matter concerning child abuse, neglect and racism. Look at this child." He pointed at Bennie who still wore a bandage on his face from his street fight. "I understand that this young man is not even allowed to go to school? You're employing an underage child-at-risk. You sir, are no better than a plantation owner and appear to be completely lacking in cultural competence."

Bennie interrupted. "Missa Wilsa, I believes there is some fried chicka in the icebox, you wants I should get ya'll some?"

Glen wore a constipated expression. "Not right now Bennie, thanks."

"Mister Wilson, why isn't this child in school!"

Thinking quickly, "Because Bennie is being home-schooled?" he offered.

"Then where is his registration paperwork? Where is his portfolio as required by Alaska State regulation? Where's your daily log? Where are your attendance records? I smell injustice and it stinks to high heaven, Mister Wilson. I stand as witness to your contribution to the delinquency of a minor. Miss Chelawah-Smith represents the State of Alaska Division of Family and Youth Services. You may be liable for criminal and civil penalties and you can count on prosecution to the fullest extent of the law until moral balance has been restored. I will raise my voice to the public in an outroar unheard since the wooly mammoths roamed the tundra. We may be small in number but our swords of justice will smite the mighty and our banners of freedom will unfurl in the powerful winds of our inevitable enfranchisement."

During this speech, Bennie left the room and reappeared eating a large slice of watermelon. He let the juice dribble down his chin as he watched Glen sweat. Murphy poked her head in the room.

"Boss, mind if I make a few comments?"

"Please do," Glen replied, with evident relief.

"In accordance with Alaska Statute 14.30.010 section nine, Bennie has completed the 12th grade, so he is not required to attend school. We have a notarized statement from his custodial parent granting us provisional guardianship. In addition, we have a letter of emancipation authorization from the Florida Child Welfare Administration signed by the clerk of the Florida Supreme Court. Of course, if Bennie wants to voluntarily enter into your care, we will not hinder him in any way."

Bennie tossed down his watermelon rind and wiped his face with a napkin. To Murphy he said: "You guys are no fun. Alright, just beat it," he added for his black visitors.

"Excuse me?" Zontle-Mackle asked.

"The fun's over, so just go away."

Zontle-Mackle took a deep breath as if he was going to start one of his tirades. But, he deflated at the look in Bennie's eyes. The trio filed out of the room with baleful glances.

"Cripes, that was a close one," Glen said.

"You didn't think we'd take a minor over state lines without our paperwork in order, did you?"

"Of course not."

"Glen, I don't want you to take money or any favors from those parasites," Bennie said flatly.

"Hey a buck is a buck," Glen responded.

"Is that supposed to be a joke? I've read Huck Finn and," Bennie said with an offended tone, "I don't think you're funny. "

"Sure Bennie, whatever. Is there really some chicken in the fridge? All this jawboning has made me hungry."

"Yeah boss, a whole bucket of Colonel Sanders, get me some too, will ya?" Bennie asked while flopping down on the couch. Murphy shook her head with wonder and left the room.

"Yes, massa," Glen replied, heading for the kitchen.

Angela

Angela sat at the bar at the Petroleum Club and sipped a club soda. This quiet club was private, but they let her in. She was looking at a cubic inch of soft skin that folded over her leather belt when she leaned forward. *Fat*, she thought, *I'm getting fat. Old, and fat.* Twenty-six-years old and at least two pounds heavier than she was at 16. *This is the end. Walter is too busy to pay attention to me, the candidate is just a pig and Julio has disappeared.* She could see herself in the bar mirror. A strand of her hair fell over her face and her mascara was rough. She didn't care. Earlier, when she was rubbing Oil of Olay into her thighs, she thought she saw the beginning of a stretch mark. *I'm falling apart. Next I'll have a mustache and my tits will be pointing toward the center of the earth. I'm rotting in this muddy hell.* She sighed and placed a Virginia Slim between her lips. She was reaching for her lighter when she noted a hand holding a wooden match. Flame erupted with a flick of a thumbnail. She leaned over and accepted the light before leaning back to see who was holding the match. She almost gasped, but maintained her composure. She sat up straight and swept her hair out of her eyes. It was the Swashbuckler, People Magazine's most desirable bachelor in 2004. A wild Australian. Movie Star. Bad Boy. He made an inquiring gesture and she shrugged and pointed at the stool. He slid in and waved at the bartender.

"Baileys, rocks," he said. His accent dislodged something in the pit of Angela's stomach. Probably an ovum; her body signaling that it would be perfectly acceptable to mate with this man.

"I have to come up here every now and then to clear away the Hollywood bullshit, know what I mean? Things are more real up here. Boots, guns, dogs, pickup trucks, fishing poles. I don't like doing that stuff, of course, but I like being around it. The last American frontier. Call of the wild. North to Alaska. I like all that. You too?"

Angela did not trust herself to speak. She just nodded in agreement and stared into the mirror to see if there was any hope for her lipstick. Other than being thin in spots, it seemed to be almost acceptable. Barely.

"I have a movie starting in September. We're shooting in Mexico, something about a soldier. I haven't read the script yet, I should be doing that instead of sitting here and chatting with you. I hate Mexico and I thought I'd come up here for the contrast. One of the nice things about Alaska is that it's not Mexico, know what I mean? Do ya?"

"Sure," she managed to say.

He held out his hand for a shake. "Ronald Graff. I'm sorry, I assume everyone knows who I am, that's a bad habit."

"I know who you are."

"And you?"

"Angela."

"Angela. That is a very pretty name. Very angelic. It does you justice, if you don't mind me saying."

If you don't mind me saying? Her ova were wrestling for position and elbowing each other to be first in line. So to speak.

"Thank you."

They sipped and made eye contact in the mirror.

"You're not from here originally?"

"No, I was born in Alberta. I've been traveling a lot, first with a theatre troupe, then with Cirque du Soleil, then with Doctor Zalooq."

"Zalooq? I caught his show in Branson. I was very impressed."

"I'm one of the stage girls."

"No shit? That is really awesome. Maybe you can explain—"

"We're not allowed to talk about any of that stuff."

"Oh, sorry, I understand. Trade secrets, right?"

"Something like that."

"What's Zalooq like?"

"He's a genius. He takes all that magic stuff seriously. He's always studying folklore, spells, witchcraft and ancient medicine. He's always trying to figure out what works and what doesn't and why."

"Sounds fascinating."

"For him, maybe. How long can you sit and watch a guy read old books, surf the Internet or mix chemicals? His body can be here and his mind can be in the Yucatan or Malaysia. It's maddening. Boring."

"I suppose. Look, I'm gay of course, but I think I could get it up for a beautiful girl like you. How much?"

"Excuse me?"

"How much for a night?"

Her ova stopped their little dance. He took her for a whore. And why not, she's a single girl drinking in an expensive private bar.

"Five thousand."

"Five thousand? Bloody hell, that's a lot." He studied her carefully from sandal to earring. "But yeah, five thousand, you're worth that much."

In spite of Angela's best effort to be cool, a tear slipped from under an eyelash. "I'm a dancer and stage performer, not a hooker. I just said five thousand to see what you'd say."

"Oh look, I'm sorry luv, I've upset you." He handed her a napkin which she used to dab at her eyes, trying not to smear the mascara more than it already was. "Truly, I just assumed.... That was rude of me. I apologize."

They sat and sipped in silence.

"You won't tell anyone what I said about being gay?"

"I won't tell," Angela whispered.

"It's not something I want the world to know about the Swashbuckler."

"I understand."

"I'm ashamed of myself. Let me make this up to you. What can I do?"

"It's alright."

"No, it's not alright. Look, a friend of mine is casting Alice in Wonderland at the Community Theatre. I think you'd make a lovely Alice. He owes me a favor. What do you think?"

"Alice?"

"Yeah. It would be a lot of work and not much money, what a deal, huh?"

"I'd love it. Very much, I'd love it."

"Consider it done. It's over on 70th, meet me there about noon tomorrow. Once he gets a look at you, it will be a done deal, I know it."

"Are you just trying to get rid of me?"

"No. What can I do?" He pulled out a silver Cross pen and scribbled his cell number and the suite number of his hotel room on a cocktail napkin. "I'm completely serious."

She took the napkin and folded it into her handbag. They drank and thought their solitary thoughts for a few minutes.

"Would you really have paid five thousand?"

"You're so pretty, even at five-thousand, you'd be busy every night of the week. There's no question about it in my mind."

Angela's ova were squirming and clamoring for attention again. She realized that what she really craved was some attention from Walter.

"Thank you," she whispered to the Swashbuckler.

"You're most welcome," he replied.

Glen and Murphy

Glen was looking over the questions one last time as the make-up girl powdered his face. He admired her undulating rear after she gathered her accessories and walked away. The sound technician adjusted Glen's wireless microphone. Once all was ready, Glen walked onto the set and sat down. He leaned over and spoke with the host. Under the blinding stage lights, her make-up was garish and clown-like, but the effect was good on camera.

"We'd like to strike seven and twelve and you can add back in number three if we run short."

"You already approved the questions. It's too late."

"If you ask those questions, I'll pull off your wig on live TV and chuck it at the camera."

She looked at him for a beat then scratched at her script with a red pen.

"Fine," she said sourly. She regained her composure as the stage director ran through the count-down. Under the bright lighting at count one, she produced a dazzling smile.

"Welcome back to Fairbanks Live. I'm Sheila O'Grady and we're visiting with Glen Wilson who was recently recruited as the Democratic Party candidate for US Congress. First of all Glen, it was quite a surprise when Julia Patterson backed out of the race so soon after winning the Primary election."

"Yes, Sheila, I was surprised too. My team and I wish her Godspeed in dealing with her sudden health problems. I'm sure her doctors will patch her up and maybe we'll see her again in the next election cycle."

"We've received conflicting reports, do you know what her illness is exactly?"

"It wouldn't be appropriate for me comment. I'm told her campaign will issue a press release very soon with all the details. I don't think it's serious and I'm sure she'll be back on her feet in no time. Until then, she will be in our thoughts and prayers as we wish for a complete and full recovery."

"That goes for all of us here at Channel Three also. Do you know why you were chosen in place of the previous party front-runner, Jim Van Doren?"

"I think there are a couple of reasons for this. One, my message of responsible governance mates perfectly with the direction of the modern Democratic Party. Mr. Van Doren represents the past and I represent the future, so that was a sort of harmonic resonance. Secondarily, our polling gave us confidence that the voters of Alaska were behind our program. Finally, Mr. Van Doren signed on with the Reform Party, which probably did not sit well with headquarters. All-in-all, I guess I had the right message and the right momentum at the right time, so things just fell together. I'm pleased with how things worked out and all indications are that the national party officials feel the same. Really, it's a win-win situation for all, particularly the good people of Alaska."

"Looking to the future, you have a tough race ahead if you are to beat Bill Sanders. Our polling shows him leading you by eight points with quite a few undecided voters out there. How do you see the election shaping up?"

"Our polling shows us coming in slightly better than that. Considering where we came from, the trends are all in our favor. I've been speaking to every group that will listen and our message of shoring up Social Security, protecting the environment and encouraging a healthy business environment so we have more jobs for those who want them has met with wide approval. My sense is that the voters of Alaska are ready for a social progressive who believes in cost-effective programs to help the young and old while placing the lightest possible burden on working people."

"You are new to Alaska, how do you respond to those who criticize you for running up here instead of your home state of Washington?"

"First of all, let me say that I have been in love with Alaska since I read Jack London's books when I was a kid. I came up here for the same reason that most folks did. To enjoy the splendor of this grand territory and to preserve and protect this incredible wild wonderland. I feel a bond to the people of Alaska and their independent spirit. So far, everyone I've talked to has welcomed me into their hearts and their homes and I have not at all felt like an outsider. For that, I must thank all the kind people of Alaska and promise that I will serve their needs and desires if they choose me to represent them in Washington DC."

"You have had some adventures already. Let's look at some of this great film. You were in a plane crash?"

"Yes, Sheila, you are correct. We had the misfortune of crashing and the positive fortune to come out of the situation alive and well."

"Where did you learn to drive a dog team?"

"Like all Alaskans, when your duty calls, you just jump in and do the best you can. Alaska is for can-do people, it's no place for sissies. I'm certainly not ready for Iditarod, but when faced with necessity, I just did what any other great Alaskan hero would do."

"I understand your campaign manager and accountant had an adventure, what can you tell us about that?"

"Your sources are very good, Sheila. Indeed, you are right, two members of my campaign staff were able to disrupt a bank robbery. They were shaken up a bit, but all turned out well in the end. It was a scare, but we're back to working hard for the people of Alaska."

"Your campaign manager was formerly a policewoman?"

"Yes, she was a Florida State Trooper prior to joining my team."

"Can you comment on your relationship? Is she also your girlfriend?"

"It would not be appropriate for me to kiss and tell, but I will confirm that Margaret Murphy and I are very close."

"She is an attractive woman, is there any chance that some wedding bells will play into your future?"

"She is attractive indeed. We have an election to win, after that who knows?"

"We're coming up to a break. Are there any last messages you'd like to give our audience?"

"Yes, first of all I want to thank you for inviting us to join your program. I urge those who are so inclined to join our rallies and campaign events. I will be serving blueberry pancakes at the Russian Community Center in Tanana on Saturday, all the folks should come out for that. We put our schedule on the Internet, so be sure to surf over and take a look. I look forward to seeing each and every one of you out there."

They held their smiles and their poses until the red light was extinguished. Glen tore off his microphone and ran his fingers through his hair.

"That went okay, I think," he said.

"Sure. You don't really believe you have a chance against Sanders?"

"I'll tell you what, I'll wager on it. If I win, I get a night with you, no holds barred? If you win, I'll give you a couple of airline tickets and a ten thousand dollar gift certificate for Neiman Marcus?"

"One night? Can I just lay there?"

"Sure, whatever you want."

"That's tempting, I don't think you have a snowball's chance in Houston. Let me sleep on it and I'll get back to you?"

"I'll be waiting. Until then."

Glen waved at the crew then strode off stage. The next guest, an old man with a fiddle, was being fussed over by the makeup girl. Glen nodded at him and worked his way to backstage area. Murphy caught his eye.

"That went over well. What did you and Sheila talk about after the camera was off?"

"Just a friendly wager on the election."

"Oh," Murphy said suspiciously. "Do you hit on everything that wears a skirt?"

"I'm not sure I follow your train of thought, Murphy."

"Forget it, we have a speech at the Elks Club, let's hustle it up."

"Sure, Murphy, let's hit it."

Walter

Walter sat in the lobby and hid behind a USA Today newspaper. He had a .25 caliber automatic jammed in his front pocket and it pressed painfully into his hip. Right on schedule, there was Angela, dressed in jeans and carrying a sport bag. She walked quickly through the lobby. He could imagine the headlines and how pissed-off Glen would be. Congressional candidate staff member murder-suicide. He knew that Angela was screwing around. She was weak, she fell from grace from time-to-time, particularly when he was immersed in a project. The part that bothered him most was how happy she was in recent days. It was one thing when she was strung out and moping around. It was quite another to see her pink cheeks and cheery attitude. Whoever was making her this happy would simply have to die. Nothing fancy like Julio, just a single shot to the back of the head. Then Angela, then himself. Light's out, goodbye.

Walter slipped on his hat and dark glasses and stepped onto the street. He'd almost waited too long, Angela had jumped in a taxi and was pulling out of the hotel parking lot. He slipped into the next taxi and told the driver to follow. They turned on the Old Seward Highway and cruised south. Walter's stomach was tied in knots and he couldn't stop thinking about the little gun that was embedded into his thigh. Angela's taxi dropped her off on 70th and he watched her go in the back door of a brick building. A block up, Walter told the driver to stop and let him out. Walter leaned against a building and watched the front entrance. Angela had entered the back door of the Anchorage Community Theatre, so she was probably screwing some low-budget actor. That would make the headlines even juicier, but Walter didn't care. The theater marquee said: Alice in Wonderland Opening Soon.

After an hour of chewing gum and watching the traffic, Walter felt it was time. He walked up to the theatre and found the front door propped open. He slipped inside. The interior was dim. His eyes slowly adjusted to the low light and he checked his weapon. A bullet was in the chamber and the safety was on. He was ready. He crept to the stairwell and tip-toed up. He could hear voices. He peeked over the railing of the balcony and saw a man tugging on Angela's dress. Slowly he realized that there were other people milling around; the prop crew were touching up some paint and gaffers were adjusting the lighting. The man who was tugging on Angela's dress stood up and clapped his hands.

"Okay, once more!" he called out. Angela stood at center stage with her script held at her side.

"I beg your pardon, you had got to the fifth bend, I think?"

"I had *not*!" said a man holding a script in front of his face.

"A knot! Oh, do let me help to undo it!" Angela cried out.

"I shall do nothing of the sort. You insult me by talking such nonsense!" the man replied.

"I didn't mean it!" Angela said in an upset tone. "But you're so easily offended, you know! Please come back and finish your story!"

"Alright," the director said, "that was better. The mouse is exasperating you, Angela, driving you mad. Okay? Give me a little more outrage next time."

"Got it," Angela replied.

The director addressed someone off-stage. "Somebody help me with this goddam dress!"

Walter sat in the darkness and watched them rehearse. A man sat quietly a few seats away. He leaned over and whispered something to Walter.

"I'm sorry, what?" Walter whispered back.

"Isn't she a lovely Alice? She positively glows."

Invisible in the darkness, Walter nodded his head in agreement.

Onstage, Angela said sadly "I wish I hadn't mentioned Dinah! Nobody seems to like her, down here, and I'm sure she's the best cat in the world! Oh, my dear Dinah! I wonder if I shall ever see you any more!"

CHAPTER 15

ALASKA INSTANT POLL

September 19

ADN Survey of likely Voters (plus or minus 4% error)
31% Sanders – REP
30% Wilson – DEM
21% Undecided
8% Van Doren – REFORM
3% Other
4% Walters – GREEN
1% Gray – LIBERT
1% Patterson – DEM
1% Onkiak – AK IND

Walter and Glen

Walter walked into the command center. Glen was watching himself deliver a speech on a video recorder. With a remote, he was watching, reversing and playing a section over and over.

"Hey Walter, do you think this suit makes me look fat? I need to find a better tailor."

"The suit is fine," Walter replied. "I need to talk to you about something."

Glen continued to fiddle with the remote and watched the video intently. "I really like the part where we pan back to the kids holding their home-made *Wilson for Alaska* signs. Those native children are really cute, Chief Eddie came through for us again."

"Glen, listen to me. I want to talk to you about our ball. We're doing fine in the polls, we don't need a heavy campaign push at this party."

"Holy moly, that intern has great boobs. I wonder if she's 18? Somebody needs to get me her cell phone number."

"Glen, we don't need this party to be a huge campaign thing. We could use it for something else. I have an interesting idea I'd like to play with. Something a bit unusual."

Glen froze the screen on the smiling intern.

"Look at those melons. I have some interesting ideas about what to do with those. Some unusual ideas. I wonder if she's a virgin?"

"I want your permission to try something experimental at the ball."

"Can't you see I'm busy? Do what you want, I can't be troubled with every detail." He waved the remote at the screen. "She has a nice ass too. I gotta get me some of that."

Walter could not completely suppress a small smile as he left the room and quietly shut the door between himself and Glen.

Elke and Walter

Elke slit open the mail with a scalpel and threw contribution checks into a shoebox and entered invoices into the accounting program. There was an invoice from a company in Juneau for some equipment delivered to the Centennial Hall Ballroom. She picked up her cell phone and direct-connected to Walter.

"Walter. It's Elke. I'm wading though invoices and there are some big ones for Juneau. What's up with that?"

"I'm getting things in line for Glen's coming-out ball. It's audio and video support equipment, no big deal."

"This is not just electronic gizmos. There are bills for atomizers and humidifiers. Industrial gasses shipped in from Seattle. LED[25] lighting panels. We're up to almost a half a million dollars already. Does Glen know about all this stuff?"

"Yes, I talked to him and he approved it. It's going to be quite interesting, you'll see."

"Okay, if Glen likes it, then I guess we're okay. You did a good job with the missionaries. That was fun, more fun than counting up all these invoices. Let me know if you need me for anything."

"Sure, Elke, you got it."

Elke disconnected and grabbed another stack of mail to sort through. She found another large invoice, this time for amplifiers and subwoofers being delivered to the ballroom. She did not think twice about it, she just entered it into the accounting system and flagged it for immediate payment.

---

[25] Light Emitting Diodes, solid state electronic light sources.

Moshi

For a few minutes, Moshi watched some rubber-booted workers cursing and clearing out some saplings that beavers had felled. It had been raining and the pond was flooding. Every week, workers from the University came out to dismantle part of the dam and keep the water level in check. In the distance, in the waning light, she could see a small campfire flickering far back in the trees. Cradling her bottle of gin, she crossed a footbridge. Two figures came out of the underbrush and startled her. Stopping in the center of the paved trail, she tried to make herself as small as possible. The vagrants recognized her.

"Hey, it's just Moshi," one said. "We're really hurting, do have anything you can spare for us?"

Moshi stood quietly and did not respond. All she could think about is what she would do if they tried to take her gin. *What if the bottle broke?* She was in bad shape, her face was flushed and she felt alternately feverish and clammy. She'd only had one back-alley customer this night, a well-dressed drunk who didn't come but gave her twenty dollars anyway. He didn't hit her like some of her other impotent customers. It wasn't her fault, but being slapped and pushed around was part of the job sometimes. The main thing was to get the money so she could get the gin.

"At least you can give us a candy bar or something, we're hungry."

"Just leave her alone, she doesn't have anything."

The two figures slipped back into the brush. Moshi followed a footpath through the underbrush at the back of the Chester Creek Park. By the time she reached the camp, she was stumbling in the dark. A swarthy woman was cooking what looked like a squirrel or a small cat on a spit over a small fire. Her grin was a toothless horror. Moshi settled on the dirt in front of a spruce tree. She twisted off the metal cap of the bottle and took a long drink. Three other figures huddled around the fire and tore off pieces of the meat with their fingers. When Moshi had fed the heat of her stomach and felt the choking grip of her awful life recede, she passed the bottle to the old woman and it made its round from hand-to-hand and mouth-to-mouth. While she waited for the bottle to come back to her, she watched the moon hover over the restless trees.

Angela and Walter

One candle did not seem to be enough for Walter, so he asked the waiter to bring more. They glimmered and enriched the pink blush of Angela's cheeks. They had a booth at Sullivan's Steakhouse. Walter topped off Angela's glass with Chateau LoVecchio Ultra Reserve, the most expensive Merlot that Nicki, the wine goddess, kept in her cellar.

"I've been a complete ass. I should never neglect you like I have been. You deserve a better man than me. I should be whipped like a dog." Walter paused. "Aren't you going to say anything?"

"You're doing just fine so far," Angela said with a small smile. She sipped her wine and dabbed her lips with a starched white napkin. Above the napkin, her eyes teased in the flickering light.

"Well, I'm sorry for being so self-centered. I have bought you a little gift."

He pushed a small box across the table.

"Something that sparkles?" Angela asked laughingly.

Walter nodded solemnly: yes.

"A guy can never go wrong with a gift that sparkles. Shall I open it?"

Walter nodded and Angela tore off the wrapper. Inside was a ring with a large yellow diamond center stone set in a platinum band.

"My God, Walter, it's stunning."

"As are you, my dear."

"Does this mean what I think it means?"

"Yes, it does."

"Well then, I will. I mean I do." She slid the ring on her finger and admired it in the shimmering light. "It's not much, but I have something for you too."

She slid and envelope across the table. Inside, Walter found a single ticket to the premier performance of Alice in Wonderland at the Anchorage Community Theater.

"Thank you, dear."

Angela deflated a little.

"You already knew?"

"Yes dear, the Doctor knew. The Doctor knows all. I really appreciate the invitation, I know how much this means to you."

The waiter delivered platters of grilled salmon with blackberry sauce. They ate in silence and Angela could hardly remove her eyes from the glittering diamond. The waiter offered them dessert menus, but Walter waved him away.

"I have my own plans for dessert," he said.

He slipped a small bottle of violet crystals out of his pocket. "I created a special recipe just for you and I," he whispered as he shook the vial.

"Oh Walter," Angela said with fiery sparks in her eyes. "Get me out of here now."

"Yes my dear," Walter replied.

CHAPTER 16

ALASKA INSTANT POLL

September 30

ADN Survey of likely Voters (plus or minus 4% error)
35% Wilson – DEM
32% Sanders – REP
15% Undecided
8% Van Doren – REFORM
3% Other
4% Walters – GREEN
1% Gray – LIBERT
1% Patterson – DEM
1% Onkiak – AK IND

Lester Mike

Lester sat on the toilet and read an article about Glen Wilson. He was rising in the polls and it actually looked like he had a slim, but real, chance of winning. *Who would have guessed?* Lester fingered the bandage on his head. There must surely be a better way to make a living than skirting the law and hustling from day-to-day. Kotzebue was not quite the end of the earth, Barrow was. It was close enough however. They needed a new mayor. Lester wondered if there was still time to throw his hat in the ring. If he could get a hundred of those good-old-boys to write in his name, maybe he could win that race. If Glen could do it, why couldn't Lester? It was certainly something to consider.

The Ball

Murphy straightened Glen's bowtie. He was wearing a black tuxedo and his fresh haircut was aerosol-sprayed into stiff perfection. Murphy was wearing a knee-length black dress which showed off her full figure. She was still angry about having to wear high-heel pumps, but softened when Elke mentioned it made her calves look sexy. Elke was wearing a pink and cream pearl gown and actually found some matching elbow-length gloves. Her hair was spun into a cotton candy swirl and she had sprinkled a dash of golden glitter on her cleavage. Bennie and Emma were cute in their outfits; Bennie wore a gray double-breasted suit and Emma wore a native-themed outfit with leather and bead accents. Everyone was into the spirit of 'dress-up' for their formal debut in Juneau. All of the politicians that ignored Glen's campaign before the primary election were returning his phone calls after Glen switched to the Democratic Party. The Governor, Juneau's mayor, both senators, most of the state senators and congressmen, various union officials, and assorted other players had accepted invitations to meet the candidate (and consume his complimentary liquor). Juneau is a political town and enjoyed isolation from the population centers of Anchorage and Fairbanks where most of the taxpayers lived. Thus far, the politicos had deflected all attempts to move the state capital to Anchorage.

"Walter has been fussing over things, he's as grumpy as a rabid cat." Elke commented.

"Yeah, what's with him?" Glen asked.

"He's spent almost 700 thousand dollars on setting this up, he wants things to go smoothly," Elke said.

"700 grand! That's a lot a goddam canapés. Who authorized that kind of money?"

"He said you did."

"Bullshit. I must have been drunk. Does anyone know what he's up to?"

They looked at each other and shrugged.

"Here he comes, you can ask him yourself."

Angela was dressed in a layered chiffon. She looked like a fairy queen, missing only wings and a magic wand. Walter wore cream-white tails and a top hat. He carried a cane decorated with a wolf's head and his eyes burned with a searing intensity.

"What the fuck are…"

"Sorry, no time to explain," Walter said, raising a hand to silence Glen. "Trust me, this will be quite interesting. You have a choice, you can use nasal filters and hearing aids with notch filters or you can wear a chemical patch. Insert the filters and hearing aids as the music starts or put the patches on now, just apply them on the underside of your wrist."

The patches were small, about one-inch in diameter. The crew all took patches and applied them while looking at Walter suspiciously.

"Can I get patches for my dad and mom?" Emma asked.

"Good idea," Walter said while handing her some extras.

"I don't like the way you use the word 'interesting'", Glen muttered.

"Maybe you're not as dumb as you look," Walter replied as he walked briskly from the room.

"Who hired that damn shit-head?" Glen complained, shaking his head. "Is every one ready?"

The election team clasped hands for an instant before they realized how cheesy this looked and dropped their hands guiltily.

"Yeah, boss, we're ready," Bennie said. He took Emma's hand and they regally entered the ballroom. Murphy checked her sequined handbag for her .357 and threaded her arm through Glen's and took a deep breath. "Ready as we'll ever be, I guess," she whispered.

Mary and Chief Eddie Kleedehn, standing by the bar, waved as Glen and his team entered the large ballroom. The room was decorated with American flags and campaign posters. A mirror ball hanging from the ceiling scattered blobs of seething light. Round dinner tables were covered with linen tablecloths and had signs for the occupants. Each table had old glory and Alaska state flags arranged in the center. Security personnel, dressed in black suits and wearing headsets, were positioned in quadrants around the room. The players in Maynard Ferguson's big band orchestra shuffled their sheet music and warmed up. Glen and Murphy took their position by the main entrance as the ushers opened the double doors. The people lined up outside were craning their necks to peek into the room. Immediately, the line surged forward. A receptionist took the invitations and whispered the names to Murphy. Murphy gave Glen his cues with introductory phrases like "Good evening, Governor" and "Pleased you could make it, Councilman." Glen and Murphy shook hands, kissed cheeks, and grinned until it seemed their faces would split open. It was an assembly line of schmooze. A photographer captured each greeting with incessant flashes and muttered instructions like "lean to your left, sir" or "turn a little more toward me, ma-am". This went on for several life-times before it was time for Glen's speech. He found himself standing on a riser in front of a projection screen with a sheaf of notes pressed into his hand by the resplendent Elke.

Slowly, the room settled into relative silence. Glen was fitted with a wireless microphone and the speakers were arrayed around the room so that his voice was non-directional. With Walter's high-technology audio system, it was as if God was finally answering prayers. Glen's equalized and electronically modulated voice smoothly entered the collective minds.

"Thank you, ladies and gentlemen, for joining us for our official introduction to Juneau. I want to announce for the first time, the polls show what I've been hearing from the great people of Alaska for some time: we're leading." Glen paused to allow a round of applause to run its course. "I've been traveling around this great state and talking to people. I've talked to shop-keepers in Seward (the scene projected behind him eased into focus showing a small grocery store with patrons waving from the front porch), school teachers in Soldotna (the picture morphed into a shot of smiling children in a small classroom), mushers in Manley (the screen showed a dog team running at full-speed with steam pouring from their snouts), crabbers in Kenai (a close-up of a dripping king crab), Inuits in Iliamna (a parka-clad woman skinning a caribou), and claim jumpers in Juneau (a picture taken moments before of the incumbent Republican state senator with a grinning Glen)". This photograph earned a good laugh from the crowd. Hidden by shadow, Walter stood in the back of the room wearing a satisfied smirk.

Glen walked to the edge of the riser and continued. "Since I was a kid (shimmering Aurora Borealis undulated behind him) I have been fascinated by the unspoiled Alaskan frontier. I am honored to have been chosen, along with the Democratic Party, to represent the people of Alaska in the election which draws near. As I stand before you, I will make a confession. I am an idealist. I think the job you do, and the job I hope to earn from the voters of Alaska, is important. The school children of Alaska (a montage of smiling children waved), for all the elders of Alaska (a photograph of an old woman wearing a fur-lined parka and smoking a bone pipe), for all the working people (a clip of pipefitters maneuvering a crane-hoisted section of pipe into place), the sportsmen (a man and his dog pose by a moose carcass), the fishing folk (a bobbing boat with nets deployed), all of our citizens need us to preside over their savings, their health care system, their education establishment, their critical infrastructure, their legal and police services, and their emergency medical and fire services. Now more than ever, it is up to us to spend their money responsibly and to uphold and maintain the public trust. How am I suggesting we do this? By taxing and spending? By closing our ears to the needs of our constituents? By doing things the way we did things in the previous millennia?"

Glen paced along the edge of the riser. A pair of spotlights tracked his movements and his skin glowed as if molten. Fog from a dry ice machine roiled in a thin layer around his feet. "Shall I list a few things our people need from us? Moral courage. An unending determination to struggle for justice. Strength to fight against waste, against enemies of the environment, hatred, erosion of human rights and exploitation of the young and the old. However, it's not enough to be against things. We have to be for things too. A cleaner environment, tax relief for working families, quality and cost-effective education, and a universal safety net of medical service, all these things and more. Let me ask you where my esteemed competitor is on these important issues. Shall I tell you? Nowhere! Mr. Sanders is too busy rattling his sword to pay any attention to the problems that face our children. Mr. Sanders is too busy crafting tax schemes for corporations to notice the situations that our senior citizens face. Mr. Sanders is too busy to hear the cries for help coming from our struggling small businesses. Mr. Sanders is busy having expensive lunches with lobbyists in Washington while Alaska's children make do with macaroni and Kool-aid. While Alaska's elders are cutting their pills in half to make them last longer. While our homeless community freezes on our streets."

Glen pulled a handkerchief from his pocket and mopped his forehead. "Standing up here for goodness and decency is hard work," he quipped.

Murphy held her breath. These words were not part of the script and she hoped Glen would not get derailed. He continued and she breathed again. Behind him, images of clouds swirled around Mount Denali.

"I will spend the next few months traveling around Alaska and I will tell you the topics I will discuss. Energy independence. Saving Social Security. Improving yields from the Alaska's Permanent Fund dividend. Improving health coverage for the old, the young and the needy. Saving our environment from corporate exploitation. Rooting out inefficiency and waste in government programs. Equality and tolerance. Jobs. The Wilson campaign is going to win and I ask each and everyone of you to get on board or get out of the way. Let's have a chicken in every pot and a snowmobile in every garage. I want to thank you all again for coming. Let's relax, have a nice dinner and focus on beating Sanders in November. Thank you very much!"

The applause was polite as the servers brought out bread and wine. Glen worked his way through the array of tables shaking hands. He overheard a snippet of conversation between an older man and his wife.

"That was a long speech, did he actually say anything?"

"Your dinner is free, so shut up and eat."

This made Glen smile. He winked at the old man. Glen got to the back of the room and leaned against the wall next to Chief Eddie. Murphy stood nearby scanning the crowd.

"Good job, Glen, the presentation was very effective."

"Thanks," Glen replied.

"What's the deal with these patches?" Chief Eddie asked, pointing at his wrist.

"Something Walter cooked up. For the money, it better be damn good. Let's get some of that salmon before the pols get it all, what do you say?"

"Hell yes, let's eat, damn it."

Glen pushed his dessert plate away and patted his stomach.

"What a meal," he said. He took Murphy's hand and they strolled to the dance area and swayed to a jazzy rendition of *Smoke Gets in Your Eyes.* This broke the ice and soon they were joined by several other couples. The bar was doing a brisk business and inhibitions relaxed as the evening wore on. Glen was having an in-depth conversation about financing Social Security with a steward of the Plumbers and Pipefitter's Union who actually seemed to understand the nuances of the federal system when he noticed a thin vapor trickling from the ceiling vents. There was a rhythmic rumble coming from the sound system and the lighting seemed to be flickering with pulsating colorations.

Glen caught Walter's eye across the room; he seemed overly pleased with himself. He nodded and fussed with video cameras that were panning and scanning the room. Glen felt a slight prickling sensation on his skin and felt dizzy and disoriented, like he was separating from his body. The feeling was subtle and could have been caused by the wine, but Glen suspected something else was going on. He watched the crowd dance, drink and chat. Beside a lot of scratching, nothing seemed unusual. Then reality shifted and the scene changed into something else. Time stuttered, Glen noticed that it seemed to stretch like taffy then jump. Walter was playing some of his temporal biochemical tricks, but Glen felt there was something else going on. The Pipefitter was sweating profusely and spitting on the floor. Two men in tuxedoes rolled across the floor punching and pulling each other's hair. Two women were clinging to each other and sobbing. The band was playing Sun Ra and the lead trumpet player was standing and seemed to be trying to blow his body through his horn. Time slipped and Glen found himself sitting the floor passing a bottle of cognac between Murphy and Chief Eddie. Murphy had lost her shoes and most of her hair had escaped the tight bun. Most of the partiers were gone and the band was still performing a free jam of some sort. Emma seemed to be having an intense conversation with her mother. Glen enjoyed random glimpses of flesh from a young lesbian couple making out in a dark corner while the bartender seemed to mixing more drinks for himself than for his customers.

"Anyone have a clue what happened here?" Murphy asked, slurring her words in a slight lisp.

The room was a mess. Some dishes had ended up on the floor and, out of sight, someone seemed to be breaking glasses by throwing them against the wall. Two waiters passed a joint back and forth. Elke walked by muttering in German. Angela, with her eyes clenched closed, danced by herself in front of the band with a bundle of bedraggled yellow tiger lilies clutched in her fist. It was either pouring down rain outside or some sort of staticy white noise was faintly audible from the sound system.

"Nope," Glen said after taking a drink. He passed the bottle to the Chief.

"Me neither," the chief said. "Do you think Walter will tell us?"

"He'll tell us or I'll rip out his asparagus."

"I think you mean apparatus," Murphy suggested, "rhinoceros. Esophagus."

"Shut up, Murphy."

Bennie wandered by. "Hey Ben, are you alright?" Murphy asked.

"Yeah, I think so. I'm sleepy, can I rest here?" he asked.

Murphy held her arms out and pulled Bennie tight. "Sure," she said. Bennie laid his head on her breasts and was asleep within moments. Glen woke up with a trickle of cold fluid soaking into his pants. Chief Eddie was snoring and the cognac bottle was tipped and sloshing on the floor. Glen staggered to his feet. His watch said 3:00 but that didn't seem right. Walter touched his arm.

"The limo is standing by, boss," he said.

"Good. Let's gather everyone up and get out of here. By the way, what did we leave for a damage deposit for this place?"

"Don't worry boss, I got it," Walter replied.

"Damn straight," Glen said.

Glen and Walter

Glen tracked down Walter who was reviewing video tapes from the ball in a suite at the end of the hotel hallway. Glen slammed the door and spun Walter's chair around. Walter did not look like he had gotten any sleep, his hair was standing straight up and there were dark circles under his eyes. He was still wearing the tuxedo with claw hammer tails.

"Alright, Walter. Spill it."

Walter rubbed his face with his hands.

"Okay, I'll tell you. I've been experimenting with the way that the body experiences the flow of time. Our perception of time is not uniform, there are biochemical controls for this. If I were to attack you with a knife, your body will stretch time to allow you the maximum ability to react. While you are eating, time passes more quickly. I have narrowed down the chemical triggers and Bennie has been helping me with the bioinformatics."

"Sure, that's interesting, but it doesn't explain everything that was happening at the ball."

"Yes, you're right. I'm sure you're familiar with the double helix of Deoxyribonucleic Acid, DNA and the replication process involved with the polymerase chain reaction. Your genetic information is passed to you from your parents in the DNA sequence. We've decoded the genome and understand the sequencing pretty well at this point based the Adenosine, Guanosine, Cytodine and Thymidine DNA nucleotides. However, from our experiments with fragment length polymorphism it looks like the encoding has far more resolution than we ever expected. The carbon-phosphate sugars are not binary or even trinary. The actual coding is far more complex. In the same way that molecules are composed of atoms and atoms are composed of protons, neutrons, and electrons, and these atomic particles are composed of —"

Glen was flushed and shaking. "Damn you, Walter," he interrupted, "I don't know what you're talking about. If you don't start putting this in terms I can understand instead of scientific horse crap I'm going to kick your ass from here to the salt water."

Walter closed his eyes and lowered his head. He took a few deep breaths.

"I'm simply trying to tell you that a lot more information is passed into you, through genetics from your parents, than we ever guessed."

"I understand inheritance. We inherit traits from our parents like hair color, skin tone, facial features, even disposition and temperament. Big deal. This is not breaking news."

"I'm saying that the coding has much more resolution than we thought. You inherit much more."

"More? I don't understand."

"I have not proved this completely, it's still very speculative."

"Spill it."

Walter sighed. He held his hands out like he was praying then pointed them at Glen. "You've heard, when facing certain death, your whole life, in tremendous detail, passes before your eyes?"

Glen nodded.

"This appears to be an imprinting process. There is a download, a mass storage. Your memories and mental transfer functions are impressed into the sperm and the ovum and are locked in at conception. It looks like we inherit a rather complete imprint from our parents."

"Meaning that our parents exist inside us?"

"Essentially, yes, you are correct, and not just your parents. All of your ancestors. I told you the data content of our DNA is massively complex and detailed. It's all there. With the right chemical soup and sensory stimuli, we can tease out this information. Hypnosis only scratches the surface. By enabling a sort of nucleotide polymorphism the experiential engine that interprets stimuli and the control response can be re-written. The consciousness of the donor can emerge. This is similar to a multiple personality disorder except past lives overlay the current personality."

"This is really big. Reincarnation."

"Bigger. Use your imagination, boss. We're talking about immortality."

Glen got up, but his legs were shaky. He steadied himself with the arm of the couch.

"What about my party? What did you learn?"

"Oh, that was just for fun." Walter chuckled. "You can't learn anything from an uncontrolled population and a randomized environment like that."

"Great. You're fucking around. Are you sure this work is safe?"

Walter's eyes flicked to the corner. "Uh, sure boss, of course it is. Microscopic margin for error, safer than walking across a street. Safer than driving a car. Safer than climbing a ladder."

"Shut up. I'm going to take a nap and think about this. When I come back, I'm probably going to kick your ass. Don't do any more experiments without full disclosure first. This whole thing is making me queasy."

"Do you want me to give you something for that? I have some Alka Selzer around here someplace. Perhaps some Pepto Bismol?"

"No, I don't. I don't think I trust you. I can't think right now, my mind is a muddle. I'm trying to win an election, can't we mind-fuck the world later on?"

"Sure boss, I read you. I'll focus on the election."

Glen let himself out of the room. He staggered down the hallway with his head cupped in his hands.

"Immortality! This team is going to be the death of me," he muttered to himself.

Walter and Elke

Walter parked the rental car on Happy Lane. He held the door open for Elke and they looked around the neighborhood. It was a typical middle-class block just off the main drag of East Tudor Road. The yards were decorated with tricycles and broken plastic toys. A cat skulked by with a limp thrush in its jaws. They strolled up Folker Street and were immediately hit up for money by a scabrous and jittery young man wearing a filthy black trench coat and discolored woolen gloves with exposed fingertips. He reeked of sweat and bad breath.

"Spare change for a bowl of soup?" the youth asked aggressively while standing in front of them on the sidewalk. Walter looked carefully at the scruffy kid.

"Nah, beat it," Walter said. He escorted Elke around the bum who turned and followed them.

"Hey, I'm talking to you. You got money, just gimme enough for a sandwich."

"Blow," Walter said over his shoulder.

The bum grabbed him by the shoulder. "Don't ignore me when I'm talking to you," he said with hostility.

Walter turned and looked the bum over from muddy mechanic's boots to damp stocking cap. "Bugger off," Walter said tonelessly.

"You can spare a few bucks, bubble-boy," he said with his hands extended. "Don't you want to leave a good impression with the lady?"

Walter glanced at Elke and his mouth twisted into a thin sly smile.

"Sure, okay kid, let me see what I have." He reached into the inside pocket of his raincoat and pulled out a bank-wrapped bundle of bills. "Here you go, have a ball on me."

The bum grabbed the cash and sprinted away with a loose-limbed gait. He glanced over his shoulder a few times to see if Walter would follow.

"How much did you give him?" Elke asked.

"Ten thousand."

"Wow, this is the kid's lucky day."

"You think I did him a favor? Chances are he'll be dead in a day. Either he'll overdose on the meth amphetamine he's been shooting or someone will cut his throat and steal his stash."

"That's very subversive. It doesn't pay to upset you, does it?"

"It's important to make things work out that way," Walter replied. He took Elke's arm and steered her toward Tudor Road. They loitered near a bus stop and watched the traffic in and out of the Anchorage Rescue Mission.

"What are we looking for?" Elke asked.

"The right candidate," Walter replied.

The sun was directly overhead and hot. They watched the crowd ebb and flow. Families in rusted-out station wagons, foot traffic that more often than not dropped an empty brown-bagged bottle in a waste can before walking up the steps of the mission, and squat native women who carried away heavy boxes of canned goods. The down and out. The perpetual losers of life's cruel lottery.

"We might do better at Bean's Café."

"Just hold on, I don't want to give up yet."

"It would help if you would tell me what you're looking for."

Walter looked at her. "If I knew, I would tell you," he said. "Hush up and let me work."

After 15 more minutes, Walter stood up straight and peered at a figure shuffling toward the shelter.

"I think we have a candidate," he said.

The candidate was a thin Asian girl. Her dark hair was oily and streaked with crudely bleached accents. She stared a few feet ahead and gave wide berth to all she passed on the sidewalk. She clutched a canvas bag to her chest and took uneven steps as if she was trying not to step on cracks.

"Let's go talk to her."

Walter and Elke jaywalked across the street and intercepted the girl. She stopped and walked backwards to avoid them. She did not make eye contact. She wore a nylon windbreaker with matching running pants and her toes were poking out of her tiny shoes. She was older than she looked from a distance, perhaps in her early thirties.

"What's your name?" Walter asked gruffly.

The girl looked like she was going to bolt.

"I don't do couples," she mumbled.

Elke gave Walter a cross look and stood between them. She slowly reached out her hand and lifted the girl's chin.

"Don't mind him, we're not trying to pick you up, we just want to talk with you for a minute." Elke said.

"I don't do religion either," the girl said defiantly.

"This isn't anything like that either. Just tell us your name, dear."

The girl's eyes flicked from side to side. "Moshi," she whispered.

"Will you join us for tea, Moshi?"

She scanned the sidewalk fore and aft and considered running. "I'd rather have some gin," she said. She turned and walked east on Tudor. She did not glance back but continued her nervous scan of the sidewalk. Elke and Walter followed about 20 feet behind. Moshi stopped at a bar called the Blue Fox and stood for a moment with her hand on the door waiting for Walter and Elke to catch up before entering. They followed her into the dim entry. Moshi sat at a table; Walter and Elke joined her and ordered draft beer. Moshi ordered a triple gin, straight up. Elke and Walter looked at each other and grimaced. They sat quietly and waited for the drinks to appear. Moshi stared at the wall and slurped half her drink in one gulp. After a few moments, her hands settled to the table and her eyes did not flick as much. She glanced between Elke and Walter and her drink. She took another deep drink and slowly calmed down. Walter watched her carefully.

"Your belly hurts, doesn't it Moshi?" Walter asked.

Moshi nodded.

"Can I touch it?"

Slowly, Moshi nodded again.

Walter pressed her belly and found it swollen; hot and tight.

"You have a lot of liver damage. Do you understand that you won't last much longer? A liver transplant might save you, but you have to stop drinking." He took his hand off her abdomen and placed his fingers against her temple. "I think the real problem is here, don't you?"

Tears trickled down Moshi's cheeks. Yet again, she nodded.

"I'm going to help you," Walter said. He pulled a sheaf of papers and a pen from inside his jacket pocket. "Will you sign this release, Moshi?"

She looked at the papers suspiciously.

"For twenty-five dollars, I will sign them."

Walter chuckled. He pulled out his wallet and counted out the bills. Moshi crammed them into the pocket of her running pants. She took the pen and painstakingly signed at each line that Walter indicated.

"Very well then," he said. He put the papers back in his jacket pocket and handed her a business card. "Here is how I can be reached." He extracted a small leather case. Without letting her see what he was doing, he removed an odd apparatus from sterile wrapping and palmed it. He pulled down the collar of her jacket and pressed his palm against her neck. She flinched and shuddered as the syringe poked her. Walter held her still for a few seconds before letting her go. He removed the palm syringe and carefully packed it into a medical waste container. He lifted her chin and gently dragged a cotton swab between her lower lip and her teeth. The swab was placed carefully into a glass bottle. He used a scalpel to trim a small fingernail cutting, this went into a plastic envelope. Moshi sat passively while he did this. He stood up. She took another sip of her drink with a trembling hand.

"Call me when you're ready to take the next step," he said.

He threw some bills onto the table and took Elke's hand to help her up.

"What was that all about?" she asked as they headed toward the exit.

"I think she can be temporarily fixed. You'll see. I assure you she has nothing to lose," he replied.

ADN

November 1

Homeless Man Found Dead

Frank Hesse, age and address unknown, was found in an alley near the corner of Spenard and Fireweed. The cause of death is unknown and police are doing an investigation. Frank was arrested last August for impeding traffic on Spenard during a crackdown on panhandlers. It is believed that Frank lived in a homeless camp in the Chester Creek greenbelt. A passerby, who refused to provide a name, said that Frank had recently come into a large sum of money. Police say no money was found on the body.

Glen and Elke

Glen walked into the room that Elke was using as an office.

"I'm bored," Glen complained.

"Why don't you work on your speech for the press club," Elke said while perusing some invoices. She peered at Glen over her reading glasses.

"Because that's boring. Bill Sanders is giving a speech at the Rotary Club meeting. Which dirty tricks are we running?"

Elke picked up a printout of the day's schedule. "We bussed in some folks from the assisted-living centers and some folks in wheel chairs recruited from the disability lists. The signs say Sanders hates the old and disabled, stuff like that. We SMS'd[26] a flash mob[27] to disrupt the press conference and we hired some students to hand out a case of bullhorns, it should be quite a scene."

"What costumes do we have out there?"

"We have the cigarettes suits and the fish suits. We're getting plenty of traction on the cigarette money that Sanders is getting and the environmentalists are with us on the expansion of the endangered species act to include Copper River Salmon."

"I'd like to wear one of the fish suits and carry a sign. That would be cool."

"I'll check with Murphy, but I don't think she will like it."

"Murphy doesn't like anything. Give me something fun to do."

"You can work on the spam email. We have a mailing list that we're hiring some high school kids to blast out of Kinko's. Walter is suggesting extracts of some of Sanders' memos. Some of the clips look pretty bad when taken out of context."

"They won't get traced back to us?"

"No, they are going out with Hotmail addresses from public computers. They'll scream but we'll blame it on Patterson and they'll believe it."

"Boring. How about if I wash some oil off seagulls outside the hotel where Sanders is speaking?"

"We decided not to do that, it was a bit of a stretch."

"Sanders was a lobbyist for Exxon."

"I know, but Murphy nixed it. Too esoteric. Don't worry about it, we're winning without it."

"Alright. Remind me to pick a fun election team next time, you guys are damn dull."

"We're winning."

"Winning isn't everything. Style matters."

Murphy walked into the room in time to hear Glen's comment. She gave Elke a kiss on the cheek.

"Do you ever listen to yourself?" Murphy asked.

"Excuse me?" Glen replied dryly.

---

[26] Short Messaging Service. Messages sent to cell phones and PDAs. Kids link together in electronic cliques linked by SMS channels.

[27] Spontaneous groups that converge on a scene for various purposes. An interesting modern social construct of young people linked together via SMS and Internet chat rooms.

"Sorry, dumb question. Alright, you can wear one of the fish suits at the Sanders rally if you promise to stay out of trouble. I don't see the harm in that."

"Finally I hear a good idea." He tossed the spam papers back on Elke's desk and exited the room. Murphy kicked off her shoes and flopped on an over-stuffed chair.

"Thanks, Murphy," Elke said, "he was getting on my nerves."

"No problem," Murphy replied, winking at her before opening her notebook computer and logging in to check her email.

Walter and Moshi

Walter was writing a long email to a friend that worked at Seattle's Fred Hutchinson Cancer Center. He was not particularly interested in cancer research, but he liked having access to their expensive equipment including a PET[28] cyclotron, various biosynthesizers and a quark electroscope. His concentration was so deep it took almost a minute before Walter realized his cell phone had been ringing.

"Walter here, what is it?" he spat into the headset in an annoyed tone.

"Doctor, its Moshi. I need to see you."

It took Walter a moment to realize who she was.

"Moshi, my little gin blossom, where are you? I'll send a cab."

When he had the information, he disconnected the call. Distractedly, he picked up the hotel phone and sent the cab, then returned to his email.

He had just pressed the send button for his email when there was a gentle tap at the door. He opened the door and looked at Moshi. She wore the same clothes but now sported the scent of vomitus and stale sweat. Like a shy mouse, she walked in the room and sat in a corner with her back against the wall. Twitching uncontrollably, she scrunched up into the smallest space possible and scanned the room for danger. She had nibbled her fingernails until they were bleeding. Walter crouched before her, but she would not make eye contact.

"The gin does not work anymore, it makes me sick," she whispered.

---

[28] Positron Emission Tomography

"I know," he replied, "my synthetic Coprinus Disulfiram derivative does that. You are anxious? You are hearing voices? Hallucinations? Tremors? You can't sleep? Shadows scare you?"

She nodded in assent at each question.

"Great, that's perfect. Don't worry about it, I've put a kit together for you."

He opened a filing cabinet and pulled out a cigar box. "I've analyzed your DNA and your biochemistry. I can get you back into balance, better than new." He opened the box and pulled out a latex patch. He pulled on rubber gloves, then removed the patch from its plastic protection. He pressed the patch against her upper arm and then took out a small round bandage and placed it against a vein on the inner side of her elbow. "Replace the patch when this indicator turns blue, it should take a few days. Don't allow anyone to handle the patches, they are tuned to your chemistry and could be dangerous to others. Come see me again if you need more patches. You still need a liver transplant, so I doubt that you'll need a refill before the ammonia narcosis kills you, but it's possible I guess. Call me when you apply the last patch and I'll order up some more. Okay?"

He turned back to his computer and started scanning medical journal extracts.

"I'm dying?" she asked.

"Everybody is dying. You're just on a faster track than the rest of us. Your liver will carry you a couple of more months. The patch will balance your bio-electrochemistry. Use your time wisely, say goodbye to everyone and enjoy yourself."

"Is that all?" she whispered.

"You can go now," he said over his shoulder.

She quietly got up, left the room and gently pulled the suite door closed behind her. Walter did not notice.

Walter and Moshi

Walter and Bennie were throwing popcorn at a television set tuned to the Discovery Channel. The show was about a genomic express sequence tag project and was so filled with errors and misinformation that Walter and Bennie were jeering. While they were watching, three overnight express envelopes were handed to Bennie. He signed the receipts unconsciously. He knew all the delivery people by name; the DHL courier was an older lady named Doris who brought Bennie home-made pastries. This time she brought some blueberry tarts. Once she was out of sight, Glen wandered in, grabbed half the tarts and wandered off again. Bennie opened the first two envelopes and threw the contents into a recycle box. The third was a little more interesting so he showed it to Walter.

"Merck is offering a directorship and a hundred-million-dollar annual budget. I'd get access to the largest bioreactor in the world."

"What is the signing bonus?"

Bennie shuffled through the pages. "Four-hundred-thousand and some stock options."

"Not bad. How about a business jet?"

"They don't mention a jet."

"Pikers. Glaxo-Smith-Klein said they'd lease a Citation for you."

"Pfizer offered a geisha harem. Emma did not like that," he laughed. "The Merck offer is a good one, maybe I'll send them something."

"What?"

"I'll send them tundra rice or protein 817a, the one that helps with a specific lymphic cancer or one of the cascade mutations of protein sequences, they'll like that."

Moshi walked into the room and stood behind the couch. Walter glanced back at her then returned his attention to the TV. She stood patiently for a few minutes.

"Who are you and what did you do to me?" she finally asked.

"I'm watching the tube. Have some popcorn?"

"I need to talk to you, sir."

"Can't it wait?" Walter asked in an annoyed tone.

"Yes, I can wait," she replied.

Every few minutes Walter glanced back at her. She showed no sign of going away. Walter sighed heavily and handed the popcorn bowl to Bennie.

"I guess I'd better talk to her," he said, shrugging.

He led her into the kitchen and opened the refrigerator. He waved at the contents and Moshi took out a plastic bottle of glacier water. They perched on stools arranged around the breakfast bar. Moshi had showered recently and her eyes were clear. Walter watched her carefully for signs of tremors, but her hands were steady and sure.

"I've forgotten your name."

"Moshi."

"Yeah, I remember now. Moshi. How have you been?"

"You know how I've been. Very good except for my stomach, it hurts bad. My mind is working. Are you a doctor?"

"Not exactly. I do a little experimental work here and there."

"What did you do to me?"

"I mapped your genome and body chemistry then analyzed your protein imbalances. Your body had a screwed up transfer function. I balanced you with a Moshi-specific cocktail, mainly a synthesis of paroxetine and benzodiazepine."

"Why?"

"Because I was bored? I was just playing around with some equipment and a research team Bennie is working with in Geneva. Just for fun, I guess."

"You can fix people?"

"Not everyone. If you have severe brain damage, we might not be able to help. Besides, it's expensive."

"Why me?"

"Because you fit a profile I was looking for and you were lucky."

"I suppose I owe you thanks."

"You can thank me by leaving me alone. If you need more patches, I can get them. Otherwise, just enjoy life, good luck, farewell, so long, goodbye. Go away."

"No. I can't go away. You fixed me and I owe you something. My ki will not be fully in balance until I repay this debt."

Glen walked in with a blueberry tart in each hand that he was alternately taking bites from. He freed up a hand and opened the refrigerator. He pulled out a quart of milk and guzzled from the carton. With a drippy milk mustache, he nodded at Walter.

"Who is this lovely young lady, Walter?" he asked.

Walter sighed. "This is Moshi and she's leaving."

"Whoa, not so fast. You're a lovely thing if you don't mind me saying." To Walter, he said: "She's young and she's not wearing any rings, there's no need for her to rush off."

He settled himself on a stool and offered a sticky hand for a shake. Walter rolled his eyes and walked off muttering to himself.

"I've seen your picture in the paper. You're running for something?" Moshi asked.

"Your Democratic candidate for US Congress, at your service, young lady. How old are you?"

Moshi thought for a moment. "Thirty."

"Perfect," Glen said with delight. "You wouldn't happen to be looking for a job? What can you do?"

"Nothing, I'm afraid. I used to work on a crab sorting line. I picked berries at my parent's farm. I gutted fish in a cannery. That's all."

"Great. That is perfect preparation for answering phones and typing up fund-raising letters. You have a pleasant voice, you can record some automated messages. Do you have a boyfriend? Nevermind, I withdraw the question. Where did you meet Walter? What size do you wear? We'll get you some new clothes. Where have you been all my life? Want to come to my room and watch a movie? What am I saying, of course you do."

Without waiting for any response, Glen took her hand and led her into the main room. He pointed at Walter who was sprawled on the couch. "We'll discuss your dereliction of duty later," Glen told him sternly.

Moshi passively followed him into the hallway. In transit, Glen decided on showing 'Sleepless in Seattle', it was as close to a sure thing for softening up a girl as he could imagine. The movie had barely started when she fell asleep. Glen smoothed her hair and watched her breath. She stirred in him a gallantness and protectiveness he didn't know he was capable of feeling.

Glen and Walter

Glen found Walter in the hotel coffee shop.

"Alright Walter, what's the deal with Moshi?"

Walter groaned. "I was just screwing around. She's an experiment, that's all."

"What's wrong with her?"

"She had mental problems which I was able to balance out. She was self-medicating with alcohol and her liver is functioning at about 10%. She has ascites, fluid retention. Her liver is as hard as a rock. Haven't you noticed how jaundiced she is?"

"I haven't spent much time with Asians, aren't they always yellow?"

"Not their eyes. How can you be so ignorant and still walking around?"

"Just give me the bottom line."

"She could croak at any time, she has a few months at most."

"What's the cure?"

"Geez Glen, she needs a cloned liver transplant."

"So let's get it set up."

"She's a street kid. The transplant will cost a half a million plus about 50 grand of immune system suppression drugs like cyclosporine and tacrolimus every year. Can't you just go find yourself a healthy girl?"

"You're right, what was I thinking? She's expendable, you were just screwing around, let nature take it's course, who cares? Let me just ask you one thing."

"What is it?"

"Who is the boss around here?"

"You are, of course."

"What did your boss tell you?"

Walter threw up his hands. "Alright already. I'll get it set up. Do you want me to schedule you a brain transplant while we're at it?"

"That's very amusing."

After moment's thought, Walter warmed to the idea. "Hey, we can do a fund-raiser and get some publicity. The press will love it."

"Now you're thinking. Just so you know, I like this girl. Don't fuck this up."

"Sure, boss, I get it."

ADN

November 2

Bizarre Fight Between Costumed Campaign Workers

In a surreal scene, a person dressed in a fish suit attacked Gary Bennett, a campaign worker employed by congressional candidate Bill Sanders. Gary was dressed as a bald eagle. The ruckus started when Gary tried to prevent the protester, wearing a salmon costume, from entering the meeting room where Bill Sanders was delivering a speech to the Anchorage Rotary Club.

"The jerk hit me with my own sign and then ran off. If he comes around again, he's going to find out what eagles really do to fish."

This latest incident occurred in what has been an unusual campaign season here in Anchorage. Anchorage police request that anyone who has any information about the identity of the costumed protester to call the police station and ask for Officer O'Toole.

Glen and Murphy

Murphy found Glen in the main room eating ice cream from a two gallon plastic tub and watching TV news. She threw the ADN in front of him and tapped her finger on an article that covered an altercation between the costumed campaign workers.

"Do you have anything to say about this?"

Glen pushed the paper to the floor.

"That prick was in my face. I told him to back off and he didn't."

"You understand how embarrassing it would be if anyone finds out our candidate dressed like a fish and picked a fight like this?"

"You should have seen it. That asshole fell over like a drunken sailor."

"We can't do stuff like this."

"Tell me about it. Do know how hard it is to throw a punch when you're in a salmon costume? We have to redesign these things so I can get a good shot in."

Murphy watched Glen eat. "No more antics, do you understand?"

"Okay, Murphy. You're right, this is serious business, no more 'antics'. Now beat it, the Simpson's show is coming on and I seriously want to watch it."

Murphy closed her eyes and took a calming breath. She shrugged her shoulders and shook her head as she left the room.

At the same time, drug companies are shifting a lot of money and effort into new ways of developing drugs, portending a revolution that could save or extend the lives of millions around the world. Biotechnology-based drug development will allow drugs to be tailored to an individual or a select group of patients, avoiding major side effects. In the long term, we will begin to correlate more and more genes with particular diseases that define an individual's risk profile, which will in turn allow us to limit or avoid that risk, either by lifestyle modification or therapeutic intervention.

From an article titled *The Suffocation of Innovation* by Robert Goldberg, published in the June 30, 2003 issue of National Review.

CHAPTER 17

Moshi

The TV hanging on the wall was muted and audienceless as a daytime drama flickered. Moshi stared at the wall and watched shadows creep as the afternoon progressed. A few weeks earlier, she was living on the street and renting her mouth to disgusting strangers for ten or twenty dollars, whatever she could get. Now she was hooked up to monitors that bleeped and plastic tubes that dripped. Murphy and Elke brought magazines which Moshi tried to read, but she could not concentrate on them. She played three-handed Skipbo with Bennie and Emma until clucking nurses chased the kids out. The candidate came and went with a film crew. The thing that touched her most was he spoke kindly to her and kissed her cheek after the cameras were off.

Her mind drifted over her life. Her grandparents had survived California WW2 internment camps and then owned and operated a rural strawberry farm. Her parents taught school and worked at the farm in the summers until everything was sold to developers. The farm land was now covered with strip malls and condominiums and the grandparents retired in Hawaii. From this heritage, how did she end up on the streets of Anchorage? If only she had finished high school. If only Erik had not introduced her to crank, heroin and gin. The only friends she had were the lowlife flotsam that hovered around the band bus. The band went on to VH1 heaven and Moshi was cast adrift. Her horizon disappeared into an alcoholic haze. Individual images would drift into focus, but they were so ugly she would push them back.

This operation was not working, she could see it in the sad eyes of the doctors and nurses that came and went throughout the day. The tissues did not match properly and her body was rejecting the transplant. Sometimes the miracles of modern medical technology fizzled, no matter how much money was spent and no matter how much people wished for a better outcome. Too much damage. Too much bum luck. Still, she was happy to have her mind back and grateful for the care she got from her new friends. For as long as it might last.

It would be easy to find an end here. She could jump out of the window or strangle herself with rubber tubing. She could just give up and let her soul go free. However, she did not feel like the world was done with her yet. In spite of her broken body and many sins, there was one last thing she could do. She couldn't save Erik and she couldn't save her baby, so what would the spirits of her ancestors ask of her? It wouldn't be long until the celestial clockwork unveiled her role. She hoped the Gods would give her the strength to succeed this time.

President of the United States Allen North

The room was small and had curtains on one side, but the curtains covered only wall as there were no windows. The ceiling was high, almost 12 feet, but the floor space was limited, slightly larger than 14 by 14. Two hundred and twelve square feet. The furnishings were sparse, consisting of a desk, a leather-covered guest chair and a futon. The wall behind the desk was adorned with an over-large presidential seal. The President of the United States, the most powerful man in the world, sat in his chair, leaning back with his stocking feet on the desk, eating from a bag of sunflower seeds and reading an article about Shania Twain in Maxim magazine. He looked up in response to a tap at the door. He glanced at his desktop to make sure nothing top secret or embarrassing was displayed.

"Come," he called out.

Wanda Dickson poked her head in. "You asked to see me, sir?"

North grinned, got up and gave her a hug.

"Yes, Wanda, come in, come in. Thanks for coming over."

He looked both ways down the hall, then pulled the door closed. Wanda was dressed conservatively in a navy blue pantsuit with a paisley scarf around her neck. Holding her leather handbag on her lap, she sat on the edge of the guest chair with her knees demurely pressed together.

"What is on your mind, Mr. President?" she asked.

He waved his arm around the room. "This is the only truly private place in the building. Concrete walls lined with quarter-inch lead sheathing. Sound proofing. No phone or other electronic devices. It is scanned for bugs every day. Completely secure."

"That's great, sir," Wanda commented tentatively. "I'm glad you like it."

"Wanda Dickson. America's sweetheart. The queen of the moral majority. All innocence and white light."

"I only have a couple of minutes, sir. John is waiting for me in his office."

"John and Wanda, the royal king and queen of Utah. Don't get me wrong, I like you Wanda, I really do. Almost two years and I'm very surprised we haven't had the chance to get to know each other better."

"Everybody is so busy. We'd love to have you and Sandy over for dinner."

"You're driving me crazy. I've seen you at the gym, you don't need to cover yourself up with all this middle-American clothing. You're an attractive woman and you know of my appetites."

He walked around the desk and perched on its edge hovering over her.

"Please, Mr. President, I'm really not comfortable with this talk. Please excuse me." When she rose, North poked her in the center of her chest. She sat back down clutching her purse protectively to her chest.

"Just so we're on the same page, I know about the film. I've seen it."

"Excuse me? I'm not following you, sir."

"Provo, 1988. I have copies. Alcohol, whipping cream and the football team. I don't know how you kept this off the Internet, it's great stuff. So, there's no need to come off all prudish and shy with me. I know you as you really are."

"That was a long time ago. I was a different person. The Lord has forgiven me."

"I'm going to take a guess at something. I'm going to guess that your husband has not seen this film. I'm also going to guess that he'd be very perturbed about it, especially if this footage found its way to the networks. You could say goodbye to his presidential aspirations, I think it would be safe to say. Goodbye to your marriage and hand back your crown, yes, Miss Utah 1990? Everything you've worked for flushed right down the nasty old commode? Yes?"

"Please don't do this."

"You've been teasing me long enough. All around but just out of reach. That's over now. We'd go now, but I have a meeting in a few minutes. The next time I call you, you'd better scoot over here quickly. Once you're here I can assure you that there won't be any big hurry. I want to take my time with you. Now, beat it."

Wanda stood up and pressed a handkerchief to her streaming eyes.

"I beg you, President North, don't do this to us."

"I like the crying. I just wish I had a three more minutes, but I don't." He drew a line down the side of her face with his finger. "So scram," he said.

He shoved his magazine into a desk drawer and switched off the lights.

"Sweet," he said to himself as he left his private presidential nook.

Moshi

On the day of her discharge, Moshi sat on the edge of her bed and waited for the nurse. The next patient, waiting in the hallway on a gurney, was a cheerful little girl about eight who wore a white scarf around her bald head. Dark purple circles circumscribed her lips and her eyes. She played games on a PocketPC and grinned toothlessly at Moshi. Nurse Thomas brought in a wheel chair and gently held Moshi's arm while she eased into it. The nurse placed her box of magazines and flowers on her lap and wheeled her through the brightly-lit hallway. A crowd milled around the exit; Moshi saw the candidate, Elke, Murphy, Emma, and Bennie grinning and waving. A knot of photographers and reporters pressed in. Glen posed with her and answered some questions on her behalf. She was dazed by the attention and did not catch everything Glen said, something about healthcare insurance for the homeless and bringing the concepts of cost-effectiveness to government. Bennie took her box of magazines while Glen shooed the photographers away and helped her into a black limousine. Moshi felt faint and leaned her head back on the leather seat. They drove down Spenard and she recognized some of the street people sitting on bus stop benches, loitering outside the convenience stores, and holding cardboard signs at intersections. Her mood was fragmented. She was happy to be off the street, but she felt sorry for the people left behind. She could feel her incision weeping into the bandages; through her dampened eyes the world looked murky under the dark skies. Stopped at a light at the corner of Spenard and 26th, she lowered the window to talk to Fred the Head. Fred held up a sign that said: "Viet Vet, will work for grass, God Bless".

"Hey Fred," Moshi said weakly.

Fred did not recognize her.

"How about a buck for coffee?" he asked, blinking his rheumy eyes.

Moshi leaned back. "Glen, can you give him something," she asked quietly.

Glen pulled some bills out of his front pocket and handed them over without looking. Moshi took the limp bills and held them out the window. Fred grabbed them as the car started forward.

"Have a great day," he called after them as he eagerly pawed through the greenbacks to count his take. He quickly started walking toward the In and Out Liquor store for some wide-mouth bottles of malt liquor.

Moshi was staring out the window and crying. Glen and his team looked embarrassed and averted their eyes to give Moshi some privacy. Glen took her hand and entwined his fingers with hers. At the hotel, Glen checked her into a room on their floor. She lay back gingerly on the bed. Glen clicked on the TV and found a rerun of The Dick Van Dyke Show.

"Is this alright?" he asked.

Moshi nodded and stared at the ceiling.

"I'll look in on you later," he said as he eased the door closed.

He did some telephone interviews and watched some election coverage on a local access channel. Fidgety, he looked in the refrigerator a couple of times, but amidst the beer, sodas, and left-over Chinese food, could not find anything he wanted. He poured a couple of ounces of Chivas Regal into a paper cup and carried it around for a while, but didn't drink any, he eventually poured it out.

"I'm going to look in on Moshi," he said.

Elke and Murphy looked at him with inscrutable expressions. They glanced between themselves but did not comment. He let himself into Moshi's room with his master keycard. She was still laying on her back and staring up at the fire sprinkler fixture in the ceiling. An old episode of the Flintstones was playing on the Cartoon Network channel. He picked up the remote and muted the show. They sat in uncomfortable silence for a few minutes.

"No matter what happens to me, I want to thank you for giving me my mind back."

"Don't talk like that. You'll feel better as you heal. You have the whole of your life ahead of you. You're under my protection now, if you have any more problems, we'll get the best doctors in Alaska to fix you up."

"I owe you something because our world is out of balance."

"Don't worry about the crazy world, it is always off balance. You just rest and get well."

"You're very sweet."

Glen laughed. "Just when I thought I'd heard everything. Sweet. That's a new one for me."

He scooted onto the bed. She rolled over gingerly and put her head on his thigh. Glen clicked through the TV program guide. He settled on an old X-Files episode but couldn't concentrate on it.

"Glen?"

"Yes, Moshi."

"I think, if you're gentle with me, you can take me. You can love me. Carefully."

"Now, don't talk loonie, I couldn't."

However, it turned out that he could, softly and slowly to avoid tearing her stitches. Afterward, she cried like a virgin. "I don't think I'll ever deserve to be happy," she said through the tears. He spent the night in her bed holding her tight and had her again in the morning.

CHAPTER 18

ALASKA ELECTION RESULTS
November 3

Counts with 98% of precincts reporting
Total Votes Cast: 266,347
Republican
35% Sanders (93,221 votes)
13% Write-in (scatter) (34,625 votes)

Democrat
43% Wilson (Winner) (114,529 votes)
2% Write-in (scatter) (5327 votes)

Reform
3% Van Doren (7990 votes)

Other (scatter)
4% (10,654 votes)

The Election Team

Glen grinned into the television cameras. Murphy stood by his side and scanned the crowd. They rented the large conference room of the Marriott, it was decorated with flags, posters and illuminated by blinding camera flashes. Glen held up his cell phone.

"I just received a call from Bill Sanders who conceded the race and congratulated me on my win. You're looking at your new congressional representative. I want to thank my election team and I want to thank the fine people of Alaska. You have my word as a gentleman that I will serve with honor. Tomorrow we have to do the work of the people, but tonight, let's celebrate."

He grabbed Murphy and planted a sloppy kiss on her lips. It took a few seconds for her to extricate herself from his grasp. He picked up Bennie and Emma and spun them in gleeful circles. After he set them down he swooped on Moshi. She held her hand out to stop him and gestured at the stitches that held her belly together. She shook his hand briskly and whispered "Congratulations, boss," into his ear. He pulled her close and gently hugged her.

Holly

At the back of the room, Holly sweated under a wig and a blanket she had wrapped around her torso. She wore tortoise shell glasses with clear glass lenses and saggy support hose. The disguise was effective, she looked like a fat spinster and so unattractive that no one cared to look at her too closely. All this celebration made her head throb. She could feel Manny in the room. He was her only true love and the only man who could fill the empty spaces of her soul. He was dead and here, the wallet-man who killed him, was on top of the world. This was the right time to topple him and send him to hell. Clutching her .45, she worked her way through the crowd. She was pressed from all sides the closer she got the Congressman. "This is for Manny," she whispered as she raised the .45 and aimed carefully through the teaming mass of revelers at Mr. Glen 'Wallet-man' Wilson. She squeezed the trigger and the world erupted into roaring thunder.

Holly did not see where the Japanese girl came from but the first bullet hit the nip in the center of her chest and she flew back into Wilson. Bright blood splattered across her white blouse. Upset by the roiling crowd, Holly could not be sure of her aim as Glen and the Japanese girl sprawled across the floor, but she fired twice more anyway. She turned and raced through shouting clusters of people that were jamming the exits. She dashed down the hallway and darted into the ladies toilet. She had previously set out the yellow sign that indicated the restroom was being cleaned. Inside, she quickly stripped off the bulky clothes. She ejected the remaining .45 cartridges. With a sharp knife, she cut the cords that bound the cheerleader. The terrified teenager was dressed in the same dumpy clothes that Holly wore. Holly pressed the gun into the girl's hand and pushed her through the door.

"Run or I'll kill you," Holly hissed. The cheerleader lowered her head like a fullback and took off down the hallway. Holly could hear shouting. She stuffed her discarded garments into a nylon sport bag. Under the clothing, Holly wore the cheerleader's cute outfit; a navy blue miniskirt with sleeveless top. Tearing off the wig revealed a pert ponytail. Hearing the gunfire she was hoping for, she slipped out of the restroom and walked calmly toward the nearest exit. The whole procedure took less than ninety seconds and went precisely as Holly had planned. She mingled with some young people for a few minutes and saw a crumpled form sprawled in the parking lot surrounded by police who were shouting into their radios. Easing herself into her truck, her insides were loose and she felt warm, calm and content. Her gut told her she'd got Wilson, but even if she hadn't, she would get another chance later. The memory of Manny demanded this justice. The only pang she felt was about the gun. She was going to miss that Springfield Amory .45, it was nicely balanced and shiny. She had money, she'd just have to buy another one, that's all. The truck started up and she let it run for a few seconds until it smoothed out. Slowly, she drove toward the street exit and left the scene in her mirrors.

Glen and Moshi

Cradling her head and pressing on her wounds, Glen looked into Moshi's eyes. The crowd hovered over them. Glen could hear shouting as if it came from very far away. There was a lot of blood and he did not know how much was his and how much was Moshi's.

"It should have been me, not you," Glen muttered.

Moshi shook her head.

"No, the stringmaster picked me. Glen?"

"Yes, Moshi, my love."

"You know, one day you're going have to quit fucking around and get serious."

Glen nodded. Tears streamed down his face. "I know."

"Postpone that day as long as possible," she said faintly.

Some people believe the body mysteriously loses 39 grams at the moment of death. This is not something Glen believed, but Moshi got lighter and he knew she was gone. Medics took her from his arms and he allowed Murphy to guide him away from the scene. His mind was fractured and he could not hold a coherent thought. He wanted to analyze Moshi's dying words, but the image of the assassin tugged at him. There was something about that dumpy woman that would not leave him alone. Something familiar. The medics sedated him and the evening melted into dream.

Vice President of the United States John Dickson

Wanda Dickson checked her hair in the bathroom mirror. She'd taken a complete workup at the salon; nails, facial waxing, mud pack, hair styling and make up. She smoothed her chiffon dress over her hips. She had not been eating well the last few days and, except for some mostly-hidden shadows under her eyes, with the ten pounds she had lost, she looked good. For almost 50, she looked great, that was all there was to it. She walked through the house and checked the lunch preparations. She'd borrowed the house from a fellow church member that was on an extended vacation cruising the Mediterranean. The caterer brought steaming pans of John's favorites, lasagna and Caesar salad with fresh anchovies and garlic. Not too much garlic for Wanda's salad, she'd had her teeth cleaned and wanted everything to be perfect. Even her breath. The wine was aerating. The scent of cut flowers sweetened the stale air. Everything was sparkling and pristine. She wished they had a house like this one, perhaps in the foothills of the Wasatch Range in their home state of Utah. However, John did not believe in borrowing money, not even for a mortgage, so they still had their first house back in Provo and lived in the Vice President's Quarters in Washington. It was nice, but it wasn't hers. From a place deep in her womb, she craved a nice place of their own.

She had been married to John Dickson for over thirty years, but she did not know how he was going to react to her news. With the grace of God, they would end up in the guest bedroom and steal a few pleasant hours out of John's busy schedule. *Please*, she prayed. The doorbell sounded and Wanda let the Secret Service agent get it. The grounds were monitored and secure, John and Wanda would mostly be left alone as long as they stayed inside. Wanda made sure that her dress hiked up so a little of her knee showed. John leaned over and kissed her cheek and stood back to admire the scene.

"Absolutely stunning," he said.

"I'm glad you like the table setting."

John grinned. "Yeah, I like that too."

Wanda blushed and felt a rolling heat from her thighs up to her forehead. She waved for him to sit and they were served. John even had a half glass of wine which was unusual for him when he was working. They made small talk while they ate. Over cheesecake and coffee, Wanda found the courage to speak.

"Wasn't it lovely for the Parson's to loan us their place?"

"Yes, Wanda, it's beautiful." He leaned forward and wiped his mouth with a cotton napkin. "I assume there is something on your mind? Good news, I hope? Perhaps you're pregnant again?"

"Oh John, at our age? Certainly we're done with all that, it's time for us to start thinking about grandkids, not more children of our own."

"Who truly knows the extent of God's will? If it's not a child then I certainly am stumped. Please?"

"Oh John, I don't know how to tell you this. I hope I can find the strength through Christ. I have something unpleasant to tell you."

John's face hardened. "Out with it, Wanda. Don't toy with me."

"It's no secret that I had a wild period of my life when I was in college. I did some things that I'm not proud of."

"I know about the drugs and the drinking, we don't need to relive all that."

"No, John, it's something worse than that. There were some parties. I was out of my mind, I didn't really know what I was doing."

"Confess your sins to God. Honestly, Wanda, the things you did before we met are not my business. I'm not completely a saint either. I played cards, went to blue movies and drank. I've told you I was not a virgin when we married. We don't need to stir all this up. I love you."

"I'm really sorry John, but it's more than that. There were some team parties after football games."

John covered his face with his large hands.

"Football players. Rape?" he whispered.

"No, not rape."

"With the minorities on the football team?"

Wanda nodded as tears coursed down her face. John picked up his wine glass, drained it and threw it against the window. It bounced off and shattered on the tile floor. Wanda winced and hunched her shoulders.

"Okay Wanda, I get it. Why do I really need to know all this?"

"There was a camera. Motion pictures. Somehow, not all the tapes were destroyed."

"Internet?"

"No, as far as I know, not on the Internet, thank God."

John sat like a bronze sculpture. "Then what?" he asked quietly.

"President North has a copy and he's blackmailing me into sleeping with him."

"Have you two...?"

"No, but I'm supposed to meet him at the Four Seasons tomorrow. He says he's going to release the tape if I don't."

John seemed to move in slow motion. He stood and picked up his chair and smashed it onto the table which exploded into a shower of flying glass and flatware. The chair fractured and he stood with one wooden leg. His knuckles were white as he gripped it. For a moment, Wanda thought he would hit her with it. She had a vision of herself spread on the floor with a trail of blood gushing from her head. Instead, he threw the club through the window. The Secret Service agents poured into the room with their guns drawn. John's face was twisted and red. He opened his mouth as if to shout at her, but nothing came out except a strangled groan. He turned and stomped quickly toward the front door.

"John, don't leave me like this," she called after his retreating back.

He didn't hesitate. He slammed the front door behind him and the house seemed to shake on its foundation. Some of the Secret Service agents followed him through the door and the rest stayed behind. They did not look directly at her. The chef found a broom and started sweeping up the glass while Wanda wept into a napkin.

ADN

November 4

Death Visits Victory Party

A celebration of victory in a tough Congressional election turned to tragedy in downtown Anchorage last night. Congressman-elect Glen Wilson was slightly wounded in an assassination attempt that killed Congressional aide Moshi Sumifu. Police killed the suspected attacker, sixteen year old Alaska High School cheerleader Kathy Simons, when she refused to throw down her weapon. No motive is known and police are investigating. In a bizarre twist, Miss Sumifu had received a liver transplant two weeks ago. There was no statement from Congressman Glen Wilson's office at press time. He was treated at the scene by medics and released.

Toxic Shock Syndrome

Raz sat in his suite at the Tokyo Zen-Nik-ku Hotel. He munched on grapes from a hotel gift basket and talked to Dave the Drummer.

"Here's how it is, Dave," Raz said. "When we get back to the States, you check yourself into rehab and kick the smack or you're fired. The label will pick up the bill. Get clean or you're out."

"I have the shit under control. I thought we were brothers, man. Don't go getting all corporate on me now that we're starting to make some money. We're partners."

"We're partners if you get straight. We're ex-partners if you say no. What's it going to be?"

"Fuck you, Raz. Can't we just relax and have a good time?"

"Yes or no."

"Damn you! Alright, I'll do the program again, prick. What about Erik? He's been shooting up too."

"Erik is out. Even when he was straight he couldn't play. We need an upgrade. Remember those lines that Moshi played? I'm going to get her in the band. If you don't like that, you can walk. We'll call it creative differences and you can go start your own stoner junky band and rot in clubs until the dope kills you. Your call."

"Erik is going to shit a brick. He's been your friend since the second grade, man. Are you really such a cold-hearted bastard."

"Yes, I suppose I am. If you see Erik, tell him I'm looking for him, alright?"

"Do your own damn dirty work," Dave the Drummer complained as he left the room and slammed the door.

Glen and Murphy

The ADN had a series of front page stories about the shooting at the victory party. Glen threw the newspaper in front of Murphy. He sat on a chair and laced up his boots.

"What?" Murphy asked. "I read the coverage."

"That's not her," he said.

Murphy looked more closely at the photograph of the cheerleader. She wore pigtails and a wide happy grin.

"What do you mean, that's not her," Murphy asked in a puzzled tone.

"That is not the shooter. That's just some poor kid that got in the way like Moshi."

Murphy watched as Glen pulled on a navy watch hat and slipped on dark sunglasses.

"Don't talk crazy. The cops got the shooter. What are you doing?"

"I got a good look at the shooter and that is not her," he said, waving at the newspaper. "I know where I've seen her. Remember the chippy who has been hanging around? We saw her at the park and she came to some of the other campaign events? Reed. She said her name was Reed."

"No. You're not making any sense. Are you losing your mind?"

"I'm going underground for a while. Cover for me."

"Glen, you're a Congressman now, you can't just disappear," she said to his back as he turned the corner and was gone.

Glen

The next public event was a celebration speech at the Chester Creek Park. Glen rubbed dirt onto his face and into his jeans. He bought a half-gallon bottle of Muscatel and sat under some trees and shared it with some hobos named Slick Rick and Sal. Rick was a black and Sal was olive-skinned, perhaps an Egyptian or Jordanian. It was four o'clock in the afternoon and it was already getting dark. There was a chill to the air and leaden clouds filled the sky. To Glen, it felt like snow was coming.

"Did you vote for this guy?" Glen asked.

"Shit no," Slick Rick said. "I don't vote. I like his free hotdogs and they'll let me take as many as I can carry if there are any left. They don't care."

Sal nodded in agreement. "They're the good dogs too, not the cheap ones made out of pig snouts and roadkill. I used to work in a plant and we threw all kinds of shit in the grinder when the inspectors weren't looking. I will say, all that nasty shit made for a tasty dog, go figure."

Murphy stood at the podium and announced that the Congressman was recovering from his injuries and could not be present. She took a few questions from the press and Glen was proud of her performance, she recited their campaign messages very professionally. He scanned the thin crowd and spotted a small figure leaving. Leaving the bottle for his new friends, he got up, skirted the tree line and followed. Through some bushes he watched the slight figure get into a GMC truck and drive to the south.

He walked to the downtown Holiday Inn. The clerk was not happy about renting to a dirty bum without a credit card, but Glen's wad of cash pacified him. Glen looked through the newspaper and found a

Honda 350 motorcycle for sale. He called and convinced the seller to bring it by the motel in the morning. With winter impending, the seller was glad to get any offer.

In the morning, after completing the transaction for the motorbike, Glen cruised the streets and hoped the rain would hold off for another few days. It was cold and sprinkled occasionally, but Glen did not get soaked, for which he was thankful. It was cold, but it could have been much worse. He made a sweep of all the main streets, the parking lots and the motels. There were several GMC pickups, but none that exactly matched the one he was looking for. Mid-afternoon, as he passed the Motel 8 on Minnesota Street, he caught a glimpse of a promising pickup in his rearview mirror. He wheeled around and watched Holly drag a pizza box and a six-pack of beer into the hotel. *Gotcha*, he thought. He watched for a light to go on in one of the rooms and counted the windows to figure out which room it was. He bought a roll of quarters from the convenience store across the street and found himself standing by her door. He stood to the side and rapped. She peered through the chain-restricted door and said: "Who's there?"

Glen waited. She closed the door, unhooked the chain and poked her head out. Glen, with the quarters clenched in his gloved fist, hit her in the face as hard as he could. She fell back heavily and Glen slipped into the room. She scrambled for her gun but Glen stepped on it and kicked her in the ribs. She gasped and slithered back against the couch. Glen picked up the gun and admired it. Holly's face was already swelling and turning purple. She wiped her face and stared at the blood.

"I think you broke my fucking ribs, Wilson."

"Care to tell me why you're trying to kill me before I return the favor?"

"Manny."

Glen racked his brain. It seemed that he did know a Manny from somewhere. Then it dawned on him. *Manny Rodriquez, from Florida. Thug, drug dealer, dead man.*

"I remember. I blew him up. So what?"

"He was my one and only true love and you killed him. For that, I will kill you too."

"Hmmm, interesting. I really felt some chemistry with you. You killed Moshi and I killed Manny. I don't suppose you consider things even now?"

"Not even close," Holly spat.

"I agree."

Holly slowly pulled off her tank top. She was bare underneath. She touched the swelling of her ribs and grimaced. Glen admired her perky breasts and felt a stirring.

"Lucky for you Wilson, I like it rough. Not always this rough," she said wryly, "but this will do."

She slowly unbuttoned her jeans one button at a time.

"Perhaps you could help me with these?" she asked coyly.

"You're doing fine," Glen replied.

She wriggled out of the jeans and tossed them aside. She sat back and watched Glen watch her. She wore white bikini-style panties. She flicked the waistband and ran her thumbs around the top. She slowly eased them off and tossed them aside. Her pubic hair was neatly trimmed.

"Come and get it, big boy," she teased.

Glen tossed the gun aside, making sure it was out of her reach. He got on his hands and knees and crawled to her. She spread her legs slightly. Apparently, she really did like rough trade, she was clearly ready. Glen crawled beside her.

"What a waste," he muttered.

He slid his hands over her breasts, over her shoulders and wrapped his hands around her neck. He squeezed. She struggled and tried to tear his hands away, but Glen pressed harder. He held the pressure until her bladder released, then continued the compression until his hands cramped and he couldn't squeeze any more. He sat back and looked at her. Her tongue was visible through her teeth and her vacant eyes were crossed.

"I hope you enjoy hell, you bitch," he said.

I'd killed again. How did this make me feel? Disembodied. Adrift. My mind refused to focus; the scope was too much. There was no particular pleasure in this act; it was more of a chore, like cleaning up the beer bottles and vomit after one of God's cynical parties.

Everyone dies, the only questions are where, when, and how. And why, but that was not my problem and not my concern. Holly was a blight on the earth. In the alternate reality where she seduced me, it would be me pissing on the carpet and staring into infinity. Let there be no doubt, death lived in her eyes. It would be me standing before the universal judge and accounting for my errors and transgressions. One day, that would happen, but not today.

I suppose, in my own way, I was just as much of a sociopath as Holly. Aggressive and dangerously antisocial. What gave me the right to act as executioner? Thou shalt not murder. Except for my shepherd Glen.

On occasion he shalt, when the situation warrants, snuff some lousy creep that crosses his path. This was not a job I'd volunteered for. I'd rather watch football on the HDTV in five-channel surround sound while guzzling factory beer and eating factory snacks on a weekend break from my factory job, in my manufactured house with my friends from the factory whooping and shouting good-natured and prefabricated insults. Cartoons, sex, nicotine, beer, alcohol, caffeine, ice cream, sports, sleep, tabloid newspapers, pornography, day jobs; all the miscellaneous pharma, all the modern opiates for the masses. The fuel and lubrication that keeps our robotic bodies moving through our robotic lives. Why couldn't I relax and let the flow of normal life envelop me, caress me, sooth me, and smother me? How I long for the luxury of such mindlessness. I crave the leather-bound, air-conditioned and besotted dream in which most men live.

Did I truly know that my destiny was to live a distinguished life? Possibly my path would end in defeat, disgrace and humiliation. Perhaps one day, the cosmic father will decide to end my illusion of adequacy. You thought you were special? Join your fellow believers in Dante's Purgatory where snakes of fire consume your flesh forever. Wilson, meet your spiritual brothers and eternal Canasta partners, Gaius Caesar[29], Hitler, Stalin and Mao Zedong. But no, I may share narcissistic and ego-centric madness with these butchers, but my crimes are tiny in comparison. Minuscule. Inconsequential and trivial.

I don't know how long I sat and watched her body cool. Long enough for her blood to begin to pool and for her skin to start turning waxy and gray. What a horrid waste. That lovely slim body. Those small but perfectly-formed perky breasts. The sculpted landscape of her legs and groin. Such a flawless vessel, but filled with such evil. God's mistake, God's sick joke, God's trial and my test.

I admit that sometimes my brain gets derailed. The flywheel explodes. I could have died, but instead I lived. Holly could have lived, but instead she died. At my hand. Why? I don't really know. Would this be the end of me? The cops could burst through the door and I'd do a perp walk in front of the cameras of the world. They would love it. Newly-elected Congressman kills young girl. Jail, trial, and new support for an Alaskan Death Penalty. Prison and a hangman's noose. Could happen. Would happen if I sat around here until the maid found me here with the Holly's empty corpse.

---

[29] Also called Caligula, the emperor of Rome (AD 37-41), known for his merciless extravagance and megalomania.

Stiff from disuse, Glen's joints popped and snapped as he gained his feet. Stretching, he took a slow look around the room for evidence. He still wore the leather gloves. There might be some hair or other sources of DNA, but, if necessary, the team would prove he spent a night in this room some time earlier as explanation. His team would see to it that this sort of circumstantial evidence would not stand. He would never be connected to the scruffy biker seen hanging around. As long as the gloves, the watch cap, and the sunglasses were never found, then this crime would never be accurately solved. He grabbed a slice of pizza from the box. It was Hawaiian style and he grunted with approval as he gobbled it down. Standing by the door, he made sure all was quiet before he entered the hallway and strode quickly but casually toward the side exit. He drove the bike to the waterfront and left it parked with the key in the ignition. It would be gone within an hour. He left the helmet, but shoved the hat, gloves, and sunglasses into his coat. Then, exhausted and depressed, with his stomach roiling from the congealed pizza, he stumbled back to the Marriott.

Glen and Scott Steele

Glen was supposed to be signing pictures and 'thank you' letters for the large dollar donors, but instead, he was staring out the window. Scott Steele, with a somber expression, tapped on the door, then came in and sat on Glen's guest chair.

"First of all, my wife and I are deeply sad about the tragic murder of your staffer. We understand she was a very special person to you. You have our condolences."

Glen just grunted in reply.

"I also want to congratulate you on your amazing victory. One day I'd like to hear the real story about how you pulled this off. Can I ask, was this part of a brilliant plan or just something you stumbled into?"

"Fuck you, Steele. Just get to the point of your visit."

Steele frowned. "Okay." He opened his valise and pulled out a sheaf of papers. "You have a budget of one-point-three million and staffing considerations. Your office budget supports 20 permanent positions and five temps. I have resumes from the current staff and several of them have expressed interest in staying on if you want them."

"Aren't they Republicans?"

"A lot of the staffers are non-partisan secretaries and office assistants. They know how DC works and they can be a real asset to a new Congressman."

"I'll look at them, but tell them not to bet their mortgage payments on keeping their jobs."

Steele looked at Glen with exasperation. "Look Glen, I know we've had our problems, but we're stuck together now. How about we start fresh and make this work?"

Again, Glen just grunted.

"Fine. You have two months to get up to speed. Orientation week in Washington starts on Monday. In the meantime, there are other orientations you might want to take advantage of. For example, the Marines sponsor orientations for you and your staff. It's a one-week temporary assignment to learn about day-to-day activities for fleet command, amphibious ship exercises, assisting judge advocates, this sort of thing. They make aircraft available to you and your staff, you travel on Navy orders. It's an interesting assignment from what I'm told."

"Okay, we'll think about that one. What else?"

"There are workshops on topics like drug policy, Latin America, immigration law, congressional ethics, the diversity gap, arms control, disease risk assessment, protocols for floor debates and hearings, office procedures and rules for dealing with lobbyists. Depending on which committees you are invited to join and where your interests lie, you can pick and choose the ones most appropriate. You have invitations for Embassy parties from Chile, Belarus, Turkey, and Morocco. There will be more, so you'll need to pick and choose which ones you want to attend. The Saudis throw a good party, if you're interested I'll ask around and see if I can get you on the guest list. There are many Congressional Staff Delegation trips, you have standing invitations to visit Indonesia, China, the Philippines, and Ecuador. If your people have a specific place they'd like to visit, let me know and I'll see what I can do. Your office is in the Rayburn building, it's a shitty set of rooms in the basement, but I'll see what I can do to get you better situated. Your predecessor was on the Transportation Committee, that will be a tough one for you get on, but you can probably get on the Veteran's Affairs Committee. Of course, you'll want to get on the Resources Committee, that is an important one for Alaska. You can transfer 100 thousand dollars from your office budget to your expense account for things like domestic travel, stationery, newsletters, overseas postage and telephone service. You get free postage for mailings to your constituents, this is called franking. You'll want to use this perk often, you can get started with sending a newsletter or some sort of status report right away. If you have any business activity in the areas of real estate, insurance sales, the practice of law or medicine, or corporate officer or board member, then you'll have to stop this right away. There is a limit to other business activity, but the safest thing to do is put all that on hold. Your investments should go into a blind trust.

I want to warn you about talking to the press, they will hound you. You have to talk to them but you don't have to tell them anything, if you catch my drift. You have no political experience. Just keep your mouth shut and soak in as much as you can. Hiring some Washington insiders will be critical, there are a couple available that would be very helpful." Steele rustled through his papers. "I think that's it for now. In general, you're going to be busy. Your staff will be doing most of the work, it will be your job to select them and set direction, otherwise you're going to be a figurehead, shaking hands, kissing lobbyists, and simply listening a lot. Okay?"

Glen nodded. Steele gathered his papers and stood up. With his hand on the doorknob, he turned back to Glen.

"We'll get to know each other more as time goes on. Let me give you some friendly advice. As a freshman congressman, there are small expectations. No one expects you to change the world, really, no one expects you to really do anything much at all. My advice is to just relax and enjoy the perks. It takes years to get enough clout to actually get anything done so keep your head down and play your role and good things will come your way in the end. Make sense?"

Glen shook his head. "Is there any way I can fire you?"

Steele grinned wryly. "No," he said.

"I was afraid of that."

Second Constitutional Amendment

A well regulated militia, being necessary to the security of a free state, the right of the people to keep and bear arms, shall not be infringed.

CHAPTER 19

Glen and Murphy

Glen settled into his leather-trimmed first class seat. He sighed with relief when he turned off his cell phone, the thing had been ringing constantly for the last three days. One of the hazards of being a congressman is everyone wanted something. Farmers were looking for extensions of subsidy programs, homeless shelter managers were looking for expanded funding, teachers were looking for increased cost of living allowances and a group of dog breeders from Fairbanks was looking for relief from environmental regulations. Was there no end to the goodies that people want from the state? The novelty of fame wore off after the first day, now he just wished his constituents would leave him alone. The flight attendant, who wore a nametag decorated with the name Alice and a soaring eagle, smiled broadly, called him Congressman and offered him champagne. Glen took two of the fluted glasses and nibbled on shrimp cocktail. Alice tried to take his jacket, but Glen kept it folded on his lap.

The aircraft was a 747-Stretch and it lifted smoothly off the Stephens Airport runway. Glen inflated a pillow and wrapped it around his shoulders. He covered his eyes with a sleep mask and settled in. He'd been cruising on a few hours sleep each night and was looking forward to some downtime during the nearly seven hour flight to Chicago. In Chicago, they would change planes and hook up with a flight to Dulles Airport in Washington, DC. Glen could already tell that this long haul to the capital would get old very quickly. Murphy read a copy of Guns and Ammo and ignored his complaining. In a few minutes he was asleep and snoring softly. The plane was somewhere over Alberta when Glen's sleep was rudely interrupted.

A swarthy man wearing a red scarf on his head tore off Glen's sleep mask and screamed at him. He was speaking some form of English, but the heavily-accented words were not registering in Glen's groggy mind. The snub-nosed revolver waved under his nose roused his attention. Tucking his jacket under his arm, he let the wild-eyed man herd him to the back of the aircraft. Calmly, he patted the arm of the terrified flight attendant. Murphy's eyes were flicking over the wild-eyed hijacker and the other cowering passengers. She had a grim look on her face. The more Glen shook off his grogginess, the angrier he got.

"Will you please shoot this fucker?" Glen asked Murphy in an exasperated tone.

"I'm not armed, you dipshit. It's not legal to carry a gun on a plane."

"I can't believe this. You should always be armed. That's just common sense."

"It's against airline rules," Murphy protested.

"Bah," Glen spat. "You're supposed to be my bodyguard. I have to do everything around here."

There are some things I will never understand about people. Our country's founding fathers were screwed in the head in a lot of ways, but they also got a few things just right. They granted us the fundamental right to carry arms. Why did they do this? Because power is vested with the people and is freely granted to those we elect to act on our behalf. Where does this power reside? Partly, it resides in our ability to protect ourselves from leaders who will always try to extend their power too far.

When I get to Washington, I will solemnly swear that I will support and defend the Constitution of the United States against all enemies, foreign and domestic; that I will bear true faith and allegiance to the same; that I take that obligation freely, without any mental reservation or purpose of evasion; and that I will well and faithfully discharge the duties of the office on which I am about to enter: So help me God.

By law, any rule that violates the constitution is invalid, but we allow the regulators and bureaucrats to erode and erase our rights. Murphy is right, there are rules against carrying arms on this aircraft but I don't accept the state's right to make laws that contradict my constitutional rights. If you do, then you are a slave and I hope you enjoy your chains, because they will get heavier each year.

Airport screening got more intense after the terror attacks of September 11, 2001. So what? I bet a Federal Marshall $10,000 that I could hand him a loaded revolver on a domestic flight. I did it and the *cheap fuck eventually paid me. It wasn't part of our deal that I tell him how I did it, but it was not that big a thing, if you have a brain, you can figure it out. I put the frame into a fake hard drive case in my laptop. I slipped the chamber into a small shaving cream can and the cartridges were inserted into battery cases in my electric razor. Okay? In your carry-on baggage, you could find plenty of metal-encased places to store gun parts. Run your gun parts through a dishwasher a few times to remove telltale cordite and gunpowder residue and you'll avoid tripping the explosives sensors.*

The problem on aircraft is not that some mad Islamic terrorist can get a gun on board. The problem is that he's the only one armed. How far are paradise-bound fanatics getting with their boxcutters if 10% of the passengers exercise their constitutional right to bear arms? Thousands of people in those New York towers would be alive today and their blood is on your hands. What do you get if you let the Feds solve the problem of hijacked commercial aircraft? Clever plans that include F-16's and air-to-air missiles that protect themselves at the expense of collateral civilian casualties. You'll excuse me if I find little comfort in this style of thinking.

Personally, I will always figure out a way to be armed and dangerous. Always. I always keep ceramic or Kevlar knifes sewn into the lining of my jackets. I was experimenting with a tiny graphite crossbow that fired bolts made with #2 pencils. Plastic stabilizing fins are inserted into the ends. They are hard to aim at any distance, but you'd be surprised how much penetration you can get with a sharp pencil launched at 300 feet-per-second. No metal, so there is no problem getting them though the metal detectors. These weapons were still in development and not ready for deployment yet. My favorite weapons are guns built into pen bodies. For heavier duty action, I had .38 shells embedded in AA battery cells, but I hoped I wouldn't need the firepower because I preferred not to take any chances with a breach of the skin of this pressurized aircraft. Could get messy.

Glen pulled several chunky Mont Blanc-style pens from the inside pocket of his sport jacket. He handed one to Murphy.

"Watch this," he said, "twist the top until you feel the glass sleeve break. Now be careful, these things have hollow point .22 long rifle cartridges in them. Press the plunger and they will fire out the end. Single shot. Be careful, because the bullet is infused with a distilled Peruvian wasp venom. Don't get any of that on you. Got it?"

Murphy looked at him with wonder. "Yes, I got it," she said.

Glen stood up and walked toward the front of the plane holding his pen. A hijacker screamed at him and waved his revolver. The other passengers cowered in their seats. Glen aimed his pen carefully and, from six feet, shot the hijacker in the eye. He fell over like a bag of quivering potatoes. Glen tossed aside the smoking pen and tread on the twitching body as he walked toward the cockpit. He picked up the revolver and slid it down the aisle to Murphy. As he continued toward the cockpit he prepared another pen for firing. He knocked on the cockpit door and shot a turbaned man in the temple when he stuck out his head. The man did not die immediately but sat down hard on the deck. Blood dripped from his head and his mouth moved silently. He did not seem to understand what had happened to him. The bullet disintegrating into his temporal lobe seemed to affect his ability to think. Glen eased his gun out of his limp hand and threw it down the aisle. A couple of passengers, with new-found courage, scrambled after the gun like it were a foul ball. Glen twisted his last pen and held it in front of him. The remaining hijacker was screaming and pressing a revolver against the head of the pilot. The copilot was prone and bleeding from a deep wound in the neck. The hijacker decided to aim the gun at Glen instead. As the gun swung around, Glen shot him in the crook of his elbow from point blank range. The hijacker's arm went limp and he lost his grip on the revolver. Glen picked up an aluminum pot of coffee and hit him in the head as hard as he could. Then he slowly poured the scalding coffee on the hijacker's upturned face. Glen felt sheepish at this brutal childish pettiness, but got a primitive pleasure from the pain of his screaming enemy. There was mayhem in the cabin until the writhing hijacker was injected with tranquilizer and handcuffed to a bulkhead. The second man, apparently not liking the sad turn of events in this world, decided to die and try the next. He sat on the bulkhead with vacant eyes staring into space. Glen kicked him over and walked back to his seat. There was an impromptu round of applause from the passengers. The flight attendants shouted for everyone to return to their seats and put their seatbelts on. With shaking hands, Alice lit a cigarette, took a deep drag, and passed it to Glen.

"The Captain has turned on the no-smoking sign!" a passenger shouted shrilly. A chorus of "Shut up" erupted from some passengers. This brought a small smile to Glen's face. Everyone needed to pull themselves together.

Glen sat back down in his seat and pulled his sleep mask on. Murphy helped Alice serve free drinks. She checked the binding of the last hijacker and tightened a belt that held a dressing on his elbow. He was partially conscious and talked incessantly to himself in Arabic. His face was already covered with weeping blisters. The pilot had a nasty lump on his head and a migraine, but seemed to be alright. The copilot was sedated and covered in a blanket, he was not doing as well.

After consulting with ground control, the pilot decided to carry on to O'Hare. Murphy gathered the gun-pens and stowed them in her purse. The revolvers were locked in a compartment in the cockpit. Murphy and Alice finally had everything settled and they poured themselves coffee in the galley.

Alice pulled the curtain between the coach and First Class sections. "I'm not supposed to do this," she said as she tipped a tiny bottle of Baileys into her coffee. Murphy shrugged and poured one into her coffee too.

"I won't tell if you won't," she said.

"The congressman is full of surprises, isn't he?"

"Never a dull moment," Murphy replied.

"Does he really think it's over and he's just going to walk away?"

"I can't claim to know what he thinks."

"Are you and he…?"

Murphy laughed. "No," she said.

"Well, maybe I'll rock his world when we get on the ground. That could have been ugly. We're going to be stuck in Chicago for a while, I think."

"Have at him," Murphy replied, tapping her plastic cup against Alice's in toast.

Glen and Murphy

Glen sat up in his seat. He flipped his sleep mask over his forehead.

"Murphy," he said.

"Yeah boss."

"Get on your cell phone and find me a lawyer. Have someone call Saul Kovacek in Seattle and see if he can get someone in Chicago to meet us at the airport."

"It's against FAA regulations to use a cell phone while we're in flight," Murphy explained patiently.

Glen glared at her and his face began to flush. Murphy raised her hand.

"Okay, sorry. Can I use an Airfone instead of cell?"

"Just find a mad dog lawyer to meet us at the airport."

"Can I ask why?"

Glen snorted. "You really don't know what's going to happen when we land?"

"Tell me."

"Just make sure the meanest and nastiest lawyer you can find meets us at the airport," he muttered while flipping the sleep mask back over his eyes.

At the terminal, the aircraft was directed to stop on an unused runway. They were met with ambulances, firetrucks and a heavily-armed SWAT team. Everyone was ordered to stay in their seats while the bodies were hauled out. Medics checked the pilot. Alice gave Glen a kiss on the cheek and pressed into his hand a scrap of paper with her cell phone number. The pilot and crew were allowed to exit. Covered by M-16 rifles, Glen was handcuffed and pulled down the gangway, where they loaded him into a black Suburban. After some shouting, Murphy was also cuffed and joined him. They stared at each other.

"Hell of a way to welcome a hero," Murphy said.

"You're stupid if you didn't see this coming," Glen said drily.

They were led into a room near customs. While sitting on metal folding chairs, Murphy tried to engage the guard in conversation, but he just stared at them with a stony look. Eventually a small dapper man with a shaved head and military style mustache walked in. He was dressed in an expensive suit and chewed on a toothpick. He threw some papers on the table and looked between Murphy and Glen.

"Ron Walker, Federal Security Director of the Transportation Security Administration," he finally said.

Glen and Murphy watched him, but neither spoke.

"We find ourselves impaled on the horns of a dilemma," Walker continued. "The press are raising hell, they want pictures of the hero congressman from Alaska. The Department of Homeland Security is busting my balls. Somehow, an ambulance-chaser lawyer is on the case and is terrorizing my people. The Deputy Administrator of the Federal Aviation Administration wants your head delivered on a platter. The FBI will be here any minute and they'll want to interview you. The president's office has been on the phone and wants quarter-hour updates. What am I to do with you?"

"You could start by showing my lawyer in," Glen suggested mildly.

Walker sighed and waved for someone outside the room to enter. One of Glen's pens and a thin black knife was placed on the table by a young woman who stared at Murphy and Glen curiously before exiting and closing the door quietly. Their luggage was placed on the floor. The zippers were only partially closed, it was clear the contents had been examined.

"These pens are very clever. Where did you have them made?"

"I bought them off Ebay."

"Cute. This knife was sewn into the lining of your jacket. We find this very interesting."

He picked it up and examined the blade. The knife had knuckle grips like brass knuckles made of some oily nylon material and a fat three-inch blade. It was very thin and flexible.

"You'll want to be careful with that," Glen commented dryly.

"Oh, I know," Walker said. "One of our officers nearly sliced off the top of his hand. What is this blade made of?"

"It's a Kevlar fiber nanotube, the edge is close to one molecule thick. It will break if it hits anything hard, but passes through flesh quite nicely."

"Just the knife could get you 25 years in federal prison. Add the gun and you'll be a free man somewhere around the year 2400. However, if you cooperate with us, maybe we can discover the permits and forms that make all this stuff legal and make all your problems go away."

"You want to know where this gear comes from?"

"That would be a good start."

"That's not going to happen."

"I figured. Look Mister Wilson or Congressman-elect Wilson, whichever you might prefer, we have a big problem here. People travel because they feel safe doing it. How does it look when you mock our laws and show how easy it is for a determined man to get lethal weapons onboard a commercial aircraft? We can't screen every pen, every laptop computer, every can of shaving cream, every battery cell, every unexplained blob that shows up on the X-ray, every laser pointer and all the other damn crap the public insists on carrying on airplanes. Even if technically we could, the public would scream bloody murder if they had to wait six hours every time they pass through an airport security gate. Confidence in personal safety, that's what we need."

"I could take the blade out of a box cutter and tape it to a bottom of a Altoids tin. I could carry the plastic handle in a shirt pocket and I'd be armed as well as the September 11th hijackers."

Walker sighed. "That's what I'm talking about. That sort of thinking is not at all constructive. You're giving me a headache."

"What about the revolvers, how did the dirtbags get them on the plane?"

Walker rubbed his temples. "We think they were stowed under the smoke detector in the aft head. We don't know how they got there yet. We're working on it. We can't seem to locate one of the technicians who serviced the lavatory equipment."

"Didn't they know it's a federal offense to tamper with the smoke detectors on an aircraft?"

"Right."

"And what were they trying to do?"

"We think they were going to crash the plane into the Sears tower."

"They'll never get away with anything like that again."

"So, you saw the F-18 escort."

"You're going to call it an escort?"

"Yeah."

"Fine. Can I see my lawyer now?"

"You and I are going to have a conversation first. What do you think of headlines like 'Hero Congressman-elect Overpowers Hijackers' or 'Passengers Upset Hijack Attempt'?"

"You don't want us to mention the firearms."

"In the interest of Homeland Security. Please."

"Fine, it's a deal."

"And if you find yourself on the Transportation Committee?"

"Yes?"

"We could sure use some additional funding."

"Of course. We're free to go?"

"Be my guest."

Glen got up and held Murphy's arm. They walked out of the room and faced the news cameras and microphones. They did not mention troublesome subjects like smuggled guns or F-18's that were prepared to shoot down a commercial airliner. It took several hours for the reporters to get bored and move on. Murphy booked them onto a private jet and they made the remainder of the trip to Dulles without incident.

The Powers That Be

Terry McOlive, the chairman of the Democratic National Committee, shook hands with William 'Willy, the man' Thomas. The 'man' was a stereotypical cigar-chomping wealthy Wall Street tycoon throwback from the robber baron vulture capitalists of the Rockefeller and

Vanderbilt eras. Only the most paranoid even believed he had political power, but he contributed to both sides and didn't direct, but on the quiet, heavily influenced politics in Washington, DC. He had rubbery lips and squashed features reminiscent of a toad.

"Hello William,"

"Hello Terry, take a seat. Cigar?"

"No thank you."

"Give me a summary."

"Sure. We did pretty well against some dirty campaigning in the Midwest. Some polls had us losing 22 seats, but we only lost 16. We have a good base for going into the elections the year after next."

"Are you ready to stop bullshitting me?"

"Excuse me?"

"You dumbshits are lucky to even have a majority. If it wasn't for that wildcard in Alaska, you schmucks would be so far down the well that you wouldn't see any sunlight at all. Your Speaker lost for the first time since Foley[30] got his ass kicked in '95. What was that guy's name? That guy in Alaska?"

"Wilson."

"Yeah, Wilson saved your collective asses. You should give him a medal or something."

"Sure. We had some bad luck and couldn't even seem to buy a break."

"Bullshit! You know better than to try to peddle that nonsense with me. You were slammed because you're soft on crime and taxation issues. You're all a bunch of pussies. Pansies. The President has the war and his crime initiatives. Are you just going to stand there with your pants around your ankles and wait for the Republicans to service you? You'd better do something bold and find yourselves a figurehead that has some balls. Alright, here's my suggestion. Are you ready?"

"Sure."

"This guy Wilson is a big hero right now for whatever it was that he did on that airplane. There are two months before you elect a new Speaker of the House. Why don't you have that lame duck piece of shit Post resign and appoint this Wilson as interim acting Speaker. Use him for some photo-ops. Congress is not in session, so there isn't any damage he can do. The more I think about this, the more I like it. The press will

---

[30] Speaker of the House, Tom Foley D – Washington, was voted out of his congressional office in the 'Republican Revolution' in 1994. It is highly unusual for a sitting Speaker to lose an election.

fall all over themselves in covering this. This is better than the Starr report."

"You don't know this guy Wilson. He's a loose cannon, not a team player. He's nothing but big trouble."

"He saved a plane full of citizens. This resonates against the Sept 11 attack in a great way for your party. You can't buy great PR like this."

"I strongly suggest that we think about this for a while. Maybe it's a good idea, but there is no reason to be hasty."

"Yes sir."

"Excuse me?"

"Just say 'yes, sir', and get your ass out of here."

"Yes, sir."

Glen and the Office Staff

"Cripes, there are a lot of you," Glen said with an exasperated tone.

The election team and the office staff were gathered for the first time. Glen stood while the team sat at a large conference table in his new office.

"Okay, all of you, let me tell you how I see this. One of the problems a congressman has is that he will not have time to do everything. So, I'm not even going to try. In fact, I am not going to do anything at all. You have all met Murphy?" He gestured toward her and everyone nodded. "Good. I am delegating all my authority to her and she will act in my stead on everything. If there is something that I absolutely must do in person, then so be it. Make sure I have my speeches prepared and I am briefed properly. For all decisions, check with Murphy who will use her best judgment. I don't want any phone calls and I don't want any visitors. Anything that comes up, just handle it, alright? Now, there are not going to be any questions. Understand? Alright, are there any questions?"

Glen looked around the room. One of the interns was waving her hand.

"Didn't you hear me say there were not going to be any questions?"

"Yes, but then you asked if there were any questions."

Glen rolled his eyes. "This should not be so hard. Do you have an IQ greater than 70? Very well, thank you all very much and get back to work. I will be in my office and I don't expect to be disturbed. Are there any questions? Good."

"Wait a minute, sir. I didn't get a chance to ask my question."

"I said there are not going to be any questions, dammit."

"Then you asked if anyone had any questions. I have a question."

Murphy hid a grin behind her clipboard and made eye-contact with Elke.

"No you don't because there are no questions."

"But I do have a question."

"I'm surrounded by dimwits. Alright, go ahead and ask your question, what is it?"

"I read on the Drudge Report that you single-handedly overpowered three armed terrorists. True or false?"

"If it's on the Drudge Report then it must be true. Yes, I took them out with my bare hands. Did Drudge say anything about how I rescued a bush pilot and drove a dogsled?"

"No, I didn't see anything like that."

"Murphy, make sure everyone reads the press releases. Write something up about the hijacking, make sure it links to the dogsled story. Now repeat after me. No phone calls."

"No phone calls."

"No visitors."

"No visitors."

"If anything comes up, then Murphy will handle it."

"Murphy will handle it," the team recited.

"Since there are no questions, that will be all."

Glen walked to his office and shut the door. Exhausted, he settled into his leather executive chair and took a nap.

Glen woke with a start. Murphy poked her head in.

"Sorry to disturb you, Congressman. You have some visitors."

"I said no visitors."

"I think you should see these gentlemen. Terry McOlive and some folks from the Democratic National Committee."

Glen sighed as he straightened his necktie.

"Okay Murphy, show them in."

Glen stood and shook their hands. He recognized Scott Steele. Also, Terry McOlive was familiar from the endless TV talk shows on which he appeared regularly. There were three others in nice suits that Glen didn't know. He immediately forgot their names as soon as they said them.

"Gentlemen, coffee? Danish? I think there are still some Krispy Kreme donuts unless the staff ate them all. It was really nice of the Lockheed-Martin folks to send a couple of boxes of those things over."

The visitors all shook their heads.

"Well, if you don't mind, I'll have one." He pressed the intercom button on his Polycom phone. "Hey Murphy, send in some more of those Krispy Kremes, will ya?"

"Sorry boss, all gone."

"Then go get some, damn you. Do I have to spell everything out for you people?" To his guests, he said: "Do you have trouble getting good help too?"

His guests just looked at him passively.

"Okay. Whatever. What brings you gentlemen out here?"

"First of all, on behalf of the Democratic Party, I want to congratulate you on your fine victory. Alaska has done well to select a fine man such as yourself to represent them," McOlive said.

"Oh, you're a smooth one, aren't you? How about something more like congratulations on bringing in the seat that saved your majority in Congress. Saved your collective ass with only chump change in support from the DNC. Huh?"

"I suppose you could look at things that way, but I don't think it's constructive. Let's focus on the future instead of dwelling on the mistakes of the past, shall we?"

"I have some accrued campaign debt that you could help me with."

McOlive exchanged a pained glance with his cohorts.

"Very well, Wilson, what are we talking about here?"

"A hundred grand."

McOlive swallowed. "Alright Wilson, we'll see that you get covered for that." He managed a thin smile. "Yes, we'll be happy to assist you with those expenses. Now, if you'll allow us to get to the purpose of our visit. You may or not be aware, since the honorable Mister Post lost his election in Kansas, we will be electing a new Speaker of the House in January."

"And you're here to tell me who to vote for…"

"No, there is plenty of time for that later. We have something else in mind. Post is back in Kansas and has no desire to traipse here to DC for a few ceremonial events. Technically, at the end of the congressional term, the old Speaker's term expires and the clerk of the house acts as the house leader until Congress convenes and a new Speaker is selected. However, we're thinking of appointing a temporary Speaker until the new Speaker is elected."

Glen leaned back in his chair and whistled through his pursed lips.

"You guys took it up the ass on the war in Iran and all the terror activity around the world. You're perceived as being weak. You think a strong and heroic figure like me might be a boost for the party image. The hero of flight 193 as your titular leader for a bit. The rugged dogsled driver from the great white north. The face of the manly new Democratic Party."

"That's not exactly the way I would phrase it, but I think you have the gist of the idea. I want to make sure you understand, should we decide to do this, that the position is purely ornamental. There will be no real authority. It doesn't really matter anyway since Congress is in recess until January, so there are no official duties. We don't want you to get the wrong thought about this."

"Speaker of the United States House of Representatives Glen Wilson. That has a lovely sound to it. Are there added staff and budget that goes with the position?"

McOlive sighed. "Yes, of course, there are some extra dollars with which to run the office."

"By God, I'll do it and thank you very much."

"We're just exploring the idea for now. We'll be in touch if the party decides to go forward with the idea."

"Outstanding! I promise to be the best damn ceremonial Speaker the Republic has ever seen."

The entourage stood. Glen shook each hand in turn. As they left, he leaned back in his chair and put his feet on his desk. The inquisitive intern brought in a box of donuts and placed them on his desk. Glen studied the ceiling and daydreamed as he munched.

In the hallway, McOlive shook his head. "What's with that guy? He seemed to grasp the situation quickly, so he can't be completely dumb. Is he for fucking real?"

"I tried to tell you," Scott Steele replied.

"I hope this isn't a huge mistake," McOlive muttered.

"It's just five weeks. What could possibly go wrong?"

The President and the Vice President

The Vice President of the United States, John Dickson, nodded at the pair of Secret Service officers that stood outside the door of the room on the sixth floor Premier Room at the Four Seasons Hotel. He knew them both by sight because occasionally they rotated into his assignment.

"Is the President expecting you, sir?"

"It's a surprise," Dickson replied, grinning through tight lips. He rapped on the door and placed his thumb on the peephole.

The security officers noticed that the VP seemed to be abnormally tense, but they did not comment. The president opened the door and was startled to see Dickson.

"Uh, come in, I guess, John, I can give you a few minutes if it's important."

Dickson brushed by him. President North was dressed in a hotel robe that hung open to reveal skinny white legs protruding from a pair of purple satin boxer shorts. North instinctively locked the deadbolt on the door.

"Did you get my package?" Dickson asked coldly.

North looked confused. "Yeah, the concierge sent something up, but I have not opened it yet."

Dickson examined a bottle of Veuve Clicquot Brut Champagne that was chilling in a bucket of ice. On the table next to the bucket there were packets of ribbed and lubricated condoms and a prescription bottle of Viagra.

"Very classy. You were expecting Wanda, not me." He popped open the pill bottle and picked out the blue tablets one-by-one. As he took them out, he threw them as hard as he could at North.

"Hey, stop that, you're hurting me," North protested.

"Pain, yes, that's the right prescription," Dickson said with a contorted look on his face. Dropping the bottle, pills scattered on the carpet. He picked up the remote control and turned on the TV. Pressing the volume button, he jacked up the sound. He walked over to a long package that leaned against the large TV. He tore the box open and removed two long scabbards. Swords. Ceremonial Marine swords that were a gift from the Dickson's Commander in the Iran campaign. He threw one to North and it landed at his feet. A sliver of blade emerged from the scabbard and glowed with a shiny blue glow in the room lighting.

"Pick up your sword," Dickson commanded.

"You're crazy. I'm not going to pick up a sword." He sidled toward the door but Dickson cut him off and waved the blade in his face.

"Wanda's video is on the Internet now. Did you know that?"

"What video? Have you lost your mind?"

"Just stop it, North. One of us is dying today, so it would be appropriate to stop the bologna. For once in your life, tell the truth, if you know what it is."

"The NSA can get into all the servers and delete the video."

"No they can't. It's on file-sharing systems all over the world by now."

"Well, what's that got to do with me? I didn't do it."

"Your slimy minions dug this up and it was only a matter of time before it got on the Internet. Once that happened, it was everywhere. You can't put the genie back in the bottle." Dickson grinned and it was a horrible sight for North. "You're right about one thing and it's ironic. You didn't really do it, but one of us is going to die for it anyway. Probably you, since you won't pick up your sword. This whole thing isn't completely your fault, but I'm striking out at someone and that someone happens to be you. Life is unfair sometimes, isn't it?"

North looked at the sword at his feet.

"I'm not going to get in a sword fight with you. That would just be stupid. We just need to sit down and work this out. That's all."

"Suit yourself," Dickson said with an eerie laugh as he took a gentle slash at North.

A line of blood formed on North's arm. The blade went through the cotton material like it was tissue paper.

"You motherfucker," North said with wonder. "You cut me."

"Last chance to die with a blade in your hand. Either way, you are dead, it's up to you."

North bent down and picked up his sword. He slid it out of the sheath. "I can't believe this is really happening."

Dickson slapped at North's blade and it fell from his hand.

"You're going to have to do better than that if you intend to die with any honor. Pick it up."

North bent over slowly and picked up the sword again. "Help me!" he shouted toward the door.

"I don't think so," Dickson said under his breath.

He made a few swipes at North's blade then slapped him hard with the flat side. The blow still drew blood. Tears welled in North's eyes.

"You're killing me," he said.

"That's right, I'm killing you," Dickson replied. He jabbed at North's loose arm. The blade stuck and he had to pull hard to remove it from the shoulder joint. At this point, North realized he really needed to fight. He was not skilled in swordplay, but he swung the blade hard and drew some sparks. Dickson laughed. "That's the spirit."

North got in one glancing slash at Dickson's face and sliced into his cheek. The blade scraped on teeth and Dickson cackled madly. "Oh yes," he slurred as he jammed the blade into North's abdomen. Flicking his eyes, North dropped his sword and staggered toward a telephone resting on a desk. He managed to get the receiver off the cradle while Dickson hacked at his back. A distant voice could be heard on the earpiece. North's body fell over the desk and Dickson attacked it with a two-handed barrage. One blow severed an arm and it fell to the floor. The door burst open and the Secret Service agents stormed in. Dickson turned toward them with a crazed look. They ordered him to drop the sword but he just laughed and stepped steadily toward them. They fired and did not stop firing until Dickson collapsed and both of their weapons were empty.

In the smoke-filled room, they looked at each other with precisely the same thought.

Oh shit.

Presidential Succession

The Presidential Succession Law of 1947 addressed the simultaneous disability of both the president and vice president. Under this law, here are the offices and current office holders who would become president should both the president and vice president be disabled. Remember, to assume the presidency, a person must also meet all the legal requirements to serve as president.

1. Vice President of the United States
2. Speaker of the House
3. President pro Tempore of the Senate

Adapted from: http://usgovinfo.about.com/library/weekly/aa010298.htm

Constitutionally, gentlemen, you have the President, the Vice President and the Secretary of State, in that order, and should the President decide he wants to transfer the helm, he will do so. He has not done that. As of now, I am in control here, in the White House, pending the return of the Vice President and in close touch with him. If something came up, I would check with him, of course.

    - Secretary of State Alexander Haig, March 30, 1981, speaking erroneously after President Ronald Reagan and James Brady were shot by John Hinckley.

CHAPTER 20

The Powers That Be

"Gentlemen and gentlewomen, please take your seats."

The scene was the private dining room of the Hays-Adams hotel. The creamy walls gleamed in the afternoon sun and spotless silverware glittered under the chandeliers. The activity was chaotic and the room was filled with chattering groups. Willy Thomas smashed a ceramic coffee carafe.

"Sit down and shut the fuck up!" he shouted.

Slowly and with much grumbling, everyone took their places.

"We have to act in a dignified and unified manner or all hell will break loose. First of all, let's hear from the Secret Service."

Lawrence Baldwin stood. His hands were shaking. He read from a computer print-out.

"At seventeen-twenty-three this evening, Vice President John Dickson killed the president with a ceremonial Marine sword. He was subsequently shot and killed after threatening Secret Service agents. He was declared dead by paramedics at five-forty."

"This has to be bullshit," Cecilia Paul uttered.

Baldwin threw a sheaf of photographs across the table at her.

"It's bullshit alright, but it's still fact." The pictures documented the gory detail of the murder scene. Cecilia flipped the pictures over so she would not have to look at them. She covered her mouth as if to stifle the urge to retch.

"Settle down, folks. How long do we have?"

Peter Samuels, the press secretary, stood. "The president was due at a dinner at seven-thirty for the Rainbow Coalition. We can cancel that, so we have at few hours from his side. Dickson's wife has been calling and we can't stall her much longer. I'd say we have less than an hour."

"So, who is the president? The next in line of succession is the Speaker of the House? That old man Post?"

"I called Post and he's scared to death. He says he's not leaving Kansas. Besides, we appointed this new guy Wilson as Speaker, I think, officially speaking, he's the president."

"Does anyone here, besides Steele, know anything about this guy?"

The room was silent. "No one knows anything about our new President? What do we have to do to get rid of him?"

"I believe Congress has to confirm him. If we don't vote to confirm, then we can take another vote and appoint someone else."

"How long will this take?"

"Realistically sir, a few days to gather everyone. These votes have to be done in person. We have Congressmen scattered around the world. For example, I know Atkins is in Melonesia."

"Let's get this done in 48 hours. Get the word out to gather every possible Congressman and keep the deaths a secret as long as possible. Until then, we have to keep this Wilson on ice. Steele knows him, he and I will go talk to him. Now, we can't have this double murder. Any ideas?"

"Princess Diana?" Marshall Scott, the head of the NSA suggested.

"John Kennedy, Junior?"

"How about Senior?"

"Jimmy Hoffa?"

"Are you all dimwits? Can't you think of something original that won't blow up in our faces? Let's get a volunteer to run a high speed locomotive into the Presidential Suburban. Pick a place on the Washington to Baltimore route where there won't be any witnesses. No passengers. Make sure the engineer goes down too. Anyone see any problems with this? Very well, folks, we have a lot to do and no time to get it done. Move!"

With that, the room cleared except for Willie and Scott Steele.

"Let's go visit our temporary new president, shall we?" Willie asked rhetorically.

Glen and the Powers That Be

Glen was snoozing on a leather sofa with a Nelson DeMille novel spread open on his chest. His necktie was loose and his shoes were scattered. A string of slobber dampened the rich leather. The doors burst open and Willie Thomas and Scott Steele strode in with a team of Secret Service agents. The agents took positions at the door and by the windows. An intern trailed, waving her arms and shouting.

"The Congressman is in conference."

Glen rotated to vertical and wiped his mouth. He ran his fingers through his hair and rolled his head on his neck to loosen the kinks.

"It's okay, Sheila. Would you bring us in some coffee please?"

Sheila nodded and backed out of the room. Glen gestured for his guests to seat themselves. Without standing Glen held out his hand for a shake.

"Hello Scott. Whom have you brought to visit me?"

"You may have heard my name. I'm Willie Thomas."

"Yes, Mr. Thomas, I have heard of you. Hostile takeover of Oracle and EDS. What did you reap out of that deal, if you don't mind me asking?"

"I do mind. Look, Wilson, we don't have much time." He glanced at his watch. "In about 45 minutes the lid is going to blow off. The President and the VP were both killed in an tragic railroad accident that will happen in about ten minutes."

"I find your mixed use of present and past tense very interesting. Well, I'm flattered that you chose to let me know in person. Please excuse me, I have some stock I need to short. I'd guess airlines and retail sectors will crash for a while, I can make a few bucks off that."

"We don't have time for such. Do you understand presidential succession?"

"No, I'm sorry. Who is moving up? The Secretary of State? The head of the Joint Chiefs of Staff? I have no idea."

Willie and Steele glanced at each other.

"The Speaker of the House is next in line."

Glen sat up straight. "Excuse me?"

Sheila brought in a coffee tray with silver carafe and china cups. Looking at them curiously, she poured for everyone then tip-toed out of the room.

"This means I can use the Presidential bowling alley whenever I want."

"Yes, among other things, like you are now the most powerful single person on earth."

"I suppose there is that."

Is there any way we could convince you to abdicate? The President of the Senate would be next in line."

"Not a chance. What's the prez making now? Four-hundred grand? And Air Force One, I'm going to like that. I read somewhere there are five thousand square feet on that baby. A bedroom, offices, everything."

"Never mind that folderol. You have to give a speech in within an hour and try to settle people down. We're liable to have chaos and you know the markets hate chaos. We have writers working on the speech and it will be ready in a few minutes."

"Run it by my team and we'll take a look at it."

"There is no time, you're going to have to give the speech as we write it."

"I said: run it by my team. Yes?"

Willie sighed. "Yes, alright."

"Mr. President? Don't you mean, 'Yes, Mr. President'?"

"Don't get the wrong idea. The President is mainly a figurehead and most of the things he does are ceremonial. The President does not make policy or do anything really. Do you understand?"

"Do you understand, *Mr. President?*" Glen repeated while staring at Willie stubbornly.

"Yes, have it your way. Do you understand, *Mr. President?*" Willie repeated dutifully.

"Yes, I believe I do understand. I know there is a Presidential theater, jogging track and swimming pool. Is there a sauna too? A private sauna would be great right now, I'm a little tense."

"Yes, the President has a private sauna. I'm not sure you appreciate the gravity of our situation. In less than an hour you are going to shock the world with news of the death of two of the most important people in the world. And you'll introduce yourself as the temporary leader of the free world. We're standing on the brink of history. You need to get yourself ready for the biggest moment of modern world."

"A half hour will be long enough to enjoy a hot sauna. Would either of you gentlemen care to join me?"

Willie stood. "We'll get the text of the speech delivered to your office right away. Good day, Mr. President. Be prepared to address the world in an hour." Willie and Steele walked toward the door.

"I don't think I like this guy," Willie whispered to Steele.

"I didn't think you would," Steele replied.

"Lets hold network coverage of his speech until we see how it turns out."

"CSPAN?"

"No, not even CSPAN, I have a bad feeling about this Wilson. No cameras."

Glen inspected the three Secret Service agents who were arrayed around the room. "Can any of you guys help me find my Presidential sauna?"

The sauna was small, a cedar-sided room that looked like it had not been used for a while.

I even get towels with the President's Seal on them. I sit with my presidential penis flopping on my thigh and my presidential roll of fat hanging out over my lap. I sweat and try to clear my head. I've always known that my destiny was large, but even I never dared to dream it could be this large. President of the United States. Slowly, it began to occur to me that there is more to the presidency than all the perks. This can be very serious business. Even bigger than having use of a private bowling alley or the White House wine cellar. Instead of shaving a few points of profit in a business deal, this is worldwide. Is this why my beloved Moshi was sacrificed? Do I finally have to decide what kind of man I am, of good or evil? When you boil it right down to the core nitty-gritty truth, I don't really want to be president. Too much attention, too much pressure, too much bullshit. There are a lot of things I don't like. I don't like my fingers being chopped off, I don't like growing old, I don't like the memory of Moshi taking her last breath in my arms and I don't like stupid people with dumb ideas. I've been drifting through life just trying to shake things up, make a profit and have some fun. Maybe it's time to grow up. Crap, who needs this? Maybe I should just cut a deal and abdicate. What would they pay to get rid of me? A million? 10 million? 100 million? The President of the Senate is a good old boy, a lifelong politician who knows the game. He'd go along to get along and wouldn't create problems for the political elite. And I'd be rich. Were all my adventures leading me to a huge pile of cash? What could be better? While I'd never had much problem getting the money I need, a few million here and a few million there as necessary, my point was never just to gather dollars. I'm more interested in getting the job done, whatever the job might be. Land the big contract, conquer my enemies, steal the lady's heart, win the election, whatever. But finally, the big score is at hand. So what is my problem? Something's not right. I could see what would happen if I went against the established powers. It would not be pretty. Better to take my money off the table and go home. Where ever home might be.

This will sound stupid, but I could hear Moshi talking to me. Telling me to serve her people. The public? I hate the people with their lazy and spoiled acceptance of modern life. Television, beer, hamburgers, SUVs, traffic laws, and taxes. This will be an odd sort of confession because it's never been much of a secret, but I don't think highly of the mass of my fellow man. But here's the confessional part, I have never really given them much of a chance or the benefit of any doubt. Perhaps it is time to do something altruistic. Have all my selfish adventures been pointed at granting a final gift to humanity? I am now President to lead Americans and the rest of the world to a better life? No matter how I tried to turn the matter around in my mind, Moshi appeared before me to point the way.

In spite of Moshi's message from beyond the grave, I knew how things would end. The way sucks and leads to futility and disaster. It always does and it always will, so why should I bother? Because, that's our destiny, that's why, Moshi whispered to me.

Glen opened the door and shivered as the cold air raised goose bumps on his body. The female Secret Service agent standing guard stared at the locker room walls and pointedly ignored the naked President. When Glen asked for his shorts, she picked them up and handed them to him without looking.

"Are you trained not to peek?" Glen asked.

"Excuse me, sir?" the agent asked.

"Nothing," Glen answered despondently. *No one has any sense of humor around here,* he thought.

President of the United States Glen Wilson

Good evening, fellow Americans.

I stand before you as bearer of terribly sad news. At approximately 5:40 this evening a tragic railroad accident took the lives of both President Allen North and Vice President John Dickson. Both were killed instantly when their motorcade was hit by a runaway high speed commuter train traveling between DC and Baltimore. The National Transportation Review Board is gathering information and will report on what went wrong and will take all necessary steps to prevent a horrible tragedy like this from happening again. I will personally make sure all information is published as soon as possible. To the families of these great men, I extend deepest sympathies from myself and on behalf of all the good people of the United States.

The presidential succession act provides for the appointment of an interim president. As Speaker of the United States House of Representatives, I have accepted the oath of office and have assumed the role of your president until such time as the House confirms me. I will now repeat that oath.

I do solemnly swear that I will faithfully execute the office of President of the United States, and will to the best of my ability, preserve, protect and defend the Constitution of the United States.

I am new to the Congress and I'm new to the national political scene. It will take time for you to get to know me and my policies. It will take time for me to grow into my new role. I ask your patience and perseverance. We live in troubled and perilous times. However, the great people of America can and will rise above such horror and hardship to achieve our destiny as a free people and as the greatest nation in human history.

We have been challenged by tragedy in the past and we'll need time to mourn for our fallen leaders. Immediately and until further notice, the flags will fly at half-staff. Let's now have a minute of silence to honor our lost leaders.

May God bless and keep America. Good night to you all.

Glen walked through a throng shaking hands and hugging shocked women.

In the backroom, Willie Thomas jumped in front of Glen. "What happened the middle section of the speech?"

"It was boring so I dumped it."

"With all due respect, Mr. President, you can't just edit these speeches any way you please."

"Will all due respect back at you, fuck off."

Glen walked back toward his Congressional office.

To Steele, Willie asked "What have we created?"

"I really don't know," Steele replied.

"Well, I don't like him. He has to go."

"It would have been easier if you'd thought of that earlier."

"Well, I didn't. Come up with a plan and make this fuck go away."

McOlive sighed. "I'll see what I can do."

The Election Team

"Does anyone here know anything about executive orders?"

The election team gathered around Glen's conference table. The phones were all ringing but one-by-one they were unplugged. As they beeped and chirped, cell phones, pagers and PDAs were turned off. Finally the room was quiet, though people occasionally banged on the locked doors. Stoic Secret Service people were stationed around the room.

"Clinton's counselor, Paul Begala, was quoted as saying 'Stroke of the pen. Law of the land. Kinda cool.'" Murphy commented.

"I'm going to do something off-the-wall. You guys will never guess," Glen said mysteriously.

Angela raised her hand. "You're going to write some executive orders?"

Walter and Bennie groaned. "I think he wants us to guess what orders he's going to write," Bennie explained.

"Oh," Angela said.

"Clinton called his either Executive Orders or Presidential Decision Directives, Bush the Second called them National Security Presidential Directives and I'm going to call them Homeland Executive Level Privilege Rulings, or Helpers for short. Catchy, eh? Helpers?"

"I can't decide if that's more lame than dumb," Murphy spat.

"I want each and every one of you to know that I'm proud of you and what you achieved. President of the United States, who would ever dare to dream of such a thing? However, we're entering a new stage of things and I regret to inform you that you're all fired. Elke will divide up the balance in the bank account and I suggest you get far away from here."

"Wait a minute," Walter complained. "Just like that? You get to the top and you dismiss us? That's bullshit. After all we've been though we're supposed to just go away? You're one cold bastard."

"Wait," Bennie said, raising his hand. "Let me think a minute." He closed his eyes and concentrated. "I think I get it. How dangerous are things going to get?"

"The big machine is not going sit back and let me shake up the system. The political immune system is going to react. Very, that's the direct answer. Very dangerous. We're going against the real power structure, not the public political clowns."

"Will the result be worth risking our lives?"

"No," Glen replied. "Probably not."

"This team can handle anything."

"This team has been great. Our achievements are incredible. From here on, it's a suicide mission. I know this is abrupt and unexpected, but you guys should really clear out for your own safety."

"Go fuck yourself, Wilson. I'm not going anywhere," Walter protested.

Bennie touched him on the arm and shook his head no. "I think Glen is right. Let's go start the business we've been talking about."

Walter collapsed. "Shit Glen, this isn't the way things should end." He wiped moisture from his eyes. "We should stick together until the bitter end, go down fighting and teach the bastards not to mess with us."

Glen put his hand on Walter's shoulder. "If I live long enough, I'll make sure you get some federal grants. If there was even a remote glimmer of hope, I'd keep you around."

"If it's a losing effort, then why bother? Just work the system and make some money."

"I'm doing it for Moshi. My karma is out of balance."

"You're doing this because you're an asshole."

"That's another way to look at it."

Bennie gathered his papers. "I'll see you around, boss," he said.

Glen grasped his hand, then pulled him close for a hug. "I predict great things for you, kid," he said.

"There's an 68% chance I'll make more money than Bill Gates by the time I'm 40. Of course, there's also a 17% chance I'll end up dead in a swamp in New Jersey."

"Watch your back, kid."

"You too, boss."

"I still think this stinks," Walter beefed. He shook Glen's hand vigorously. "Look us up if you get through whatever it is you have planned."

"Consider it done," Glen said.

Angela wrapped her arms around him and Glen made sure Walter was not watching as he squeezed her rump.

"I'm not sure I'll miss you much," she said.

"I'll miss you enough to make up the difference," Glen replied.

The Secret Service agent stationed at the main entrance unlocked the door and let them out. He shut and locked the door before others could come in. An episode of banging started again and it sounded like someone was kicking at the solid door. Glen made eye contact with the agent and shrugged. The agent tried to maintain a straight face, but a small smile escaped.

"It's been quite a run," Elke said, "from Florida to Alaska to the White House. I don't regret joining up with you. Farewell."

"Wait a minute," Murphy said with a strangled voice. "I'm not going anywhere. If we go down in flames, then so be it. We'll go down together."

Elke looked at Murphy, then nodded her head. "Yeah, I'm staying too."

"I'm serious, guys. You're fucking fired, so take off."

"I may be fired, but I'm staying. Blow it out your ass if you don't like it."

"Why do you have to be so stubborn?"

"Look who's talking."

"I shall withdraw your termination order on two conditions."

"Yes Wilson, what are your conditions."

"First of all, you'll have sex with me on the desk in the oval office."

"Condition rejected, sir. I'd rather allow weasels to gnaw at my living entrails, I'd rather be buried up to my neck next to a fire ant colony with my tongue coated with honey, I'd rather..."

"Okay, Murphy, I get the picture. How about on one of those presidential helicopters?"

"No! What is your real condition for us to stay?"

Glen collapsed into his chair. "When the serious guys in suits come for me, for the sake of Elke, you'll clear out and not look back."

Murphy seemed to age a decade. After a minute she spoke softly. "We agree. What do we do next?"

Glen sat down at the table. "I need time to think things through."

"Shit," Murphy said. "You're going to get drunk and dream up something stupid." She gathered up her handbag and laptop. "We'll be around when you need us. Let's get some dinner, Elke, I'm starved."

As the agent let them out, Murphy pointed her finger at Glen and sternly said "Don't even think about going anywhere without us."

"Okay, Murphy, whatever," Glen replied. To the agent he said, "Well, what do you think?"

"I'm not paid to think, but it's certainly been interesting so far."

"Yes, it certainly has. Can you call someone and get some single malt whiskey and cigars brought in?"

The agent hesitated. "We're not supposed to do stuff like that, but sure, why not," he said.

"That's the spirit," Glen replied, "and see if you can get some cheese pizza, nothing fancy, just Dominos or something. I'm running on empty here."

"Sure, boss," the agent said, grinning.

The Powers That Be

The Fenix Oil Company building in Alexandria was a cylindrical 10 stories of mirror-like glass in the middle of a parking lot. The business complex was newly-finished. The building entry, an open area three stories tall, was filled with brushed aluminum and glass. Bennie was seated in a Herman Miller Aeron chair. It was adjusted to its lowest level, but Bennie's legs still dangled. A kindly-looking older man entered the room and nodded at the guard. He sat at the conference table and cocked his head in curiosity.

"What is your name, sir?" Bennie asked.

"I'm Mr. Doe."

"Then you must be his brother," Bennie said, gesturing at the guard, "because his name is Mr. Doe too."

The older Mr. Doe looked pained. "How old are you, son?"

"Almost 13," Bennie replied shyly.

"I'm told you work for Glen Wilson..."

"Oh no, sir, Glen was sort of a guardian, that's all. Like an Uncle."

"I need to know all about your Uncle. Did you get to know him well? What did he talk about? Who did he meet? What makes him tick? What motivates him? What's his real agenda?"

"I don't know anything about all that stuff. I just played video games and watched TV. Glen was never around much."

"I'm confused about your relationship. Why were you traveling with him? Why did he take you to Alaska?"

Bennie shrugged. "I don't know nuthin' about nuthin'."

Mr. Doe sighed. "Did Glen ever touch you in a way that made you uncomfortable?"

"Oh no sir. I know all about that stuff and it wasn't anything like, you know, sexual or anything. Glen's just a nice old guy. Like a grandfather to me."

"I suppose this was some sort of outreach to the minority community or something. I can't figure it out. Isn't there anything you can tell me about the time you spent with Wilson and his team?"

"Um, he burps a lot?"

"Okay, son. If I send you on your way, do you have someplace to go?"

"Sure, my Aunt Angela will watch me."

"Alright, go with Mr. Doe and he'll make sure you get to her."

After Bennie was gone, a man came through a door that had a barely visible seam.

"Kind of a cute kid, but none too bright if you ask me."

"Just a black token for photo ops, I suppose. Shall we waste him? Disappear him?"

"No, let him go, he's harmless to us. Who's up next?"

"Walter Crawley. He's a curious character. An entertainer."

"I hope he knows more than the jig."

"We'll see, I guess."

The side of Walter's face was swollen and he walked with a severe limp. He was pressed into the interrogation chair where his arms and legs were bound with leather straps. A technician pressed EEG sensors onto his scalp and monitored a Truth Analyzer 3000. He was still wearing his business suit, though the sleeves were slit and his shoes were missing. Walter had been X-rayed and MRI'd so even the smallest pieces of metal had been excised from his clothes. The interrogator entered the small room. He was a small man with a blotchy birthmark that covered the left side of his neck and cheek. He pulled a revolver from his lab coat pocket and slowly removed all the bullets. He held up one shell for Walter to see and inserted it into the cylinder. He set the cylinder spinning and placed the barrel in Walter's eye socket.

"I appreciate all the great new drugs and technology, but I'm partial to the old fashioned methods. If they were good enough for Stalin, then they're good enough for anyone."

He pulled the trigger and the hammer clacked down on an empty chamber.

"Fortune shines upon you, Mr. Crawley. If you are determined to carry Glen Wilson's secrets into the grave, then so be it. Round and round like a roulette wheel. Do you prefer I spin the cylinder again or will you take your chances with the next chamber?"

"Spin it," Walter said.

"Very good, you know something of probability." He flicked the cylinder and it clicked as it rotated. "We're reasonable people. We just want some leverage over Wilson and we don't like things we don't understand. The American people need a leader they can trust who will maintain the course. In a few hours, the House will have an emergency election and it won't matter anymore, so I find your intransigence particularly inexplicable. And on the other hand, of course, your cooperation will be greatly rewarded. It seems like you have everything to gain and nothing to lose. So, one more time, just tell me what we're dealing with. Is Glen a fool or master strategist? What does he want? What is the right approach for controlling him?"

"I. Don't. Know." Walter replied deliberately.

Walter was convinced he would not survive. His body was covered in hot sweat. There was a hint of metal in the air, a scent similar to dry cleaning fluid. Walter had infused a complicated chemical into his t-shirt and it slowly reacted with stress byproducts that contaminated his sweat. The interrogator put the gun barrel into Walter's eye socket again.

"Please point the gun at your own head," Walter suggested reasonably.

The interrogator smiled at this suggestion, but his smile was replaced with one of confusion as the gun rotated. Confusion gave way to panic as the barrel approached. The technician watched with an open mouth.

"Go ahead and pull the trigger."

The room was filled with noise and a spray of blood.

"Please release me from these bindings," Walter said calmly.

The technician slowly removed the straps. Walter stood and rubbed his wrists.

"Let's exchange clothing now."

The white hospital scrubs that the technician wore were very small on Walter, but he managed to squeeze into them. He didn't look anything like the photograph on the ID card. *Who really looks at the pictures?* Walter thought. *They won't start today, I hope.* The technician advised him on the best route to leave the building and Walter soon found himself blinking in the bright sunlight on K Street. He flagged down a cab and, in an instant, was gone.

The Final Act – Murphy and Elke

Murphy and Elke looked up as the door opened. A huge black man, dressed impeccably in a tan suit and glossy black shoes, walked confidently through. Murphy stood. She recognized the man, Steve Stephens, from her days in Florida. She didn't think of him as a friend, but he was a man she respected. He shook hands with both the ladies then flopped down in the visitor's chair. Murphy threw her pen onto the papers of her desk. Exhausted, she pulled the hair clip out of her hair and fluffed her hair around her shoulders.

"They sent you," she said.

"They sent me," Steve said in agreement. He nodded toward the heavy door of Glen's office. "What's the big man been up to?"

"We're not sure," Elke replied. "He's been writing all night and stinking up the place with expensive cigars. Some kind of Presidential Directives, but we have no idea what's in them."

"Knowing Glen, I'm sure they're fascinating. Too bad they'll never see the light of day."

"Too bad," Murphy agreed. "So, it's time?"

"Sorry Murphy. The emergency session has convened and the vote will be recorded in," he said, while consulting his huge watch, "about eight minutes."

"Who did they pick?"

"Folger."

Murphy shrugged. "He seems like a decent enough old guy. What's going to happen to Glen?"

Steve spread the pale palms of his large hands in supplication.

"It's out of my control."

"Can we go in and say goodbye?"

"No."

The ladies gathered their handbags. Steve got up and held the door open for them. They held hands as they exited the room. The hallway was filled with a troop of heavily-armed silent SWAT team members. They were dressed in black and carried automatic weapons. Murphy made a quick count and determined there were over 30 in this squad. The Power's That Be were clearly taking no chances. Steve escorted the ladies out and herded them into a waiting limousine. They were waved out the east gate. Wiping at their tears, they did not look back.

The Final Act - Glen

The Secret Service Agent's earpiece squawked. Glen stubbed out his cigar and leaned back in his chair. His hair was tousled and his skin was gray and loose. He looked tired and old. He closed the word processor program and copied his Presidential Directives file onto a thumb drive. He stuffed the drive into a pre-addressed padded envelope which already had postage affixed. Sealing it, Glen walked up to the agent.

"Gotta run, eh?"

"I'm being called back to HQ."

"They gave me more time than I thought they would. It's been interesting, hasn't it?"

"To say the least," the agent replied. "I think I would have enjoyed serving under you."

"So it goes. Can I ask you a favor, man to man?"

The agent exchanged glances with the other agents in the room. They looked on expressionlessly.

"Okay."

Glen handed him the padded envelope. "I don't think my email is going anywhere. See that this gets posted, but not too close by, maybe in Virginia or Maryland?"

The agent hesitated before taking it. "Okay," he finally said.

He stuffed it in his belt under the back of his jacket. He nodded at the other agents and they filed out. Glen made eye contact with each and nodded respectfully at them. He went back to his desk, leaned back in his chair and put his feet up on the desk. He poured a glass of whiskey and lighted a cigar. This is how the SWAT team found him when they stormed the room.

A democracy cannot exist as a permanent form of government. It can only exist until the voters discover that they can vote themselves largesse from the public treasury. From that moment on, the majority always votes for the candidates promising the most benefits from the public treasury with the result that a democracy always collapses over loose fiscal policy, always followed by a dictatorship.

From 'The Decline and Fall of the Athenian Republic'

- Alexander Fraser Tytler, 1776

EPILOGUE

Moshi

Raz placed his bundle of carnations on Moshi's grave next to a red rose. He pulled his parka close. The wind ruffled his purple hair and drove icy daggers into his thin frame. The grave was on the edge of the Cedar River valley. His limousine idled on the driveway and his girlfriend leaned out the window and hollered for him to hurry up. He waved her away impatiently.

A groundskeeper was trimming grass around the nearby monument for Jimi Hendrix. A figure on a bicycle rode up the driveway. He dumped over his bike and jogged over. He picked up the red rose and unwrapped another one, which he placed on the grave.

Raz stopped him before he ran off.

"Hey, what's with that rose?"

"We have a contract at the flower shop, she gets a fresh one every day."

"For how long?"

The kid shrugged. "Forever, I guess. They gave us a credit card number that doesn't expire. I'd never heard of one, but I guess they exist. Gotta run."

Calling after him, "Who is doing this, her parents?"

"We don't know. I don't think it's her parents, though."

Raz turned back to the grave. "I swear by my soul, Moshi, I'm sorry," he whispered. "I really am."

He paused as if listening for an answer, but there was nothing except the wind whistling across the graves. Wiping his runny nose on his sleeve, he plodded back to his car.

Walter and Bennie

They were having dinner at Seattle's Space Needle Restaurant. The city lights slowly rotated by their window seats. Emma wore a sweater with real fur trim, native Americans could do this sort of thing and still get a free pass from the militant anti-fur groups that protested regularly in the Seattle streets. Chief Eddie wore a sport jacket and string tie and his wife, Mary, wore an evening gown with an elaborate turquoise necklace. Walter wore a jacket with claw hammer tails, he'd reluctantly surrendered his silk top hat to the coat room attendant. Bennie wore Dockers and a rumpled Oracle tradeshow polo shirt. They had taxied in from a Bach performance by the Seattle Symphony. Bennie tapped his fork against his water glass, then stood up. He looked tired and his eyes were bloodshot.

"I have a small announcement. I have lined up some seed money for our company."

He pulled a wrinkled check out of his pocket and passed it around. Chief Eddie's lips moved as he counted the zeroes. He whistled with appreciation. "Four million. That's outstanding. Is the check any good? Does this Oracle company have this kind of money?"

"Larry Ellison signed it personally. It's good," Bennie replied.

"I thought you were selling to Microsoft?" Walter commented.

"They only offered 3.5 mil and I didn't like the fine print in their contract. Screw them."

"Bennie, watch your language!" Mary Kleedehn scolded.

Bennie looked ashamed. "I'm sorry, mom."

"Alright, I'll bite. What did you sell?"

"A week's worth of work on a code word database program and some market research."

"How does it work?"

"There are two subscription models, one for providers and one for consumers. The providers pay $99 a month and the subscribers pay $9.99 a month. Providers pay to list products for a month, then the database automatically changes. The program is a look-up table."

"I still don't get it."

"It's illegal to sell certain things. Let's say you're Rush Limbaugh and you want to buy Tylox." Bennie referred to a scrap of paper. "This month the code word for Tylox is Scooby-Doo pencil. On an online auction site, bid on a Scooby-Doo pencil and you will get Tylox."

"What if you want a real Scooby-Doo pencil?"

"You communicate via encrypted email to confirm what you're getting. Besides, there are no real Scooby-Doo pencils."

"This sounds illegal."

"The lawyers checked it out, it will survive a court challenge. We're not selling anything but a database service. How it gets used is not our problem."

"I don't like it, Bennie. It sounds like dirty business to me," Mary complained.

"I'm sorry, mom. I'll tear up the check if you want me to."

Eddie placed his hand on Mary's arm and shook his head. Mary stared at the check. "I don't suppose we have to go that far," she said quietly. "Just be careful, Bennie, don't go too far with this."

"Okay, mom, I won't," Bennie said, leaning over to give Mary a hug. "I promise we'll use the money to create something important."

Walter made eye-contact with Bennie. He nodded slightly and raised his glass of wine in toast.

"To the future of Immortality, LLC," he suggested.

"Can't we toast to something more traditional, like long life and good health."

"Same thing," Bennie commented. His hand found Emma's and their fingers intertwined. All tapped their glasses together and they drank.

Lester Mike

Lester eased his 4WD pickup forward until the cable pulled tight. The tires spun for an instant, then caught on the sandy ice as he gunned the engine. Slowly, the truck moved forward and he pulled the SkiDoo out of the frigid and frothy water. He stopped and water cascaded out of the soggy snowmobile. He put crampons on his cowboy boots, placed his watch cap squarely on his head and jumped out of the cab onto the icy roadway. Sam Jimmy, the teenager who borrowed the SkiDoo from his dad for some skimming, was huddled under a wool blanket. The Kotzebue deputy who drew the short straw waded through the water toward shore. He was wearing hip waders which kept him dry, but it was still savagely cold out in the water. However, someone had to get out there and attach a cable to the sunken snowmobile.

Skimming was a local sport that consisted of roaring at full speed across the snow, then skimming across open water to the other side of the channel. It worked well unless you didn't have enough momentum or the engine died. Then you get wet and spend a few weekends rebuilding an engine. To be brutally honest, there wasn't that much else to do in Kotzebue in the dark and harsh winter. Together, they heaved the SkiDoo onto its trailer. Lester patted Sam Jimmy on the shoulder.

"Come on up to the office and we'll get you dried out," Lester suggested.

They tromped across the snow with their heads down against the bitter wind.

The mayor's office was in the back of the police building. They stomped snow off their boots and Lester hung up his crampons inside the door. As they walked through the building, Lester nodded at Sheryl, the girl running dispatch. In the office, a pot-bellied stove radiated intense heat. Lester opened the grate with an oven mitt and tossed in some lumps of coal. He strolled around the desk and flopped into his leather chair. With his boots on the scarred desk, he paged through an old Billboard magazine that one of the tourists left behind. They both started when the phone rang. Lester heaved himself forward and picked up the receiver.

"Mayor Lester Mike here, how can I help you?" he asked briskly.

Glen

The orderly, a large dark-skinned Native American, opened the administrator's door and ushered Glen in. The administrator was a dapper man with a full slicked-back head of gray hair. He wore a mottled gray-brown goatee and small round glasses. The nameplate on his desk said Martin Floyd. In a companion chair, a prim middle-aged woman sat quietly. Her nametag said Blakely. From a stray lock of her hair that escaped her tight bun and a pink flush on her neck, Glen deduced that they had recently enjoyed vigorous sex. Glen wore loose-fitting hospital pajamas and bare feet.

"You can leave us, Chad. Just wait outside," Floyd said to the orderly. With a scowl, Chad left the room and closed the door.

Floyd opened a folder on his desk. "We haven't had a chance to chat yet. I want to welcome you to our facility and answer any questions you might have."

"You could start by telling me where the fuck we are, Doctor Freud."

"It's Doctor Floyd. Oh, I get it, you're funning with me. That's amusing. However, I must insist that you refrain from using harsh language, it displays an unhelpful and disrespectful attitude. To address your question, the closest town is Turtle Lake, North Dakota, something like thirty-five miles away. The official name of our facility is the Prairie Meadows Federal Medical Research Institute, but we just call it The Meadows for short."

"How long will I be here?"

"Your court order assigns you to us for an indefinite period."

"Forever, huh?"

"I'm not comfortable with extreme terms like forever," Doctor Floyd chuckled, "but I would have to affirm your general thought regarding your expected tenure here at the Meadows. I hope you'll work with us to address some of your issues. For example, your file states that you think you are the President? Would you care to comment on that?"

"Do you know who the current president is?"

"We're not really up to date on political affairs of state, but I believe the President is a gentleman named Folger. We have enjoyed the company of Jesus Christ and Elvis —", the woman interrupted by holding up two fingers, "yes, Ginger, I believe you are correct, we've had two Elvis's or Elvi if that is the correct pluralization, but never a Commander in Chief of the United States before. Oh, Penny Osborn thought she was Joan of Arc, that was an interesting case, but that's neither here nor there. While I'm thinking about it, I want to ask you about something." He held up a glassine envelope which held a thin and nearly transparent disk about two inches in diameter. "We found this inserted in your abdomen, it turned up on your MRI and we took the liberty of extracting it for you. Could you tell us please what is it?"

Glen held out his hand. "Excuse me? Might I see that for a moment?"

Floyd stretched his hand out to give it to Glen, but Nurse Blakely coughed and Floyd jerked his hand back. "Ginger is quite correct, it would be against the Meadow's policy to hand this to you, I'm sorry. What exactly is it?"

"I couldn't say."

"Very well. There is a note in your file that says you've been giving your neighbor, Mister Pantalone, your medication. I must ask you to please refrain from doing that. If we have to, we'll have the orderlies force feed you, but that would be unpleasant, wouldn't it? If you refuse to cooperate, we could strap you down and inject your chemical cocktail? Will that become necessary?"

"No, I will take the damn pills. Could I please have access to a computer?"

"That's quite impossible, I'm afraid. This is a secure facility and we don't have any electronic connection to the outside world. We've found that electronic communication is counter-indicated for many of our patients. Even if we had a connection, your court order specifically and strictly forbids any access to electronics of any kind. It seems a little extreme to me, but you're not allowed to be within 20 feet of television or radio. You're to be isolated from portable stereos and other types of personal electronics. No electric razor, electric toothbrush, blow dryer, and they even specifically listed ultrasonic jewelry cleaners, not that we have much call for such here at The Meadows, yes Ginger?" Floyd laughed. "I don't even know what a GPS is, but you're restricted from its use."

"Seems like they thought of everything," Glen commented wryly.

"The whole kit and caboodle. No books, no magazines, no maps. This is the most detailed court order I've ever seen. Can you enlighten me as to the reason for of all this?"

"Nope," Glen said, "it's a mystery to me too."

One of my strengths is adapting to my environment. It would be easy to give up and let the bastards win this time. I confess, I gave into despair for a period. How long? A month or two, I don't know. I took their pills and stared at the wall. The food was okay and this place is peaceful enough. What could I do? There is little metal here and even when I was working in the kitchen they inventoried the utensils twice a day. Still, as time passed, I fought back however I could. The drugs muddled my thinking, but I was able to get them to change my medication by faking some side-effects. They eventually put me on Triazolam, which totally screwed me up, but this stuff was expensive and had good street value. The orderly started substituting jellybeans and this worked great for both of us. My head cleared and he made a few bucks selling this stuff in Bismarck. They would not let me have any books, but I talked my neighbor into ordering some textbooks. In particular, I found Malvino's Electronic Principles very helpful. At night, my neighbor would whisper the formulas to me.

I spent hours in the yard watching the sky and thinking. I watched aircraft fly over at 36,000 feet overhead and I was able to determine the schedules of commercial airplanes that flew by this fly-over part of the Midwest. Malvino helped me with the resonant frequency formula. Take the inverse of two times pi times the square root of LC. VHF Omni-Range (VOR) frequencies were somewhere around 110 Mhz. What were inductance values for bare wire? Capacitance? These were the things I spent day-after-day thinking about. It seemed like a large aluminum cooking pot could be used as a dish antenna and that, with enough wire, the wall power could be used to excite this resonant network. The first time I tried it, I blew out the circuit breaker, but the next attempts seemed to be working. I had no way to verify, but I kept trying. Insane? Dumb? Desperate? They did a good job of burying me here, but as long as I was alive, I would try to escape and seek my revenge.

Revenge is a beautiful word, a word worth living for. While I rotted in this desolate hell, I settled on my scheme. A giant flaming stick to poke into the eyes of my enemies in the US Government.

Afterward - Two Years Later

Murphy walked through the apartment door, Elke was lounging on a couch watching TV. She jumped up and hugged Murphy tightly. Murphy tossed her briefcase aside and kicked off her shoes.

"I'm totally hammered," she said.

"How was the tour?" Elke asked.

"Exhausting, I don't know how those kids do it. The more I get to know Raz, the more I've grown to respect him. He's no dummy. Underneath the makeup and the devil worship bullshit, he's a bright kid, a great businessman and one hell of a fine musician. Did you know he cleared four-hundred thousand dollars in cash at the Shea Stadium performance? I was in charge of the cash and it got rough a few times. I had to break up a couple of fights and some thugs tried to grab the cash in Cleveland. He wants me to sign on for his Fall tour, but I'll have to think about it. We need the money, but I'm not sure it's worthwhile."

"Can I get you some tea?" Elke asked while massaging Murphy's neck.

"A beer would be great. I'm glad to be home."

"We can go to bed, you look like you could use some sleep."

"That sounds great, I just want to look over Bennie's report and see if anything popped up."

"It's been two years, don't you think we'd find Glen by now if he was still alive?"

"What is your gut feeling? Do you think they killed him?"

Elke stared at the carpet. "No —, my intuition tells me he's still with us somewhere. The story doesn't feel over yet."

"I agree, so I've got to keep trying."

Murphy received summary data from deep web search algorithms designed by Bennie. A sasquatch sighting was reported near Harrison Lake in British Columbia. Unexplained lights in the sky were being reported on the coast near Savannah, GA. Aircraft pilots were complaining about interference in their VOR receivers in mid-North Dakota. Murphy sighed. She had followed many leads like this that went nowhere. Odd SETI data logged in up-state New York, mysterious postings on Internet USENET groups and letters to the editor in community newspapers. All came up dry. Still, the search would continue. She made a note to get someone to call some pilots and try to find a reasonable explanation for the radio complaints in North Dakota. She wasn't even completely sure where North Dakota was. Somewhere near Utah she guessed.

Elke walked into Murphy's office carrying a frosty mug of beer.

"How's it going?" she asked.

"Same old shit, same old shovel," Murphy said wearily.

Elke rubbed Murphy's neck to work out the kinks.

"He'll turn up someday," Elke said.

"I know," Murphy replied. "Someday."

THE END